MW01130820

Collisions
Of the
Damned

By James Young

Copyright © 2015 James Young
All rights reserved.
ISBN: 1517135656
ISBN-13: 978-1517135652

Contents

Dedication

To the "ragged, rugged warriors" of the ABDA Command. Gone but not forgotten

.

STANDARD SHIP DIAGRAMS

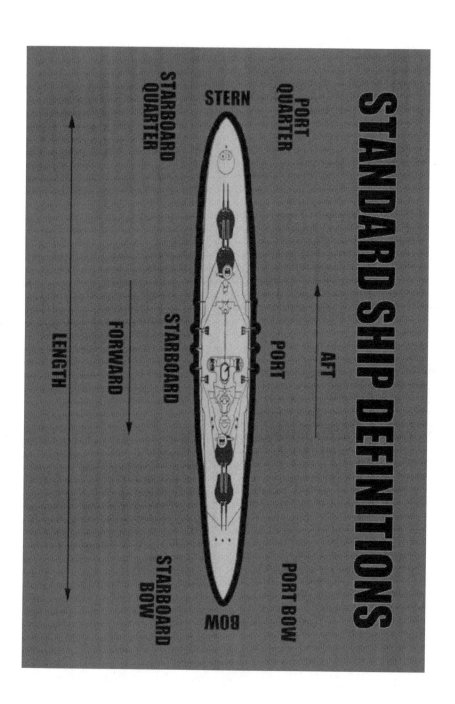

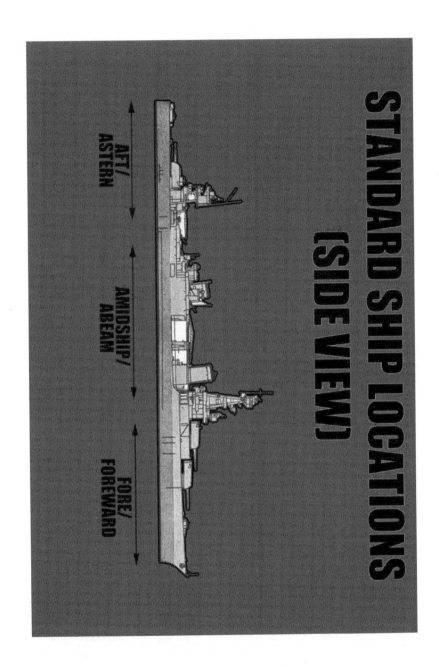

STANDARD SHIP LOCATIONS (SIDE VIEW)

AFT/ ASTERN

AMIDSHIP/ ABEAM

FORE/ FOREWARD

JAMES YOUNG

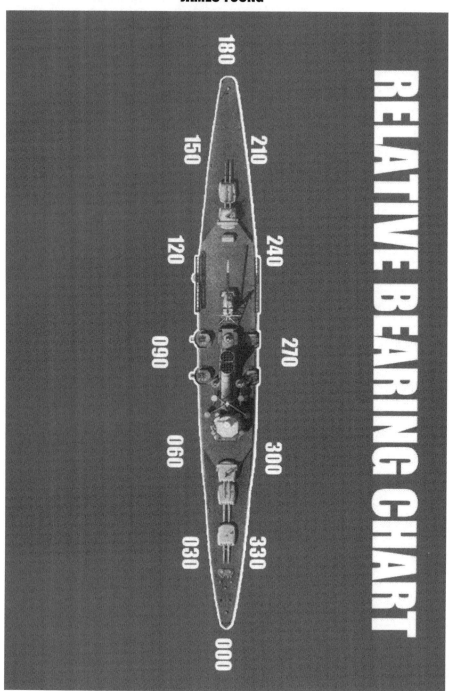

MAPS OF THE EAST INDIES

JAMES YOUNG

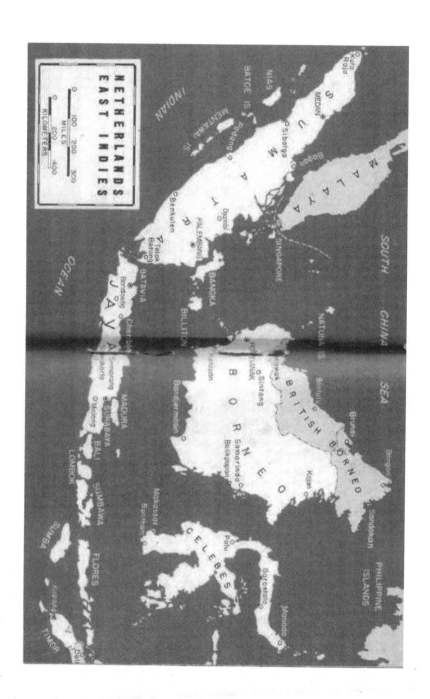

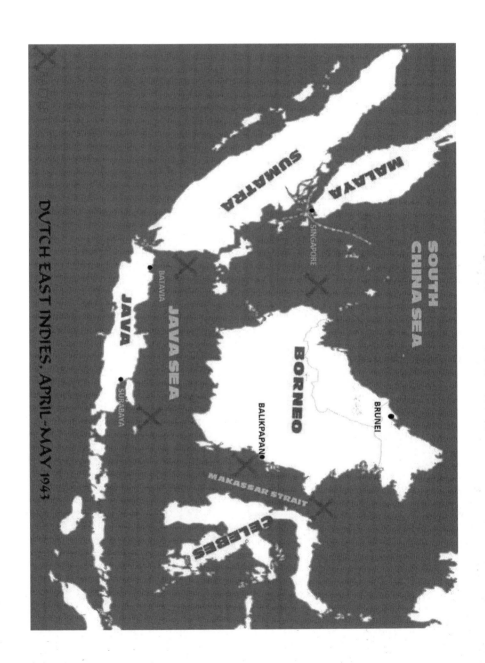

DUTCH EAST INDIES, APRIL-MAY 1943

CHAPTER 1: JUNCTIONS

War means fighting, and fighting means killing.—**Nathan Bedford Forrest, CSA.**

Red One
Gulf of Mexico
0530 Eastern Time
29 March 1943

The explosion, low on the horizon to his starboard in the predawn darkness, caused Major Adam Haynes to whip his head around in a Pavlovian response. His hands reflexively tightened on the *Wildcat*'s stick and throttle, a subconscious dance born from years of living and killing in the cockpit. As the stocky Marine major watched, the bright flash transformed into a dancing, yellowish glow that reflected off the water.

Tanker, he thought, blue eyes narrowing. *The Krauts are getting downright brazen in their submarine attacks. That ship can't be more than twenty miles off the coast!*

The Second World War or, as some were calling it, the Usurper's War, had resumed a little over seventy-two hours before. According to their preflight briefing, more than two dozen ships had been struck up and down both coasts of Florida. Nazi Germany, it seemed, had been far more prepared for war than the United States.

Or at least, that's what I gather from having to send **fighters** *out to try and spot submarines*, Adam thought with disgust. *At least there weren't enough bombs to go around to us.*

"Red One..." his wingman, First Lieutenant Griffin Teague, started to report.

1

"Saw it, Two," Adam affirmed resignedly. He brought the short, tubby *Wildcat* into a gentle turn. "Red Three, take Four and go up to ten thousand feet, heading three five oh true," Adam barked into his throat microphone. "Two, open it up, we're going down to angels three. Kill your navigation lights."

Pushing his nose down, Adam checked to make sure Three and Four had understood his implied order to keep their lights on. Seeing that the pilots had, he watched as his altimeter unwound to three thousand feet. Satisfied with his built up airspeed and that Red Two was sufficiently distant as to give them both room to maneuver, Adam kept his throttle just below the maximum as he hurtled northward.

"Any aircraft this frequency! Any aircraft this frequency! This is U.S. Army Locust Flight, please respond!" a call crackled through his headphones crackled.

Locust Flight? This better not be a Kraut tri... Adam started to think. The stream of tracers that shot up into the dark sky and intersected with a slightly blacker shape in several bright flashes brought that thought to a halt. His eyes on the stricken aircraft, Adam did notice that it had released several bombs until there was a series of waterspouts in close proximity to the tracers' point of origin. Before the spray from the bombs had finished falling, the bomber fell off to one side, dipped a wing, and cartwheeled into the Gulf of Mexico in a brilliant cascade of flame and sea.

Holy shit! Adam thought, his mouth suddenly cotton. Kicking his rudder, he brought the *Wildcat*'s nose around to a westerly heading to maintain separation from the tracers' origin.

"Locust Flight, this is Buccaneer One," Adam replied, a sickening feeling in his stomach. "Locust Flight, this is Buccaneer One."

The ominous silence in return told him that the bomber in question had probably been Locust Flight.

Looking to his starboard, he sighted a white wake on the ocean, and was able to follow it to the German submarine below.

Well at least it's bright enough to see now, he thought. The glint of sunlight on glass to his north, and slightly higher, also told him that the dead bomber had indeed been Locust Leader.

Dammit, what was that Army frequency again? Adam wondered. Before he could start breaking out his knee pad, his headphones crackled.

"Navy fighters, Navy fighters, this is Locust Two," a very shaken Southern drawl echoed in his headphones.

"Locust Two, Red One," Adam replied quickly. "You carrying any ordnance on that thing, or are we waiting for help?"

"I've got four depth charges," Locust Two replied after a moment. "We've called for help, Eglin Field says it will be at least twenty minutes."

"Red One, Red Three," his second section leader, First Lieutenant Mark Butler, interrupted. "I have contacted Homeplate and they report we will have aircraft on station in ten minutes."

Ten minutes from now that submarine should be dived, Adam thought with a flash of anger. *In fact, I don't know why he's not diving now.*

"We don't have ten minutes, Red Three," Adam replied, his tone matter of fact. Keeping his fighter in a bank as he circled the submarine, he realized he could see figures running to the conning tower from the large gun on deck.

"Hell, we probably don't even have five," Adam snapped. "Red Three, come on down with Four, set up on that bastard's bow. Locust, you want to come in from astern or one of the sides?"

There was a long pause. Just as Adam was about to make the bomber pilot's decision for him, the Army officer

3

replied.

"Astern, Red One," the man stated, his voice shaking even further.

"Red Three, me and Red Two are coming in from the bastard's port quarter," Adam said. "When I give you the word, your section comes in from the starboard bow. Clear that damn conning tower, Locust Two you come in from astern and kill the son of a bitch. Everyone clear?"

There were three acknowledgments of varying certainty as Adam circled to the submarine's port side. As he looked over the Nazi submarine, Adam realized that the sun was starting to glisten off a trail of oil streaming from the U-boat's starboard beam.

Might explain why he hasn't dived yet, Adam thought. *In these waters that'd stick out like a sore thumb.* Taking one last look around, Adam saw that the bullet shaped Army bomber was making its final turn. Cursing mentally, he pulled his own fighter up into an Immelman, the *Wildcat* growing sluggish as it lost velocity.

*I want my damn **Spitfire** back*, Adam seethed, the F4F finally finishing its reversal. With one more quick look to see Red Two on his wing, the B-26 starting its attack run, and Red Three and Four in their own dives, Adam pushed his nose down and advanced the throttle. The Pratt & Whitney began thundering in the cramped cockpit, the vibration thrumming up his arm. Watching his instruments, Adam lessened the angle of his dive as he passed five hundred feet, leveling off barely two wingspans above the waves.

"Red Flight, do *not* pull up until you're past the submarine, whatever you do," Adam warned as the four fighters hurtled towards the U-boat. With his naked eye, Adam watched as the German vessel began to turn towards him, giving the Army pilot a much narrower target. With a strangely detached thought, he realized that the conning tower had three additional platforms, two of which held twin

4

cannons and the last with a quadruple mount. Deciding the fighters were a lesser threat, the crew of the last weapon swung aft towards the approaching bomber.

That's the bastard who has to die, Adam decided, bending down to his sight as he passed roughly a half mile from the submarine. The conning tower jumped into sharp relief as he stared into the glass, and Adam had a split second to register several sharp flashes directed towards him before he was squeezing his own trigger.

The next handful of seconds was a cacophony of sights and sounds that his mind only dimly registered. Only later would Adam realize the several loud bangs he heard were the sound of the German gunner briefly finding the range to his fighter. Or that the red mist at the edge of his sight picture was Red Two's fire blasting apart a lookout's head and simultaneously mortally wounding the U-boat's commander.

In the moment, Adam watched as his own six .50-caliber machine guns briefly concentrated their fire on an area the size of a window pane before once again scything across the submarine's deck as the *Wildcat* closed through its convergence range of two hundred yards. In those pair of horrible seconds, his guns placed over a hundred rounds into the quad mount's gunner, three of the 20-mm Oerlikons, and both assistant gunners. All three men slumped to the flak platform's deck as Adam released his trigger, flashing over the submarine in a blur of gray and roar of propeller.

Seeing his flight leader was past, Red Three opened fire at just over three hundred yards. His burst of fire caught a lookout just as the man stood up to try and reman the forward anti-aircraft gun. The German's sailor's scream, subsequent trip overboard, and hailstorm of half-inch slugs convinced the remaining bridge watch to continue hugging the conning tower's deck. As Red Three and Four roared overhead, the Army bomber's nose guns added another burst of motivation just before Locust Two's bombardier released his weapons.

Dropped from under one hundred feet, the four depth charges separated from the speeding B-26 and arced downwards towards their target. As Adam brought the *Wildcat* around, the first charge landed astern of the turning U-boat. Even as the submarine was shaking from that blast, the next charge exploded underneath the submarine's stern, sending her spinning propellers out of the water. Before the turning, glistening blades had dropped back out of sight, the third depth charge struck at the base of the conning tower with a bright flash and eruption of debris. The fourth charge's failure to detonate was lost in the violence of the blast, the U-boat heeling over to starboard before returning to an even keel with smoke pouring from her amidships.

Pretty sure that's done her in. The vessel's slowing and settling reinforced Adam's thought, and he saw a hatch open at the vessels's stern. With a smile that would have been horrible to behold had someone else shared the cockpit, Adam finished bringing the *Wildcat*'s nose back onto the U-boat two miles away. Grimly, he closed with the mortally wounded submarine at a far slower rate than he had begun his previous strafing run.

Oh no, you bastards, you don't get off that easy, he thought with a satisfied rage. Even as he dived, Adam noted that the *Wildcat*'s engine sounded far rougher than it had just a few moments before. Ignoring the sound, he lined his sight up on the men struggling to get out of the hatch.

"Red One, there's a white sheet forward," Red Three stated.

I don't give a shit... Adam thought. He watched as two of the men on deck struggling with a raft turned and looked back towards Adam's approaching fighter. One man dived over the side, the other leapt back towards the hatch just as another German sailor had poked his head out. Adam

COLLISIONS OF THE DAMNED

began laughing uncontrollably as the exiting sailor took two boots to his face, his comrade bending awkwardly in a way that almost certainly indicated a broken leg.

Give my regards to Goering when you get to Hell, Adam thought, starting to squeeze the trigger.

"Red One! Red One! They're surrendering!" Red Three cried.

"*Fuck you!*" Adam screamed, pulling back on the stick. His breathing gradually slowed as the rage began to leave him, the *Wildcat* vibrating as his arm shook on the stick.

I hope I did not activate the throat mike when I started cursing at Three, he thought.

"Roger Red Three," he replied, realizing that the *Wildcat* was still shaking although his tremors had passed. Glancing over at the control panel, Adam could see that his RPMs were fluctuating and that it was not his imagination that the *Wildcat* was vibrating much worse than normal.

"Two, look me over, I think I took some damage," Adam stated, stepping on the rudder pedal to bring the *Wildcat*'s nose on a heading back to Pensacola.

"Roger One," Teague replied.

Looking around the cockpit, Adam could see no visible signs of damage around his seat. Glancing out over his cowling, however, he could see that a section was clearly holed, the lips of the penetration mushrooming back into the airstream.

"One, this is Two," Teague said. "You've taken some hits in your fuselage and there's a large hole in your left nose."

That explains why the engine is shaking like an unbalanced washing machine, Adam thought grimly. *Guess I found out one thing the **Wildcat** can do better than the **Spitfire**: take a punch.*

"Roger Two," Adam replied.

Shit, he thought. *Might want to get off another report to Homeplate. Especially if I'm going to be stepping out over the side.*

"Homeplate, Homeplate, this is Buccaneer Leader," Adam intoned. Leading with his position, Adam quickly summarized the events of the last five minutes as he crossed the Florida coastline. Listening to his engine, he realized the Pratt & Whitney didn't sound like it was getting worse.

Today might be my lucky day.

"Buccaneer Leader, this is Homeplate," the controller at the other end replied. "We have your position. Are you going to need assistance?"

"Negative Homeplate," Adam said, looking down at Pensacola's outskirts passing underneath his wing. "At this point you'll just be able to look for the smoke cloud if this doesn't work."

There was a long pause.

"Roger, Buccaneer Leader," Homeplate acknowledged. "You are clear to Runway One, all traffic is out of your way."

"Roger," Adam replied. Reaching over, he grabbed the *Wildcat*'s landing gear handle, then began cranking the fighter's wings down while cursing Grumman's designers. With a final turn, the wheels locked down as he entered Pensacola's pattern.

You didn't like that, did you? he thought as the *Wildcat* began skidding from the turbulence.

"One, only your port wheel's locked down," Red Two said worriedly. "Your starboard one is flapping back and forth in the wind."

That explains a lot.

"Roger Two," Adam said. "I'm going to try and lock it into place." Grabbing his stick, he violently waggled the

Wildcat's wings. There was a loud *thunk!* followed immediately by a shudder and the Grumman skidded even more violently across the sky.

"One, you just lost your starboard gear!" Red Two said.

Fuck me, Adam thought, the *Wildcat* shuddering as it started to head into a stall. Shoving his throttle forward, Adam was rewarded with even more vibration. The engine made a distinctly unhealthy sound as he crossed the last mile towards the runway's end.

"Going to be a little hot coming in, Homeplate," Adam snapped. "I just lost my starboard gear and I don't think this engine's going to let me go around." Dimly hearing the controller's acknowledgement, Adam began concentrating on lining his fighter up with the asphalt ahead and simultaneously preparing for a crash landing.

This makes three times the damn Germans have sent me home with a sick kite, Adam thought grimly. *Hopefully what they say about the third time being when the shit hits the fan is a bit misguided.*

The port wheel touched down and he immediately cut the throttle. Adam then braced himself as the *Wildcat*'s starboard wing slammed down into the ground. Miraculously, the fighter did not ground loop as he stomped down on the rudder to try and counteract the imparted spin. Instead, proving his luck was indeed not gone, the port gear snapped back into the fighter's fuselage in a shower of sparks, the impact throwing Adam up against the back of his seat in a teeth jarring collision. Through his blurred vision, Adam watched as the prop disintegrated, pieces flying sideways and back over his head as the Grumman slid to a stop.

Got to get out! Adam thought, fighting to stop the world from spinning. Fumbling with the canopy, he finally got it to slide back. Stumbling as he stood, Adam flopped onto his starboard wing with as much grace as a newborn foal. Reaching out to steady himself, he felt a stabbing pain in his hand.

Dammit! Adam thought, jerking the hand back as he felt as sharp pain in his palm. Looking down, he realized that a portion of the *Wildcat*'s wing was peeled back like someone had started into it with a can opener. Not wasting anytime to at the damage, Adam began to stagger away from his fighter. Belatedly, he realized that the crash truck was only four hundred yards away and coming to a stop. Looking back at the *Wildcat* with a slack jawed expression, Adam realized that despite the rough landing and damage, the Grumman was not even smoking.

Grumman Ironworks indeed, he thought, than sat down heavily.

"Major Haynes! Major Haynes! Are you okay?" he heard someone shout. Looking up, he saw a pair of medics approaching him.

"Just got…some cobwebs," he replied, waving weakly. As if his words had awoken some crazed gnome inside his skull, his head began throbbing where it had smacked against the canopy. The first of the medics reached him and crouched down, making eye contact.

"How many fingers do you see?" the man asked, holding up his thumb and pinky.

"Two very blurry ones," Adam responded, blinking.

"C'mon buddy, let's get you back to the truck," the man replied. Nodding to his friend, the duo bent down and hauled Adam to his feet.

I hope the mornings get easier than this, Adam thought woozily. *I've already been on the losing side once in this damn war, don't feel like doing it again.*

George One
No. 625 Squadron, Royal Australian Air Force

COLLISIONS OF THE DAMNED

25 Miles NW of Brunei Port, Borneo
0130 Local (1130 Eastern)
30 March (29 March Eastern)

It is always concerning when one's pilot is in a state of high dudgeon, Flight Lieutenant Russell Wolford thought to himself. *Doubly so when it's darker than the inside of a cow outside. Idiot should be paying more attention to where we're going. There's a damn war on.*

"What makes it worse is that Dutch bastard gives me a look like he is doing me a bloody favor!" Flying Officer Carl Bellingsley snapped, his Welsh accent growing stronger as his anger grew. "Oh, I'm sorry, we're just busy trying to save your home! Hope we didn't wake you!"

Dear God, please let the Japanese show up, Russell mentally begged. As the navigator/radar operator for *Killer Koala*, or "Double K" as her crew chief called her, Wolford was the *Beaufighter*'s ranking officer. While technically that meant he could have told Bellingsley to shut the hell up, odds were the tall, stocky Welshman might have taken some umbrage to that once they returned.

Last thing I want is him sulking for the next three days now that the festivities have begun, Russell thought grimly. *I miss my Mosquito. I miss England. Most of all, I miss Maggie.*

"Okay, there's the *Australia*'s homing signal," Bellingsley reported. After a moment, Russell heard the tone in his headset also. Looking forward down the *Beaufighter*'s fuselage as Bellingsley turned the aircraft to port, Russell felt a touch of vertigo as the stars swung past the narrow cockpit window.

Even the stars are different here than back in Europe, he mused. *Oh well, at least we don't have to worry about night fighters.*

"I hate flying over water," Bellinsgley snapped.

11

"At least it's warmer than the Channel," Russell replied grimly.

"Aye, and it's also got more sharks," his companion replied. "I'll take freezing to death over being gnawed apart by giant fish."

"I'll pass on both," Russell chuckled. "I was just thinking I wish I was back in England."

"I imagine it's a little inhospitable now that the war's resumed," Bellingsley retorted. "The ol' Usurper would have your head lopped off, more than likely."

Hopefully not before I told ol' King Edward what I really thought of him, Russell thought. *'You had your chance on the throne, you stupid bloke.'*

"Wouldn't change the fact that Her Majesty still has more balls than he does," Russell replied aloud. "Which will be true in fact and not just theory if she ever gets a hold of him."

"I do hope she would not truly have the man hanged, drawn, and quartered," Bellingsley replied, his tone carrying a shiver. "Her Majesty seems like such a proper lady."

"Why not? The man's cavorting with the people who killed her father," Russell snapped, then calmed himself. "Let him go join ol' Adolph in Hell without his wedding tackle."

"You are a bit harsh, don't you think?" Bellingsley replied. "I mean, I am not saying you are wrong, but lopping off a man's naughty bits seems a bit extreme…"

"Charles One, Charles One, this is Dogcatcher Base," their radio crackled. "We have trade. I say again, we have trade."

Looks like the Japanese are actually off Brunei this time, Russell thought, feeling a surge of adrenaline.

"Dogcatcher, Dogcatcher, this is Charles One," the calm, measured voice of No. 625 Squadron's commander,

Squadron Leader Cairn Spence replied to the *Australia*'s radio transmission. "Send range and bearing to your trade, over."

"Range is three five miles, bearing two seven oh, angels nine," the *Australia*'s fighter direction officer responded. "Speed is one five oh knots."

Must be a Jap float plane, Russell thought quickly. *Which means there's likely enemy vessels about.* Russell took a swig from his canteen to clear his suddenly dry mouth.

"All right Bellingsley, look sharp," Russell said, his voice far calmer than he felt. "That bloke is probably coming up from the southwest, so we need to set course for one nine zero true. Charles flight has the snooper, let's go find where he came from."

Squadron Leader Spence's plan to support the American-Commonwealth-Dutch-Australian, or ACDA, task force sweeping north towards Brunei had been quite simple given No. 625's sixteen available fighters. Since half the Australian unit's strength consisted of *Beaufighters* N.F. Mk. IIIs whose radar was only good for finding airborne targets, Pence had decided to organize these into Charles and Michael flights.

The remaining eight *Beaufighters* carried the most recent radar that allowed both airborne targets and medium-to-large surface ships to be hunted. After several experiments in the last month, Spence had decided that George and Oliver flights would ACDA operations by attacking Japanese vessels out at sea.

Great theory, but I guess now we'll see if it works, Russell thought as the *Beaufighter* came around to its new heading.

"Hope those chaps in No. 640 are giving the Japanese hell tonight," Bellingsley said. "

I hate nervous chatterers, Russell thought, even as he grunted his assent.

"Flying a *Blenheim* over Singapore, even at night, is not how I'd want to start my war," Bellingsley continued.

"Were you not just complaining about sharks? I do not remember there being sharks in Singapore before the Germans kicked us out," Russell snapped, then cursed inwardly.

"Sorry Sir," Bellingsley said stiffly.

Now is not the time to sulk, you idiot, Russell seethed. He looked down at the radar set, willing a blip to appear as the *Beaufighter* continued on its southeasterly heading.

"Charles One, this is Charles Two," Spence's wingman stated. "I have visual on trade, two contacts, slightly below us, two miles, bearing oh one oh."

"Righto, you have lead," Spence barked.

Charitable man, our squadron leader, Russell thought. *Of course, he's got ten kills, is probably tired of staging around up here like we are, and just wants to get this over with.*

Before Russell could spend any more time thinking about Charles One's contacts, a bright green blip on his own radar.

"We've got a contact, Bellingsley," Russell said. "Bearing oh one oh from us!" The three blips were just to the right of the *Beaufighter*'s current heading, and Russell began fiddling with the set's knobs to figure out the range to their prey.

"Charles One, this is George One. We have trade also, working up bearing and range now," Bellingsley intoned into the net.

"All right chaps, it appears that our friends have deigned to join us this evening," Spence replied. "All aircraft except Charles Two, climb to angels twelve and await developments."

Aboard Charles Two, the pilot and radar operator were already closing with their prey. Adopting a pursuit curve, the inexperienced pilot did not realize how quickly he was closing until the target's biplane silhouette was almost filling the windscreen. Reacting quickly, the man mashed the trigger down for a full second before he hauled back on his yoke.

The *Beaufighter*'s massed firepower of four 20mm cannon and six .303-machine guns had been designed to saw apart German heavy bombers. Against the lightweight Aichi E13A floatplane it was the equivalent of using a battleaxe to chop chicken wings. Exploding in flames underneath the climbing *Beaufighter*, the biplane's demise served as a bright indicator that battle had been joined.

"Charles Two, are you all right?!" Charles One asked, his voice concerned.

That's a valid question, Russell thought. The explosion had been insanely bright even from their location miles away.

"Yes, I'm good. I think that's a kill," came the shaken response. "Watch it, these kites are flying slow."

"Not anymore. His partner's just taken off like the devil was after him. Tallyho," Spence replied.

A few moments later another flaming comet fell down from the scattered clouds to be quenched in the waters below. In a little under two minutes Charles Flight reigned supreme over their corner of the night sky.

"Now, George Flight, you are free to deal with your trade," Spence asserted, his tone somewhat triumphant.

Several thousand feet below the *Beaufighters*, a pin could have dropped the I.J.N.S. *Jintsu*, George One's surface contact.

15

"I believe that the *Nachi*'s aircraft have collided," the *Jintsu*'s master, Captain Masatori Kimura observed solemnly. He continued more quietly, "I knew it was far too dangerous to fly with these clouds."

The group of staff officers looking stricken at the rear of the bridge was the reason for Kimura's drop in volume. The *Jintsu* was the flagship for Rear Admiral Raizo Tanaka, commander of Destroyer Squadron (Desron) Two of the Imperial Japanese Navy. Behind the *Jintsu* evenly spaced at four hundred yard intervals were the destroyers *Hayashio*, *Hatsukaze*, *Kurashio*, *Yukikaze*, *Tokitsukaze*, and the *Amatsukaze*.

"Sir, shall we launch our aircraft?" *Jintsu*'s officer of the deck, a senior lieutenant, bellowed. Captain Kimura favored the man with a deadpan face that spoke wonders to those who knew him. *Jintsu*'s master watched as the younger officer's face nearly split into a smug grin before the senior officer turned away to hide his own smirk.

Question my pilot's courage, will you? Kimura thought savagely, his righteous anger focused on the commander standing stiffly at the hatchway to the light cruiser's flag plot. Squinting, he studied the six shapes three thousand yards off of *Jintsu*'s port quarter. Leading the column and clearly visible was the destroyer *Natsushio*. Behind the small vessel were the hulking, menacing shapes of the heavy cruisers *Nachi* and *Myoko*, followed by destroyers *Asagiri*, *Minigumo*, and *Asagumo*.

We do not need aircraft aloft to conduct a shore bombardment, Kimura thought, stepping briefly out onto the port bridge wing. The wind from the *Jintsu*'s movement combined with what appeared to be a rather westerly wind caused him to stagger before catching himself. Turning, he looked aft to where *Jintsu*'s own plane remained in its catapult, then quickly stepped back onto the bridge.

"Tell Warrant Officer Matsuoka that he will not be

launching tonight," the light cruiser's master ordered, daring Rear Admiral Tanaka's staff officer to contradict his order. "I'm reasonably certain he will be safer here than up there."

"Easy does it Bellingsley," Russell warned, fighting to keep the worry from his voice as the *Beaufighter* rapidly descended through increasing turbulence.

I didn't come all this way to die because you're sulking, Russell thought worriedly.

Spence and his flight leaders had worked out simple methods for attacking enemy shipping. Aware of vertigo's dangers, the senior officers had determined they would conduct most of their operations via level bombing at masthead height versus using torpedoes. While the latter were far more effective, a very long and straight run in the dark without a reliable horizon just begged for pilots to start smacking into wavetops. Bombing, on the other hand, allowed the *Beaus* to stoop on their prey like hawks from any direction, and with slightly less exposure to anti-aircraft fire.

Too bad the low-flash rockets haven't been quite perfected yet, Russell mused. The squadron had found that flying the standard aerial rockets, while likely to be very effective, was like looking into a series of bright camera flashes. Searchlights and tracers were effective enough in ruining night vision without adding in "own goals."

"Beginning flare run now," Bellingsley reported. As the first aircraft to make contact, George One had responsibility of illuminating for the rest of the flight.

If I didn't know better, I'd swear he's almost relishing the possibility of killing us both, Russell thought, slightly perturbed as he prepared to count down the range.

"Three thousand…two thousand…one thousand…flares, flares, flares!" Russell chanted. There was the rattle of the flare canisters falling out of their aircraft, then a few moments later the night lit up behind them with the

17

bright magnesium orbs falling under their parachutes. As the eighth and last flare fell out of the dispenser tube in the *Beaufighter*'s belly, Bellingsley threw the fighter into a tight turn to spoil possible gunnery solutions. Russell felt the twin-engined fighter shudder briefly on the edge of a stall, the aircraft's ordnance making it handle sluggishly. Before the senior officer could call out a word of caution, the pilot leveled the aircraft off and dipped the nose to regain airspeed.

Bellingsley need not have worried about evading anti-aircraft fire. The bursting magnesium caught the *Jintsu*'s crew by surprise, the *Beaufighter*'s muffled engines barely audible over the cruiser's own throbbing turbines. Before the gun crews could even begin to clear the white spots from their eyes, first George Three and then Four swept towards the cruiser from her starboard bow and port quarter.

Three's aimpoint was the illuminated light cruiser's superstructure, the pilot squeezing his trigger as his pipper passed over the ship's forward armament. Beginning at the base of the structure, the sparkling impacts of ball rifle ammunition and bright flashes of twenty millimeter hits climbed the *Jintsu*'s bridge like a malevolent zipper of destruction. The storm of fire cleared the *Jintsu*'s bridge in seconds, decapitating Captain Kimura and mortally wounding the helmsman, a talker, and both junior officers of the deck. Rear Admiral Tanaka, just stepping onto the bridge proper to give the order to launch *Jintsu*'s aircraft, was stopped in his tracks by a .303 round to his abdomen and splinters that sliced open his arm. Crumpling to the ground, the Japanese flag officer found himself pinned under two bodies of his staff.

Captain Kimura's last order had been for a hard turn to port in order to clear the flares. With the helmsman's headless body still dragging the wheel to the left, the light cruiser heeled hard over, throwing unsuspecting crewmen off their feet and causing blood to begin sloshing across the bridge and out of the wings. Just as men were struggling back towards their feet and rushing towards the ominously silent bridge, George Four opened fire from the darkness. Thrown off by the cruiser's turn, George Four's fire only briefly connect with its target. The damage, on the other hand, was all out of proportion to the dozen 20mm shells and almost a hundred rounds of .303 ammo that struck *Jintsu*'s hull. First the cruiser's aircraft burst into flames, then her starboard forward torpedo mount.

In the case of the former, the hapless Warrant Officer Matsuoka did not have enough time to register his danger before the Kawanishi E7K floatplane became the funeral pyre of both him and his observer. The five men servicing the aircraft had just begun shrieking in agony from their impromptu immolation when 20mm hits on the torpedo mount became several intense, torchlike jets of flame forward of their position. Burning with bright, white intensity, the fire from the twin 24-inch weapons bathed the light cruiser's deck in a dancing, horrific light that was visible from every ship in the task force.

As the flaming light cruiser continued to heel to port, the remainder of the Japanese group belatedly realized she was out of control and that they were under attack. Commands rang out aboard a dozen bridges as anti-aircraft crews began firing wildly into the air, across the horizon, and, in least a couple of cases into their fellow vessels. In the port column, the *Natsushio*, *Nachi*, and *Myoko* surged ahead as their masters rang up all ahead flank. Aboard the *Asagiri*, the destroyer's captain barked orders to turn to port, the signal lamp at the rear of her bridge passing this message to the *Minegumo* and *Asagumo*.

Dammit Two, where are you? Russell thought angrily as he watched the Japanese vessels scattering on his radar.

19

Before he could click his radio to ask, their wingman answered the question for him.

"George Two, resuming attack run," came an angry report. Looking, Russell could just barely see the *Beaufighter*'s rushing shadow passing through searchlight and tracer fire. A burst of gunfire suddenly came close to the attacking fighter's wing, causing the *Beau*'s pilot to jerk as he released his payload. Both of the *Beaufighter*'s bombs missed long, exploding off the *Jintsu*'s port side.

Bloody hell! Russell thought. *I doubt that was close enough to do anything other than shake her up.*

"We're going to have to give it a go," Russell barked, as the last of their flares winked out. There was a series of small explosions on the *Jintsu* as Bellinsglsey brought them around, and from his perspective Russell could swear the cruiser was starting to slow to a stop.

"You don't want me to try and get some of that larger trade we saw?" Bellingsly asked.

"No, let's get the bird we've clipped!" Russell snapped. "Just make sure you put the damn bombs on her!"

"Right then," Bellingsley seethed, and Russell felt his stomach dropped as the *Beaufighter*'s nose dropped. Having no job now that they were in their attack run, Russell could look around the sea below. He watched as the wakes that had been following the staggering light cruiser into her turn suddenly began scattering, their weapons continuing to fire at phantoms. Suddenly the sea was lit brightly again as George Three dispensed its flares near the burning light cruiser. Russell realized there were three destroyers near the larger vessel.

Too late to get cold feet now, Russell admonished himself. *Just hope Bellingsley doesn't screw this up.*

Russell need not have worried, as his pilot was determined to get a hit even if it killed them both. Cutting diagonally across the *Jintsu* from starboard bow to port quarter, Bellingsley made a textbook drop. George One's first 500-lb. bomb passed through *Jintsu*'s starboard lifeboat, reducing the craft to kindling on its way to piercing the cruiser's lightly armored deck. Equipped with a delay fuse, the bomb slammed all the way to the vessel's forward fire room in a storm of fragments and spall before exploding. The blast killed every Japanese sailor in the compartment, opened the *Jintsu*'s machinery spaces to flooding, and began a fierce bunkerage fire that further illuminated the light cruiser for all to see.

Bellingsley's second weapon was far more damaging. Hitting the light cruiser near her stern, the weapon began to pass out of the starboard side before detonating. This had a mining effect on the *Jintsu*'s hull, shaking and torquing the keel as if the light cruiser had been grabbed by a giant monster. Moreover, the explosion separated the starboard shaft, sending the propeller spinning into the inky blackness of the South China Sea. With a sound like a load of pipes rattling in the back of a lorry on a rutted road, the *Jintsu* began to vibrate as she continued to turn to port. Her harried executive officer, having already ordered a reduction in speed, screamed for the engine room crew to stop the vessel.

"Good show Bellingsley, good show!" Russell shouted, looking back over the *Beaufighter*'s tail. He was about to give another exhortation when a sudden series of bright flashes appeared in the night sky above and to George One's right side. A lurid orange streamer of flame blossomed from a point where the sky was somewhat darker, revealing a diving George Three as the *Beaufighter* attempted to finish *Jintsu* off. Before Russell could even begin to order George Three to retreat, multiple Japanese gunners focused on the flaming comet, catching the ablaze *Beaufighter* in a spider web of tracers. Even as the two bombs dropped from the twin-engined fighter's wings, Russell could already see the stub-nosed aircraft starting to fall off on one collapsing wing.

21

George Three continued staggering to the side, then slammed into the South China Sea at over two hundred knots, the resultant plume tinted orange before returning to darkness.

Bloody hell! Russell thought, watching as the two bombs landed close board the rapidly slowing *Jintsu*.

"George one, George One, this is Geor..." George Four began, before the squadron frequency was suddenly filled with a loud trumpet blaring.

"What the fuck?" Bellingsley snapped, his shoulders visibly tightening as the sound blared into his headphones. A moment later, there was a pause in the music filled by an accented voice screaming insults in badly accented English.

"We're being jammed!" Russell shouted over the *Beaufighter*'s roaring engines. Reaching over, he switched the radio frequency on the fighter's set.

"...say again, break off George Flight!" Spence's voice roared in Russell's headphones. "Slattern! Slattern! Slattern!"

Shit! The Navy's almost in range! Russell thought. "Slattern" was the agreed upon phrase indicating Australian aircraft needed to clear the area lest they find themselves on the wrong end of friendly ships' gunfire. While some had theorized the aircraft could operate at the same time, Russell was firmly in the camp that getting hit by fragments from a friendly hit or, even worse, an actual shell did not sound like a good plan.

Would have liked to put at least one set of bombs on those big bastards we saw, Russell thought. *Then again, a 500 pounder might just bounce off their hide.*

"What do we do?" Bellingsley asked, just as the *Beaufighter* was buffeted by a strong updraft. A few moments later rain began hammering against the observation dome over Russell's head.

"Back to Brunei," Russell said, his voice shaken as George Three's fate fully registered. "Jettison our bombs."

Deveraux had a wife and family back in Suffolk, he thought. *I don't even know how we notify them. Hell, I don't even know if the Usurper's goons will deliver the news.*

George Flight had left chaos in their wake. The *Jintsu,* having completed almost a complete circle and forced the IJN's port column to avoid her, was ablaze and stopped with the *Hayashio, Hatsukaze, Asagiri, Minigumo,* and *Asagumo* beginning to close with her to render aid or scattered in her general vicinity. The *Kurashio, Yukikaze, Tokitsukaze,* and *Amatsukaze,* having steered to starboard away from the crippled flagship, were continuing almost due east at top speed, their gunners intermittently shooting at shadows as they put distance between themselves and the battered *Jintsu.* Forming a third group, he *Natsushio, Nachi,* and *Myoko,* had also initially continued east at top speed, but were beginning to loop back around to the north to rejoin the rest of the Japanese group.

None of the Japanese vessels realized that something far more malevolent than George Flight was bearing down on them.

U.S.S. Houston
South China Sea
0145 Local (1145 Eastern)

"Bridge is asking the lookouts if they see anything again," stated the young sailor at the rear of Battle Two.

Commander Jacob Morton, the *Houston*'s executive officer, found himself wanting to reach through the talker tube and strangle Rear Admiral Glassford himself. A tall, wiry man with a shock of white hair underneath the "pie plate" steel helmet and flash hood he was wearing, Jacob peered out into the rain squalls and new moon darkness himself.

*We don't have that gee whiz system the **Australia** and **Boise** do, Admiral*, he thought disgustedly, rubbing his blue eyes in a vain attempt to clear some of the rain from his face. *Maybe you should have made one of them your flag? New moon and no reference points, we're lucky we haven't had a collision ourselves.*

The ACDA Striking Force, as the group of destroyers and cruisers were known, was in a long, snakelike column in part to minimize the likelihood of just such a merger. It was only in a grudging acknowledgment that, yes, the Japanese Navy *did* have submarines that the old "four piper" destroyers *Peary* and *Whipple* were one thousand yards to the column's port. To starboard, the the two elderly destroyers' sister ships *John D. Ford* and *Pope* maintained their anti-submarine watch at an equal distance. Between each duo, the H.M.A.S. *Vendetta* led H.M.A.S. *Australia*, U.S.S. *Boise*, the *Houston*, H.M.C.S. *Exeter*, H.M.A.S. *Perth*, H.M.C.S. *Electra*, H.M.C.S. *Jupiter*, and H.M.C.S. *Encounter* through the murk.

"Lookouts are reporting they saw some flares briefly but then the squall covered them," the talker reported. "Now there's just a fire on the horizon, nothing else so far."

I imagine the lookouts aren't much happier about being constantly questioned than we are hearing about it, Jacob thought. He glanced over at the makeshift plot, squinting as he stared at the map.

"At least this time we know we're not going after a wild goose chase," someone muttered in the darkness. There was a low murmur as the offending sailor was quickly and abruptly shushed by one of the petty officers, but Jacob found himself agreeing with the man's sentiment.

No, unlike a couple days ago, sounds like someone has actually seen something rather than some Dutchman being scared by what was apparently a submarine, Jacob thought. The ACDA had been rushing north towards Sumatra when that particular error was discovered. The ships had almost been back to Surabaya when they had received the report of Japanese forces being sighted west of Brunei in the South China Sea.

"Sir, *Australia* reports multiple contacts, range twelve thousand yards, bearing three two oh to oh eight oh" the Talk Between Ships, or TBS, talker said excitedly. "Requesting permission to fire."

In an instant, Battle-2 became more still than a closed funeral parlor. Every man could hear the dull throb of *Houston*'s turbines as she pushed forward through the South China Sea and the sound of the aft turret starting to orient towards the reported contacts off the column's port side..

"Admiral Glassford is telling them to stand by, wait for positive visual identification," the talker continued.

*What in the hell is he doing up there? We **know** there are no friendly vessels out here!* Jacob wondered in alarm. That last point had been made quite clear shortly before nightfall by the ACDA staff. As a sudden rainfall began to roar across *Houston*'s decks, Jacob felt his stomach start to clench.

Aboard the Japanese destroyer *Yukikaze*, one lookout turned away from the spectacle that was the burning and exploding *Jintsu* drawing rapidly astern. As the destroyer began turning to starboard to lead her three fellows back towards the stricken flagship, the junior rating brought his night glasses back up to cover his assigned sector to port. Still shaking from the excitement of the air attack, the young man took a deep breath…and realized he was staring at phosphorent wakes even if he could not see the ships causing them in the dark. Feeling his bladder and bowels loosen in fear, the lookout took a precious moment straining to identify the vessels. It was only after a few moments he realized that there was no way they could be Japanese.

"Enemy ships to starboard!" he turned and screamed,

the binoculars slipping from his wet hands.

Unlike the Allied fleet, there was no hesitation nor confusion engendered by the report. *Yukikaze*'s captain, as demonstrated by his decision to immediately surge away from the flares laid down by No. 625 squadron, was a man of decisive action. Shouting orders at the top of his lungs, he quickly began barking orders for his torpedo officer to begin sighting on the enemy ships and the main battery to load starshell.

"Guns, fire!" Captain Fitzpatrick, *Australia*'s snapped. "I will not be rammed by some Japanese vessel because some damn Yank cannot pull his head out of his arse!"

The Australian heavy's cruiser's firing gong rang out in the darkness a moment before her eight 8-inch guns opened the Battle of the South China Sea.

The *Australia*'s broadside flashed and rumbled across the darkness. Jacob jumped, just as startled as the rest of the Battle-Two crew. Eight glowing orbs shot out in the darkness to merge with something in a shower of sparks and at three distinct explosions. Moments later, starshells burst behind the targeted vessel, the high intensity flares descending like beautiful, oversized snowflakes. Bringing up his binoculars, Jacob sighted at least three vessels suddenly scuttling in the illumination.

"*Australia* confirms identification as Japanese vessels," Seaman First Class Teague, Battle Two's senior talker, stated rapidly.

"Guns is looking for targets!" his companion, Seaman Second Class Rodney Bass added.

"All vessels are given permission to fire," Teague stated. "Van destroyers have been instructed to turn to starboard to clear the firing angles!"

Jacob was about to respond when the *Houston*'s 5-

inch guns began barking starshells out at the enemy vessels.

"All right people, one at a time!" Jacob barked, making all of the talkers pause for a moment. Twelve thousand yards distant, the *Houston*'s starshells added to the bright illumination. The *Boise* fired again, the hits from her salvo leading to her switching to shooting as soon as her main guns could be reloaded.

"Roger," Jacob shouted, watching as the light cruiser's outline repeatedly strobed in front of him.

*I hope **Boise**'s gunnery officer knows what he's doing,* Jacob thought. A few moments later, *Houston*'s aft turret ceased searching and the heavy cruiser's firing gong began to buzz.

As one of those misfortunes of war, Jacob's desires were not being met. Both the *Boise* and *Australia*, firing with the aid of range finding radar, had straddled with their first salvos, then hit with the second. Unfortunately, the two cruisers were both engaging the hapless *Yukikaze*. *Boise* followed the *Australia* as the latter turned to starboard to unmask her stern turrets. As a result the unfortunate Japanese destroyer was subject to the full attention of twenty-three 6 and 8-inch guns.

The effects on the light-skinned *Yukikaze* were devastating. As a destroyer, she was never designed to stand and trade gunfire with a light and heavy cruiser. Even as her torpedoes were disgorged into the water at the bright flashpoints that were *Boise*'s guns, *Australia*'s second salvo had blasted a a hole in the waterline as it detonated just below the anchor. Belatedly, the destroyer's 5-inch guns began attempting to respond, belching out a single salvo before *Australia*'s second 8-inch hit carried away the *Yukikaze*'s gun director. In addition to shredding the DD's gunnery officer, the fragments from the impact also killed the sharp eyed lookouts who had initially spotted the Allied column, and shoved splinters through the roof of the destroyer's bridge.

The *Yukikaze*'s captain had just enough time to realize his right arm was as cleanly as if a butcher had cleaved it when *Boise* found the range with three, then four, then five more hits in the space of sixty seconds. The hail of explosions finished massacring the bridge crew, knocked out the destroyer's entire main battery, and exploded her boilers in a gout of steam and screaming men. Beginning to slow from her thirty-four knot advance, ablaze across her forward half, in under three minutes *Yukikaze* ceased serving any purpose other than as a coffin for her crew and superfluous target to the *Boise* and *Australia*'s energetic gun crews.

The flash and blast from *Houston*'s guns swept across Battle Two like a giant's breath. The glass portholes, removed and placed in their holders, all shattered as the heavy cruiser shook with her first broadside of the war.

Temporarily stunned, Jacob attempted to blink away the bright dots still clouding his vision. Beside him, Chief Petty Officer Roberts, Battle Two's non-commisioned officer in charge (NCOIC), swore loudly as he staggered around partially blind. Sticking out a hand, Jacob steadied the shorter, heavyset man until the NCO had regained some of his night vision. The sulfuric smell of expended black powder washed over them as *Houston* passed through her own gunsmoke, the heavy cruiser's thirty knot passage making the passage mercifully brief. Even so, Jacob felt this throat burning and fought the urge to cough.

Dammit Sloan, you better have fucking hit what you were shooting at, Jacob thought angrily.

Lieutenant Commander Sloan, had selected the *Amatsukaze* as his target. As the *Houston*'s 5-inch guns continued to lay starshells at a rapid rate, the turning Japanese destroyer had been a clear target in his sight. With the range at slightly under 10,000 yards and all three turrets able to bear, Sloan had made the decision to clear his nine guns of armor-piercing (AP) shells so that the next blast could be the more useful high explosive. Unfortunately, *Amatsukaze* made a fortuitous last minute turn that caused the first salvo to land barely a hundred meters short.

"Son-of-a-bitch," Sloan muttered disgustedly, bringing nervous looks from the director's other occupants. *Can't even hit a damn destroyer at ten thousand yards*, the blonde, handsome gunnery officer thought to himself.

"Hot damn, look at *Boise!*" someone shouted from the lookout station below. Sloan did not flinch from his sight, continuing to track the rapidly evading Japanese destroyer as he waited for the *Houston*'s gun crews to reload.

Even as *Amatsukaze* was dodging the *Houston*'s fire, the *Yukikaze* finally met her end. Firing as the range closed through eight thousand yards, the *Boise*'s eighth salvo found the destroyer's forward magazines. With a bright initial flash, followed by a thunderous explosion the 2,500-ton destroyer and her 240-man complement ceased to exist in a corona of debris. Every man who watched the fiery demise of the *Yukikaze* aboard the Allied ships broke out in a spontaneous cheer. For one vessel, these cheers were suddenly broken off by explosions.

The three Japanese destroyers had unleashed twenty-four Type 93 torpedoes upon their initial sighting of the Allied force just under five minutes earlier. With a top speed approaching fifty knots and the Allied column turning towards them, the weapons had closed the intervening distance far more quickly than the Allies would have expected. Nearly wakeless, the 24-inch weapons carried warheads designed to eviscerate a full-sized battleship with one blow, nevermind the gaggle of cruisers and destroyers they faced that night.

For the majority of the Allied force, the horrible angles the Japanese torpedo officers had chosen made the chance of hits very slim. *Australia*'s turn to unmask her full broadside and errors made by terrified torpedo crews still shaken by sudden aerial assault all combined to worsen these odds. However, even bad percentages were still greater than zero. The bulk of the *Yukikaze*'s hastily fired torpedoes passed astern of *Houston* and *Exeter*. The latter's lookouts, startled by seeing detonations in their wake, had just shouted a warning to the bridge when the *Tokitsukaze*'s spread found the *Perth*.

In his haste, the *Tokitsukaze*'s torpedo officer had failed to put a proper angle between the torpedoes. As a result, the eight fish from the destroyer had barely fanned out as they set upon their runs. Had he misjudged the Allied line's speed this would have resulted in a complete miss. Unfortuantely for the Australian cruiser's complement, it was not their Japanese counterpart's night to be unlucky. Three of the Type 93s intersected with the *Leander*-class cruiser's port amidships. The *Electra* and *Exeter* were treated to the spectacle of three almost indeterminate explosions that killed every man in the vessel's aft engine room, destroyed the bulkhead between that space and the boiler room behind it, and broke the cruiser's back. Steaming at thirty knots, the damage forced the *Perth* to tear herself apart, splitting in two just aft of her second funnel. The aft portion, almost open to the sea its entire length, sank in moments. As the stern went under, witnesses aboard the *Electra* saw the cruiser's screws still turning at full revolutions.

The forward section, ablaze towards its aft end, gradually lost momentum. As the *Electra* put her helm over to pass *Perth*'s remnants to starboard, the mangled, burning section began to slowly roll to port as it settled. In the half light of the blazing fuel oil pouring out into the surrounding ocean, *Electra*'s crew were treated to the ghastly spectacle of men racing up the sinking light cruiser's side. With a roar, the maimed vessel's 'A' turret fired one last blast to port, the shells smacking into the water barely eight hundred yards away.

"*Exeter* and *Electra* report *Perth* has been hit by a submarine!" Teague screamed. "*Exeter* has been near-missed!"

"How bad is *Perth* hurt?" Jacob asked, fighting to keep his voice calm while fixing the excited young sailor with a baleful gaze.

"She's blown in half, Sir," the talker replied, much quieter but visibly shaken.

"Goddamit Teague, *she* who?!" Jacob barked.

"*Perth*, Sir," Teague said, visibly shrinking under his own helmet. "*Exeter* and *Electra* report she went straight down." A moment's pause. "The *Whipple* and *Peary* are being directed to search for the submarine and pick up survivors."

Jacob nearly lost his footing as the *Houston* suddenly lurched to port. Gazing at the helm indicator, he belatedly realized that Battle-2 was bathed in light, the deck outside clearly visible.

Starshells! Jacob thought, just as the *Houston*'s forward turrets thundered at the *Amatsukaze*. Jacob fought the urge to try and hide from the illumination rounds. Instead, he turned his head around as he heard several cheers from the closest 5-inch gun crew.

Sloan's sixth salvo had finally found paydirt. Almost carrying over, one of the cruiser's 8-inch shells hit the *Amatsukaze*'s No. 2 funnel. Detonating with a bright flash and sparks, the high explosive shell spewed a scythe of fragments into the aft torpedo mount just as the crew was completing reloading. Through some miracle, the mount remained serviceable. Its crew, however, suffered the usual fate of men caught in the open by artillery, their screams carrying across the destroyer's deck.. The Japanese vessel lurched under the impact, funnel smoke pouring back down into her engineering spaces seconds later. Coughing and sputtering, the men tried to doggedly continue working on their tasks.

Amatsukaze's captain, feeling his ship staggered by the hit, struggled to keep his face calm.

"Sir, should we switch shells?!" his gunnery officer called down the voice pipe.

"No! Continue to fire starshell!" the destroyer captain responded. *Any moment now*, he thought.

"Why is that bastard firing only star shell?" someone asked on the *Australia*'s bridge.

"It's not like it's needed with the Yanks firing!" came the response from another talker.

The Commonwealth cruiser had quieted her own guns in order to avoid interfering with the *Boise* and *Houston* as they engaged the two Japanese destroyers. While their less disciplined American lookouts had done everything but break out the popcorn for the show, several months of fighting in the Mediterranean had made the *Australia*'s crew a little more disciplined.

"Ships! Three enemy ships to three points off the port bow!" the young rating sang out.

"Hard a port! Watch for torpedoes! Guns, engage enemy vessels to starboard!" Captain Fitzpatrick barked as he ran across the *Australia*'s bridge. Leaning down towards the sighting glasses on the bridge wing, Fitzpatrick saw the two enemy vessel's wakes clear as day even if he could not make out their shapes. A few moments later, *Australia*'s starboard secondary guns began firing even as the cruiser's four turrets began turning to bear on the new targets.

"Sir, *Australia* reports enemy ships to starboard!"

"What?!" Jacob asked, turning to Teague. His question was lost in the *Houston*'s guns firing their next salvo.

Commander Sloan had begun to figure out the *Amatsukaze*'s evasive patterns. Out of the nine shells from *Houston*'s broadside, four were near misses that completed the slaughter of her torpedo crews, knocked out her No. 1 turret, and began leaks below the vessel's waterline. Two more shells hit the cruiser, destroying her steering room and starting a bunkerage blaze amidships. With water pouring into her stern and her helm no longer answering, the *Amatsukaze* began to slow, carrying on in a straight line.

The *Amatsukaze*'s travails were minor compared to that of the *Tokitsukaze*. Even as *Houston* was hitting the former, *Boise* found the range to the latter with a 6-gun half salvoes. Seeing that most of his shells hit, *Boise*'s gunnery officer immediately began rapid fire with both port secondaries as well as the six-inch guns. While gun malfunctions had robbed him of three weapons, it still meant that the light cruiser was throwing four salvoes every sixty seconds. Even as *Australia* was throwing her helm hard to port and warning of additional vessels, the *Tokitsukaze* was hit by first two, then three more shells.

With the first two shells, one to the gunnery director and the other to the engine room, the destroyer ceased to be an effective fighting unit. The next three, hitting the rudder controls, blasting a massive hole in her waterline, and, finally, detonating the torpedoes being reloaded in her forward banks, caused the the destroyer to cease being a ship. With a bright white flash, the barely two-year-old destroyer broke violently in two, her demise condemning seventy-six more men to the embrace of the South China Sea's marine life.

"*Australia* just turned to port!"

Jacob gestured for the TBS headphones, wanting to hear what was going on himself. What he heard chilled his heart.

"Torpedoes! Torpedoes to starboard!"

Captain Takahiko Kiyota *Nachi*'s master and the senior officer present, had immediately responded to the late *Yukikaze*'s initial sighting report. The man's first order had been for all gunners aboard the two heavy cruisers to cease engaging airborne targets. The second was to shut off their search lights. His third had been for all three ships to reverse their northern flight away from *Jintsu* and come to a generally eastern course while he assessed the situation. The fourth and final order directed all destroyers vessels except for the *Hatsukaze* and *Miniguomo* away from the blazing *Jintsu* and onward to the attack with the intent of catching the large Allied force between two pincers.

Three minutes before *Australia*'s lookouts had sighted the two heavy cruisers and the accompanying *Natsushio*, the trio of IJN ships had launched their torpedoes at the targets illuminated by the *Amatsukaze* and *Karushio*'s star shells. The three vessels had then angled slightly to port on a course that would bring them parallel to the enemy line at a range of roughly ten thousand yards just as their torpedoes were impacting. Seeing the *Boise*'s shape outlined in the flash of her own guns, Kiyota believed himself to be facing a *Colorado*-class battleship and had ordered all three vessels to concentrate their torpedo fire accordingly. It was only after *Nachi*'s gunnery officer had repeated the target's speed that the senior officer had realized his error. It was as he was giving counter orders to the destroyers approaching from the southwest that *Australia* made her sudden turn to port and began engaging the *Natsushio* with her secondaries.

"Illuminate targets! Target the third vessel!" Kiyota barked disgustedly. "Open fire!"

Unfortunately for Kiyota's intent, two things disrupted his perfectly planned pincer. First, the *Jintsu* suffered several secondary explosions as her fires finally set off torpedo warheads amidships. This event, startling in its ferocity, allowed to the lookouts aboard the *Whipple* and *Peary* to see the approaching trio of Japanese destroyers that had previously attended *Jintsu*. Frantically signaling a warning both visually and over TBS, the duo of American four-stackers surged forward to engage their opposite numbers. The *Jupiter* and *Encounter*, having just passed the *Perth*'s foundering bow, also turned to port and began to close with the approaching IJN vessels.

"Enemy destroyers bearing two oh oh!" Teague shouted, just as *Nachi*'s searchlights swept over Battle Two.

Jacob had a brief instant to register the report and attempt to see the chaotic plot in his head before the Battle of the South China Sea degenerated into barroom brawl rather than a controlled sea battle.

The crew of the *Boise*, suffering target fixation as their guns switched to the *Karushio*, took precious moments to react to the *Australia*'s sighting message and sudden turn. Realizing the *Australia* was not as nimble as his newer ship and fearing a collision should he immediately put his helm over, *Boise*'s captain resolved to wait until his vessel reached the area where *Australia* had begun her emergency turn. With his bridge awash in the intense white light of the *Natsushio*'s searchlights and the enemy cruisers having just presented themselves, it was reasonable to assume the light cruiser had the thirty or so seconds to wait. Unfortunately, as the lookouts finally spotted the nearly wakeless Type 93s' to

35

starboard, the man had enough time to realize it was an incorrect choice based on his vessel's own armament and a peacetime mentality.

The *Boise* was the target of over thirty torpedoes. While the vagaries of night targeting, her changed course, misjudged speed, and pure dumb luck made the overwhelming majority of these weapons miss, the light cruiser's fate was almost pre-ordained. The first tin fish to merge with her was set for a battleship's draft, passing underneath the light cruiser's three forward turrets. The second tin fish, hastily and improperly handled during reloading drills when the *Nachi* had been departing Cam Ranh Bay, hit with a dull *thunk* that was audible throughout the light cruiser's forward half. Less than ten seconds later, *Myoko*'s first torpedo ripped open *Boise*'s No. 1 fireroom, killing all hands where they stood. The blast threw almost every man aboard the cruiser off their feet. The lights flickered once, then went out throughout much of the ship, causing panic among the crew of the adjacent compartments as water began flooding into the engineering spaces. As old hands and petty officers began restoring order, yet another torpedo speared the light cruiser's bow, shaking the entire vessel and completing the process of knocking circuits askew in her main generator room. Hard hit, unable to fire or steer, the light cruiser began to come to a stop with a fire beginning to glow in her midsection.

The remainder of the Japanese torpedo salvo continued through the Allied formation, with two of the Type 93s passing just forward of *Houston* while three detonated in the heavy cruiser's wake. Feeling the vessel shake, Jacob ran to the starboard side of Battle Two to look behind the vessel. To his surprise, Jacob realized that the *Exeter* was no longer behind the *Houston*, and that his vessel's own 8-inch guns had almost completed swinging to starboard. Ducking back inside Battle Two's hatch, Jacob turned to ask the talkers a question just as all hell broke loose.

Seeing that their salvo had only crippled one target and completely missed the other, the *Nachi* group suddenly found themselves with a tiger by the tail. Aboard the *Nachi*, Kiyota had a brief moment of indecision as he first ordered the main battery to fire at the *Houston*, then countermanded his order and ordered the guns to fire on the *Boise* and the cruiser's generators to begin making smoke.

The *Boise*, heavily damaged by her torpedo hit and slowing, was all but sitting duck. Her crew had just begun responding to the disemboweling torpedo attack when the *Nachi*'s searchlights swiveled to illuminate her in stark relief. Firing on manual control, the American cruiser's starboard 5-inch guns managed to get off a hurried volley at the lights before the *Nachi* unleashed a full ten gun broadside at her. While not the virtual machine-gunning that *Boise* had delivered to her two victims, the heavy salvo was tightly grouped due to the Japanese Navy's *Sokutekiban* device. As a result, all ten shells either near missed or hit the light cruiser in a forest of waterspouts and cacophony of dull explosions that sliced the cruiser's forward funnel in half, blinded her aft director, killed many of the secondary battery's crews, and jammed the No. 5 turret with a hit to the barbette. Wallowing from her torpedo damage, the *Boise*'s guns remained silent as her crew fought to save the vessel's life.

For the *Myoko*, trailing astern of the *Nachi*, the gunnery officer had lost sight of the *Australia*, which was masked by the burning *Boise*. Switching to the *Houston* as *Nachi*'s first broadside thundered out, the Japanese commander was startled to see the American cruiser's own 8-inch guns turning towards the *Nachi*. Hurrying his shot, the officer put his first salvo over two hundred meters short of the *Houston*.

The beauty of night combat was that searchlights worked both ways. Even as his own ship was lit up like King Kong on the Empire State Building, Lieutenant Commander Sloan took aim at the heavy cruiser battering the *Boise*. At under eight thousand yards and closing thanks to Captain Wallace's aggressive decision to turn towards the enemy vessels, Sloan made a quick range estimate and fired the six guns loaded.

The broadside was on for range, but Sloan had misjudged the *Nachi*'s course. As a result, only one 8-inch shell hit the IJN vessel. Streaking in like a meteor from the starboard bow, the shell pierced the *Nachi*'s thick belt and detonated with a low order explosion in A turret's handling room. Miraculously, none of the Japanese cruiser's own shells exploded in a sympathetic detonation, although every man in the compartment was killed by the resultant powder fire and fragments. High up in the vessel's director, the Japanese gunnery officer felt the slight tremor and realized that he was shooting at a sitting duck when another American vessel was trying to kill him.

"Got him!" Jacob shouted as he saw the bright flash of the hit on the Japanese cruiser.

Someone had finally remembered the *Houston*'s new speaker system in Battle Two and belatedly switched on the TBS. Radio discipline had gone completely to Hell, and Jacob could hear Rear Admiral Glassford trying to order the destroyers that had been to starboard but fallen behind to attack the Japanese cruisers. Meanwhile, the *Australia* was attempting to break in with a report of more destroyers mauling the *Whipple*, *Peary*, *Jupiter*, and *Encounter*. The *Electra* and *Exeter* were strangely silent.

Jacob had just enough time to process all this information before the *Myoko*'s second broadside arrived with the sound of ripping canvas. The *Houston* staggered as Jacob heard a series of explosions amidships and forward.

"Damage report!" he barked, turning to the talkers as the TBS continued to yammer away.

"Zig zag pattern two!" Teague responded, not having understood what Jacob was asking in the cacophony of sound.

Yes, it might be time to start dodging, Jacob thought. Amazingly, he did not feel any conscious fear. He was too focused on trying to keep track of the battle to realize that the *Houston* was outnumbered two heavy cruisers to one and was currently fighting all by herself at point blank range.

The firing gong sounded again, and Jacob closed his eyes while bracing himself.

Myoko had just fired her second salvo, observing at least four hits, when the *Exeter* made her presence known. Having turned to starboard to unmask his main battery, Captain Gordon had found himself in the pleasant position of "crossing the T" in front of the Japanese cruisers. With her own radar finally unmasked from behind *Houston* and the Japanese force conveniently illuminating themselves with searchlights, the *Exeter* had waited an extra minute to be sure of her firing solution. The patience paid off, as her half-dozen 8-inch guns caught the *Myoko* completely by surprise.

Whereas all of the Allied cruisers had been designed in strict, if not overly slavish, compliance with the 10,000-ton limit of the Washington Treaty, the *Myoko's* designers had not been able to cram all that they desired into the cruisers hull and give her adequate protection. When confronted with the hard physics equation of only so much equipment being able to fit into a given mass, the designers had simply ignored the limit when designing the vessel. The resultant design choices simultaneously saved and cursed the heavy cruiser as *Exeter*'s salvo thundered home with four hits.

Two of the shells were rejected by the *Myoko*'s armor

due to the sharp angle they impacted at. However, there were plenty of vulnerable things not protected by the vessel's belt, and the third shell found a starboard AA mount. In a stunning pyrotechnic display, the mount was completely demolished, its ready ammunition exploding in a manner that caused great consternation on her bridge. The final shell, continuing a theme for the night, detonated just below the port forward torpedo mount. Fortuitously for the cruiser, the shell's detonation did not detonate the Type 93s warheads. Less fortunate for everyone in the surrounding area, the flame jets from the weapons' oxygen fuel immolated almost the entire crew. The few survivors, horrifically burned, managed to trip the electrical trigger for the mounts to try and save their ship. The three Long Lances ejected from the tubes snaked out from the *Myoko*'s port side and fell towards the bottom of the South China Sea. The oxygen fed flames briefly lit the waters near the cruiser's hull with their eerie glow before falling out of sight towards the bottom of the South China Sea.

As the flames from two seemingly major fires lit his bridge, *Myoko*'s captain barked orders for the heavy cruiser to turn hard to port and engage the *Exeter* even as his guns fired again at the *Houston*.

Jacob had just gotten his bearings back when *Nachi*'s salvo had arrived close aboard. Whining splinters slashed over the *Houston*'s open decks, and another shudder told him that the heavy cruiser had been hit somewhere underneath her waterline. Just as Teague was complying with his first request for a damage report, *Myoko*'s salvo began heading over the water seemingly right at him.

"Shit!" Jacob muttered as time seemed to dilate, fear loosening his bowels as the shells seemed to head right for him. In that instant, he felt suddenly aware of everything that was happening inside of Battle-2.

The sound of the talkers updating information from the bridge…

The petty officer in charge of the plotting table cursing at a man for making an error…

The bright light as a Japanese searchlight swept over the position…

The yelling and shouting from the 5-inch gun crew nearest to where he was standing.

Time resumed its normal speed as the tight Japanese salvo filled the area around the *Houston*'s stern suddenly became alive with more whizzing steel, screams, and the *crump* of explosions. The eight shells that hit the American cruiser all hit aft of the vessel's No. 1 funnel in a fury that harkened back to a Napoleonic broadside. Jacob would never know how near he came to death himself, as a secondary explosion threw him to the deck just as a splinter passed into Battle Two. One of the compartment's runners was not as lucky, the sailor falling to his knees with his left arm raggedly cut off just above his elbow. Jacob looked at the man in horror as the young sailor stupidly waggled the limb, then began screaming in agony.

"Litter party!" Chief Roberts bellowed, cuffing one of the sailors standing mutely in shock. "Get this man below!".

"Sir!" Teague screamed, jerking Jacob out of his reverie. "I have Damage Control!"

Jacob took the preoffered sound telephone even as the *Houston*'s own guns roared out a retort at the *Nachi*. Looking to port, he saw the *Australia* heading almost one hundred eighty degrees the other direction, her guns seemingly pointed right Jacob's head as the big cruiser prepared to reenter the battle.

"This is the XO! Report!"

As Jacob listened to the voice of Lieutenant Commander Caspin Nye, he felt himself cursing the *Houston*'s designers. As with her sisters, the *Houston*'s

41

designers had underestimated the amount of ship they could have squeezed from 10,000 tons. With a philosophy the exact opposite of their Japanese counterparts, the U.S.N.'s designers had been almost fanatical in their adherence to the letter of the Washington Treaty. The *Houston*'s No. 3 turret was now jammed in train, the aft magazine was being flooded due to a shell hit that had started a massive deflagration, and nearly destroyed the cruiser.

That explains the flame that went by, Jacob thought grimly. He was immediately thankful for the stiff breeze that blew past Battle Two, as he was sure the smell of burnt flesh would otherwise have filled the compartment.

As the forward armament roared again, Jacob snapped himself back to paying attention to Nye's report. The engineering spaces were starting to slowly flood, indicating damage to the vessel's bottom. While the pumps could slow the process, Nye believed it was well past time for the *Houston* to disengage or he could not guarantee power for much longer.

Jacob started to inhale in order to shout across Battle Two, then immediately felt a sharp jab of pain in his chest that caused him to double over. Attempting to take a deep breath, he felt the same agony again and realized what it was from past experience.

Cracked some freakin' ribs, he thought to himself. *Haven't done that since that bar fight in England as a lieutenant.*

"Sir, are you all right?!" Chief Roberts exclaimed, clearly concerned. Jacob nodded, waving him away. He felt the *Houston* start to turn to port.

"Sir, we're leaving the fight!" Teague said.

Looking around the compartment, Jacob realized they were no longer illuminated, and no more fire was inbound. There was the sound of gunfire astern, and he realized that the *Australia* was engaging a target.

The reason for *Houston*'s succor was the *Nachi* and *Myoko* having much more pressing problems. Like a back alley tough jumping a larger opponent, the Commonwealth cruiser had been shooting as rapidly as possible even as *Myoko*'s guns began swinging towards her. For her part, *Nachi* had fired one more salvo at *Houston* before also turning to look for the Commonwealth cruiser as well. Unlike the *Boise*, however, the *Exeter* was equipped with flashless powder and managed to rattle off eight full broadsides and fired her torpedoes before either IJN cruiser had a chance to bring their searchlights to bear.

The damage to *Myoko* was horrible. As her gunnery officer finally found his target, the *Exeter*'s fire had holed the heavy cruiser's bow and forward spaces, started several fires, and necessitated the flooding of No. 1 and 2 magazines. Grievously injured, the *Myoko* nevertheless brought her searchlights to bear to aid the *Nachi*'s targeting. The bright lights pinned *Exeter*, the heavy cruiser's dual stacks and staggered deck making her identification almost immediate.

It was at this moment that the *Ford*, *Pope*, and *Electra* forcibly reminded the Japanese force of their presence. The *Natsushio*, having continued to fire at the *Boise* as her torpedo crews reloaded, suddenly staggered, a huge wave of water going up as one of *Electra*'s torpedoes found her amidships. With her power immediately knocked out, the destroyer slowed and became a navigational hazard for the *Nachi* just as her gunnery officer was taking aim at *Exeter*. As lookouts screamed about additional torpedoes inbound, Captain Kiyota barked orders for the heavy cruiser to turn hard to port. To the gunnery officer's disgust, his ten shells all missed the *Exeter* due to the emergency turn, the smaller Commonwealth cruiser lost in the neatly spaced waterspouts.

Even as *Electra* tin fish were paid to the *Natsushio*, the *Ford* and *Pope* were closing on the two Japanese heavy cruisers from almost directly bow on. Both four-pipers dated from World War One, and as such lacked a central director that allowed all guns to be simultaneously targeted or fired. Offsetting their age was the fact that the vessels' individual captains had relentlessly drilled their crews over the last six months. Now as both destroyers charged the *Nachi* and *Myoko*, their training paid off. Hardly able to hurt the cruisers with their guns, the "four pipers" managed to land several punishing hits as they closed to five thousand yards. Turning simultaneously to starboard as *Nachi* and *Myoko* began their turn away from *Exeter*, both destroyers launched torpedoes from the heavy cruisers' starboard quarter then started to turn away into their own smoke. *Nachi*'s starboard secondaries managed to enact some measure of revenge for the shellfire striking her, landing two 5-inch shells on the *Ford* before that vessel disappeared from view. The two shells exploded amidships on the destroyer's port side, detonating just above the waterline. Hard hit, the *Ford* began slinking away into the darkness with the *Pope* circling worriedly back to render aid.

The *Nachi*'s gunnery officer never had a chance to celebrate his success as the *Australia* found the range. Shooting high, the Commonwealth put four 8-inch shells into the *Nachi*'s superstructure and turrets. While *Nachi*'s designers had blatantly violated the tonnage limit their nation had agreed to in the Washington Treaty, they had not placed massive protection everywhere. In an effort to keep the cruiser from being top heavy with all of her protection and heavy broadside, the designers had decided to provide the turrets with only enough armor to keep out splinters. As a result, the shell that hit dead center between B turret's twin guns shell cut through like an ice pick through a soda can. Detonating just as several powder charges arrived from the *Nachi*'s magazine, the shell's detonation caused a secondary detonation that blew the structure's roof off and back into the cruiser's bridge.

Pandemonium was a gentle word for the carnage that ensued as several tons of steel slashed into the massive pagoda structure. Like a fistful of razor blades flung into a darkened bijou, the roof's remnants ricocheted around the enclosed compartment. Captain Kiyota, having governed the fight as aggressively and professional as possible after Rear Admiral Tanaka's incapacitation, was rewarded by having his entire left side slashed open as a huge piece of steel slammed him to the compartment's rear. The officer of the deck and the cruiser's talkers were all similarly dispatched by either the initial entry of steel or the horrible ricochet as the fragments bounced off the surrounding bulkheads.

The *Nachi*'s junior officer of the deck (JOOD), having stepped briefly out onto the starboard bridge wing, took in the macabre scene inside the structure. Before he could step inside, he heard screams from above him and a recurring grinding sound. Realizing that the director had taken a direct hit, the young lieutenant stepped back into the bridge and promptly slipped on a puddle of blood and fell to his knees on one of the many casualties. As the man groaned underneath him, the JOOD fought back to his feet at grabbed the sound powered telephone at the back of the bridge. Screaming into it, the officer informed the *Nachi*'s executive officer that he was now in charge, as the bridge was a charnel house.

Maimed, the *Myoko* had started to slow as she turned back into her smoke screen. With the *Exeter*'s accurate fire still landing around her, the *Myoko*'s captain ordered a zig back to the north. It was at this point that the *Nachi*, fires burning throughout her pagoda structure and her stern turrets firing almost full astern, came charging through the smoke her sister had laid. Screaming in rage, *Myoko*'s captain ordered her helm put back to starboard. The the heavy cruiser's bow stopped its motion to port, then slowly came around to the inside of the *Nachi*'s path.

The two cruisers passed close enough that the *Myoko*'s crew on deck could see *Nachi*'s men carrying the dead and wounded from her bridge in the sudden light of an *Electra* star shell pattern. The *Nachi*'s men, for their part, could see *Myoko*'s ruined forward half, damage control crews playing hoses on the numerous fires still burning in front of her bridge. Just as the two ships finished passing port to starboard, the American destroyers' torpedoes finished their painfully slow journey.

In the end, five torpedoes, two from *Ford* and three from *Whipple*, struck the *Myoko*. In contrast to the allegedly superior Mk 14 and 15s which had replaced it, the elderly Mk 8s had a lower dud rate. Only one of the weapons failed to detonate, the other four stabbing the heavy cruiser's bow, abreast the already flooded magazines, amidships, then just forward of where her props joined the hull. Her rudder carried away, her aft engine room opened to the sea, bunkerage suddenly set alight, and the damaged bow suddenly acting as a brake to her progress, the *Myoko* undulated like a stabbed, living beast then stopped.

The *Nachi*, her steering capability belatedly restored, continued to hurtle west into the darkness. As her weary crew looked after, they watched as their sister was hit again, first by *Exeter* then by *Australia*. Belatedly, her executive officer radioed the directive to retreat to the Japanese destroyers still dueling their opposite numbers to the southwest In contrast to *Nachi*'s pell mell retreat, that of the *Karushio* and her new companions was well executed. Having sunk the *Whipple*, crippled the *Peary*, and forced the *Jupiter* and *Encounter* to retire at the cost of only moderate damage to the *Asagiri*, the pack of four Japanese DDs had been busy stalking the *Australia* when the *Nachi* ordered retreat.

Aboard the *Karushio*, the news was met with a great deal of anger. Having watched his comrades die, the *Karushio*'s master had been looking forward to possibly gaining some measure of revenge with the other three destroyers close behind. As he received news that torpedo reloads were complete, the Japanese commander bit out orders for the torpedoes to be fired against the burning, stationary *Boise* once the *Karushio* had come back about to the west and the following *Asagumo, Asagiri*, and *Hayashio* to be informed of this target. Two minutes later, all four DDs unleashed their ship killers, then made best speed back towards the still burning *Jintsu*.

For the second time that night, the *Boise* became the focus of a swarm of Japanese torpedoes. Unlike the first time, there was no mistaking her for a capital ship or misjudging her speed. Just under eight minutes after their launch, as the *Pope* and *Ford* were approaching the crippled cruiser from her starboard quarter, four of the massive Type 93s struck the light cruiser from bow to stern.

The crew of the *Ford* had just enough time to register the hits before one of the torpedoes that had missed *Boise* astern slammed into the four piper just underneath her bridge. Throwing the entire crew off their feet, the Type 93's warhead snapped the tin can's keel like a grown man breaking a celery stalk. The pressure of the DD's speed caused the bow to snap off just behind the bridge, the structure gouging another hole in the DD's side as it bounced to port. Shuddering to a stop, the *Ford* immediately began to settle.

The destroyer's destruction, as horrific as it was to those viewing from her sister ship, was merely a preamble to the *Boise*'s demise. Already heavily flooded, the cruiser's keel and several amidships bulkhead suddenly gave under the inrush of additional water. With a sound that would haunt all who heard it until the day they died, the *Boise*'s hull jackknifed. For ninety horrific seconds, her bow and stern were both horrifically outlined by a spreading pool of burning fuel oil floating atop the South China Sea.

Broadcasting a frantic warning about submarines, the *Pope*'s commander put his helm hard to starboard and reversed course away from the sinking *Ford* and *Boise*. Hearing the call, Rear Admiral Glassford immediately ordered the *Exeter* and *Australia* to cease their pursuit of the *Nachi* and retire south to regroup. Despite bitter commentary the bridge of both vessels, the two Commonwealth cruisers complied after firing one last desultory salvo after their fleeing opponent. As they passed the crippled, sinking *Myoko*, each heavy cruiser fired three more salvoes into the battered IJN vessel. The *Australia*, at barely five thousand yards distance, fired four torpedoes and was rewarded with two more hits to the listing *Myoko*'s port side. Absorbing far too much damage for even her overweight hull, the IJN cruiser visibly lurched then quickly slipped under the waves bow first.

Peeling off from where she had been leading her larger brethren, the *Electra* began pinging her sonar as she closed on the rapidly settling *Ford*. Receiving no returns, the Commonwealth DD continued easing forward slowly while settling a listening watch on her hydrophones. As a result, she was still two thousand yards distant when the *Ford* finally slipped beneath the waves, the survivors yelling for help from the visible ship. The Commonwealth crew were just readying nets and lines when these cries were cut short by a series of bright flashes and explosions from beneath the water, the *Ford*'s depth charges detonating as her wreck passed three hundred feet. Horrified, the *Electra*'s commander ordered the destroyer's advance quickened. Despite this effort, the *Elecra* would haul only twenty of the *Ford*'s crew out of the waters.

There was one final act to the night's drama. Despite the explosion of her torpedoes, the *Jintsu*'s executive officer had managed to maintain some semblance of stability with *Hatsukaze* and *Minigumo*'s aid. Unfortunately, what he did not have was the ability to repair his rudder or fully extinguish the fires that continued to threaten his magazines.

Even worse, the executive officer had no clue of the science that had made the night air attack possible, but figured that it would not be prudent to risk any more of the Emperor's ships when the sun rose in a few hours. Giving an order that disgusted him to his core, he instructed charges to be laid and the Emperor's portrait to be transferred to the *Minigumo*. Ten minutes later, as he stood on the *Minigumo*'s stern with Hirohito's picture clutched in his hands, the commander watched as the scuttling charges detonated the *Jintsu*'s secondary magazine and remaining torpedo warheads. Her hull utterly shattered, the light cruiser rolled over to starboard and sank into the South China Sea's depths.

"Jesus Christ, is that clock broken?" Jacob asked, looking at Battle Two's rear bulkhead as *Houston* began to slow from her pell mell retreat. Splinters had scored the metal around the device, and Jacob could not believe the time piece's face was correct.

"Yes, Sir," Chief Roberts said wearily. "It's correct."

I cannot believe that fight was less than forty minutes, Jacob thought, shaken. *One hundred twenty-five men aboard this vessel alone are dead, nevermind how many went down with the **Perth***. Regaining his composure, he nodded.

"Understood Chief," Jacob intoned solemnly.

The two men were interrupted by Teague.

"Sir, Captain Wallace for you!" the young sailor said. Jacob took the sound powered phone.

"Sir, Commander Morton," Jacob said.

"XO, I can't get a hold of Damage Central from here, and my last runner has not come back," Captain Wallace said, his voice angry. "What's our status?"

"Sir, No. 3 turret is locked in train and it will take a yard trip to get it to move again," Jacob informed *Houston*'s captain. "The handling room is also burnt out, and the magazine has been flooded as a precaution. We've got

JAMES YOUNG

flooding in both engine rooms, but at the moment the bilge pumps are keeping ahead of it. Lieutenant Commander Nye is still assessing the damage forward, but most of it appears to be flooding and nothing that will affect the ship's ability to fight."

There was a long silence.

"You go find Nye and tell him that he needs to get better communications going with this bridge," Wallace snapped. "Rear Admiral Glassford is ordering a retirement— some Jap submarine just blew the *Boise* and *Ford* out of the water."

Jacob felt his face pale.

"Aye-aye, Sir," Jacob replied. "I'll go find Commander Nye right now."

"Report to me on the bridge when done," Captain Wallace ordered, his tone only slightly more neutral. "We'll discuss some changes to procedures."

"Sir, do you need the division heads?" Jacob asked.

"No, I think you're quite capable of passing along my guidance," Captain Wallace said. "Get moving."

"Aye aye, Sir," Jacob said, then realized he was talking to a dead phone.

"Lieutenant Locher!" Jacob barked after a moment, looking around in the darkness.

"Sir," Chief Roberts said quietly, gesturing for Jacob to step away from Teague.

"Yes, Chief?" Jacob snapped.

"Lieutenant Locher's overboard," Chief stated.

"What?!" Jacob asked, similarly dropping his voice.

"He jumped when we took the hit to Turret Three," Chief Roberts said, continuing to make sure no one was present. "One of the runners saw him do it. I was going to inform you right when Captain Wallace called."

Jacob recoiled and opened his mouth to yell at Chief

50

Roberts. Regarding the man's face and considering what he'd said, he stopped.

Panic is catching, Jacob thought. *We were all so distracted by the casualties that we didn't even notice, and it's not like we would have stopped for him.*

"Thank you, Chief," Jacob said after a moment, then took a deep breath. "That was a good decision."

"Thank you, Sir," Chief Roberts replied. "I would suggest you inform the captain, and only the captain, when you see him next."

"Agreed," Jacob stated, his tone grim. "See that he's listed with our casualties as 'missing' when you provide your report to the Surgeon."

"Aye aye, Commander," Chief Roberts replied.

With that, Jacob stepped out onto the *Houston*'s deck for his journey down to Damage Central.

Pearl Harbor
0900 Local (1400 Eastern)
4 April 1943

"Well Lieutenant Cobb, I don't mean to be rude, but we need your bed," Commander Rolland Sampson, USNR, drawled in an attempt at humor. "If these were normal times, I'd keep you here, as I am particularly worried about your shoulder blade. But you're ambulatory, and that means you can convalesce at home."

Lieutenant Eric Cobb, formerly of the carrier *Hornet* by way of the flattop *Ranger*, fought to keep his face neutral. Sampson's expression was very apologetic, the man's brown eyes sad underneath his dark brown hair.

That would work if 'home' wasn't currently at the bottom of the North Pacific, Eric thought, his blue eyes narrowing. He had *just* been allowed to roll over onto his backside and sit up in his bed after the wounds he suffered during the Battle of Hawaii just over a week past. It was still painful to move due to the sixty stitches in his back and cracked scapula.

Unfortunately the bastard's got a point, Eric thought, his gaze falling on the empty bed across from him. The grievously wounded sailor that had occupied the space had given up the ghost sometime the night before, slipping into death despite the doctors believing the *Minneapolis* man might make it.

"Sir, I'm going to need to make a phone call," Eric stated, wincing as he sat up.

"Understood Lieutenant," Sampson replied. "We will give you some medications for the pain. It is absolutely imperative that you do not drink while taking these."

"Aye aye, Sir," Eric said.

Although maybe sweet oblivion wouldn't be so bad after all, he thought, then mentally shook the words away. *I'm not a quitter*.

"You'll have to come back in four days so we can take the stitches out," Sampson continued, gesturing for two orderlies to help Eric stand up. The younger officer was able to do so without help, but only after grunting involuntarily as the pain shot all across his back.

"You're not going to be able to fly for at least six weeks," Sampson continued. "I'm serious, Lieutenant Cobb."

"Sir, I'm not even sure what squadron, if any, I'm assigned to," Eric said disgustedly, then caught himself. "Sorry, Sir."

Sampson gave Eric an understanding look.

"Lieutenant Cobb, I know that you've been through a lot," Sampson said. "I think I'd be rather disgusted at your luck to this point myself. Hopefully you'll be able to get some rest as you recover. You'll need to go see the adjutant for your orders after Nurse Bowden gets you a sling."

"Aye aye, Sir," Eric responded, walking gingerly towards the doors out of the ward, the orderlies close behind him.

Two hours later, Eric stood in fresh khakis with his right arm in a sling. Beside him, a rolling clothes rack held three garment bags with a new set of whites and three more sets of khakis enclosed within them. A short, attractive nurse stood holding the other side of the rack in order to keep it from rolling away with the strong breeze blustering in from the harbor. Looking across the choppy blue waters, the sun sparkling off the waves, Eric watched tugs gingerly moving the battleship *Maryland* towards the dry dock.

"She doesn't look good, does she?" Nurse Bowden asked, her brown eyes narrowing as she studied the *Maryland*.

"No, no she really doesn't," Eric replied. He gave the woman a sideways glance as the wind moved her shoulder length brunette hair. The two of them waited a few more minutes in silence.

"I hope being this late will not reflect badly on my brothers' next fitness report," Eric said, annoyed. In addition to being head nurse for the casualty ward, Beverly Bowden was married to one Major Max Bowden, the commander of Marine Fighter Squadron (VMF) Fourteen.

"Well your sister-in-law probably had to take them the car over at Ewa," Beverly replied quickly. "That's okay, I needed some time from inside the ward anyway."

Eric nodded at that last statement.

"I can only imagine how hard it is for all of you every day," Eric replied. "Just how bad is the bed situation?"

"Now that they've plucked everyone they're going to out of the water, we're over three hundred beds short," Beverly replied lowly after glancing around. Eric looked at her, stunned.

"My god," he said. "How many dead?"

"I haven't been shown the full casualty figures." Beverly's voice was strained as she continued. "*Arizona, Saratoga*, and *Pennsylvania* went down with over half their crews. *Colorado* was not much better. That's over three thousand men right there. We've put two hundred more in coffins since the 27th ourselves."

Eric wished he hadn't asked as he watched Beverly become more agitated as she continued talking. Before he could say something, a familiar voice behind him stopped the conversation.

"Lieutenant Cobb!" Ensign Charles Read said, genuine joy in his slightly twangy voice. Turning, Eric was similarly overjoyed to see the tall, lanky Missourian also in suspiciously fresh-looking khakis. To Eric's surprise, the man's dark hair was buzzed in a very severe crew cut. Read's right arm was also in a sling, an injury suffered when his SBD *Dauntless* had been gunned out of the sky by Japanese fighters.

*In some ways, I wish I **had** taken your bird from you when mine went down*, Eric thought. *At least then I might have been able to defend myself. Then again, **Dauntless** versus fighters probably wouldn't have gone well even if you'd seen them.*

Like Eric, Read was accompanied by a nurse dragging a clothing rack. To the senior officer's bemusement, the sandy blonde woman was even shorter than the dimunitive Nurse Bowden. Her blue eyes met Eric's with an easy smile, the grin making her oval features and aquiline nose even more attractive.

"Is this the famous Lieutenant Cobb I've been hearing about for the last two days?" she asked, her voice a high alto.

"I'm sorry, miss, but you have me at a disadvantage," Eric drawled, giving Read a speculative look. "It appears many women talk about me in Hawaii, so I may be mistaken in assuming it is Ensign Read who has spoken of me."

Eric saw the woman's smile waver a little bit, and realized what he said could have been misconstrued.

"Jennifer, he's on pain meds," Beverly said with a laugh of his own. "What he means is that his sister is out here, as well as his three brothers. Two of them fly with Max."

"Oh, your poor mother," Jennifer replied, genuinely shocked.

"Well she didn't have all of us at once," Eric replied dryly, drawing a laugh from everyone. Jennifer blushed slightly.

"No, I mean to have all of you here at risk," Jennifer said quickly, looking sheepish. Eric noted that Beverly stiffened at the other nurse's statement, then quickly relaxed. "Oh, and as Beverly said, I'm Jennifer, Jennifer Zempel."

Eric nodded towards Jennifer and instantly regretted it, pain shooting up his back and neck as he moved.

"My apologies," he bit out.

"No, mine," Jennifer said quickly, dropping her hand and stepping towards him concerned.

"He's got stitches in his back," Beverly explained. Eric noted that she surreptitiously checked to make sure he hadn't ripped any of them.

"Perils of doing business," Eric gritted out. A car horn honked behind him, as a battered Packard sedan pulled up to the building. To Eric's surprise, it was not neither Sam nor David Cobb that hopped out from the passenger seat, but his youngest brother, Nicholas "Nick" Cobb.

"What, you were expecting a gorilla with mug that sorta looks like yours?" Nick asked, noting the surprise on Eric's face as he moved around to open the door. Unlike any of his three brothers, Nick was rail thin and clearly under six feet in his whites. While his build hid a wirty strength and athleticism that had served him well for several years, it was pretty clear the Cobb gene pool had been all out of "monster juice" by the time it got to Nick.

"Just because Mom apparently stunted your growth is no reason to compare poor Sam and David to King Kong," Beverly said with a laugh.

"I go with the theory that Mom would have murdered Dad in his sleep if she'd had another baby the size of Mr. Bowling Ball over there," Nick said, thumbing towards his brother.

"I see you intend to take full advantage of my injured state," Eric bit out.

"Oh this is going to be more fun than when Sam got that hernia in eighth grade," Nick said. "Especially since you don't have a twin to set up a cruel trap for me."

Jennifer looked from Eric to Nick, gaze lingering on the younger Cobb.

Y didn't get our size but you sure got an extra helping of handsome, Eric thought, suppressing a wry grin.

"Are you two always like this?" Jennifer asked wryly.

"Only when they're worried about each other and don't want to show it," a female voice chimed in as Sadie Cobb, Eric's sister-in-law, stepped from the other side of the car.

What in the Hell is going on here? Eric thought.

"Where are Sam and David?" Eric asked, turning to look at Beverly. The nurse simply smiled thinly, then gave Eric a very gingerly delivered hug.

"I'll let your brother tell you," she whispered in Eric's ear. "They were fine when I last saw them."

The hairs on the back of Eric's neck rose up as Nurse Bowden stepped away. He saw that her eyes were glistening, and she quickly turned away from Eric.

"Come Jennifer, I think we've got work to do," Beverly declared

"I'll write," Jennifer said cheerfully, giving Charles a hug. She turned to Eric.

"It was nice finally meeting the famous Lieutenant Cobb," she said with a smile and a wave. With that, the short, friendly nurse turned to follow Nurse Bowden back towards the hospital's front doors.

"Kind of shocked to see you in khakis already," Nick commented, looking his brother up and down.

"Yes, I'm just as amazed as you are," Eric said. "I don't see it happening with whites though."

"I wouldn't be surprised, Sir," Charles intoned. Eric turned to look at the man.

"Why is that, Ensign Read?" Eric asked.

"Because they've taken all the deceased men's uniforms they could find from ships that made it back and put them with whatever clothes they had on hand," Nick muttered, fixing Read with a hard look as he grabbed the last of Eric's clothes.

Eric stopped dead in his tracks.

"What?" he asked.

"Yes Sir, we're both likely wearing some dead man's clothing," Read said, his voice full of gallows humor.

"Ensign Read, where are you going to?" Sadie queried.

"I was waiting on a taxi to take me to the BOQ, Ma'am," Charles replied, speaking of the Bachelor Officer's Quarters.

"Nonsense," Sadie snapped. "There's room at our house."

Nick and Eric both looked at their sister-in-law with a stunned expression.

"Oh don't give me that look, either of you," Sadie

57

said. "That is, providing Ensign Read can sleep on a sofa bed. You know if he goes to the Bachelor's Quarters his survivor leave's going to end up with him on duty a lot."

Nick and Eric both shrugged, knowing their sister-in-law had a point.

"You signed out to the BOQ's, Read?" Eric asked.

"No Sir, they just told me to sign out as "survivor's leave" and to pay attention for a general recall," Read replied evenly.

"All right, looks like you're coming with us," Eric replied.

Five minutes later, after he had slowly and excruciatingly eased into the back seat behind Sadie, Eric finally had a chance to follow Beverly's advice.

"Okay, where are those two lugs and why does Beverly look like she saw a ghost?" Eric asked as Sadie shifted gears.

"This goes no further than this car," Nick said, looking pointedly at Read. "Sam and David are aboard the *Long Island* and shipped out last night."

"What?!" Eric asked, jerking upright and instantly regretting it. "I thought they were getting sent back to the mainland?!"

Sadie laughed bitterly at that, drawing a sorrowful look from Nick.

"Apparently Captain Browning, Vice Admiral Halsey's Chief of Staff, pointedly asked why the only Marines who 'actually killed something' were being sent *away* from where the action was," Nick explained. "I met him when they gave me my Navy Cross. He's an asshole."

Strangely, I can't argue with his logic, Eric thought. *Even if it puts my brothers at risk.*

"Do you know where the *Long Island* is headed?" Eric asked aloud, then almost yelped as Sadie hit a bump.

"Sorry, got distracted," she said. Looking at her in the rearview mirror, Eric could see her eyes begin to glisten slightly. Looking away before she looked up at him, he turned back to Nick. His younger brother was looking at Sadie, then at Read.

He knows, Eric thought.

"I would suspect that if I were a spy, Nick, I probably wouldn't have come to pick up your brother and left so quickly," Sadie said reproachfully. "So that leaves Ensign Read, and somehow I don't think the Japanese are going to get anything out of him."

"It is possible that I've gone turncoat," Eric joked lightly.

"It's also possible I'm going to click my heels three times and go back to Kansas," Sadie replied wryly. "But anyone who has heard me sing knows that I'm not Judy Garland."

"Can't be worse than Patricia," Eric said, then stopped.

"To quote a certain man we all love, 'You make Patricia sound like an angelic choir,'" Sadie said ruefully.

"Sam said that?" Nick exclaimed, his eyes suddenly wide.

"David, actually," Sadie said with a slight smile at her trickery. "But you know if David said it…"

"…Sam was thinking it," Eric finished.

"Wake," Nick said after a moment. "They're heading to reinforce Wake."

Eric hoped that his face did not look as scared as he felt.

"Scuttlebutt has it that Vice Admiral Pye is *not* looking for a fight," Nick said. "Unfortunately, Vice Admrial Halsey *is* gunning for one."

"Is he insane?" Eric asked bluntly. "I mean, I know

he's got new aircraft, but the Japanese…"

"The Japanese are a discussion that can wait," Nick snapped, looking over at Sadie.

Eric was about to snap back at his little brother then stopped.

"Since when did you start becoming the wise one?" Eric asked, incredulous.

"When I nearly died," Nick replied. "It appears it doesn't always take with some of us."

Eric heard Ensign Read's sharp intake of breath.

"You now, little brother, someday these stitches are going to heal," Eric said, his tone making it clear there was no real heat behind the words.

"Hopefully they'll stop having me as a gopher around SUBPAC headquarters by then," Nick replied with a smile. "I don't think you can hold your breath long enough to come get me on a boat."

"When you hear something knocking on your conning tower hatch, I hope you'll rethink that assessment," Eric said.

U.S.S. Long Island
1300 Local (1800 Eastern)

I really need to consider a new profession, Captain Samuel Cobb thought to himself as he banked his *Wildcat* into a gentle clockwise orbit orbit around the *Long Island*. *Because I don't recall agreeing to taking off and landing from somea postage stamp in the middle of the damn ocean when I signed up for the Corps.*

"Okay Red Flight, let's get aboard," Major Max Bowden ordered into his radio. "We'll leave Green Flight to bore some holes in the sky."

Sam shook his head at Bowden's cheery demeanor as he listened to Red Flight's acknowledgment over the squadron net. He adjusted his Mae West and seatbelt, moving his massive frame around the *Wildcat*'s tiny cockpit in a manner that kept the fighter from scooting too much around the sky.

I mean, I'm not **scared** *of the water, but I went Marines for a reason*, Sam continued to muse. VMF-14 should have only been expected to hitch a ride aboard the *Long Island* to within range of Wake. Instead, the unit's *Wildcats* were part of the combat air patrol, or "CAP," orbiting over the *Long Island* and her near sister, the *Archer*. The latter vessel had entered Pearl Harbor just long enough to unload the two squadrons of *Hellcats* that had been lashed to her deck, then promptly loaded on two squadrons of orphaned *Dauntlesses* from the sunk *Saratoga* and *Lexington*. Looking down at her, Sam remained doubtful of her ability to actually fly the dive bombers off when the time came. Still, Vice Admiral Halsey's staff had issued the orders, so *Archer*'s crew were going to try their damndest.

I'm not so sure I like being the bait on a hook either, Sam thought grimly. He scanned the screen arrayed around the two escort carriers and six fast troop transports in two columns behind them. Technically Vice Admiral Halsey and the carriers *Yorktown, Enterprise*, and *Victorious* were acting as a "covering force," but in reality the three carriers had been acting almost independently due to their superior speed. As a result, the five operational battleships of the Pacific Fleet were plowing through the seas a few thousand yards off the convoy's starboard bow, with the entire force shepherded by fifteen destroyers.

"Green One, Green Three," his brother David drawled. "Action, eight o'clock."

It's bad enough that we're both out here, Sam thought. *They didn't have to go and break us up too*. The Cobbs had been wingmen ever since they'd arrived in Hawaii. While Major Bowden had initially pondered the wisdom of the arrangement, he had come to rely on it. Apparently that hadn't been enough for one Captain Browning.

Someone needs to teach that son of a bitch the old saying about not sticking your nose in someone else's business lest it get broken, Sam thought. *Glad he got put in his place by Major Bowden and Lieutenant Colonel McKenna.*

Motion on the ocean beneath him caused him to turn his head. Two destroyers were turning sharply from the *Long Island*'s screen, and black smoke began pouring from both vessels' stacks as they began adding speed.

"Red One, Green One, there's some DDs going after a sub," Sam said.

"More likely a whale killing," someone muttered from one of the two flights.

"Those boys better be careful, or they're going to run out of depth charges," another pilot answered on the squadron frequency.

"Belay the chatter," Bowden snapped as he settled into the *Long Island*'s landing pattern. The little escort carrier was coming into the wind and steaming as fast as she could. Turning back to the destroyers, Sam watched as one of the two vessels began her attack run on the suspicious contact.

I don't blame them for being jumpy, Sam thought. *The Japs apparently learned something from the Germans in the last few months, as their subs have been downright annoying.*

As Sam watched, depth charges flew from the destroyer's side even as more 'ash cans' rolled off her stern. The single stack vessel briefly continued on a straight path to clear the blast radius, then put her helm hard over to starboard. As the ship's bow began to come around, the water leaped behind the vessel as the pattern of charges went off.

Well there goes a few hundred fish, Sam thought disgustedly.

"Schoonover Base, Schoonover Base, this is Clipper One," he said, radioing the battleship *California*. "How do you read this station?"

"This is Schoonover Base," came the staticky reply. "We have you five by…"

The controllers transmission was cut off by a sudden scream and dull *crump* that both sounded so up close Sam reflexively shoved his stick over to port and added throttle. His wingman, startled, immediately followed his section leader, while David and his wingman broke to starboard. Even as completed what Navy pilots were starting to call the Thach Weave, Sam realized that the sound he'd heard wasn't from any airborne source.

"Rejoin on me, Green," he barked, pulling up and scanning the ocean beneath him. Full pandemonium appeared to be breaking out, as the *California* was ablaze from her No. 2 turret aft on her starboard side and coasting to a halt. While Sam watched, the battleship began to drunkenly roll to starboard.

What in the hell? Sam thought, looking around the skies.

The "what" in this particular instance was the Japanese submarine I-19, and "the hell" was the plucky I-boat had managed to put four 21-inch torpedoes into the *California*'s starboard side from the nearly point blank range of three thousand yards. Even had the torpedoes been the standard weapons which the IJN had developed prior to 1941, the wounds would have been grievous. When equipped with the special *Sandaburo* warheads that the IJN had developed from the German transfer of the captured British explosive TORPEX, the resultant effect was like the difference between being stabbed with a hunting knife versus slashed with a katana.

Amazingly, the weapon that penetrated the *California*'s torpedo bulge and vented its wrath into the vessel's forward powder magazine only stirred a runaway deflagration rather than a hull-shattering explosion before being quenched by seawater, but this was of little comfort to either Captain McWaters, her master, nor to Vice Admiral Pye and his staff. Even as the former was returning to the bridge from the latter's map room, he found himself having to fight the battleship's sharp list as water rushed into her hull. In the two minutes it took for him to reach his post, the inclinometer had already reached ten degrees. In the ensuing two minutes it took for him to get any semblance of a report, it was at fifteen. By the time McWaters made the decision to have the crew abandon ship, it was far too late for him to affect anything resembling an orderly evacuation. The vessel's sudden and violent capsizing spared him both the burden of making any further decisions or the inconvenience of answering questions at any ensuing Courts of Inquiry.

Sam felt himself starting to shake as he looked at the *California*'s glistening hull.

Oh my God, it's happening again! he thought, frantically looking for Japanese aircraft. Reaching to slide the canopy back, he stopped himself. Screaming in frustration, he punched the side of the cockpit, the pain bringing him back from the edge of insanity. Breathing rapidly and roughly, he watched as the *Long Island* and the rest of the convoy put their helms hard over to port to turn away from the attacking submarine. To his horror, Sam watched as two of the torpedo tracks continued towards the line of transports. Before he could click his radio in warning, one of the weapons connected with the last vessel in the port column. With a black tinged waterspout that went higher than the vessel's masts and gout of steam, the transport came to a stop.

Hit her stern, Sam thought disgustedly. *She probably just lost power. Which means she's going down.* Searching, he realized he'd lost track of the last weapon. Scanning, he saw the errant weapon heading harmlessly past the *Long Island*'s starboard side...and four more inbound towards the escort carrier and the *Archer*.

"*LONG ISLAND, LONG ISLAND, TORPEDOES INBOUND!*" Sam screamed into his radio.

Even had the *Long Island*'s captain had Sam teleport onto his bridge and point at the weapons, there was nothing that could have been done. Already engaged into the hard turn to port that had brought her into the crosshairs of the lurking *I-168* when the Japanese submarine fired its bow tubes at her, the *Long Island* lacked either the speed or the rudder capability to take any evasive action. Even as Sam's panicked warning was echoed by her lookouts, the bridge crew could only watch as the duo of torpedoes aimed for them closed at fifty knots. Astern, the *Archer*'s crew remained blissfully unaware of their own danger, as the second half of the I-boat's salvo remained unseen thanks to the lookout's focus on the capsizing *California*.

Whereas misfortune had placed *Long Island* in the current situation, it would be poor design that sealed her fate. A former merchantman, *Long Island* lacked any of the protective measures enjoyed by her larger fleet carrier brethren. Had she been built with any semblance of armor, the greed of Commander Tanabe, *I-168*'s captain, would have potentially resulted in a grievously damaged vessel. Instead, seconds after the first torpedo passed just under the *Long Island*'s bow, the second slammed into the carrier's starboard side abreast her avgas storage.

To describe the subsequent explosion as violent would

have done it a grave injustice. With a roaring *whoompf* and accompanying fireball that vomited from the escort carrier's open hanger, the *Long Island*'s aviation fuel immediately transformed into a roaring conflagration that rippled aft like a flaming flood tide. Staggering out of line, the carrier began immediately suffering from secondary explosions as aircraft being readied in her hangar began to explode. Major Bowden, having just returned to the VMF-14 ready room with his flight, had just enough time to order the eight other pilots in the compartment out toward the flight deck before the blazing tidal wave overtook him.

Aboard the *Archer*, her captain had only enough time to register what had happened to the *Long Island* before his own vessel was struck. Unlike the *Long Island*, the *Archer* was not hit directly in her avgas. Instead, the first weapon struck her far enough forward that the vessel might have survived the ensuing flooding…had the second weapon not struck at the juncture of her engine room and bomb magazine. If the *Long Island*'s secondary explosion had been violent, the detonation of several dozen bombs and depth charges was positively cataclysmic. In an instant, the *Archer*'s entire aft end ceased to be, fragments hurled in a three quarters circles that saw steel landing on the light cruiser *Honolulu* steaming over six thousand yards off her starboard quarter.

Above the two stricken carriers, Sam felt tears running down his cheeks. Stunned, he watched as the *Long Island* continued to leave a snail's trail of burning avgas and fuel oil behind her as she slowly came to a stop. His mouth dry, he belatedly realized he was flying erratically, his flight strung out behind him.

Do your job, dammit, Sam berated himself.

"Green Flight," he rasped, then swallowed. "Green Flight, follow me. Time to go find someplace to land."

"Roger Green One," David replied. "I have the

Enterprise's homing beacon already."

"Roger Three, you have lead," Sam said, leading Green Two around to reform on his brother's wing.

Behind Green Flight, the angry destroyers that had initially gone after a contact were rushing up the turned convoy's starboard side. While several of their brethren furiously hunted the *I-19* to no avail, twenty minutes after the *Long Island* had been struck, the *Sims* and *Hammann* spotted the *I-168*. Commander Tanabe, aggressive as always, had shifted his position while his torpedo room crews reloaded. Hearing the *Archer*'s breaking up noises, Tanabe returned to periscope depth to see what other targets he might claim. The maneuver was his undoing, as the *I-168*'s scope was sighted barely two thousand yards off *Sims*'s port bow. Seeing the danger as he performed his first sweep of the ocean, Commander Tanabe ordered an immediate retreat to the depth. The maneuver was futile, as first the *Sims* then the *Hammann* made runs over the crash diving submarine's position. While the ensuing oil slick and debris field was nowhere near as expressive a finale as the *Archer*'s demise, the subsequent plunge to the depths was no less fatal for the *I-168*.

The *Long Island* would continue to burn for over an hour as her surrounding vessels rescued the crew that had escaped. Finally Vice Admiral Halsey, able to see the smoke over the horizon from the *Enterprise*'s island, had finally had enough. Ordering the *Long Island* scuttled, Vice Admiral Halsey then disgustedly directed the Pacific Fleet sortie to come about. Wake Island, and its defenders, were not worth subjecting the already battered fleet to additional attrition. As the *Long Island* sank beneath the waves after receiving another torpedo from the destroyer *Blue*, the Pacific Fleet's ability to conduct offensive operations went with her.

JAMES YOUNG

.

CHAPTER 2: NEUTRAL CORNERS

Go Sir, gallop and don't forget that the world was made in six days. You can ask me for anything but not time. --
Napoleon

Pensacola, Florida
0840 Eastern
7 April 1943

Adam could not believe the words he heard coming out of Lieutenant Colonel King's mouth.

"You mean to tell me that Captain Bowles will *not* be receiving a court-martial for having extra-marital relations with another officer's wife?" Adam snapped. "Just because his father had the misfortune to get burned to a crisp?" He paused, aware that his tone was bordering on the belligerent.

A knock on the head has a way of making a man just not give a damn, he thought angrily. *So much for this guy not being a careerist.*

Lieutenant Colonel King fixed Adam with a steely gaze, green eyes locked with Adam's blue ones. After several long ticks of the clock behind his superior officer, Adam broke the glare, eyes focused on a spot above King's head.

"My apologies, Sir," Adam gritted out.

"For a moment there, Major Haynes, I was confused as to which one of us was in command of this air wing," King observed, his tone icy. "I would think the fact that I initiated court martial proceedings against Captain Bowles for his tryst and offered to immediately transfer him from your squadron would have served to indicate my feelings on the matter."

Adam winced internally, though his expression remained completely neutral.

"However, I will merely chalk up your insubordination to your injuries and not gross ignorance of military discipline," King continued. The underlying *"Unless you do this again..."* was quite clear.

"Yes, Sir," Adam said.

"Now, as I was saying, Captain Bowles will be reinstated to your squadron as soon as he returns from survivor's leave," King continued, reaching inside of his desk.

"Tell me, Major Haynes, are you an avid reader?" King asked. Adam blinked twice, not sure if he had heard his superior correctly.

"I read when I can, Sir," he replied, his tone uncertain.

"I used to firmly believe," King stated in measured tones, "that an officer should take an interest in the popular press as part of his professional duty. My usual reasoning for this is so that officer may stay abreast of the world situation."

With that, King took his hand out of the desk and tossed a copy of LIFE magazine on the desk.

"Another reason I will now add is so that he does not believe his boss is a two-faced jackass," King said with a slight grimace.

One look and Adam knew why the Bowles was not receiving a court martial. Pictured on the front page of the magazine was one Captain Bowles embracing a tearful older woman. Two other officers, both of flag rank, looked on. The headline was in huge white letters with black borders. It read:

THE FACE OF OUR NEW

WAR

'Dead Hero's Son Embraces Mother'

"Admiral King's Chief of Staff called me personally to discuss this news story," Lieutenant Colonel King stated. "You can imagine how well things went over when I told him young Captain Bowles was up for court martial."

I imagine that was a very one-sided and profane conversation, Adam thought, feeling a twinge of genuine remorse for having judged his wing commander so harshly.

"I'm surprised they didn't try to transfer him, sir," Adam said, crestfallen.

"They did. You're not the only one with markers, Major Haynes," King observed. "I just used most of mine to ensure that Mr. Bowles didn't suddenly find himself in a training command somewhere."

King's disdain was evident by how he spoke of the junior officer. Hearing it, Adam was amazed that King had used some of his own favors to keep Bowles within the squadron.

He has to know that this will not end well for Bowles, Adam thought.

"Thank you, sir," Adam replied. "I will make every effort to ensure Captain Bowles receives numerous opportunities for professional development."

I hope I didn't sound too malevolent, Adam seethed.

"Before you go off and figure out some way to do the young captain in, Major Haynes," King said, his tone indicating the seriousness of what was about to follow, "I suggest you consider a few things. One, understand that if Captain Bowles dies in any sort of 'accident', it will likely mean the end of your and my career, no questions asked."

Adam nodded, hoping that the disappointment was

71

not obvious on his face.

"Two, Bowles is reinstated as a flight leader immediately," King continued. "In the story he is listed as a flight leader, and the last thing the Commandant wants is for it to hit the papers that our young lover boy has been demoted. Apparently Mrs. Bowles is a decent lady and doesn't deserve to have that happen to her."

Adam remained silent while he mulled over which flight he would have to give back to Bowles. Captain Kennedy hadn't worked out that well as a flight leader, plus it was a different flight than Burke's or the one Bowles had led prior to his emergency leave.

"Sir, I'll be giving him Yellow Flight," Adam stated.

"Good. Finally, you've got to give up two captains in order to fill out a couple of other squadrons that are being raised out of this last crop of trainees."

"Walters and Seidel," Adam said without hesitation.

"That was quick," King stated, obviously surprised. "I take it you're not pleased with either officer?"

"Sir, neither one of the two of them will ever be capable leaders while Bowles is in the squadron," Adam responded. " Not to mention that I busted them the same time as Bowles and can't return him to flight leader status while not doing the same for them."

King looked at Adam with a raised eyebrow.

"I don't know Major, I think you're actually starting to gain my confidence in you being a little bit more than a hired gun," King observed dryly.

"Sir, you're starting to restore my faith that there are truly warriors in the Corps," Adam retorted.

King chuckled at that.

"I don't know whether that was a compliment or an insult, but either way we both have work to do," King said. "The orders detailing these changes will be at your office by this afternoon."

"Thank you, sir," Adam responded, coming to attention. "Permission to leave?"

King shook his head.

"There's one more matter," King stated. "Please, have a seat."

Adam looked at his wing commander skeptically as he gingerly sat down. He'd apparently torqued his back worse than he had thought.

Guess a banged up head and fragments weren't quite enough, Adam thought.

"First off, let me tell you that I think there's likely a medal in your future," King said. "Vice Admiral Thompson has endorsed you for a Silver Star, and each of your men for a Distinguished Flying Cross."

I'm sensing another big "other shoe" directly overhead if that's the opening gambit, Adam thought.

"Thank you, Sir," he replied, hoping to conceal his desire just to get things over with.

"There are, however, some concerns," King continued. "There is the little matter of you using profanity over an open channel. Although you were in the heat of the moment, you will never use that word again over an open radio while you're a member of this wing. Do I make myself clear?"

*We'll see how well proper language holds up when the bullets begin to fly past **your** head*, Adam thought.

"Second, there is the little matter of what led to you cursing at your section leader," King continued briskly. "First lieutenant Butler stated that you were apparently in the midst of strafing the submarine again even though it was clearly sinking. Is this true?"

I might need to get Butler a new home, Adam thought, carefully considering his answer.

"Sir, the submarine had not surrendered," he stated after a long pause.

"That's not what I asked, Major," King replied, green eyes hard. "But your answer speaks volumes. Did it ever occur to you, in your blood lust, that live Germans might be more use to us than dead ones? Or that if we start making it impossible for people to abandon ship then the Germans might do the same to us?"

There were several clicks on the clock before Adam realized that the questions were not rhetorical.

"Sir, I will not pretend to be inclined to show the Germans any mercy," Adam said. "I've watched those Kraut bastards shoot my friends in parachutes, and I think what they did to London speaks for itself."

King pressed his lips into a thin line.

"I see," King replied evenly. "So you are saying that you are unrepentant?"

"Sir, if you order me to take every possible measure to make sure I don't harm any more Germans than I absolutely need to, then I will of course follow orders," Adam stated. "But other than that, no, I don't regret for an instant attempting to kill them."

"Major Haynes, I realize we're at war," King started slowly. "I also realize that you've not only seen the elephant, you keep running up to give it hugs. That, however, does not excuse war crimes. Yes, I am telling you that for future reference you will no longer kill men who are attempting to abandon ship or are jumping out of their aircraft. Is *that* clear?"

"Yes, sir," Adam replied, once again making his face blank. He watched as King searched his visage for any signs of duplicity. Either being satisfied or, more likely, realizing Adam was not going to openly defy him, King relaxed.

"Enough of that," he said. "What are your plans for today, Major Haynes?"

COLLISIONS OF THE DAMNED

"Classroom instruction, sir," Adam replied. "I'll be giving a class on air-to-air gunnery, followed by aircraft recognition. Need to make sure the men understand the difference between a *Spitfire* and a 109."

King raised an eyebrow.

"Expecting a visit from a German aircraft carrier?" he asked, his tone only half-joking.

"Understand there were a lot of folks in Hawaii not expecting a Japanese one to come calling," Adam said. "I certainly wasn't expecting to be strafing a submarine either."

"Point taken," King allowed with a slight smile. "I'll probably drop in."

"Always welcome, sir," Adam said easily.

IJNS. Akagi
1454 Local Time (0054 Eastern)
11 April (10 April)

Vice Admiral Tamon Yamaguchi looked out across Kure's harbor as the damaged I.J.N.S. *Shokaku* was eased towards the installation's dry dock. Listing and down by the bow, the IJN flattop's wounds were both clearly visible and very severe.

It's a wonder she made it back, Yamaguchi mused. *Which is better than we can say about her sister.* With his narrow, almost feline face set in a scowl and almond eyes narrow, Yamaguchi looked like he was ready to spring at some unseen enemy as he watched the tugs do their work.

"You are certain that you sunk the second *Yorktown* carrier?" Admiral Isoroku Yamamoto, commander of Japan's Combined Fleet, asked from beside him. A distinguished, athletic man with a permanently shaven head, Yamamoto stood in a plain, navy blue uniform. The senior officer's maimed left hand clutched his hat as the two men stood on the carrier's bridge.

"Yes," Vice Admiral Yamaguchi replied. "One of *Chikuma*'s aircraft reported that the crew was abandoning ship when it turned back towards the task group."

Yamamoto pursed his lips, bringing his binoculars up so he could study the ravaged *Shokaku* more closely.

"It will be at least six months before she returns to action, sir," Yamaguchi stated.

"I have told the repair yard they have four," Admiral Yamamoto asserted firmly. "The *Taiho* will be ready in September, at which point you will again have six carriers."

I'm not sure I think those two vessels should be division mates, Yamaguchi thought. *Although at this point, I do not believe I am being asked my opinion.*

"We will hopefully have enough pilots to man all of them," Yamaguchi stated. He was about to continue, then stopped as Yamamoto gave him an appraising look.

"Inoue-san openly wondered if perhaps your concern for your pilots is a means of masking a loss of heart," Yamamoto intoned solemnly.

Yamaguchi fought to keep his face calm.

"Perhaps Inoue-san should worry more about how two squadrons of fighters and some shore guns managed to repulse his initial attack," Yamaguchi said, his calm voice completely belying his white-hot rage. "I wish to conserve my strength for the Decisive Battle, not use my sword to cut my neighbor's underbrush."

Yamamoto regarded his subordinate for a few moments, then began speaking.

"I was not quite as blunt as you, Yamaguchi-san, but I conveyed those same feelings."

Yamaguchi allowed himself a brief smile as Yamamoto continued.

"Our submarines reported sinking two American carriers and a battleship, and there were several subsequent

COLLISIONS OF THE DAMNED

sightings of the force heading back towards Pearl Harbor. Inoue-san expects to conduct his final assault by tomorrow."

The two men were interrupted by one of Yamamoto's staff officers.

"Begging your pardon, sir," the young commander said, bowing to both admirals. He handed Yamamoto a message flimsy. The senior officer looked down at the paper, his face growing progressively more grave as he read it. Finishing, he turned to the commander.

"When was this message received?" Yamamoto asked, his voice strained.

"Four hours ago, sir," the commander replied.

"Dispatch orders for Vice Admiral Fukudome to scuttle the *Shoho*," Yamamoto barked. "Where is Vice Admiral Ozawa's report?"

"We have been attempting to contact Vice Admiral Ozawa for the last twelve hours..." the commander began. Yamamoto opened his mouth, then closed it, his view speculative.

"What was his last position relative the reported location of the British carriers?" Yamamoto asked.

"Three hundred miles northeast as of last night," the commander replied.

Yamamoto turned and looked at Yamaguchi.

"Vice Admiral Fukudome was attacked last night in the darkness by British single-engined aircraft," Yamamoto said. "The Commonwealth seems to have been practicing a great number of night maneuvers based on what happened to Tanaka-san and now Fukodome."

*I would practice night maneuvers too if my front-line torpedo aircraft was a **biplane***, Yamaguchi thought.

"Where is Ozawa-san?" Yamaguchi asked, bewildered.

"I dispatched Vice Admiral Ozawa with *Ryujo*,

77

Junyo, and *Hiyo* to Singapore a week before you departed for Oahu," Yamamoto replied. "His orders were to raid Darwin, then head south and strike at Perth. Simultaneously, Fukodome was to depart Madagascar and be in position to strike the Royal Navy base at Ceylon with *Shoho* and *Zuiho*."

Yamaguchi's eyes widened.

No wonder Inoue was asking for help from two of my carriers, Yamaguchi thought. *We appear to have stripped all other areas of not only carriers, but aircraft to man them.*

"My assumption, of course, was that the Army would not be taken by complete surprise in Singapore," Yamamoto muttered, furthering Yamaguchi's look of surprise.

"Sir, I am not sure I follow?" the latter stated.

"The Army was prepared to launch a predawn strike against the Dutch on the first day of the war," Yamamoto said. "Apparently those jackals have been so wonderful to the local populace that they lit signal fires to help guide British night bombers to the airfields."

Yamaguchi winced and grunted, not needing to know much more.

"The Army refuses to answer how many aircraft they lost, but they have stated that the invasion of Sumatra must be postponed until the Philippines operations are complete," Yamamoto said.

"What did the Army do to prevent the British from having their path lit again?" Yamaguchi inquired.

Yamamoto gave him a grim look.

"The same thing the Army always has done: Kill lots of people who had nothing to do with it in an attempt to cover up their incompetence," Yamamoto spat disgustedly.

"What of Nagumo-san's aircraft?" Yamaguchi asked, his face puzzled.

"What aircraft?" Yamamoto asked with a barked laugh. "As directed, he shifted his aircraft north through

Siam and Indochina. Those he did not redeploy flew aboard the *Chiyoda* and *Chitose* the first day of the war and were used to surprise the Americans at Clark Field."

I wondered how we managed to catch them unawares after they attacked Formosa, Yamaguchi thought. He'd heard of the great attack that had crippled the Americans' air support but not the details.

"How long until the Army believes the Americans are defeated?" Yamaguchi asked. "I understand the Army reached Manila this morning."

"Probably another week and a half unless there is naval interference," Yamamoto replied. "Kondo-san planned his attacks well, and Ozawa's attacks seem to have made the enemy cautious even if they did catch Fukodome."

Yamaguchi thought for a moment, mentally recalling a map of the Philippines in his head.

"If we are needed for the Southern Operation, we can sail the Second Division by the end of the week," Yamaguchi said quietly.

Yamamoto looked pensive for several minutes. Finally, he spoke.

"No, you are right—as Fukodome just showed us, if I stretch our forces too thin I risk losing your carriers in penny packets," Yamamoto said. "We will take some of your pilots, but leave their ships—I will need them whole for the Decisive Battle."

"How soon do you think that the Americans will attempt to advance again?" Yamaguchi asked.

"I would like to think that they will sue for peace if we complete the Southern Advance quickly enough," Yamamoto answered. "Unfortunately, we both know from our time there that the Americans are a proud people. You stung them practically in their lair but, at the moment, they are likely telling themselves it was a fluke at the moment."

"If not for our allies, we would have struck them far

JAMES YOUNG

harder back in 1941," Yamaguchi stated bitterly. Yamamoto turned to look at him.

"True, but it is best not to question a great gift," Yamamoto said. "If we had not gone north, the Army would still be in charge of the nation and we'd be pouring material into China that can be better used building and repairing our ships."

Yamamoto had started to gesture towards the *Shokaku* with the last, but had caught himself.

"I think the fuel oil is more important," the junior admiral replied. Yamamoto nodded sagely at that.

"A full year's worth is more than we would have ever been able to save on our own," he said. "We would never have been able to pull of so many simultaneous operations if not for the oil the Germans gave us. We have Singapore in almost pristine condition and were gifted another year to train your force. I think that the gods smiled on us."

Yamaguchi could see his superior's point.

"But still, we could have caught our enemy asleep and unprepared rather than alert and full of fight," Yamaguchi replied.

"When attacking a sleeping giant, one must ensure that the first stroke is fatal," Yamamoto said. "You handled your force with great aggression and skill, your losses the due that Fate requires for great gambles. There is no other commander that I would rather have had in your place."

Yamaguchi drew himself erect, a great feeling of pride filling him. Disguised in language designed to save face, Yamamoto was saying he was happy Yamaguchi had been commanding the *Kido Butai* rather than Nagumo. It was extremely high praise from the usually taciturn commander.

"Remember you estimated that you would lose two carriers, Yamaguchi," Yamamoto said. "I will gladly take one in exchange for three carriers and four battleships."

80

Yes, but even at that exchange rate we will have no navy in three years, while both of us know the Americans will have an ever larger fleet on the seas, Yamaguchi thought to himself. *My victory was great, but the next one we have must be even greater.*

"Hopefully our German friends will continue to keep some of the Americans' strength tied down in the Atlantic," Yamamoto said.

"How many of my pilots will you need?" Yamaguchi asked.

"I will consult with the staff," Yamamoto said. "We will take all of the orphans from *Shokaku* and *Zuikaku* to fill the ranks, then have Fuchida-san pick once the rest once they have returned from their three day passes. Hopefully by that point we will have bases in the Philippines for them."

U.S.S. Shark
0100 Local (1230 Eastern)
13 April (12 April)

"Lieutenant Commander, General MacArthur would like a word," a dry voice stated from conning tower's hatch.

Lieutenant Commander Anthony Todd, United States Navy, bit back his first response to the voice's owner. Lowering his night binoculars, he found the entire bridge crew looking at him rather than watching their respective sectors.

It would not do to cuss out a flag officer, even if he apparently got the rank by making sure his nose was firmly attached to a four-star's ass, Todd thought. *Really starting to wish Mrs. Sutherland had talked her husband into pulling out.*

"Gentlemen, I believe you all have work to do," Todd snapped, causing the sheepish bridge crew to turn back to their tasks.

Not that you can really do it in this murk, he thought. A truly stupendous fog had begun rolling into the Sulu Sea, and Todd wished he'd given the island of Palawan a wider berth.

Glad I ordered a slow down, Todd thought to himself, fuming. *Which robably what that Army dumbass is upset about.*

"Lieutenant Graham, tell the XO that now would be a good time to charge the batteries," Todd said. "We're not going to be going much faster than this until we're past Palawan Island or the fog clears, whichever comes first."

"Aye aye, Sir," Graham said, then began speaking down the hatch into the control room.

"Lieutenant Commander Todd…" the Army brigadier said again, clearly nonplussed at being ignored.

"Sir, with all due respect, I am busy commanding my vessel," Todd stated. "Perhaps General MacArthur is not aware of Navy custom, but typically captains stay on our bridge."

There was a tense moment of silence, then the sound of footfalls on the ladder as the voice's owner finished coming all the way up into the night air.

"You listen here, *Lieutenant Commander*," the man snapped as he emerged. "I do not need a lecture from you on common military courtesies."

"*Lieutenant Graham*," Todd barked, his face set in a mask of rage as he turned away from one Brigadier General Sutherland, USA.

"Yes sir?" the officer of the deck asked, turning away from his own sector.

"Take the good *general* here below to the rear torpedo room!" Todd shouted. "He is to be confined there under bread and water for the remainder of our voyage."

"*What?!*" Sutherland roared. "I will…"

"Enemy vessel, four points off the starboard bow!" one of the lookouts screamed.

Todd turned to where the frightened man was pointing just in time to be blinded by the searchlights of the Japanese destroyer *Awikaze*. Moments later, the destroyer's forward turret roared as the DD's gunnery officer attempted to find the range. The two shells screamed across the intervening distance and landed four hundred yards short of the *Shark*'s hull.

"Crash dive! Take her down!" Todd shouted. Two of the lookouts shoved past the bewildered Sutherland on their way to the hatch, followed by the officer of the deck.

"Move you stupid son of a bitch!" Todd shouted, shoving Sutherland towards the hatch.

The Army general was turning to protest this treatment when the *Awikaze*'s next shell ended the discussion with explosive finality. Striking level with the lookout platform on the conning tower, the blast simultaneously killed Sutherland and Todd and the *Shark* incapable of diving. Lieutenant (j.g.) Graham, having just begun his descent into the boat, dropped unconscious to the control room's deck with fragments through his head and chest.

To his credit *Shark*'s XO, Lieutenant Morris, responded remarkably well to the hits. Shouting at the control room crew to get a hold of themselves, Morris countermanded Lieutenant Commander Todd's final order, then barked orders for the crew to battle surface. Easing himself through the perforated conning tower, Morris reached the *Shark*'s bridge in time to see the *Awikaze* less than two thousand yards away and closing, another brace of shells striking the *Shark* aft. The next duo of shells ended any more of Lieutenant Morris' concerns as well as rendered the *Shark* capable of being effectively conned as they destroyed the control room, conning tower, and the deck gun in the midst of the latter being manned.

As fuel oil spurted from the submarine's shattered tanks, the *Awikaze* continued to close even as the *Shark* began to settle into the water. Believing the American submarine was trying to escape, the Japanese destroyer captain ordered depth charges to be readied. It was only as the *Shark* began rolling to port that her assailant's master realized the American submarine was mortally wounded. Calling for full astern, the *Awikaze* drifted to a stop barely one thousand yards from where the *Shark* slowly slipped beneath the waves.

Curtly ordering the searchlights cut, the *Awikaze*'s captain curtly asked for the depth at their current location. Informed that there was only eighty feet under the keel, the man's fet set in a hard scowl. There were shouts for aid from the darkness ahead of the destroyer, an occurrence that made the Japanese officer's face become even more menacing.

"Set the depth charges for sixty feet, all ahead full," he barked. Black smoke belching from her stack, the destroyer began accelerating towards the spreading oil slick. A little over two minutes later, as a six charge spread rolled off her stern, the *Awikaze* ensured that there would be no personal plea for aid from General Douglas MacArthur, Commanding General, U.S. Army Philippines.

Pearl Harbor, Hawaii
1630 Local (2300 Eastern)
15 April

"With all due respect, Sir, I would rather be reassigned to a boat at the earliest possible convenience," Nick stated, standing stiffly at attention.

There was a menacing chortle from behind the desk in front of him.

"You hear that, Commander Freeman? *Lieutenant* Cobb believes *Rear Admiral* Graham's order that he be reassigned to his staff is rather inconvenient," Captain Daniel Davis, commander Submarine Squadron Six, said snidely. The heavyset senior officer sat behind his desk, his jowled face and ruddy expression making him look like a brown eyed boar hog.

"I think Lieutenant Cobb's request is reasonable," Commander Jason Freeman, former commanding officer of the U.S.S. *Nautilus*, stiffen beside him. Slightly taller than Nick, Freeman was almost as slender and wiry. His sandy blonde hair was short and slicked back in a barely within regulation Clark Gable haircut. The man's mustache was similarly trimmed, the complete style making him appear like a Hollywood lothario in his service whites. The Medal of Honor around his neck glinted in the room's overhead lighting.

"Well, pardon me, *Commander*, but for some damn reason I remember not arguing with flag officers when I was a lieutenant," Davis barked.

"Sir, I meant no dis..." Nick started to say, feeling Commander Freeman stiffen beside him.

"Shut up, Lieutenant Cobb," Davis said, his voice cold as ice. "Just because you and Commander Freeman happened to luck into helping sink a Japanese carrier does not entitle you to the privilege to talk back to the commanding officer of your squadron. Do I make myself clear?"

"Yes, sir," Nick replied in the loudest voice possible.

The fact I just sounded like a plebe answering a particularly ignorant upperclassman is purely coincidental, Nick thought. *Or at least that's what I'll swear to on a stack of Bibles if it comes to that.*

The fact that Davis suddenly looked like he was going to burst a blood vessel indicated to him that his tonal effect was right on.

"Get out of my sight, both of you," Davis snarled.

"Now."

"Aye-aye, sir," Nick replied, saluting and executing an about face that was straight out of Bancroft Hall. Commander Freeman offered a more lackadaisical salute, its meaning as clear as Nick's hyper reaction, then turned and exited Davis's office also.

"I guess we could have handled that a little bit better, Lieutenant Cobb," Commander Freeman observed a few minutes later as they stepped out into the bright Pearl Harbor sun.

"Sir, I can't believe he won't recut my orders so I can go with you to the *Herring*," Nick seethed. "What good is giving every officer in a wardroom Navy Crosses if they're going to break the gang up?"

Freeman laughed at that, returning the salute of two passing commanders. Nick greeted the two officers, receiving a pair of nods in return.

"That is going to take some getting used to," Freeman observed, looking down at his award self-consciously.

"Well Sir, you can imagine my surprise at my own award," Nick replied.

"Seems like your family makes a habit of collecting the things," Freeman joked, then stopped at the pained expression crossing Nick's face.

"Sorry sir," Nick stated sorrowfully. "My brothers are all a little banged up at the moment."

Freeman nodded sagely.

"I imagine watching your entire squadron die in front of you has that effect," he noted.

"Yes sir, it apparently does," Nick replied. "I don't think either of my brothers has slept a full night since they have returned. Between notifying the next of kin and boxing up effects, they've been busy."

"You ever think maybe you should embrace this

assignment, Lieutenant Cobb?" Freeman asked. "Perhaps for your mother's sake if nothing else?"

Nick looked sideways at his former commanding officer.

"Sir, I figure you're my best ticket to getting out of this war in one piece," Nick replied. "Followed closely by Lieutenant, I mean *Lieutenant Commander* Banes."

"Ol' Stringbean will make a great commander, but he needs to get his own folks," Commander Freeman observed. "You guys lower down the totem pole didn't notice it much, but we definitely had different styles."

Nick looked at Commander Freeman in surprise.

"Let me guess, you figured we were both hyper-aggressive?" Freeman asked with a smile.

"Sir, are you saying Lieutenant Commander Banes wasn't?" Nick asked, genuinely curious.

"No, I'm saying Stringbean makes me look calm and reticent," Freeman replied with a twinkle. "Still think his boat is a safe bet?"

Nick shrugged.

"Sir, we attacked an entire Japanese task force," Nick replied. "I don't think there's an aggression setting higher than that."

"You'd be surprised," Freeman replied, looking at his watch.

"Don't you have to be at Rear Admiral Graham's headquarters soon?" Commander Freeman asked.

"Yes, sir," Nick replied.

Freeman looked at him askance.

"It's a bad look to be late to your new job," Freeman said sternly. "Especially since you know there was a phone call saying when we left."

"What are they going to do, sir, send me to sea?" Nick asked with a sneer.

"I think you'll find yourself back out on a boat soon enough," Commander Freeman said. "Be late and it will be some Sugar boat heading up to Alaska."

Okay, I had not considered that possibility, Nick thought.

"Thank you, sir," Nick said, coming to attention and rendering a proper salute.

"Till we meet again, Lieutenant," Freeman said, returning the gesture. He turned and began walking away towards his billets.

Nick watched his former commander go for a few moments, returning the salute of a couple of sailors, then turned the other way and looked down the street towards his own fate. He had no idea what his future as a staff officer held, but he was sure it was going to be painful. As he passed by the empty submarine docks, Nick gave a wistful gaze towards the U.S.S. *Tautog* as that vessel was taking on provisions.

Maybe I could stow away, he thought briefly, then quashed the thought. *While I have no idea what people do at SUBPAC headquarters, I am well aware that it has to beat the brig.*

"Well, guess it's time to take my whippin' like a man," Nick muttered as he reached the square building serving as SUBPAC headquarters. Making one last check of his uniform, Nick strode up and presented his identification to the Marine NCO standing guard with a bayoneted rifle and old World War I helmet at the door. The man looked over Nick's identification and his orders, then handed them back to the officer with a salute.

"Well, everything looks in order Lieutenant Cobb," the gunnery sergeant said. "Do you know where the admiral's office is?"

"Negative Gunnery Sergeant," Nick replied.

"Very well, you pass through this door and go to the

end of the hall and take a right," the grizzled man replied. "Don't worry, there's no gallows in there, sir."

"Thank you," Nick said with a grin. The NCO came to attention and saluted once again.

"Good luck, sir," the man replied.

"Thanks Gunnery Sergeant," Nick replied.

Nick followed the directions and soon found himself standing outside the chief of staff's door. Raising his hand, he knocked three times.

"Enter!" came the shout from beyond the door. With a last deep breath to stiffen his resolve, Nick entered the chief's office.

Sitting behind his desk, a lit cigar throwing up a thin trail of smoke, was Captain Kevin J. Donze. A tall man, Donze's physique could be described as "grizzly." A mustang, Donze was known for his low tolerance of idiocy and, much to the horror of his "refined" peers, an almost ever present cigar.

Rumor has it that the man does not carry matches for his cigars, as he simply lights them on the flaming remnants of the staff, Nick thought. He came to a position of attention precisely three steps in front of Donze's desk and snapped off a perfect salute.

"Lieutenant Nick Cobb reporting as ordered, Sir," he said flatly.

Donze returned the salute, then gestured for Nick to sit down at one of the two chairs just in front of his desk.

"Coffee or a smoke Lieutenant Cobb?" Donze asked, reaching for the open pack of cigars on his desk.

"No thank you, sir," Nick replied, sitting stiffly in the chair.

"Lieutenant, you need to relax in this headquarters," Donze said, a slight smile on his face. "Just because some of us happen to have all this extra braid on our caps doesn't mean we've forgotten how the rest of the submarine force lives."

Nick allowed himself to relax into the chair, still keeping his back straight as he looked around.

"While I'm sure you've heard this until you're ready to puke, great job on that Jap carrier," Donze said. "So what exactly do you think your new job is going to entail?"

"Sir, I'm not quite sure," Nick said. "I was not briefed prior to coming over."

That's the understatement of the year, he thought to himself.

"Well, I might be a bit responsible for that," Donze allowed. "Captain Davis was a bit slow in ordering you to move up here, so I suggested to Admiral Graham that he might need 'encouragement'."

Nick fought back the urge to grimace at that one. Suddenly the reason behind Davis's attitude became a lot clearer.

"Admiral Graham believes that there is a lack of "big picture" understanding at the boat level," Donze said. "Quite frankly, he doesn't think most of our commanders understand the reasons behind their orders—something that was exacerbated by the late Admiral Bowles believing that he ran this building as well as serving as CINCPAC chief of staff."

Nick kept his face expressionless at the mention of the late flag officer.

I'm probably going to Hell for thinking getting roasted in aviation gas was a fitting end for that man, Nick thought.

"In order to fight this problem, Admiral Graham has decided that he needs a junior officer, that being yourself, to write out a weekly strategy update," Donze continued. "The report needs to be geared towards officers of your rank and experience, the intent being to given them an idea of what's going on outside of their boat."

Nick was thunderstruck.

"Uh, Sir, are you sure you have the right Lieutenant?" Nick asked. "I mean, I just barely passed English while at Annapolis?"

Donze chuckled at that.

"Don't worry, Lieutenant Cobb," Donze said. "If necessary, we'll get one of the local teachers to help you."

Nick wisely decided not to push the issue. His mother had not raised any fools.

It's also been made clear to me today that a lieutenant's opinion isn't worth an admiral's fart, much less consideration, Nick thought bitterly. *Guess I'm pretty much stuck with this job*, he thought to himself.

"Don't worry, Lieutenant, we're not planning on keeping you here forever," Donze said. "You'll be here for six, maybe eight months top before we'll have you on the next new boat that shows up from the States."

Not forever, Nick thought, feeling genuinely horrified. *It will just seem like it by the time we're done. Is it too late to learn how to fly?*

Several miles away, Sam and David would have happily traded places with their brother.

I almost wish we were back to doing notifications, Sam thought, hammering down the lid on yet another crate of personal effects. *I don't know how many more wives' pictures I can see.*

"It'd be nice if they had just told us to do the officers," David seethed. "I mean, it beats hearing kids scream at us to 'bring their Daddy home,' but…"

Sam looked over at his brother as the other man let his voice trail off. He could see that his twin was fighting back tears, and reached past him to grab the form.

"Read the next item, David," he said. "I'll buy first

round after we get done here."

I hope I never have to do that again as long as I live, Sam thought, waiting for his brother to regain his composure.

"Picture, five by seven, in frame," David said heavily. The woman in the picture was a pretty brunette in a patterned white dress, obviously something quite important to the late Captain Abraham Finkel of Brooklyn, New York. Sam made the notation, then took the picture and began to put it in the crate.

"His sister, Celia," Sam said softly. "Told me if I had been a Jew he would have happily set us up together, thought we would have gotten along great. She even wrote me a couple of letters."

David looked at his brother in shock.

"You never told me about that," he said, surprised.

"Yeah, well, figured if you could run off and get engaged I could meet someone's sister," Sam replied. He sighed heavily. "Really sweet girl, I wonder how she's taking this."

"Poorly," David guessed. "You know, Sadie really not taking this whole thing well."

"You think?" Sam snorted. "Sorta puts things in perspective when most of the men your husband has introduced you die on the same day."

David looked at him like a kicked puppy, and Sam was immediately regretful for his tone. Like many big men, beneath their gruff exteriors neither Cobb twin liked seeing people hurt.

At least he's got Sadie and his church family to fall back on, Sam thought grimly.

"I wish you weren't so flippant," David said lowly. "Sadie's been trying to do what she can as well with the wives. The school and church have been delivering a lot of casseroles."

"I guess I should try that holy roller thing once in awhile," Sam said. David looked at him aghast.

"You know, Mom *and* Patricia would both flay you alive if they heard you talk like that," David replied. "I would think after all that's happened you'd be more inclined to consider getting right with God."

"He's kept us together this long, David," Sam said with a slight grin. "I don't think he's going to split us up on the other side."

David exhaled, shaking his head at Sam's tired joke.

"Patricia is right," David observed. "You will never be reformed."

"Patricia is one to talk," Sam replied. "At least I haven't left anyone at the altar."

"No, but you're apparently too blind to see someone wants to take you there," David replied.

Oh geez, here it comes, Sam thought, rolling his eyes.

"You know, I think you can at least go visit the two of them," David continued. "I mean, we know that Eric and Lieutenant (j.g.) Read are getting good home cooked meals on a daily basis, but I have no idea what you're doing to feed yourself these days."

Mainly sitting at home having cold sandwiches and drinking myself into oblivion, Sam thought.

"I'm not sure I'd be great company right now," Sam stated.

"Tootsie worries about you, Sam," David blurted, exasperated. "I think she's afraid you're going to crack."

Sam started laughing at that, drawing a suspicious look from David.

"Sorry," Sam said. "I just had a mental image of your conversation where Tootsie revealed that to you."

"Well she has a point," David said, stopping Sam's laughter in its tracks.

"Apparently she's not the only one," Sam snapped. He stopped, then felt his face start to color.

"Sorta just proved your point for you, didn't I?" Sam asked grimly.

"I've got this," David replied. "Take off for an hour, then come on back to find me."

Sam stretched his arms out and made a sound approximating that of a *Wildcat* running up as he stood up. David shook his head at his brother.

Twenty minutes later, Sam was rapping on his sister's door. To his surprise, Jo answered it.

"I see that communication remains a family weak point," Jo said. "Patricia's out having a picnic with Lieutenant (j.g.) Read—Eric was supposed to tell you."

"I've been a little bit busy boxing up dead people's stuff," Sam replied. "I don't think my brother knew."

"Okay, for her next act the amazing Josephine will stick *both* her feet in her mouth," Jo stated, stepping back from the door. "What brings you to our humble abode?"

"I was told to stop avoiding my little sister," Sam said.

"More correctly, you were told to stop avoiding your little sister's roommate who awkwardly professed her feelings for you in a time of great stress," Jo stated flatly.

Sam was taken aback.

"Well..." Sam started to say.

"I just received a telegram from my father," Jo said. "It was slightly sparse on details, but he wanted to make sure I knew that he was capable of sending telegram should someone 'stop by the house later.'"

Sam looked up in shock as he heard the tremor in Jo's voice.

"Good thing Western Union is faster than the Pacific

COLLISIONS OF THE DAMNED

Fleet's casualty office," she said, the last part trailing off in a sob. Sam strode over and embraced her, wrapping the shorter woman in his arms.

"So I made it a new rule to just start telling people what I'm thinking," Jo continued, tears in her voice. "How am I doing so far?"

"I can't complain," Sam allowed, squeezing her tighter.

"So why don't you give it a try," Jo said, squeezing him back then switching to a mocking Southern drawl. "Jo, I think you're a swell gal, but just not the one for me…"

"Stop it, Jo," Sam said, leaning back so he could look into Jo's eyes. "You know it's not that."

"Then what is it, Sam?" Jo asked, her eyes wet.

"I look at David with Sadie," Sam replied, "and I realize that I am just not ready to be that man with anyone. You of all people deserve someone who will treat you like you deserve."

There was a moment as Jo scanned Sam's face.

Well maybe I should have stayed with David after all, Sam thought for a moment, bracing himself.

He looks so vulnerable, Jo thought to herself. *Damn you, Sam Cobb.*

"I simultaneously want to slug you and kiss you, Sam," she finally said.

"I think we should hold off on the kissing," Sam replied jokingly, holding her slightly away from him.

"Geez, you could try and not act like that you'd sooner lock lips with Medusa," Jo observed.

"I'm not like my brothers and sisters, Jo," Sam retorted. "Woman kisses a man, she's going to get kissed back. That will lead to something we will both regret."

"I'm pretty sure only one of us would really regret it,"

Jo muttered, stepping back from him. "Jesus Christ, maybe I need to jump on Read before your sister does."

"Before his sister does what?" Patricia asked from the kitchen, causing Jo to nearly jump high enough to hit the roof.

"Make dinner," Sam said, not even missing a beat.

This is why I love you, Sam, Jo thought, as Eric and Charles walked into the living room.

"Well you're moving a lot better," Sam said, going to give his brother a hug.

"Easy you big lug," Eric stated. "It's the pain meds, they're actually starting to work."

"Charles," Jo said, nodding at the befuddled Lieutenant (j.g.) Read.

"Jo," Read replied. "Captain Cobb."

"Congrats on the promotion, Read," Sam said, nodding towards the young pilot's collars.

"Thank you, sir," Charles said. "I feel like I cheated to get it though."

"Getting shot down isn't cheating," Sam replied honestly.

Well they seem to be rather accepting of Read, Jo observed, mentally raising an eyebrow. *Is it because Eric's vouched for him, or because the young man hasn't actually made a move for Patricia?*

"It's my turn to cook, Jo," Patricia observed, walking into the dining room. "Sam, how long are you here?"

"I need to go back to give David a chance to go home in about twenty minutes," Sam said.

"Pork chops it is, then," Patricia replied. "Jo, you want to start some potatoes?"

"Certainly," Jo replied. Read stood up as she started to leave, prompting Sam and Eric to start doing the same as Jo waved them back down.

"Thank you gentlemen, but you all three need to relax while you can," she said, shaking her head as she entered the kitchen.

"What's this Western Union telegram on the table…" Patricia started to say lowly, then stopped dead in her tracks as she saw Jo's expression. "Oh my God!"

"Calm down, Dad's fine," Jo stated lowly. "Or at least, as fine as you can be when you've qualified for a Purple Heart."

Sydney, Australia
1030 Local (1930 Eastern)
22 April (21 April Eastern)

"XO, when was the last time you slept?" Captain Wallace asked as he walked up behind Jacob on the starboard wing of *Houston's* bridge.

Dammit Captain, this is not the time to start showing concern for my well-being, Jacob thought. Turning from where he was watching another load of 8-inch shells being passed down into the vessel's forward magazine, Jacob brought himself erect and tried to force the fatigue from his eyes.

"Sir, with all due respect, I have slept as much as the men," Jacob replied.

"That was not the question I asked, Commander Morton," Captain Wallace replied. "Judging from the clumsiness of the evasive maneuver you just attempted to pull, I'd say it's been at least forty-eight hours."

Forty-eight would be a generous guess, Jacob thought. *That's just been since I've slept, not slept well.*

"Sir, judging from the scuttlebutt, we're needed north," Jacob replied. "In your absence I was doing my best to expedite that process."

97

"Well, give me a status report then," *Houston*'s master replied.

"The *Vulcan*'s crew finished the last repairs on No. 3 this morning," Jacob said, gesturing towards the heavy cruiser's stern. The *Houston* was currently sitting in dry dock where she'd been since arriving in Sydney a little over three weeks before. Once the water had been pumped out from around they heavy cruiser's hull, it had been possible for the Cockatoo Yard's specialists to begin performing adequate but swift repairs beneath the waterline. For their part, the American repair crews aboard the *Vulcan* had used the massive dockside crane to lift out the No. 3 turret and its guns.

"I trust that they were satisfactory?" Captain Wallace asked, eyebrow raised.

"Sir, I'm not necessarily comfortable with their quality," Jacob replied, "but the turret turns and we have nominal flash protection back. Commander Sloan thinks we can fight well enough, but he would have preferred the repairs be done at Pearl."

"Wouldn't we all?" Wallace asked sarcastically.

"Commander Sloan has only informed me of the issues he has, sir," Jacob replied. "Our hosts have been nothing but gracious."

"I'm sorry that I was away for so long, XO," Wallace stated, changing topics. "As you alluded to, a lot has happened since I was over in Fremantle, and that disrupted the conference. Then we were waiting for Vice Admiral Somerville to return from his carrier hunt and General MacArthur to join us."

Jacob looked to make sure they were alone.

"How did that go, sir?" he asked lowly. "The papers are reporting that it was a great victory, but the rumor mill says that it was a bloody draw."

"General MacArthure is dead, as is Vice Admiral

Somerville" Captain Wallace said heavily. "The *Furious* was sunk, the *Warspite* was damaged, and at least three of the Japanese carriers got away towards Malaysia."

Jacob suddenly felt his fatigue wash over him again.

"The only good news is that Admiral Phillips doesn't think the Japanese will try and hit Ceylon again," Captain Wallace observed. "But that was a pretty steep price to pay."

Ships are dropping like flies, Jacob thought, woozily.

"XO, you need to get some sleep," Wallace stated.

"Sir, I'm needed…" Jacob protested.

"Jacob, you're no good to me if you drop off the side of this bridge into the dock beneath us because you're too tired to stand up straight," Wallace said. "Come with me to the chart room, and after that you are going straight to bed."

"Aye-aye, Captain," Jacob replied.

"And you will remain in your bunk for at least seven hours," Captain Wallace continued. "Am I understood?"

"Aye-aye, Sir," Jacob replied.

"The fact that you're not putting up more of a fight makes me even more sure you haven't slept since I've been gone," Captain Wallace observed.

As to the two men headed back into the bridge, Jacob looked out into Sydney's harbor. The *Vulcan* was the closet vessel to the dry docks, with the hulk of the destroyer *Peary* tied up alongside.

Can't believe that shot up tin can made it back here, Jacob thought. *The Japanese destroyers are clearly as powerful as we worried about.*

Just beyond the *Vulcan* and *Peary* was the newly arrived U.S.S. *Phoenix*. A twin to the *Boise*, the *Phoenix* had escorted the *Vulcan* on her journey from the West Coast. Admiral Hart had directed that the light cruiser would remain in Sydney until the *Houston* was repaired, then both vessels would move together back north towards Darwin in company with a foursome of destroyers that was expected within a couple of days.

It's not safe out there for unescorted ships, Jacob thought. *Plus he's probably thinking that **someone** needs to be ready to defend this place after the last few weeks.*

Just before they passed out of the bridge, there was the sound of several ships whistles from further towards the harbor mouth. Both men stopped in their tracks.

Speaking of defense, Jacob thought, looking around to find out where the nearest helmet was. After a moment, he realized the whistles were not signals of an imminent attack.

"Holy shit," someone exclaimed on the starboard deck below. Both Jacob and Captain Wallace ran out onto the bridge wing on that side. After a moment, Jacob saw what had caused the expletive below.

Holy shit indeed, Jacob thought.

The vessel limping up the harbor, her movement like a crippled prize fighter, was the heavy cruiser H.M.A.S. *Canberra*. It was clear that the *Australia*'s sister ship had been in a major fight from the blackened impact points along her hull, and her bridge was smashed to ruin. The vessel's A turret was still trained to starboard, its guns knocked askew, while smoke wafted up from her amidships. A moderate list to port and the way her hull laid low in the water indicated underwater damage as well, a broad oil slick behind her looking like a wounded animal's blood trail.

"What in the hell happened to her?" a sailor asked. Both Captain Wallace and Jacob turned to look at the offender, causing the man to decide to be somewhere else, quickly. Taking a look around, Captain Wallace saw that no other sailors were within earshot.

"What happened to her were Japanese bombers," Wallace replied. "Apparently our friends have a little bit more range than we expected."

"Where was she?" Jacob asked.

"Couple hundred miles south of Sumatra," Captain Wallace replied. "Saw a snooper two days ago, called for help. Japanese arrived before the *Beaufighters* did."

Jacob gave a low whistle.

"Too bad she didn't have the *Australia* with her," he said. "Radar probably would have helped a bit."

Captain Wallace turned and looked at Jacob.

"The *Sydney* was with her," he replied. "She had radar."

The past tense was not lost on Jacob.

"How bad is she hit?" Jacob asked, gesturing towards the cruiser.

"She took a torp forward on the starboard side, and you can see the bomb damage to her turrets. Her guns hit some Jap bastard and he did in the bridge," Captain Wallace answered. "Her XO was hit by a fragment, so the gunnery officer's her CO right now."

"Quick promotion," Jacob noted with no mirth.

"Part of the discussion in Fremantle was the heavy Australian losses," Captain Wallace said. "That's two light cruisers sunk in the last month and both of their current heavies damaged. Vice Admiral Crutchley is starting to become a little incensed at his command getting shot up from under him."

Jacob felt a cool chill that had nothing to do with the freshening breeze.

As bad as the news from Pearl is, we still have the Atlantic Fleet plus the new vessels that we're building, Jacob thought. *The Aussies don't have shit coming, and the Commonwealth are just as bad off.*

"...especially with the Dutch seeming hesitant to come to grips with the Japanese," Wallace was saying, causing Jacob to wonder what the first half of the sentence was.

"Not sure I follow the last, Sir," Jacob said wearily, finally giving up on trying to fill in the holes.

"There was a probing sweep down the Makassar Strait by some Japanese cruisers," Wallace explained patiently. "They were detected by an Aussie seaplane, and Admiral Phillips ordered one of the Dutch admirals to attack that night. The Dutch refused, saying they were conserving their forces for landings only."

"Well that's awfully nice of them," Jacob observed bitterly. "I imagine that played really well with a Commonwealth admiral."

"Admiral Phillips tried to have the man relieved," Wallace replied. "Admiral Helfrich refused and complained to the Combined Staffs back in Washington. The Brits allegedly told Phillips to back off."

The *Canberra* glided stop aligned with the doors of the *Houston*'s dry dock. Captain Wallace looked at the cruiser with a grim set to his face.

"*Marblehead* was also with them," Captain Wallace stated after a few moments. "She came out of the attack with a couple of bomb hits, nearly capsized. Her captain took her to Surabaya where the Dutch are trying to fix her in the floating dry dock. Probably good for her, as she was going to go home through the Indian Ocean—and that would have meant she'd probably have been caught by those carriers."

"Even without the carriers, that's a long trip across the Indian Ocean," Jacob replied, shaking his head. "Sir, we're getting the shit pounded out of us."

"Yes, things are taking a turn for the worse," Captain Wallace replied. "Which is why this vessel will be departing back north in forty-eight hours, two days earlier than we thought. Admiral Phillips seems to think that the Japanese are preparing to make a play for Java, bypassing Borneo."

"What about the Philippines?" Jacob asked.

"That's what I was going to talk to you about in the

chart room, XO," Captain Wallace returned. "The Japanese have pushed the Army back onto the Bataan Peninsula."

"What?!" Jacob said.

"It probably wouldn't have made a difference if he were there, but MacArthur's defensive plan was for shit," Captain Wallace said. "The Japanese outflanked both ours and the Filipino Army's troops in North Luzon. At that point it was all over but the shouting, and they were lucky to save what they did to fall back on Bataan. Lieutenant General Wainwright's calling for help"

Jacob could detect the tone of weariness in Captain Wallace's voice.

"Let me guess—he's blaming the Navy," Jacob replied.

"To everyone that will listen," Captain Wallace replied. "There's some kook even claiming that MacArthur was set up by President Roosevelt to eliminate a political competitor."

"I don't know why he didn't just fly out," Jacob observed.

"That was the plan when he got down to the East Indies," Captain Wallace stated. "They didn't have anything with the necessary legs left after trying to bomb the invasion beaches, plus everyone is still jittery after Darwin and Perth. Thought it'd be a crying shame if the senior general in the United States Army got blown out of the sky flying to Australia."

"That would be a bit of a problem," Jacob allowed. "Fitting given how badly the Army's apparently bungled the war, but still a problem."

"Yeah, well, still feel sorry for that damn boat skipper," Captain Wallace allowed.

"True." Suddenly Jacob felt every bit of fatigue that had been accumulating for the last twenty-four hours. He turned to face Captain Wallace.

"Get to bed XO," Captain Wallace said, seeing Jacob's eyes. "I don't want to see you awake before 1630, or you won't be my executive officer anymore. Clear?"

"As crystal, Sir," Jacob replied, already heading for the passageway off of the bridge.

Clark Field
1000 Local (2200 Eastern)
23 April (22 April)

The roar of several dozen radial engines in close orbit around Clark Field was a familiar one for the residents of Manila. However, the nationality of the circling aircraft was a sight that scared even the most stalwart Filipinos' hearts.

Lieutenant Isoro Honda, formerly of the carrier *Akagi* but now of the Tinian Wing, Imperial Japanese Navy Air Force (IJNAF), kept his head swiveling around as he applied rudder to bring his *Shiden* into alignment with the asphalt field below.

It has been an eventful month, he thought, still shocked to find himself getting ready to land on what had been one of the largest American base in the Pacific. *From Hawaii to the Philippines, with kills in both places.*

The *Kido Butai*'s supplements to the Tinian Wing had been well received, especially when an amphibious assault had allowed them to be shuttled into the Philippines by the light carrier *Chiyoda*.

*She is not the **Akagi**, but she seems to make a very good taxi,* Isoro thought. *I can only imagine how surprised the Americans were when they were returning to this very field to find us waiting for them.*

Honda made one last check of the area around the landing pattern, his movement demonstrating why his comrades called him "Sea Snake." Satisfied that his two wingmen, Warrant Officers Watanabe and Sawato, were in proper position with no American fighters about to attack, Isoro made his final approach.

Twenty minutes later, Isoro and the other nineteen *Shiden* pilots present were gathered around Commander Fuchida to find out what was coming next. With his tall and gangly frame, Isoro found himself once more standing in the back row

"In five days, we will begin our attack against the Dutch East Indies," Fuchida began. "The fate of the Empire and our entire war plan rests on all of your shoulders."

There was a slight shuffling in the Philippine heat at that statement, several of the newer pilots looking at one another. For his part, Isoro's face remained expressionless.

If you were not prepared to have to do heroic things, you probably should not have joined the IJNAF, Isoro thought. *Japan needs us now mor than ever.*

"Honda-san," Fuchida said, startling Isoro out of his thoughts.

"Yes sir?" Isoro asked.

"We are a long way from Hawaii, no?" Fuchida asked with a slight smile.

"Yes, sir, we really are," Isoro said, grinning momentarily himself.

"Tell me, how has the hunting been for you fighter pilots?" Fuchida asked. "It seems forever since I have helped bag a battleship."

Isoro smiled at that last part.

"The hunting has been excellent, sir," Isoro said.

"Are you ready to try your luck with the Dutch?"

"Commander, as always we are your sword," Isoro replied with a broad smile.

"Isoro-san, I am glad to see my faith in you is

completely justified," Fuchida replied.

As if I truly had a choice, Isoro thought without any trace of rancor. *In this time of need for Japan, a warrior must be prepared to make sacrifices.*

CHAPTER 3: CENTER RING

*The first blow is half the battle—**Oliver Goldsmith***

Makassar Strait
0345 Local (1545 Eastern)
26 April (25 April)

"Apparently these chaps have never understood the concept of concentration of force," Flying Officer Bellingsley observed dryly.

"Or they realize that we can't stop them everywhere," Russell replied, looking at his radar screen. He was desperately tired, especially of looking at the green screen in front of him.

We've been busy since the Japanese started probing out of Singapore two nights ago, Russell thought, rubbing his eyes.

"Damn moon is far too bright for my liking," Bellingsley stated nervously.

"It's only because the sky is bloody clear for once," Russell stated, scanning the sky.

"George Flight, Charles One," Squadron Leader Pence's voice echoed in Russell's ear.

Glad he survived that bloody cock up a few days ago, Russell thought. *Damn wing commander ordering us out to help the **Canberra** ought to have been shot. Gee, who could have foreseen there'd be damn Nip fighters escorting the bombers? **Anyone with a bloody brain, that's who***.

"This is George One," Russell replied.

"When was the last time you heard from Black Cat Six?" Pence asked.

107

I have no idea, Russell thought, looking at his wristwatch. *The bloke is staging around in a **Lancaster** near a Japanese task force. He might be slightly busy.*

"Charles One, this is Black Cat Six," the *Lancaster* pilot replied, his New Zealand accent deepening with annoyance. "Be advised there's at least one cats eye fighter about. He was bloody persistent, so I thought that might be more important than answering the telly."

Seems that Black Cat Six has not been having a good night, Russell thought. *Still, good thing they decided to send a **Lancaster** up there rather than a **Catalina**.*

"What is your report, Black Cat?" Pence replied, his voice clipped.

"There's at least one carrier, probably two," Black Cat Six replied. "Radar operator counted four more large contacts before the...*look out!*"

There was the brief sound of gunfire over the radio before Black Cat Six ceased transmission. Russell spotted a stream of tracers a dozen miles or more ahead of them, followed by a bright fireball that quickly winked out.

Hope that wasn't Black Cat Six, Russell thought.

"Persistent bugger," Black Cat Six said. "Let's see what that bloody *Beau...*"

The *Lancaster* pilot stopped once he realized he was talking over the open radio.

"What I want is you to finish your report, Black Cat Six," Pence stated, sounding positively perturbed.

"Five large blips, at least one carrier," Black Cat Six snapped. "Enemy fighters about, just splashed one. Take a course of three four oh true, fly for about five more minutes, and I doubt you'll miss them!"

"George, Michael Flights, did you copy?" Pence asked.

"Roger," Russell said.

"Roger," Michael One replied.

Well here's to hoping those blokes in the **Bostons** *know what they're about*, Russell thought.

"Charles Flight, let's try and clear the way," Pence stated. Peering out of the *Beaufighter*'s observation dome, Russell watched as Charles Flight began to accelerate away from the bomb-laden George Flight and Michael Flight's A-20s.

"Let's start letting down," Russell said, looking back at his scope.

"Going down," Bellingsley replied, his voice nervous.

George flight began to spiral down from ten thousand feet, the circles moving gradually north. As they passed seven thousand feet, the sky to their north suddenly became alive with shell bursts.

"Well looks like we're not the only people out here with radar," Pence stated. "Tallyho, multiple ships, bearing three five five true, four...*AAAAAHHHHH*!"

Russell had seen the burst of tracers a split second before the screams began. Charles One's demise as as impressive as it was sudden, the *Beaufighter* spinning out of the sky like a macabre Catherine wheel. Russell felt his stomach in his throat as he watched the falling fighter.

"Gotcha you bastard!" Charles Three cried. A moment later there was another bright explosion as the *Zero* fighter that had shot down Charles One met a less spectacular if just as incendiary death.

Blimey, was all Russell thought. He snapped out of it as George One leveled off just above the dark waters of the Makassar Strait.

"Charles Three, keep your eye up there for any more of those bastards," he barked, smoothly assuming control of the squadron. "Michael Flight, orbit east and stand by. George Flight, we're going to try alternate attack pattern three tonight."

There was a moment of silence.

"Roger," Charles Three replied, followed quickly by Michael One and George Three.

Well the 500-pounders we've got won't even dent a battleship, but they should hurt a carrier, Russell thought. *Here's to hoping we and the **Bostons** guess right on who is who.*

Attack Pattern Three required all four of George Flight to attack simultaneously, with each pilot picking out his target.

"Bellingsley, we're taking a target at oh three oh relative, range twenty one thousand...*CHRIST!*"

The entire Japanese formation had suddenly erupted in small arms, medium caliber and, in at least two cases, main gun fire. In an instant, the sky had gone from relatively placid to one of the largest anti-aircraft displays that Russell had ever seen. Directly ahead of their aircraft, a pair of destroyers switched on their searchlights and began to wildly sweep the surrounding skies. As George One passed five thousand yards, two of the searchlights locked onto the approaching *Beaufighter*. The simultaneous sharp *crack*! of anti-aircraft explosions above and behind their fighter caused Russell's bowels to loosen, and he had to concentrate to keep from losing his bladder.

Oh bloody hell, Russell thought, the *Beaufighter*'s cabin lit up from the intersecting beams. To Bellingsley's credit, he quickly sideslipped, but not before there were several *thumps* back along the fuselage that told them the destroyers had managed to find the range with their automatic cannons. Russell felt the *Beaufighter* slew sickeningly to the left before Bellingsley corrected, their target growing ever larger in front of them. To Russell's relief he saw the distinctive flat top outline as the vessel put her helm hard over to port and away from them.

"Port engine's losing power!" Bellingsley shouted.

The next twenty seconds were the longest of Russell's life. Behind him, he watched as George Three lost both of its wings, the fuselage and surfaces all spinning down into a huge splash of spray.

"Charles Three, break!" his headphones crackled.

"Michael One, Michael One, you're on fire!" came another voice. Russell didn't spare a glance backwards, his focus forward as he stood up in the observation dome. The carrier's entire starboard side was seemingly aflame from her anti-aircraft battery, the tracers reaching out towards their fighter in the darkness. Just as Russell was about to scream at Bellingsley to release, he saw a stream of tracers lazily arcing towards them.

Oh Lord, he thought, just before a 25mm shell smashed into the fuselage just in front of the dome. In a flash of light, rush of air, plexiglass, and fragments, Russell felt several sharp stings on his face and across his upper torso and a sharp blow as a particularly large piece of observation dome caromed off of his goggles.

Shit! he thought, falling back into the fuselage. Stunned, he heard Bellingsley shouting oaths at the top of his lungs and the *Beaufighter*'s armament roaring as they approached a Japanese destroyer. To Russell's surprise, the strafing attack silenced several of the vessel's smaller guns, and he had a momentary image of the main battery trying to depress from where it had been firing at high altitude.

"Hit! *George One, you got a bloody hit!*" he heard George Four's exuberant voice.

"Are you hurt?" Russell asked, feeling blood pouring down his own face.

"Yes, Sir, I am," Bellingsley choked out as they passed out of small arms range. "We're losing oil pressure in the port engine, I'm going to have to feather it."

"Bloody bastards got me in the face," Russell said, shouting over the roar of wind above his head. "Let's see to

111

you first."

"George One, Charles Four! I'm getting the bloody hell out of here! Charles Three has been rammed, and Charles Two was shot down by flak," came another report.

"Roger Charles," Russell said, suddenly feeling weary.

Oh God, am I hurt worse than I thought? he wondered.

"Bloody hell," Bellingsley said. "Starboard engine is starting to overheat as well. We're likely going to have to ditch."

Russell looked up from where he was digging into the first aid kit. As he did so, he realized blood was running down the side of his goggles.

"Dammit! There's a submarine supposedly out here on the surface," he said, making his way up to where Bellingsley was flying one handed. Turning to look back through the starboard windows as they headed south, he saw a large blaze on the water.

"Charles Three, this is George One," Bellingsley said into his microphone. "We're going to have to put her in the water."

"Roger George One," Charles Three replied.

"George One, this is Four," George Four broke in. "I have you in sight. Do you want us to drop flares?"

Yes you idiot, I want the people we just bombed to totally know where we are, Russell thought uncharitably.

"Negative Four," Russell replied.

"George One, this is Black Cat Six," the *Lancaster* pilot broke back in. "State your position."

Oh shit, I do not know where we are, Russell thought.

"About four minutes southwest of that damn task force, mate," Bellingsley barked over the radio. Maybe about to be six minutes. Speed about two hundred knots!"

"Roger George One," Black Cat Six replied. "Standby."

"Oh take your time, lad," Bellingsley snapped. "We'll just have a spot of tea from my damn engine."

"Easy Bellingsley, he is trying to help," Russell barked, unconsciously going to wipe his face with his flight jacket collar. He immediately regretted that decision, the sharp pain of glass splinters and cloth across cuts causing him to grunt.

"Sir, how bad are *you* hit?" Bellingsley asked, worried.

"I'm okay, just got glass and part of the damn fuselage in my face," Russell replied, checking over the *Beaufighter*'s life raft. To his relief, he saw that the package had not taken any damage.

"All right then, I'm going to put her down," Russell said, as the starboard engine began vibrating. "Rather make a powered ditch. Brace yourself, sir."

Russell was pleasantly surprised at how smoothly Bellingsley put the big fighter down on the smooth waters of the Makassar Strait. In a mad scramble, both men hustled out of the aircraft as water began flooding into the numerous holes in their fuselage. Barely three minutes later, the drenched aviators watched from their dinghy as George One put its nose down and slipped under the waves.

"I guess now is a terrible time to mention it, but my uncle runs an aquarium," Bellingsley said nervously. "He said something about the Dutch East Indies has some of the most aggressive sharks in the world."

Russell looked over at his companion.

"You're bloody fucking right, Bellingsley," he snapped. "That was the worst time to mention it!"

Before Bellingsley could say anything, there was another round of firing to their north.

"Looks like they scared someone else up to take a swing at our friends," Bellingsley observed.

"Yes, yes they did," Russell replied. He suddenly started to shake, his stomach rotating without warning. Moving swiftly, he nearly upset the dinghy as he vomited over the side. Wiping the back of his mouth, he suddenly wished he had not been sick as a large, sinuous shape swished by the side of their craft.

"You just had to mention the bloody sharks," Russell seethed.

Bellingsley's response was drowned out by a low throbbing sound and their low horizon suddenly sprouting another shape.

"Bloody hell, I hope that's friendly," Bellingsley said. Russell reached up and unlatched his holster, leading to a snort from his pilot.

"Laugh if you want," Russell snapped. "I heard what those blokes were doing in the Philippines from one of those American pilots that passed through a couple days ago. No thank you, I'd rather die fighting."

The dinghy suddenly jerked to the side as something bumped it from underneath.

"You still might die fighting, just not how you think!" Bellingsley observed.

Russell realized why they had not seen the submarine sooner: its decks were awash as it came towards them. In a daring feat of seamanship, the vessel eased underneath their dinghy, then lifted them out of the water.

"If you blokes are quite done riling up the local tourists and wildlife, could you move lively and get aboard?" a distinct English accent asked.

Guess that answers that question, Russell thought, springing to his feet. *It just might be our lucky night.*

"Roger Two," Wolford replied, then switched to

intercom. "Let's see what we've got down here," he said to Bellingsley.

U.S.S. Houston
1025 Local (2225 Eastern)
27 April (26 April)

Houston's senior wardroom was once more the location for a council of war, each department head and present to find out their new mission. The compartment's walls bore grim testimony to her hasty repairs, a new coat of paint not really hiding the fact a shell had exploded in the space at South China Sea. If one took a deep breath, it was hard to miss the slight odor of burnt paint from the fire that had been started by a *Nachi* 8-inch shell.

Barely enough time to get refueled at Surabaya, Jacob thought, looking over the grim faces. *Not that that place doesn't seem like it is under siege.*

"Gentlemen, we have been ordered to rendezvous with the remainder of the ACDA strike force north of Kangean Island in the Flores Sea," Captain Wallace stated. "Yesterday the Japanese established a beach head at Balikpapan despite air attacks from our allies."

Hard to get a good air strike off when you're constantly having to defend your own harbor, Jacob thought. *Especially since the damn Japs seem to have figured out a way to blind the freakin' radar.* Apparently the British had a name, "Window," for what the Japanese had dropped.

Odd name for something that prevents you from seeing rather than helping you see, Jacob thought. *No matter, just hope they don't figure out how to use that shit at sea.*

"As you can see, we have the *Australia*, *Phoenix*, and two Dutch destroyers with us," Wallace said, referring to the *Isaac Sweers* and *Banckert* that were to port and starboard respectively. "Unfortunately, those fighters overhead are going to have to go home in about thirty minutes, and no more can be spared from attempting to attack in the north."

Jacob hoped his fear wasn't quite obvious on his face.

"The Japanese also landed in West Borneo near Brunei and Sarawak," Commander Sloan began. "With the establishment of enemy airfields in the Philippines, we will be unable to interfere with these landings using surface assets."

Jacob winced inwardly at that last statement. While the Commonwealth divisions were fighting tenaciously in Sumatra, the combined Allied Air Forces were being slowly ground to pieces by the Japanese aircraft. Even the Allies' best fighters, the *Spitfire,* was having difficulty with *Zero,* while the extended range of Japanese bombers necessitated that all surface ships could not move into a region of contested airspace. Only the near suicidal-bravery of the Dutch, Australian, and Commonwealth pilots kept the Java Sea from becoming a Japanese lake.

"Admiral Phillips' intent is to force the Makassar Straits this afternoon with the destroyers and cruisers of our command in order to compel the enemy to commit his covering force," Captain Wallace continued. "At that point he will bring forward his own battleships to seek an engagement under cover of darkness. I will be followed by Commander Morton," Wallace concluded.

Jacob stood up, straightening his tie as he strode to the briefing chart. Taking the pointer from his captain, he rested it on a point about twenty-four miles north of Balikpapan.

"Yesterday, Australian aircraft attacked a force of warships to include one aircraft carrier," Jacob said. "Reports are still unclear, but apparently one of the Aussies hit the carrier with a bomb, then another one put his bomber into it with a full load."

Proves that our opponents don't have a monopoly on suicidal crazies, he thought, looking the shocked faces of his fellow officers. *Of course, person has to be half crazy to be an aviator anyway.*

"Dutch and Commonwealth aircraft have been attempting to attack this group as well as the transports arrayed off Balikpapan since dawn," Jacob continued, remembering what he'd been hurriedly told by the Asiatic Fleet staff. "There are no reports on their success."

Moving the pointer a little bit further south, Jacob moved on to the next portion of his briefing.

"What the returning aircraft have reported is that there are several large warships, possibly to include two battleships, located here, about eighty miles east of Adang," Jacob said. "Further north are five to eight destroyers protecting around twenty transports just off of Balikpapan, while somewhere out there is apparently another Japanese carrier,"

There were several murmurs that went around the room. The ACDA command had only one flattop left after the *Furious*'s untimely demise. The old *Hermes* was not expected to put the fear of God in anyone, and if the Japanese had brought the carriers which had decimated the Pacific Fleet at Pearl Harbor forward, the ACDA was as good as dead.

"Gentlemen," Captain Wallace said sharply, "we do not have time to give voice to our doubts. We have been waiting for this day for almost a month now, and I for one am ready to give these damn Japs another beating. Anyone who feels differently just let me know, and we'll be sure to put you off at the next port."

Captain Wallace's glare and tone had the desired effect, making the wardroom so quiet that a pin could have dropped.

"We will be accompanying the destroyers and light

117

cruisers north in order to give them some needed backup," Jacob said. "Upon gaining contact with the enemy fleet, we will attempt to fight our way through to the transports or until we sight enemy heavy units. At that point we will come around and sail south until we are met by the advancing Main Body under Admiral Phillips. I will be followed by Captain Wallace."

Captain Wallace strode to the chart with a purpose, his face set in a hard line. He did not even bother looking at the chart as he turned to face the gathered officers and NCOs.

"Gentlemen, this vessel will be performing the mission for which she was designed in less than six hours," Wallace said, his eyes meeting those of every other individual in the room. "Remain calm, do your jobs, and we will succeed in kicking the Japanese asses for finally coming out from under their damn rocks. Dismissed to your departments, all except for the XO and Guns," Captain Wallace said firmly.

The wardroom quickly cleared, leaving Jacob and Commander Sloan alone with their captain. Jacob looked around at the room, taking a moment's pleasure in the amount of excess equipment that had been removed at his direction.

*We would have burned like a candle if I hadn't had that talk with the **Perth**'s XO the night the war started*, Jacob thought. *I'd totally strip the paint off the bulkheads if I could be sure the metal wouldn't rust in this humidity.*

"Just a couple of things I want to make sure you know as well as me, but aren't for popular consumption," Captain Wallace began once the room was empty.

Jacob and Sloan looked at each other briefly.

News withheld from the wardroom is never good news, Jacob thought, seeing a mirrored expression on Sloan's face.

"The Japs got the *Hermes* with a fish just before our

briefing started," Captain Wallace said grimly. "It cost them, badly, but she's out of the upcoming fight."

Jacob hoped the shock did not show on his face. The *Hermes* had been shipping a full complement of *Sea Hurricanes* that had been expected to keep a near constant cover over the battle squadrons. It was not a good sign that she had been hit by a torpedo, especially if she was damaged bad enough to be out of the upcoming battle.

"The Main Body has been repelling air attacks throughout the morning," Captain Wallace continued. "So far *Hermes* is the only major casualty. We can expect air attacks ourselves within the next hour as we close with Admiral Phillips."

"I only hope our guys are giving the Japanese as much hell as they're giving us," Jacob muttered.

"Judging from the reports the Aussies' gave us, I think that's a fair bet," Captain Wallace said.

Balikpapan Beachhead
1115 Local (2315 Eastern)

Isoro knew things were going to be bad when he saw the merchantmen explode from roughly twenty miles away. From the shape and size of the explosive cloud, he knew that the vessel had been a fully loaded ammunition ship.

While simultaneously assaulting both sides of Borneo was impressive in its daring, he thought, *it may prove to be ultimately costly.*

It was all supposed to have been so simple. With the seizure of airfields in the vicinity of Davao, Philippines, the IJNAF had been at the extreme limits of fighter range to Balikpapan. In order to add a large margin of error, the *Ryujo, Hiyo,* and *Zuiho* had been intended to act as emergency landing stations for the land-based *Zeroes* and *Shidens.* Unfortunately, judging from the condition that

119

Isoro had seen the *Ryujo* in a few moments before as she limped underneath is aircraft, nothing was landing on her deck...if she made it home.

I could have stayed aboard my damn carrier rather than coming out here to some dusty hell hole, Isoro thought bitterly. *A dusty hell hole where the damn food is doing terrible things to my intestines.*

As if triggered by his thoughts, his stomach gurgled and shot through with sharp pains. Grimacing, he summoned all his determination to avoid fouling himself, scrunching his sphincter tightly. Closing his eyes, he felt the sweat break out on his forehead.

The sound of cannon fire made him snap his eyes open, reacting instinctively with a climbing turn to starboard. In the end, the move saved his life, as tracers whipped just underneath his fighter. The pain in his bowels forgotten, Isoro quickly rolled his fighter inverted to look through the top of his cockpit to see who his assailant was. Out of the corner of his eye he saw a flaming comet descending towards the ocean, apparently one of the aircraft from another *chutai*. Another blurry shape hurtled just barely underneath him, the enemy aircraft unable to match his roll.

Hurricane, Isoro thought to himself, having studied identification cards during their five day wait. Continuing his roll, he pursued the rapidly diving enemy fighter, ensuring that he still had both of his own wingmen behind him. As he watched, his Number 3, Sawato, turned after his prey's wingman, cutting the approaching *Hurricane* off with a burst from his own cannon.

Seeing his tail was clear, Isoro turned back forward, pulling hard on the stick to begin a tight turn. Gradually his nose continued to come around, the enemy fighter starting to disappear as he gained enough lead. Realizing that he could not escape the *Shiden* in a dive, the enemy pilot attempted to reverse his turn, the worst thing he could do as it made the

Hurricane hang as a perfect target for a moment. That moment was all Isoro needed, as he mashed down the triggers for his guns. With a bright flash and gush of flame, the *Hurricane*'s fuselage tank burst from the impact of the heavy cannon shells.

Zooming past the doomed fighter, Isoro saw the pilot imprisoned in a sea of flame, frantically trying to get his cockpit open. Forgetting his victim, Isoro whipped his head around to make sure he did not have another enemy fighter on his own tail. Scanning around, he saw a kaleidoscope of chaos all around him, the skies having gone from empty to suddenly full of enemy aircraft.

Damn you all, Isoro thought, again feeling his stomach clench as he looked for targets. Seeing another enemy fighter, this one apparently one of the more nimble *Spitfires*, on the tail of a *Zero* above him, Isoro put his aircraft in a sharp climb. Wishing for the umpteenth time that he and his fellow pilots had reliable radios, Isoro watched helplessly as the *Spitfire*'s wings sparked with its eight machine guns, blasting the hapless *Zero* out of the sky.

Just as Isoro was about to fire in revenge, the *Spitfire*'s wing flew off, another *Zero* catching the enemy fighter with a fast overhead run. Turning in his seat, Isoro saw the *Zero* execute a fast wingover, another *Spitfire* trying to turn onto the fighter's tail. Realizing that he had been seen, the *Spitfire* attempted to disengage. Unfortuantely for the Allied pilot, his *Zero* opponent was an apparent maestro at maneuvering his aircraft. As Isoro came around to cover, the *Zero* pilot dispatched the enemy aircraft with a burst of cannon and machine guns that shattered the *Spitfire*'s tail, sending it spinning out of the sky.

As he joined up on the other *Zero*, Isoro recognized the aircraft as belonging to one of the Tinian pilots.

It's that man named Nishizawa, Isoro thought, looking around for his own wingmen. Sawato joined up on his port wing as Nishizawa flew off to rejoin his own *chutai*.

Where is Yoshida? Isoro asked.

There were suddenly puffs of anti-aircraft fire below and to his starboard side. As he looked, Isoro suddenly saw several objects heading towards the *Ryujo* at low altitude and slow speed. Pushing his nose down, he saw Yoshida slide into position on his port side.

Bastard, Isoro thought to himself, then turned his head back around. As he rapidly began to overtake the aircraft below, he suddenly had to rub his eyes as he believed that he had to be seeing things from his childhood.

Biplanes?! These idiots are using **BIPLANES?!** he thought to himself, watching as eight enemy became seven with a stream of tracers from *Ryujo*'s escorts.

"Enemy bombers above us!" Yoshida shouted. Looking upwards, Isoro saw that Sakai and several other *Zeroes* were moving to intercept a gaggle of large aircraft that were moving in at high altitude towards the beach head. From a distance Isoro recognized the four-engined aircraft as American *Flying Fortresses* and felt his stomach clench in fear. Those aircraft had already grown legendary with the telling of the *Zuikaku*'s demise by the *Shokaku*'s crew.

'Crane killers', Isoro thought to himself, then turned back to focus on his targets. Leveling off just above the ocean, Isoro suddenly realized how much of an advantage in overtake speed he had. Skidding desperately, he realized that he was moving too fast to get his guns on target. Where a neophyte would have pulled up, Isoro realized that would expose his belly to the seven tail gunners who even now were blazing away at him.

His fighter suddenly lurched as an anti-aircraft shell exploded near his tail. Realizing he was in as much danger from friendly fire as the enemy, pushed his throttle up against the firewall and remained low and fast, leaving the enemy planes to the destroyers and *Ryujo*'s own guns. Climbing and looking back, the Japanese ace watched as the five remaining biplanes pressed their attack.

There's no way they'll make it, Isoro thought.

Two of the biplanes inexplicably survived the gauntlet, smoke pouring from their engines as they aimed their weapons at the nearer of *Ryujo*'s two escorting destroyers. One aircraft crashed immediately after release, a crewman's body visible as it hurtled above the spray. The second managed to stagger into a turn before being intersected by five different streams of tracers, the canvas wings bursting into flames before the aircraft lurched into the drink. The pair of dropped torpedoes spurred the destroyer to add on more speed and turn to avoid them, masking some of her guns. This gave a flight of four more biplanes that Isoro had somehow not seen an almost free pass.

These are brave men, Isoro thought grudgingly, even as he circled around to see if more aircraft were inbound. The lead biplane suddenly detonated in a huge cloud of black smoke as a 25mm round found its torpedo The last two biplanes released at the same time, taking into account the creeping *Ryujo*'s last clumsy attempt to evade. In the next moment, tracers from the carrier's guns smote both aircraft from the sky, following the burning carcasses down into the flames.

It took only moments for the final act of the combat. With a sickening feeling in his stomach, Isoro watched both torpedo wakes arrow directly towards the *Ryujo*'s side. The first weapon was off a bit in speed, passing just ahead of the carrier's bow. The second weapon was perfect, hitting the carrier amidships with a waterspout that towered over her still smoking flight deck. With a visible vibration, the carrier began to coast to a stop and start to list.

Dammit! Isoro pulled back on the stick, continuing to climb away from the torpedoed warship. Jumping, he looked at his fuel gauge, realizing that the few minutes combat had used up the last of his reserves. If he intended to return to the Philippines, he had to depart now. If not, he needed to find the *Zuiho* or *Hiyo*. Looking around, he saw that the closest enemy aircraft were the rapidly receding *Flying Fortresses*. Searching, he saw that they had attacked the merchantmen near the beach. Amazingly, the bombers had missed, the water still disturbed by their dropped weapons.

Perhaps luck is on our side, Isoro thought. With that thought, he resolved to remain in the area. In order for the attack to be successful sacrifices had to be made, and that included landing on a carrier far from his own bed, such as it was.

Not that this is much of a sacrifice, he thought, his stomach rumbling again with a vengeance. *Indeed, I desperately need to visit the head.*

Seeing the *Hiyo*coming into the wind, he started to head for the small carrier.

Houston
1345 Local (0145 Eastern)

"Enemy aircraft, bearing three five zero, range twenty-five thousand yards," Seaman Apprentice Oliver Wedgewood, Battle Two's new talker, stated in his high, reedy voice. A *Boise* survivor, Wedgewood had bounced around several departments before catching the eye of Chief Petty Officer Roberts, the NCOIC of Battle Two. A smart, intelligent lad, Wedgewood had an uncanny memory and the ability to recall information hours, if not days, after he had first heard it.

I'll be damned if he's actually nineteen years old, or whatever bullshit it says on his record, Jacob thought. *Oh well, if he's old enough to have faked his records, he's old enough to face the consequences.*

"The ship is ready for air action in all respects,"

124

Roberts said from the other talker station. The *Peary* sailor they had inherited to man the second station was busy vomiting in the head, the stress having finally gotten to him.

They really should have given those poor bastards survival leave, Jacob thought.

"All right men, looks like we're just in time to meet the next enemy airstrike," Jacob said laconically. "Lieutenant Foncier, you have the station, I'm going out to watch the festivities."

"Aye-aye, Sir," Lieutenant Paul Foncier drawled from just behind Battle Two's helmsman. The large, broad-shouldered Cajun was also a *Boise* survivor, his younger brother having been killed aboard the cruiser *New Orleans* at Hawaiian Islands. The man had earned Jacob's impeccable trust during their journey up from Sydney.

Nice to be able to step outside and see what in the hell is going on without having to look through those damn portholes, Jason thought as he stepped out onto the deck, his binoculars around his neck. *I trust Chief Roberts, but he's still not an officer.*

The enemy aircraft were still invisible to the naked eye, the report having been passed from *Australia*'s radar, but their likely targets were visible on the horizon. The ACDA Main Body had already repulsed four air attacks so far that day. The heaviest and by far the most deadly had come just one hour before, thirty-six twin-engined bombers storming into the outnumbered CAP and *Beaufighters*. Twenty of the bombers had managed to press into anti-aircraft range, with all but two of those surviving to release their weapons.

The *Hermes*, already damaged earlier, had taken another fish on the opposite side. The carrier was currently stopped and low in the water three miles to *Houston*'s starboard, a pair of destroyers close aboard.

She's not going to survive another hit, simple as that,

Jacob thought. *I'm not even sure I'd bet on her surviving the two she's taken.*

Turning back to look north, Jacob could see a column of smoke coming from the battleship *Revenge*, a bare mile and a half away. The vessel had taken a torpedo hit and was still fighting the resultant fires, slowing the entire Main Body's battle line to fifteen knots.

She's going to have to go back to Surabaya, Jacob thought. As if reading his mind, the battleship hove to port away from the rapidly forming battle line, black smoke pumping from her funnel as she attempted to increase her speed. Two Commonwealth destroyers turned to help the battleship out, laying smoke to obscure the larger vessel's movements. The battleship's wallowing turn brought her back towards *Houston*, the large 15-inch turrets swinging out towards the approaching Japanese aircraft.

"Aircraft port beam!" a lookout screamed from somewhere forward. Lifting his binoculars to see where the enemy was, Jacob bit back a curse. Like predators sensing a wounded member of the herd, the approaching enemy formation was turning and starting to track towards the *Revenge*. Jacob watched as the six *Sea Hurricanes* and six Dutch *Hawks* that were airborne as CAP closed towards the approaching specks. Through his binoculars Jacob could tell that the approaching enemy aircraft were single-engined and heavily outnumbered the CAP.

"Sir, we're moving to assist the *Revenge*," Foncier called. Looking astern, Jacob could see the *Houston's* repaired aft turret swinging out towards the approaching enemy aircraft, now rapidly growing. As he watched there were several falling comets, the explosions eliciting cheers from the *Houston's* waiting gun crews.

Might want to make sure those are enemy aircraft before you start cheering, Jacob thought. He was suddenly nudged in the back by a hard object. Whirling, he was prepared to rip someone's face off when he realized it was Chief Roberts holding out his pie plate helmet.

"Hard to make the men keep theirs on if you're not wearing yours, Sir," Chief Roberts said quietly. "More importantly, I'd hate to have to train up Commander Sloan…he's sorta deaf."

Jacob took the helmet, getting ready to retort, when the cruiser's port 5-inch guns opened fire at the approaching enemy aircraft. Turning to look, Jacob saw the shells burst far short of the approaching enemy aircraft.

"What in the hell is Sloan doing?" Jacob asked. Turning he moved quickly into Battle Two, listening as the talkers counted down the range to the approaching Japanese aircraft.

Unbeknownst to Jacob, the aircraft he had seen falling out of the sky had indeed been Japanese. The combined first strike of the *Hiyo* and *Zuiho*, the approaching group had consisted of ten A6M *Zeroes* and twelve each *Vals* and *Kates*. For once the FDO aboard the *Prince of Wales* had managed to place the CAP in a superior position to use their heavier aircraft in a slashing dive attack, his task aided by the timely arrival of six American P-38 *Lightnings*. Striking with a ferocity all out of proportion to their numbers, the CAP had managed to destroy two of the *Zeroes* outright to get amongst the bombers. As a result, the strike was disjointed, the six remaining *Vals* and eight *Kates* attacked as a stream rather than one concentrated group.

"There was an error in range from the *Australia*, Sir," Foncier said as Jacob came in. The 5-inch guns spoke again as one volley, then began firing as rapidly as the crews could reload. Turning, Jacob could see the enemy coming in a loose gaggle, the torpedo bombers descending almost to sea level.

127

"Main battery preparing to engage torpedo bombers,"
Wedgewood said, his voice several octaves higher and
breaking. Jacob's eyes met Roberts, the NCO already on the
way to talk to the young man.

Captain Wallace's original intent had been to try and
draw off some of the approaching enemy planes by
presenting his ship as a nearby target. The ruse was
unsuccessful, the surviving Japanese pilots suffering an
extreme case of target fixation as they began rushing in
towards the *Revenge*. Seeing that his ruse was not going to
work, Captain Wallace barked for the wheel to be put hard to
port, bringing the *Houston* around in a sharp turn towards the
enemy aircraft.

Just as the heavy cruiser was heeling over, the nine
eight-inch guns roared out their first salvo. Six miles away
nine perfectly spaced geysers rose up like an instant waterfall
in front of the charging Japanese torpedo planes. The
approaching eight aircraft continued to advance, the pilots
arcing undeterred through the falling salt water. A few
moments later the *Revenge* tried her luck through the smoke
screen laid by her consorts, the geysers from the 15-inch
shells far more impressive but just as useless.

Bastards are approaching too fast, Jacob thought.
He had been aboard a ship under mock air attack several
years before during his time at BuPers. A pilot that had been
observing the attack had explained the intricacies of aerial
torpedo dropping to Jacob. As the *Houston* continued to
come around in her tight turn, the vessel's 1.1-inch pom-
poms began engaging the enemy aircraft as they hurtled
across the ship's path from starboard to port. As Jacob
watched, one of the enemy aircraft shed a wing, rolling and
cartwheeling into the ocean.

Then the aircraft were past to port, the range fouled

by the passing *Phoenix* as the light cruiser inexplicably crossed between *Houston* and the approaching Japanese strike.

Fucking idiot, Jacob thought, his opinion obviously shared by several others in Battle Two judging from the angry cries. The light cruiser made up for her interference by winging one of the enemy aircraft as they passed overhead.

"Dive bombers!" a lookout shouted from the crow's nest above him. Looking up, Jacob felt his heart stop.

Two *Vals* were diving directly at the *Houston*, their approach almost unnoticed except by a solitary 1.1-inch crew that had tracked the bombers the entire way in. Belatedly the numerous machine guns located around the cruiser's deck opened up also, but it was far, far too late.

Jacob stood transfixed as both bombers released their weapons, the black dots separating from between the bombers' fixed landing gear and growing larger. The Japanese pilots fired their cowl-mounted machine guns as they pulled up, the bullets impacting forward of Battle Two amongst a 5-inch gun crew. Jacob watched as the falling bombs seemed to elongate, instinctively realizing that this meant they were going to miss.

It wasn't by much, both bombs landing close enough on *Houston*'s starboard side to jolt the heavy cruiser and spring a couple of leaks in her engine room. The sound of metal on metal and screams told Jacob that the fragments had struck several of the exposed men manning the ship's machine guns and secondary mounts.

Dammit, can we go one engagement without the surgeon getting work? Jacob thought crazily. Suddenly he realized he smelled gasoline, and looked forward to see aviation fuel leaking onto the deck from one of the *Houston*'s seaplanes.

"Damage control to the catapults!" Jacob barked back into Battle Two. "Get those damn planes overboard!"

He turned to see both *Vals* weaving away out of range, one of them smoking slightly with its rear gunner blazing away at the *Houston* despite being far out of range.

Go ahead and waste your ammo, you stupid SOB, Jacob thought. Turning away from the fly by shooting, Jacob looked back towards the *Revenge*.

The old battleship was heeled over in a turn to starboard, coming around slowly to comb the approaching torpedo tracks. Versus the pilots of the *Kido Butai*, she would have been meat. Against the less well-trained pilots attacking her, the evasive turn, heavy fire, and the smoke screens were just enough for her to narrowly avoid the weapons launched at her.

The turn was not enough to avoid the attention of the four *Vals* that survived to push over on her. Three of the bombs missed at varying ranges, the closest two hundred yards off of the battleship's starboard bow. The fourth, and last bomb, landed on *Revenge's* 'X' turret, blasting the battleship's seaplane into flaming junk while expending its fury without penetrating the turret's roof. Looking back at the flaming battleship, the *Val's* tail gunner believed that the bomb hit had been a fatal one.

"Oh shit," an older petty officer muttered from behind Jacob. "She's done for." Jacob brought up his binoculars, focusing on the burning area. A quick glance showed the turret still operational, the crew starting to bring it back into train.

"She's all right," Jacob observed. "Going to need a new paint job on her stern turrets, but she's not that badly hurt."

"Sir, the aviation department's reporting the port SOC has also been holed," Foncier reported.

"Instruct them to jettison both aircraft," Jacob replied

disgustedly.

"Roger," Foncier replied, gesturing for the information to be passed to the aviation department.

The *Houston* began to slow in order to match speed with the *Revenge*, weaving back and forth to avoid steaming too far away from the battleship. Astern, the *Phoenix* and the two Dutch destroyers resumed their journey to join the Main Body.

"Sir, Captain Wallace requests your presence on the bridge," Wedgewood reported. Jacob noted that his voice sounded somewhat deeper and shook his head.

I don't care what Roberts says, I'm not having a damn fifteen-year-old as my talker, Jacob thought as he walked out of Battle Two to make his way forward. Moving quickly, he found himself at the bridge a couple of minutes later, just as the aviation division was pushing the damaged SOC over the cruiser's starboard side.

Captain Wallace was standing on the starboard wing of the signal bridge looking back as the biplane tumbled into the sea. From the look on his face Jacob could tell he was not pleased.

"XO, I am told you gave authorization to jettison that aircraft," Captain Wallace said lowly as he walked up.

Oh shit, Jacob thought.

"Yes Sir, I did," he replied just as lowly.

"While I appreciate your initiative and understand the logic given the fine example on our larger brethren," Captain Wallace said, gesturing at the *Revenge*, "please give me some warning next time."

Next time I'll let the bastard catch on fire, how's that sound? Jacob thought.

"Aye-aye, sir," he replied.

"We've been given new orders by Admiral Phillips," Captain Wallace said. "Apparently our opponents didn't pay attention to that part about not splitting one's forces when facing a superior enemy." With the last, he handed Jacob a flimsy. Reading it quickly, Jacob looked up in surprise.

"This has to be a feint," he said. "They're trying to draw forces off to the other end of the Java Sea."

"I thought the same thing until I saw the transports," Captain Wallace replied. "The Dutch have sent another couple of aircraft to confirm, but it appears that they're trying to flank our forces on Sumatra while our back is turned up here."

"What are our orders?"

"We're being joined by the *Phoenix*, *Exeter*, and *Australia*," Captain Wallace said. "Those two Dutch destroyers and three Dutch cruisers will join us as soon as we get the *Revenge* back to harbor. *We* are still going to Balikpapan, the Main Body is going back to Sumatra."

If that's what's happening to battleships, we cruisers don't stand a chance, he thought fatalistically.

"Sir, signal from the *Exeter*," a lookout called. Both Jacob and Captain Wallace turned and look aft to where the Commonwealth cruiser was rapidly approaching at her full speed. The signal was in mid-sentence when they began being able to read it.

...GLASSFORD SENDS: REQUEST YOU HEAVE TO SO THAT I MAY BOARD MY FLAGSHIP. GREATLY ENJOYING THE REFRESHMENTS HERE, BUT NEED A CREW THAT SPEAKS PROPER ENGLISH.

Both Captain Wallace and Jacob started laughing, quickly followed by the signalman.

"Acknowledge the signal," Captain Wallace replied. "Tell the *Exeter* that we're pleased to have her in our 'little coterie' again.'"

"Aye-aye, Sir," the signalman replied, then began transmitting the message.

Same old dancers, same old tune, Jacob thought. *Hopefully we'll hurt them a lot more than last time.*

Pearl Harbor
0845 Local (1415 Eastern)
27 April

"Danny, how in the hell are you?" Vice Admiral William F. Halsey asked as he strode into Rear Admiral Graham's office.

You know, maybe Vice Admiral Pye's death was a blessing in disguise, Nick thought as he sprung to his feet. *Halsey's an aviator but he's already visited this office more times than his last two predecessors combined.*

"Doing well, sir, doing well," Graham replied, coming from around his desk to take his boss's preoffered hand. "What brings you down to my lovely sweatshop?"

Looking at Halsey, Nick suddenly realized that the man's smile was not meeting his eyes.

"I was in the area and thought I'd stop by," Vice Admiral Halsey said. "Lieutenant Cobb, why don't you excuse us for a moment?"

That was not a request, Nick thought.

"Aye aye, Sir," he said, leaving the two admirals and Captain Donze inside Graham's office.

Stepping outside, Nick passed by the desk of Agnes Nunes, Admiral Graham's secretary. An olive-skinned, dark-haired woman, Nick had heard Agnes originally hailed from New Mexico by way of Portugal. Although he had entered the office ignorant of secretaries doing anything but dictation, Nick had quickly come to realize the folly of that

133

assumption.

Who knew that the office executioner wears a dress? Nick thought.

"I was wondering how long it was going to take you to make your exit," Agnes observed in her contralto voice.

"Not soon enough," Nick replied with a smile. Agnes gave a slight laugh at that, covering her mouth with her hand.

Hmm, no rings, Nick said.

"You remind me of my fiancée," Agnes replied with a smile.

Which apparently doesn't mean a damn thing, Nick thought bitterly.

"Well hopefully he knows when to run for the hills himself," Nick replied evenly, hoping his regret didn't show in his voice. ""When two large bulls are in a rather small pen, it's best for the smaller farm animals to leave, quickly."

A sad look passed briefly over Agnes' face.

"His name was William Clayton," Agnes said. "He was XO of the *S-27*."

Nick paled.

"Oh Jesus, I'm sorry," he replied.

The *S-27* had been one of the "Sugar" boats, the *S-class* that had been designed to defend the coastal waters of the United States and her possessions, not range the entire Pacific like the current "fleet" submarines. As such, she had been assigned to guard the Panama Canal zone, where she had been sunk on December 23rd the previous year by the U.S.S. *Anderson*.

That explains why she gives everyone the cold shoulder, Nick thought, repressing the urge to shudder. *Horrible accident, and all because the DD's signal officer had looked at the wrong day's recognition signals.*

"No need to apologize, Lieutenant Cobb," Agnes said after a moment. "You're not the idiot who sank her."

True, Nick thought. *Or else I'd be wearing stripes and living in Kansas.* Initially the Panama Canal Zone's commander had resisted court-martialing the *Anderson*'s commander. Rumor had it that Admiral King himself had put a kibosh to that course of action.

Man's lucky he wasn't shot, from what I understand of Admiral King from Eric, Nick thought.

"No, but I am the idiot who just made you think of him," Nick replied. Agnes cocked her head and gave Nick a speculative look.

"Yes, yes you did," she replied.

"If you don't mind me asking, how did you end up working for Rear Admiral Graham?" Nick asked, glancing warily at the door. Agnes chuckled.

"You are very funny, Nick," she said, shaking her head. "For all their stars, they are still just men, men who put their pants on the same way you do."

"Yeah, except both of them have a lieutenant to help them," Nick replied with little mirth.

"He likes you, you know," Agnes said. "Says you remind him of how he was back when he was a young officer."

Nick turned and looked at the woman with a quizzical look on his face.

"And how's that?" he asked.

"Like a man running around with his hair on fire who can't seem to figure out why he smells smoke everywhere he goes," Agnes said, her smile broadening as she dropped the other shoe.

Their banter was interrupted by Captain Donze coming out of the room, his face stricken.

"Agnes, no one is to disturb Rear Admiral Graham for the next hour. *No one*," Donze said severely.

"Yes Captain Donze," Agnes said, raising an

eyebrow.

"If anyone has a problem with that, they can come see me," Donze continued. "Cobb, follow me to my office."

Nick had never seen Captain Donze look so shaken. He followed the senior officer into his room, closing the door behind him at Donze's hurried gesture. The captain stared out the window for a moment, taking a couple of deep breaths.

"Cobb, what I'm to tell you stays in this room until you hear otherwise," Donze said resignedly, gesturing to the chair in front of his desk.

"Aye-aye, Sir," Nick replied, suddenly glad that he knew where all of his brothers were.

"Rear Admiral Graham was just notified by Vice Admiral Halsey that his son's submarine, the U.S.S. *Shark*, is overdue and presumed lost," Captain Donze said. "It is believed that she was lost with all hands."

"Oh God," Nick replied, just as shocked as Donze.

"Did you know Lieutenant Graham?" Donze asked, seeing Nick's ashen expression.

"Yes," Nick said. "We played baseball together at the Academy. Ted Guinn, another teammate of ours, just reached the *Shark* before the war started. What happened?" Nick asked.

"We don't know yet," Donze said gently. "She was was detached on a special mission to Corregidor," Donze replied. "They picked up General MacArthur with orders to deliver him directly to ACDA headquarters in Surabaya."

My God, Nick thought distractedly. *How many people that I know are going to die in this war?*

"Lieutenant Cobb, did you just hear a word I said?" Donze asked sharply, causing Nick to jump in his chair.

"Yes Sir," Nick replied, shaking himself out of it. "Just a little shocked is all."

Donze's face softened.

"I apologize Lieutenant," Donze said. "I've known Justin since he was ten, so it is a great blow to me also. If you would like me to stop...?"

"No Sir, I want to know what happened," Jacob replied.

"The *Shark* apparently ran afoul of a Japanese destroyer near Palawan," Donze said, his voice suddenly breaking. "The *Perch* was supposed to rendezvous with her and provide an escort. Stated she heard gunfire, then depth charges. When she went through the area a little later there was a shitload of oil and a couple of bodies, that was all."

"Holy shit," Nick breathed.

Just like that, more friends dead, he thought.

"Go ahead and take the rest of the day off, Cobb. We don't need you here," the senior officer said.

"Aye aye, Sir," Nick said numbly. He got to his feet, then went to collect his cap from Agnes's office. Seeing the look on his face, Agnes stood from behind her desk and handed him a slip of paper.

"Call me, Lieutenant Cobb, if you need someone to talk to," she said, meeting his eyes. Nick was shocked at the depth of emotion in her eyes.

"I know what it is like to get bad news and not have anyone to speak to it about," Agnes said. "It is not like you need to worry about letting something slip to me."

All Nick could do was numbly nod, his mind still in shock from the loss of his friends.

"Good. I will be home around seven o'clock," she said. With that, she was back to her normal professional self, sitting down to type up some reports. Nick quickly moved to the exit, leaving the building into the bright Hawaiian sunshine. As he left, a flight of *Dauntlesses* thundered over. The aircraft made him think of his brothers.

They'll understand, he thought to himself. He knew exactly where to find Sam and David, and set off for Ewa field.

CHAPTER 4: UPON THE SEAS OF JAVA

*It is warm work ; and this day may be the last to any of us at a moment.—**Lord Horatio Nelson at Copenhagen***

Houston
0100 Local (1300 Eastern)
29 April (28 April)

"Sir, the Dutch are entering the harbor," Wedgewood said quietly, as if he was trying to keep his voice from passing out of Battle Two.

"I think if the enemy is close enough to hear your voice, Wedgewood, they'd probably be shooting by now," Jacob snapped. "Speak up, dammit."

"Aye-aye, Sir," Wedgewood said, the hurt clear in his voice. Jacob suddenly felt like he had kicked a puppy. He fought back the urge to apologize, instead looking back out Battle Two's starboard portholes.

The Japanese force trying to open a second beachhead on Sumatra had almost pulled it off. Admiral Phillips' decisiveness in ordering his vessels to the west appeared now to have been the only thing that could prevent a terrible disaster for the ACDA forces on the Dutch island. Reports had begun filtering in shortly after nightfall of landings being conducted near the port of Palembang, the harbinger of which had been at least three enemy cruisers beginning the pre-landing bombardment.

Should have known the idiots wouldn't keep trying their luck up around Medan, Jacob thought wistfully. The Dutch had been surprisingly fierce in their defense, throwing back several Japanese amphibious attempts from Malaya on

139

the Sumatran port. Judging from the intel report Jacob had quickly reviewed, it appeared as if the Japanese Army, not the Navy, had been in charge of these amateurish attempts.

That's what you get for allowing your Army to try an amphibious operation, stupid sons of bitches, he thought triumphantly. *Need the navy to hold the water before you get ashore.*

"I hope those Dutch bastards are as good as they think they are," someone muttered inside the darkened Battle Two. There was a low response to that comment from Chief Roberts, Jacob recognizing the man's menacing growl anywhere.

I don't care how good they are, it would be a very bad idea for us to go that close to Banka Island with our charts, Jacob thought with little mirth. So far the ACDA force had been lucky about grounding on the poorly charted shoals and reefs around the East Indies, with only a couple of Australian corvettes and a gunboat coming to grief.

Stupid bastards have had these islands how long? Jacob thought incredulously. *Brave fellows at the lower level, but apparently everyone in charge over there is an idiot.*

"It's dark as hell out there, Sir," Rogers said, gliding up with a cup of coffee and startling Jacob. "I don't envy those Dutchmen going into that anchorage, even with good charts."

To their surprise, the ACDA Striking Force had not faced any more air strikes once separating from the Main Body. Indeed, it had been almost eerie that their only contact had been a lone snooper that United States Army P-38s had dispatched while returning from a beachhead strike.

I'm not one to look a gift horse in the mouth, Jacob thought. *But I've got to wonder where in the Hell the Japanese carriers are now.*

"We're coming to course three six zero true,"

Wedgewood said, as the *Houston* turned gently to starboard. Peering to port, Jacob tried to imagine the geometry of the upcoming fight. Commanded by Rear Admiral Karel Doorman aboard the light cruiser *Tromp*, the flotilla consisted of the other Dutch cruisers *Java, De Ruyter, Sumatra* and *Jacob Van Heemskerck* with five destroyers in escort.

'Bout time their navy joined in the dying, as their ground pounders and airedales have been giving it all they've' got, Jacob thought. *I don't think those divisions on Sumatra are really interested in hearing about 'fleet in being.'*

"I can't say I disagree with you about going into that harbor, Chief," Jacob replied aloud. "Those clouds are going to make it hard to use starshells."

"We'll have to go with searchlights," Chief Rogers replied. "Going to be close-in work tonight, I'm afraid."

"Glad we brought the *Phoenix*," Jacob replied, gesturing astern where the light cruiser was trailing the *Exeter*. "Before the *Boise* took those torps, she was wrecking those little bastards with her six-inchers."

"Yeah, well, see what that got her though," Rogers replied.

We're lucky that we have ammo that works, Jacob thought. *I guess flashless powder was just too much money for Congress to spare.*

"We'll just have to make..." Jacob started.

His retort was cut off by a contact report coming over the Battle Two speakers followed by the *Phoenix, Exeter*, and *Australia* all opening fire. With that massive set of sensory input, the Battle of Balikpapan began.

The Japanese destroyer *Asakaze*, accompanied by the *Awikaze*, had been pursuing a submarine contact for the previous four hours. Moving along at barely ten knots, the pair of destroyers had been wholly focused on their task in the gloom. Neither had been aware they had been steaming blithely towards a line of Allied warships. For the *Asakaze*, cognition came in the form of a half dozen 6 and 8-inch shells hitting the destroyer while the rest of the broadsides hid her in a forest of waterspouts. The hits were more than enough, at least two of them touching off both her forward and aft magazines.

"Enemy destroyer, bearing three four oh, range eight thousand yards!" Wedgewood shouted, sounding like a man being goosed with a cattle prod.

The visual sighting relayed from the lookouts was only possible due to the brilliant flames from the *Asakaze*'s sudden and violent demise. With her bridge crew's night vision ruined by the explosions and her captain stunned, the *Awikaze*'s reaction to her fellow destroyer's death was far too slow. Even as *Houston*'s searchlights reached across the eight thousand yards to transfix the destroyer in their beams, Commander Sloan was aligning the heavy cruiser's main armament.

"Shoot, shoot, shoot," Jacob muttered urgently. Sloan was already ahead of him, pressing the trigger up in the CA's director. *Houston*'s firing gong buzzed, then all three of her turrets spit her broadside towards the slowly accelerating *Awikaze*. Four out of nine shells hit, knocking out the vessel's powerplant, setting her bunkerage afire, and blasting her forward guns into wreckage.

"Holy shit!" someone shouted in Battle Two, the destroyer's *extremis* visible with the naked eye. Jacob had to agree with the sentiment, shocked that the cruiser's first salvo had so devastated the intended target. He felt the ship shift underneath him as Captain Wallace ordered a sharp port turn. Looking out past the *Houston*'s smokestack, Jacob could see the *Australia*, the lead ship in the formation, also turning towards hard to port.

"What in the Hell is that Aussie bastard doing?" he shouted to one of the talkers, rushing his words to get them in between the firing of the 5-inch secondary.

"[T]hat Aussie bastard" was reacting to the reports from his radar plot of four large contacts at range twelve thousand yards bearing down at thirty knots from the north. Unable to make a visual sighting, Captain Fitzpatrick had ordered the emergency turn to give his main battery time to train to starboard. The *Houston* had just made her own turn when the *Mogami*, lead vessel of the IJN's 7th Cruiser Squadron, became visible to the *Australia* at just under ten thousand yards. Aboard the Japanese cruiser, the *Australia* becoming backlit by the two burning destroyers now behind her was the first realization the squadron had they were in true danger. Even as the *Mogami*'s captain was barking order to put the heavy cruiser's own helm over to starboard, the *Australia* opened fire and turned on her searchlights.

In the *Houston*'s director, Commander Sloan watched as the *Australia*'s eight gun broadside rolled over the *Mogami*'s forward half like a typhoon of steel. The American gunnery officer watched as an 8-inch gun barrel flew through the glare of the *Australia*'s searchlights, the weapon coming from the *Mogami*'s annihilated No. 2 turret.

"Enemy heavy cruiser, bearing oh seven oh!" one of the *Houston*'s lookouts shouted. Turning the director to look where the lookout's report was, Sloan saw the second Japanese cruiser in line, the *Mikuma*. Having seen her sister hit, the *Mikuma*'s guns had already been searching for a target. By happenstance, they were already trained most of the way towards the *Houston*.

"Oh fuck me," Sloan breathed, even as the *Houston*'s starboard 5-inch guns began banging away in defiance.

143

That was when the *Exeter* belched fire from behind the *Houston*, her forward guns unmasked from the *Houston* beginning her turn. The four 8-inch shells straddled the *Mikuma*, hitting so close that splinters killed several men on her decks. They were shortly followed by a single American 5-inch shell hitting the cruiser's port catapult and igniting the float plane there.

Neither the *Exeter*'s intervention nor the belated hit from the *Houston's* secondaries delayed the *Mikuma*'s firing. Ten 8-inch and four 5-inch guns exploded in one massive broadside towards the *Houston*'s starboard side. In the chaos of the sudden fire, the *Mikuma*'s gunnery officer had overestimated the range to the *Houston* by over two hundred yards. Still, six shells, a pair of 5-inch and four 8-inch, hit the American heavy cruiser down her entire length. The remaining eight passed over or through the ship's superstructure.

The first 8-inch shell destroyed the secondary anti-aircraft director, blasting it completely off the mainmast just above Turret Three. The resultant splinters cleared away many of the men manning the 5-inch guns as well as pelted the roof of Turret Three with debris. The second 8-inch, fired from the same turret, impacted the foreleg of the mainmast without detonating, punching a neat round hole before continuing on to the other side of the cruiser.

One shell of each type slammed into the hangar just forward and below Battle Two. Normally the structure would have been occupied by two fully loaded seaplanes, but Jacob's earlier decision to jettison the aircraft bore dividends. While the blast and fragments killed several of the air department men nearby, the resultant fire was only a moderate one, not a roaring conflagration that would have resulted from ignited aviation fuel.

The final two shells both impacted the heavy cruiser around her bridge. The 5-inch shell exploded in *Houston*'s chart room, while its 8-inch counterpart penetrated the conning tower and detonated within. The end result was to send fragments ripping through the heavy cruiser's control spaces, the hot steel making almost literal mincemeat of the conning tower's occupants and incapacitating almost every man on the bridge. Her rudder still to port, *Houston* circled away from the advancing *Australia*.

One instant Jacob had been looking at the Japanese cruiser and waiting for *Houston*'s own guns to open fire. The next he found himself crumpled on the aft bulkhead of Battle Two, spots in front of his eyes and shooting pain in his right shoulder. Looking down, he could see that the joint was clearly dislocated. Standing up, he suddenly felt a huge shifting of warmth down his leg. Feeling dizzy, he looked down to see his uniform's leg soaking through with blood down by his calf.

Oh shit, he thought as he crumpled back to the floor in an undignified heap. Battle Two was chaos all around him, Chief Rogers attempting to regain order. Wedgewood was down, half of his body laid open in a clearly fatal wound. Jacob watched as the young boy's face, utterly serene, met his.

"Sorry Sir," the sailor said clearly and quietly, then died.

With a roar, *Houston*'s main armament replied even as the cruiser continued out of control through her turn to port.

"Damage report!" Jacob barked, forcing his mind to focus.

"We can't raise the bridge, sir!" Chief Roberts replied. "Sky Two is *gone*, we're still trying to figure out where else we got hit."

"Does the bridge have control?" Jacob asked stupidly, then kicked himself.

"No response, sir!" Foncier reiterated.

"Continue the turn to port, bring us around," Jacob shouted to the auxiliary helmsman. "Tell the *Exeter* we'll be coming back up behind the *Phoenix!*"

"Look at that bastard burn!" one of the lookouts shouted. Struggling to his feet again, Jacob saw exactly what the man was referring too.

Holy shit we're hitting her hard, Jacob thought excitedly, looking at the *Mikuma* with his binoculars.

Through the intense study of Japanese vessels' pictures, Sloan had trained himself to recognize most of *Houston*'s likely targets. Noting that the center split of his second salvo was slightly short, *Houston*'s gunnery officer added two hundred yards. In the gloom, he could not see that *Mikuma*'s turn to starboard was much sharper than her sister ship's had been, meaning that the heavy cruiser had actually stared moving back towards his previous range estimate. As a result, the three shells that did hit impacted low on the *Mikuma*'s hull where her belt was thickest.

In effect, the belt made the damage merely bad as opposed to devastating. In a stroke, the Japanese cruiser was suddenly left with half of her machinery spaces, with fragments and water killing many of the engineering crew and steam cooking many of the survivors. Staggering from the blow, the *Mikuma*'s second salvo was off, several shells near missing the burning *Houston*. *Houston*'s third salvo, on the other hand, was dead on as Sloan corrected his aim.

Only the main armament's inherent dispersion prevented all nine 8-inch shells from slamming into *Mikuma*. As it was, six shells were more than enough devastation to end the *Mikuma*'s active participation in the night's festivities. Two hits found stern turrets, blasting the barely armored structures to pieces in a pyrotechnic display that both immolated their inhabitants and caused several members of the crew belowdecks to panic. Another hit the cruiser's aftmost funnel just below the point where it joined with its foremost twin, exacerbating the damage from *Houston*'s first salvo even further as smoke and fumes were suddenly forced back into those boiler rooms not already flooding.

The last two shells exploded around the cruiser's storage torpedoes, splinters splitting the oxygen canisters which gave the Long Lances their phenomenal range. In a chain of events that was becoming all too familiar to Japanese surface warfare personnel, the casks once more became impromptu torches that incinerated the men surrounding them. In *Mikuma*'s case the carnage was far worse, the flames sweeping through men whom had just begun the torpedo reloading process.

Slowed, and with a brilliant blaze springing from her midsection, the *Mikuma* heeled over even further into her starboard turn. Belowdecks, the IJN cruiser's damage control officer, the blood of several sailors upon him from the hurricane of spall that had ripped through his compartment, began screaming for the aft magazines to be flooded. In the confusion and bedlam, the order was misheard to flood *all* the magazines. Emasculated, with her turrets suddenly down to only a handful of shells, the *Mikuma*'s night grew even worse as the final two functional boilers snuffed out. Starting to coast, the Japanese cruiser's sudden drop in speed caused Sloan's next salvo to miss forward.

They've got to be breaking every rule in the book inside the turrets, Jacob thought, his ears ringing from the *Houston*'s most recent blast. *Oh well, I'll risk a mishap rather than getting blown out of the water!*

"Captain Wallace is ordering that we switch targets!" the replacement talker reported breathlessly. "He is wondering why we are shooting at the same heavy cruiser as the *Australia!*"

Jacob looked at the plot, confused.

"What is he talking about?" Jacob asked, aghast. "Belay that order, we're shooting at a different Jap! Is the bridge taking back control?!"

The talker pressed sound powered phone closer to his ear as *Houston*'s secondaries continued to fire. Looking forward, Jacob could see that the *Houston* had almost completed a course reversal.

Sloan has to be hating me right about now, he thought.

Jacob should have been more worried about the vessels behind him. Having started to follow the *Houston*'s turn, the *Phoenix* realized the flagship was out of control and came back to starboard to follow the *Australia*. The decision was nearly a fatal one, as Sloan just barely saw the light cruiser fouling *Houston*'s firing angle before squeezing off another salvo.

The *Houston*'s gunnery officer need not have worried about engaging the *Mikuma*, as the *Phoenix* proceeded to take up where her older comrade had left off. Unlike the late captain of the *Boise*, the *Phoenix*'s master was far more conservative and had directed his gunnery officer to wait until visual identification was achieved before engaging any target. Having received a thorough butt chewing for ignoring this directive with the *Asakaze*, the young commander in *Phoenix*'s director made sure that he had not only seen his next target, but had watched *Houston* put a pair of salvoes into her.

Now, with the *Mikuma* definitely identified, aflame, and at less than ten thousand yards, the *Phoenix* opened rapid fire on what her gunnery officer had designated "flaming datum number two." Like the *Boise* during South China Sea, the *Phoenix* seemed to erupt in flashes as all fifteen of her 6-

inch guns and secondaries began spitting a round every six to eight seconds. Unfortunately for the Japanese, unlike her late sister the *Phoenix* had been equipped with radar that provided an almost precise range to her staggering target.

The results were both ironic and hideous. *Phoenix* and the other cruisers of the *Brooklyn*-class had been designed in response the 7th Cruiser Squadron due to latter's large 6-inch armament. The Imperial Japanese Navy, desiring a heavier shell and longer range, had believed that placing five 8-inch turrets in the *Mogami*-class would be far more effective than their original guns at all ranges. This had been done over the ship designers' strenuous objections, but the IJN's senior officers had stated "better a lesser number of decisive blows than a flurry of annoying ones."

The crew of the *Mikuma*, had the older admirals been present aboard their vessel, would have been happy to have a discussion pointing out that quantity had a quality all its own. In a cacophony of metal on metal, detonations, screams, and the horrible sound of flames, the *Mikuma* was pounded into a hulk in the space of three minutes. Suffering over twenty blows that quickly overwhelmed her damage control officer's abilities shortly before ending his earthly concerns, the disabled heavy cruiser erupted in flames.

The only thing that stopped the *Phoenix*'s mugging of her assailant was the untimely arrival of the *Mikuma* and *Mogami*'s torpedoes. Launched immediately upon being taken under fire, the spread had initially been aimed at the *Australia* and the *Houston*. With the former having come hard to port upon seeing the torpedo launch flashes along the *Mogami*'s flank and the latter having turned completely around, only the *Phoenix* had the misfortune of blundering in front of a Type 93. The weapon smashed into the light cruiser's bow a few feet ahead of Turret No. 1 and partially severed structure. The pressure from *Phoenix*'s full speed passage completed the rest, as with the sound of tortured steel and a horrific vibration, almost the first third of the cruiser peeled back to slam down her port side.

Astern of *Phoenix*, the *Exeter*'s bridge crew saw the all too familiar waterspout of a torpedo hit and the *Houston* seemingly out of control five hundred yards off their port bow. Scanning further left, Captain Gordon saw the *Australia* continuing a harder turn to port roughly four thousand yards beyond both American cruisers. The Australian warship was continuing to engage an unseen assailant at bearing three four oh from her position while signaling frantically about torpedoes. Barking orders, Captain Gordon directed the *Exeter* starboard rather than head into what was pretty obviously torpedo water.

The first outcome of Gordon's decision was a positive one, as he watched the heavy cruiser *Kumano* come steaming out of the gloom on a reciprocal course, her guns turned to engage the *Phoenix* even as *Exeter* sat six thousand yards off her port side. As the Japanese heavy cruiser illuminated the damaged American light cruiser, *Exeter*'s own guns swiveled to engage the fast moving Japanese cruiser. Both heavy cruisers fired simultaneously, and once more the *Exeter*'s wartime experience allowed her to get the drop on a larger, heavier opponent.

In the space of sixty seconds, the Commonwealth vessel fired three full salvos. Before *Kumano*'s captain had time to register just what his lookouts were screaming about, the *Kumano*'s aft turrets, seaplane hanger, and No. 1 boiler room was knocked out. Having attracted the *Phoenix*'s attention by hitting with her own first two salvos, the *Kumano* suddenly found herself caught in a crossfire as the light cruiser responded to this new assailant. Firing a ragged salvo that straddled the *Exeter*, the *Kumano* put her helm hard to port and began making smoke as she attempted to reverse course. On her bridge, the heavy cruiser's captain barked for torpedoes to engage both Allied cruisers while the guns remained focused on the *Exeter*. It was the man's last order before *Phoenix* put two shells into the *Kumano*'s bridge structure.

That plot has gone completely to hell, Jacob thought.

"Bridge has control!" someone shouted. A moment later the firing gong rang again, as Sloan resumed firing at the blazing *Mikuma*.

"Cease fire! Cease fire!" the talker shouted. "Captain Wallace is asking the plot room where in the hell the *Exeter* is!"

"The *Australia*'s been hit!" someone else yelled.

The *Australia* had indeed been struck. The fourth and final member of the 7th Cruiser Squadron, the *Suzuya*, had put her helm hard to starboard when the *Mogami* had begun taking damage. Listening to the excited yammering on the radio and watching as the three ships in front of him were engaged in turn, Captain Kimura Masatomi, the *Suzuya*'s master, had passed to starboard of the blazing *Mikuma* and just missed being run down by the *Mogami* as that vessel had disengaged from the *Australia*. The *Kumano*'s entrance had bought him additional time as well as firing starshells that illuminated the Allied group.

As the *Mikuma* had been receiving her punishment from *Phoenix*, Masatomi had been stalking the still firing *Australia*. As the Allied heavy cruiser had put her helm over to comb the spread of torpedoes that had deprived the *Phoenix* of her bow, the *Suzuya*'s own torpedo officers had taken their bearings then fired the heavy cruiser's six portside Type 93s. Seeing that he *Australia* was still engaging the *Mogami* despite that vessel moving ever further away, Masatomi ordered the *Suzuya* brought back around in a hard starboard turn to unmask her starboard torpedo tubes.

Thus it was one of the *Suzuya*'s port torpedoes that caught the *Australia* as she was heading roughly southwards in parallel with the *Mikuma* and *Mogami*'s weapons.

Distracted both by the *Awikaze*'s final death throes and her own attempts to hit the *Mogami*, the *Australia*'s lookouts never saw the Type 93 coming. One moment the heavy cruiser was firing a four gun broadside...the next her machinery spaces were being ripped open by the 24-inch torpedo's warhead. Burning oil swept backwards towards the cruiser's stern, the flames providing illumination even as the *Australia*'s main lights flickered then died.

Masatomi, hearing his lookouts reports and seeing for himself that the solitary torpedo had seriously injured the *Australia*, turned to see that the *Kumano* and *Mikuma* were both clearly done for, at least one if not two Allied cruisers were still hammering the former, and that the *Northampton*-class cruiser his lookouts had initially sighted was now somewhere in the gloom. Just as Misatomi was attempting to figure out which vessel to engage with his guns, there was a large explosion from the west in the direction of the anchorage. Recalling that his primary mission was to protect the transports, the *Kumano*'s captain barked for the starboard torpedo tubes to finish the burning Australian cruiser.

"Is Captain Wallace injured?" Jacob asked Chief Roberts, looking as the medical teams carried Wedgewood's body away. He jumped as *Houston*'s guns fired once more, the nine 8-inch rifles putting three more shells into the hapless *Kumano*.

"No, and he's the only person on the bridge that isn't," the grizzled noncom replied, listening to the sound powered telephone. "Good thing he wasn't in the conning tower, as it got ripped up pretty good."

"Looks like ignoring fleet recommendations on where a ship should be fought from worked out in this case," Jacob observed.

"Yeah, I don't see Admiral Hart ripping Captain Wallace's ass for fighting from the bridge next time,"

Roberts stated with a shake of his head. Both men felt the *Houston* coming around to starboard and pointing her nose to the southwest.

"Captain Wallace is taking us towards the anchorage," Chief Roberts reported. "The Dutch are asking for immediate assistance."

Jacob looked towards where the *Australia* sat fighting her fires and the *Phoenix* was continuing to barely creep along.

I don't know what help they're expecting us to give, Jacob thought wryly.

"All right, everyone except for one talker get the hell out of here and go help with that fire!" Roberts ordered. "We've still got more asses to kick tonight!"

As the *Suzuya* headed southwest towards the transports, she passed her staggering sister. The *Mogami* was clearly hurt, her aft turrets askew, a fire on her amidships, and her stern visibly lower in the water. Still, as the *Suzuya* headed towards Balikpapan Bay, she signaled that she had reloaded her torpedoes and stood ready to support *Suzuya*'s attack. Responding, Captain Misatomi directed her battered sister to ensure whatever vessels were finishing off the *Kumano* and *Mikuma* did not reenter the anchorage behind her.

Stationary, with her burning bunkerage presenting a nice aim point, the *Australia*'s bridge crew could have done nothing about the incoming Type 93s even if they had seen the nearly wakeless torpedoes. While all six weapons had been fired without accounting for the *Australia*'s residual drift from currents, in the end the *Suzuya*'s torpedo crews demonstrated the worth of the IJN's repeated pre-war exercises. First one Type 93 crashed into the *Australia*'s bow just forward of her A turret, then the second completed the devastation of her engineering spaces. Feeling his ship's sickening lurch and immediate list, Captain Fitzpatrick immediately knew his command was done for.

Aboard the *Exeter*, Captain Gordon had reversed course to close back with his fellow cruisers. Seeing that the *Kumano* had been brought to a halt, her final functional turret silenced by *Exeter*'s seventh salvo, Gordon gave orders for the torpedo flat to engage the crippled Japanese cruiser, the main battery to cease fire, and for signals to obtain further instructions from the *Houston* or, failing that, the *De Ruyter*. It was just as his own torpedos entered the water that the *Australia* suffered her last two impacts. Cursing, Gordon ordered the *Exeter*'s crew to stand by to rescue the *Australia*'s survivors.

"What the hell just happened to the *Australia*?!" Jacob asked.

I swear I just took my eyes off her for a second, and now she's looking like she could roll over any time, Jacob thought.

"Lookouts report she took two fish," Chief Roberts replied. Without warning the *Houston* heeled into a sudden, sharp starboard turn.

"Bridge lookouts think they saw a fish porpoise just off the port bow," Roberts grunted, holding on to a stanchion as the *Houston* leaned into the turn. Jacob held on to the plot table, his wounded leg throbbing even as he tried to avoid putting weight on it.

"Captain Wallace is ordering us to wait on the *Exeter*," Chief Roberts stated, then stopped. "Belay that, Sir, we are now going to stand by the *Phoenix*. *Exeter* reports she just torpedoed one of those Jap heavies."

Jacob felt a wave of dizziness pass over him.

"Sir, you're bleeding again," Chief Roberts said, his voice alarmed. "Corpsman!"

"I'm fine," Jacob barked. "Why aren't we going to go help the Dutch?!"

"Captain Wallace is stating he wants us to be able to see what in the hell we're blundering into," Chief Roberts said. "The *Exeter* is stating she will be taking off the *Australia*'s survivors."

Jacob turned to look towards the *Australia*, the heavy cruisers blazes making her starkly visible in the otherwise Stygian night. Before he could respond, there was large explosion ten thousand yards off the *Houston*'s port bow.

"What was that?!" he asked, then waited as Roberts listened.

"*Phoenix* reports that second Jap cruiser just blew up," Roberts replied. "She's about to get underway, they've shored up her forward bulkheads best they can."

"What's going on in the anchorage?" Jacob asked.

"No idea, sir," Roberts replied. "But the radio room is saying they have not heard from the *De Ruyter* for the past ten minutes." "

"We've got to head into that anchorage," Jacob muttered. "We're never going to get this close again."

Had Foncier and Jacob had the ability to see events unfolding to their southwest their opinion may have changed. Rear Admiral Doorman, in a maneuver that would have brought an appreciative smile to the shade of his flagship's namesake, had led his force single file into Balikpapan Bay at slow speed. With the burning flames from Balikpapan's refineries helpfully backlighting the Japanese transports, Doorman had ordered his force to launch torpedoes as they headed deeper into the Bay, holding their gunfire until sighted or the initial weapons struck. Thus it was only when a 15,000-ton ammunition ship exploded, followed shortly by torpedoes hitting three more transports, that the IJN guard force realized that the rolling gunfire to their northeast was not the only problems to be had that night.

Unfortunately for the Dutch, the IJN's warships were not the only armed vessels that they needed to be concerned about. The armed merchant cruiser *Sasebo Maru*, a former whaling factory serving as a converted heavy vehicle transport, was sitting directly athwart the Dutch force's path as Doorman's forces opened fire. Surprisingly for a vessel so large, the factory ship was armed only with four old 6-inch guns in open deck mountings, with a number of smaller anti-aircraft guns complementing the main battery. However, the *Sasebo Maru* was commanded by a former naval officer named Koji Kaneko. A man whose discipline was harsh even by Japanese standards, Kaneko had constantly drilled the four crews during the three months the vessel had been in Cam Ranh Bay. Indeed, so rigorous had Captain Kaneko's drills become, the *Sabebo Maru*'s crew had derisively started a wager on how many times the *Sasebo Maru* would actually fire at another ship once the Southern Operation commenced. Given that Kaneko had shown no compunction in blasting hapless Vietnamese boats, floating pallets, or whatever impromptu target happened to present itself, the gun crews had joined Vietnamese fishermen in thanking their lucky stars when the *Sasebo Maru* had finally weighed anchor.

This training had quickly paid off when the Dutch ships turned on their searchlights to illuminate targets. Unlike Kaneko's drills, the explosions of torpedoes and a pair of friendly ammunition vessels had persuaded the crew to move with amazing alacrity. About the same moment that the *Australia* had begun engaging the *Mogami* in the Makassar Straight, the *Sasebo Maru* began shooting at a rate that would have made a regular IJN crew proud. More important than their rapidity, however, was the crew's accuracy. The *De Ruyter*, as both the lead and largest vessel in the Dutch contingent, was a natural target. Heading at an angle away from the *Sasebo Maru*, the cruiser's port side was exposed to the whaling vessel, turrets facing to starboard. With the range under three thousand yards, the *Sasebo*'s crew took full advantage before the *Tromp*, as the next ship in line, could begin returning fire.

If the *Sasebo*'s shells had been armor-piercing, the battle would have ended almost immediately. Instead, the older ordnance was pure high explosive, lacking even the benefit of a delay fuse. As a result, the *De Ruyter*'s minimal belt still served to keep the shells out of the light cruiser's vitals. However, the *Sasebo Maru*'s eight shell found the rear of the *De Ruyter*'s B turret. The effect of the hit against the almost wholly unarmored gun house was devastating, with the the structure suddenly becoming alive with spall that sliced crew, ignited powder bags, and decapitated several of the *De Ruyter*'s crew topside. Two more shells hit the Dutch cruiser amidships, one blasting the vessel's Fokker seaplane overboard, the other destroying two of her twin 40mm mounts. The ready ammunition in the destroyed positions began exploding, making the cruiser look like a traveling skyrocket factory.

The *Sasebo Maru* had made the one critical mistake in all forms of combat—she had drawn attention to herself. The *Tromp*, sailing behind the *De Ruyter*, missed short with her initial salvo. Joining the *Tromp* in returning fire, the destroyer *Piet Hein* put her shells into the whale factory's superstructure, starting a fire in one of the galleys. The *Tromp* regained her honor a moment later, hitting with three of her 5.9-inch shells into the large vessel's engine rooms. Between the two salvoes, the *Sasebo Maru* lost power to all of her guns and had a fire start in her galley's cooking oil. Moments later, the *De Ruyter* and *Java*'s guns silenced the *Sasebo Maru*'s open mounts, killed several of her crew, and ignited another fire amidships amongst several parked and crated light tanks.

The Dutch triumph over the *Sasebo Maru*'s gun crew

was short lived. Having seen and heard the ammunition ship blow up, the Japanese destroyers *Yunagi* and *Oite* had immediately reversed course. Moments later, as the Dutch force opened fire and dispelled both captains' assumption that a submarine had snuck into Balikpapan Bay, both destroyer captains fired their torpedoes and came about to port. With the range just over ten thousand yards, the crews of both DDs had time to watch the *Sasebo Maru*'s brave stand as their older 21-inch weapons covered the distance.

The Type 91s were neither as fast nor as potent as their larger Type 93 brethren. Against the unarmored, lighter Dutch warships they did not need to be. The destroyer *Kortenaer* was the first vessel hit, a Type 91 hitting her amidships and snapping her keel in half. The destroyer's momentum caused the ship to rip in half. Rolling to starboard, the *Kortenaer*'s fore half flipped backwards as the aft half continued along for a brief couple of minutes before its bulkheads collapsed.

Seeing the *Kortenaer* hit, the captain of the *Java* put her helm hard to starboard to attempt to comb the torpedo tracks. The rudder had just barely begun to swing the light cruiser's bow around when two of *Oite*'s torpedoes struck her. Either weapon would have been fatal, as the first bore through the cruiser's hull into her forward magazine while the second carved out her propulsion. Almost immediately wrapped in flames, with everything forward of the bridge disappearing in the mammoth magazine explosion, the *Java* served only to split the Dutch formation as the *Tromp* and every vessel astern of her turned hard to starboard.

In one of the true ironies of the war, the five weapons that passed through the Dutch formation continued heading up Balikpapan Bay towards the *Sasebo Maru*. Three of them rewarded the *Sasebo Maru*'s crew with a blown out side for their good shooting. As the vessel immediately began settling, the crew got to conduct an operation they had not drilled for during their journey—abandoning ship.

COLLISIONS OF THE DAMNED

Aboard the damaged *De Ruyter*, Rear Admiral Doorman reacted to the *Java*'s demise by ordering his mixed force immediately come about. Those ships astern of the *Java*, having already reversed course to avoid possible torpedoes, assumed their commander was ordering them to rejoin on the *De Ruyter*. It was at this point that the *Yunagi* and *Oite* briefly continued their counterattack, firing their meager broadsides in an attempt to draw attention away from the transport anchorage. A brave charge, it served its purpose by focusing the remaining Dutch vessels' attention on the two destroyers.

The *Oite* was the first to be hit, her foremost torpedo tubes being destroyed by a shell from the *De Ruyter*. This hit was followed by a 4.7-inch shell from the *Van Ghent*, the shell exploding in the destroyer's wardroom. Disturbed by the Dutch shooting, *Oite* reversed course and made smoke, moving away from the onrushing Dutch ships. The *Yunagi*, fixed in a searchlight from the *Evertsen*, was struck next by a pair of shells that began flooding in her engine room. Following the *Oite*'s example, the older destroyer reversed course into smoke.

Realizing that he was losing control of his force as the *De Ruyter*'s gun crews nearly engaged the *Tromp* as the latter approached from the direction of Makassar Strait, Rear Admiral Doorman gave the much simpler order of FOLLOW ME to the ships of his command. Heading out of Balikpapan Bay at thirty knots, it was at this point that Rear Admiral Doorman began asking for Rear Admiral Glassford's forces to rejoin his. Receiving a garbled response in return, Doorman was in the midst of repeating his request when the Japanese struck once again.

The *Oite* and *Yunagi*, fleeing pell mell from the advancing Dutch force, were heading east when they were confronted by the advancing light cruiser *Yubari*. At the head of four destroyers that had been northeast of Balikpapan as part of the transport fleet's covering force, the *Yubari* served as the flagship of Rear Admiral Sadamichi Kajioka. Angrily inquiring as to where the duo of destroyers believed they were going, Rear Admiral Kajioka ordered them to fall in behind the destroyers *Kisaragi, Mochizuki, Mutsuki, Yayoi* of his squadron. It was this force that, having sighted the Dutch in the light from the burning *Java*'s hulk, unleashed a massive torpedo spread. Once more, the IJN turned back into the darkness and waited the almost eight minutes for their twenty-eight weapons to arrive.

Had Rear Admiral Doorman changed his course even somewhat, he might have saved his force. Unfortunately, the perpetually underfunded and obsolescent Dutch East Indies Fleet had never been provided with radar or advanced night glasses. Believing that Rear Admiral Glassford's cruisers had managed to either attract or destroy the majority of the transport's escorts, Doorman had no reason to entertain the thought his alert ships could still be surprised.

As it was, the bugbear of speed estimation once more reduced the IJN's effectiveness. From Doorman's perspective, this would be cold comfort as the *Tromp, Jacob van Heemskerck, Witte de With*, and *Evertsen* were all hit by one or more torpedoes. For the *Witte de With, Evertsen* and *Jacob van Heemskerck* the mergers were fatal, the Japanese tin fish having the same effect as poison spears through a man's abdomen: certain, albeit not instantaneous, death. The *Tromp*, on the other hand, took three fish and simply vanished in a brilliant globe of flame and smoke as multiple magazines detonated.

The *Yubari* and her companion's subsequent gunfire only served to exacerbate Rear Admiral Doorman's shock. Realizing that he was completely outnumbered, and with most of his force either sunk or sinking, the Dutch admiral ordered a general retreat. This was hastened by the arrival of the *Suzuya*'s reload torpedoes, the Type 93's passing close astern of the *De Ruyter*. With the *De Ruyter*'s own guns struggling to respond to the *Suzuya*'s first broadside, Rear

Admiral Doorman swiftly decided discretion was the better part of valor. For the Japanese, having already been unpleasantly surprised by Allied aggressiveness that night, the decision to not pursue was an easy one.

"Rear Admiral Doorman is ordering a general retreat," Chief Roberts said. "He has ordered rafts to be dropped for the *Australia*'s crew, and all vessels to make their best speed south.

Looking to where the *Australia* had disappeared just ten minutes before, Jacob could not argue with the Dutchman's logic. As *Houston* continued to zig zag ahead of the plodding *Phoenix*, Jacob did some quick math.

Sun will be up in a few hours, Jacob thought. *If this crappy weather breaks, we might have to leave the **Phoenix** behind.*

Balikpapan Airfield
1030 Local (2230 Eastern)

"Not only does this area have nocturnal visitors, but the weather is abysmal," Isoro noted, rain blowing sideways into the edge of their tent.

"This front should be moved through by this afternoon," Lieutenant Eiji Makioka, Isoro's friend and Eta Jima classmate observed. "Our visitors are lucky that the weather gods are apparently taking pity on them."

Isoro grunted noncommittally, watching the rain continue to pound the ground outside. The low rumble of an explosion from Balikpapan Bay was a grim reminder of the previous night's activities and his own lack of sleep. A similar sounding but vastly different rumble through his abdomen served as a less subtle reminder that he and the other members of his squadron were lucky to have a day to rest.

Four sorties yesterday, he thought. *At least it appears that the Allies are finally conceding the landing here.* Isoro rubbed his eyes, images from the previous day coming unbidden as soon as he closed them. His first kill of the day, a *Lancaster*, locked in a flaming flat spin before it hit the jungle. His second, a Douglas bomber, simply falling out of the sky with a shattered cockpit. A *Zero* exploding as...

"Isoro, wake up!" Eiji chided, shaking him. Isoro jerked awake, looking at his friend ruefully.

"Sorry Eiji," Isoro said.

"We are all tired," Eiji allowed. "I'm just glad that soldiers have managed to clear out the last of the snipers."

Isoro shuddered. The "sniper" hadn't looked more than sixteen, his uniform two sizes too large for him. That had not prevented the Army from torturing him, finding out where he lived, and brutally executing his entire family in front of the boy.

I am certain being decapitated was a relief for him after what they did to his sister, Isoro thought. Part of him could understand the Army soldiers' frustration, as it had been on of their pilots that the sniper had killed. On the other hand, he wondered how the soldiers slept at night. The distant crump of shell fire from inland ceased his introspection.

"We are fortunate that the Westerners have been pushed beyond artillery range," Eiji observed.

"Especially with your large aircraft, Eiji-san," Isoro replied, gesturing to the twin-engined Mitsubishi G4Ms at the end of the paved runway. "Even the Dutch cannot miss those when they are on the ground."

Eiji gave his friend a harsh glare.

"You kill the Emperor's enemies one by one. I kill them by the dozen, if not the hundreds in the case of his ships," Eiji said stiffly.

"That will be a great deal more difficult now that your torpedoes are at the bottom of the ocean," Isoro replied somberly. "It is most unfortunate about the ammunition ship."

Eiji exhaled heavily. His bomber group had flown into Balikpapan each carrying a torpedo. The remainder of their ordnance had been embarked in the merchantman whose detonation had sent them all scrambling from their bed the night before.

"I do not think those Dutch idiots will ever realize just how many of their countrymen they likely saved," Eiji said fiercely. "Until more torpedoes can be ferried down, we are restricted to only attacking capital ships."

"Has anyone thought to use the ones off of the carriers?" Isoro inquired. "From what I have seen they have no use of them."

"We have sent a request up through channels back to Tokyo, as Admiral Kondo continues to believe that the carriers will receive new aircraft," Eiji said, causing Isoro to snort in disbelief.

"With the losses we took off of Hawaii and in the last few days, Admiral Kondo will be lucky if he gets any reinforcements at all," Isoro snarled. "Maybe he will get his wish for a surface battle after all."

"You speak like a defeatist, Isoro," Eiji said quietly.

"No, I speak like a man who an do math," Isoro replied. "Look at ook at your losses. Look at my unit's losses."

"Our losses have not been excessive..." Eiji snapped.

"No?" Isoro sneered. "You will be leading one of our vics this afternoon if the weather clears. I am the senior *chutai* leader on this airfield. We are both mere lieutenants."

Eiji did not have an immediate reply to that. He was saved by the arrival of an orderly, the man bowing in deference and averting his eyes.

"Sir, your presence is requested by Commander Fuchida," the man said stiffly. "They are beginning the brief for the attack on Surabaya."

Isoro was about to respond when there was the sound of wild firing in Balikpapan Harbor. All three men crouched down, as the merchantmen and warships anchored inside the formerly Dutch port were not known for their fire control. As if to prove their prudence, a tight group of shells terminated their parabolic arc in a cluster of explosions at the southern end of the runway. A few moments later, there was the sound of a hollow *crump!* indicating that Eiji and his comrades were not the only capable torpedo bomber pilots in theater.

"Those damn Australians," Isoro seethed. "I cannot believe they are flying in this!"

"I hear the Army has taken to calling that twin-engined fighter of the Australians 'The Whispering Death'," Eiji observed. "Something about not being able to hear it before it has already started its attack run."

"How can those bastards even see?" Isoro asked. "First the *Ryujo*, then these attacks!"

"Desperation, my friend, desperation," Eiji replied.

"Oh to be somewhere far, far away from here," Isoro replied. "I am sure the cherry trees are beautiful this time of year."

"You should worry more about Commander Fuchida than flowers," Eiji pointed out. Isoro pushed himself off the ground.

"I sincerely believe people thousands of miles from here have no idea what is going on," Isoro replied.

Honolulu, Hawaii
1630 Local (2300 Eastern)
14 April

Jo muttered a very unladylike swear word, fighting to hold on to the pot of noodles as she maneuvered them towards the sink. Setting the pot down, she started the cold water, running her hands underneath the cold tap. The sound of approaching heels meant that the target of her ire was moving within range.

"Where in the…*heck*," Jo said, making a conscious effort not to swear at Patricia, "are my *good* potholders?!" she asked, screaming nearly at the top of her lungs. Patricia, her hair still wrapped underneath a towel, shrugged.

"I don't know, maybe you should have cleaned the kitchen rather than asking someone who just came out of the bathroom," she returned snidely.

Okay, I've had about enough out of you, Jo thought. Her face must have reflected it as Patricia quickly held up her hands as if to ward off an attack.

"Jo, I'm just saying everything that looked like it was stained or dirty I put in the laundry," Patricia said slowly.

"Is that another one of your 'Southern sensibilities', that things we *use every freakin' day* can't be just a touch dirty?" Jo asked archly. Bringing both of her hands out of the sink, she put them to her chest and looked up at Patricia, rapidly batting her eyelashes.

"Oh my *gawd*, I can't have *company* seeing dirty potholders," she said in her best breathless Southern drawl. "Since when have you cared about what your brothers see?"

Patricia looked at Jo furiously, then suddenly started to turn beet red as Jo suddenly struck a pose like she had just had an idea.

"Oh wait, it's not your *brothers* who have you stressed out, it's the dashing Lieutenant (j.g.) Read," Jo chided.

"You are *not* amusing Jo," Patricia said seethingly.

"I'm not the one trying to keep up appearances," Jo pointed out. "Or hide the fact that I find someone attractive."

"Charles is just a..." Patricia stammered.

"Stop!" Jo said fearfully, throwing both her hands up. Patricia did just that, looking at her like she had lost her mind.

"Sorry, just didn't want you to burn in Hell for eternity for telling that big fat fib," Jo said, her face the picture of concern.

"Oh I could hit you sometimes," Patricia said, balling her fists.

"Yeah, but then you'd feel all guilty for messing up my looks even more than they already are," Jo replied snappily. Patricia *harrumphed* at her, turning to stir the simmering tomato sauce.

"You know, for someone who is chiding me about keeping up appearances, I notice that you're wearing a dress I've never seen before," Paricia said. "I know it's not for Sam, bless his heart, so that leaves...oh, wait, *Eric.*"

Okay, that's hitting a bit below the belt, Jo thought.

"I think that your brothers have all made it clear that I'm the second little sister they wish your mother had," Jo replied, tone despondent. "Besides, they're all crazy."

Patricia laughed at that comment.

"Eric is actually the sanest one," she replied.

"That's not much of a stretch in your family," Jo said drily. Patricia favored her with a dirty look for that comment.

"Well, you gotta admit, Patricia, Sam and David finish each other's sentences, Nick goes underneath the ocean in a sardine can, and you're fanatical about your beau seeing dirty potholders," Jo replied.

"He is *not* my beau," Patricia replied.

"Yet," Jo retorted, "but fine, you ran away from your

parents because they wanted to get you *married*."

"To a man who thought my purpose in life would be to sit at home and have his babies," Patricia replied sharply.

"Yes, but wasn't he *rich*?" Jo responded. "You could have been on easy street for the rest of your life."

"Pardon me if I believe in having a man who appreciates me for having a brain," Patricia replied. "I grew up reading fairy tales and watching my parents. Someday I'll find a man who wants me for a *partner*, and then we *will* live happily ever after."

Well, we sort of thought you had found one, Jo thought. *Then he had to go get himself killed by the Japanese.*

"Yeah, well, let me know when you find one," Jo replied. "Where are your brothers, anyway?"

Charles could probably be forgiven for thinking that he's somehow been transported to a hilltop above a certain famous river in Montana, Eric thought, fighting to control his own annoyance as he listened to Sam, Nick, and David. *One little night at the church social, and suddenly he goes from being their sorta pal to Public Enemy No. 1.*

The five men, miraculously all on pass at the same time, were making their way to Patricia and Jo's house for dinner. Sadie had begged off, stating that she really was not feeling well.

Except Custer probably went quickly, Eric thought, nothing that Sam and David both had his former wingman sort of boxed in.

"I mean, it's not that we don't like you Charles," Sam explained, his voice somehow menacing in its utter levelheadedness. "It's just that Patricia's already had one man not come back, and we don't want her hurt again."

"Shouldn't Patricia get a say in that?" Eric inquired,

drawing a look of ire from both twins.

"Maybe you should have made sure you didn't introduce them, Eric," David snapped.

"I'm sorry, I was a little bit distracted *by the freakin' holes in my back*," Eric retorted, his tone hot.

"I would just like to state, for the record, that Toots is going to poison both of you," Nick stated.

"No, they have a point," Charles said, his tone apologetic. "I mean, I've already gotten shot down once, haven't I?"

"This is some bullshit," Eric finally snapped. "Look you big oafs, I didn't know this Peter guy and I don't' really give a shit what happened to him."

That stopped both Sam and David in their tracks. Eric noted that Nick scurried into the street in order to avoid getting caught in what was shaping up to be the worst fratricidal violence since Genesis.

"Peter was our friend," Sam seethed.

"A great man," David added without missing a beat.

"Okay, and he's dead," Eric stated defiantly. "You think you two jackasses have a monopoly on dead friends who were great people?!"

Whatever his brothers were going to say in return was interrupted by the the crack of a bat followed by the wet sound of a baseball striking flesh.

"*Crap!*" Charles exclaimed, causing all three brothers to suddenly look at the younger officer. He had dropped the flowers he'd been carrying for Patricia and Jo in order to grab his nose, and blood was running between the fingers of his hands onto his whites.

"What in the Hell?!" Eric asked, grabbing his handkerchief out of his pocket.

"Oh my gosh! Mom, Timmy hit a man in the face!" a little girl shouted from the picket fence behind Nick. Sam and David turned to look at the blonde haired little girl, her freckled face still looking at all four men in shock. As they met her eyes, she turned shyly away and ran back around the corner of her house.

Patricia did say something about little kids having just moved in and raised a racket, Eric thought. A couple seconds later a little boy poked his head sheepishly around the corner of the house, obviously 'Timmy' from the guilty look on his face. Taking one look at Charles bleeding all over his whites, that look turned from guilt to sheer terror as he dropped the bat he was carrying.

"Oh Lord," came a heavily-accented woman's voice from the front step. Standing in a dress and apron was a tall, statuesque blonde that was clearly Timmy and his sister's mother. She muttered a phrase in Russian and began moving towards Timmy, her statement and obvious intent causing both Sam and David to start laughing.

"Mother, he did not mean any harm," Sam said quickly. His flawless Russian caused the woman to stop dead in shock, whipping her head around so quickly that Sam genuinely thought she was going to harm herself.

"Our friend's nose is quite large—the ball could not help but hit it," David continued, also in the same language as his brother.

The woman looked at them stunned. Timmy, realizing that he had just been granted a huge reprieve, made eye contact with Charles.

"Sorry Mister!" he called. Then, turning to run, he stopped and remembered something. Nick was there ahead of him, walking over to hand the boy the ball.

"I would go to the backyard if I were you," Eric heard Nick say softly. "My brothers have your Mom distracted. Go into the house crying so your sister thinks you got tanned, then wash up for dinner. By the time those two are done talking to your Mother, you should be safe."

169

Timmy looked up at Nick in awe. Nodding twice, he took off like a bat out of hell. A few moments later they could all hear him screaming bloody murder like he had just received the beating of his life, followed by a little girl's laughter.

Oh sibling rivalry, Eric thought, sharing a knowing look with Nick. The commotion caused the front door to open, a man just a few years older than Sam and David stepping outside the door. Seeing his wife in animated conversation, he began walking across the yard.

"Is there a problem, Niole?" he asked in English, looking at the four men.

"*Your* son hit that poor man in the face," Niole replied in the tone all mothers use when discussing wayward children. "It is somewhat fortunate, as I found out these two men speak Russian and, apparently, so does our neighbor!"

"Oh," the man said, extending his hand to Sam. "My name is Alf, Alf Olrik," he said. Listening, Eric could detect a very faint accent, leading him to think that the man was a second-generation American.

"Hello Mr. Olrik," Sam said. "I am Sam, and this is my brother David."

"Uh, yes, I see the resemblance," Alf said with just a trace of irony.

"Yeah, we get that a lot," Sam replied with a grin. "That is my youngest brother, Nick, and standing over the unfortunate Ensign Read is my other brother, Eric."

"Your poor mother," Alf said, looking at all four of the Cobbs. "I know what it is to be from a house full of boys."

"Yeah, never a dull moment in the Cobb household," Nick observed, walking up.

The front door to Patricia's house opened, revealing the youngest Cobb.

"Sam, I thought I heard your...*Oh my God!*" she shrieked, looking at Charles. Turning and looking at her four brothers, her face transformed from curious to rage as if a switch had been thrown.

Hell hath no fury like a woman scorned, Eric thought.

"Sam, David, Eric, Nick!" she snapped, her Southern drawl suddenly so thick it threatened to coat the yard with honey. Jo, coming up behind her, stepped back in shock. "Someone want to explain to me why my *guest* is sitting on the ground with his nose bleeding?!"

As Eric and his brothers fought the urge to lean backwards, he could see the same thought going through all their minds.

My God, she looks just like Mom! Minus the thunderclouds and lightning, of course.

There was a stunned silence as all four brothers looked at each other, causing Niole to start tittering.

"You are all dead," she said in Russian, holding her hand up to her mouth and moving away quickly.

"Only if they don't answer me," Patricia snapped in the same language.

Not sure I've ever heard Russian done with a drawl that thick before, Eric thought. *The Duchess would be proud. Who knew having a White Russian "aunt" would bring Toots closer to her neighbors?*

"Well, is someone going to tell me what happened?" Patricia continued. "My God, I thought you four were supposed to be my *older* brothers, not children I've got to keep from fighting!"

"Wait a second Toots..." Nick started.

"Don't you start, Nick Elrod Cobb," Patricia snapped. "Eric, the least you could do is bring the man inside rather than have him standing out here bleeding all over himself!"

"I didn't..." Eric started in turn, cut off by his sister

171

pushing past him to take Charles' arm.

"No, of course you didn't think, you guys never do. Just like you haven't thought that maybe the blood is not going to come out of that uniform now that you've let it set," Patricia snapped, tugging the younger officer towards the door. "I thought you guys grew out of bullying people when you went to the Naval Academy, but apparently your bad names have followed you."

"Patricia, we didn't do anything!" David exclaimed plaintively.

"Right, I suppose the skies opened and dropped something on his nose?" Patricia said, looking at her brother. Standing just behind her, Charles looked back at the four Cobb brothers, a speculative look on his face.

"Why you little," Sam muttered. Patricia whipped around quicker than a striking water moccasin.

"You know what, Sam? I think David and you can find dinner somewhere else tonight," Patricia said finally. "I know Sadie isn't feeling well, but maybe Nick's new lady friend would like to have you over."

"Wait, what?!" Nick asked.

"Patricia, they didn't..." Eric started.

"Hush Eric, the only reason you're not going with them is because I know you couldn't throw a punch right now if your life depended on it," Patricia said flatly.

"Aw Patricia, that's not fair!" Nick said, looking at his sister.

"The fair comes once a year, Nick, and I don't see any ponies," Patricia snapped. She smiled in a manner that was in no way friendly. "However, what I do have cooling in the kitchen is Mom's pecan pie, so I guess I can see why you were confused."

There was dead silence, the three banished brothers looking at Patricia like she had just told them their parents had died and left her the entire family estate. Alma Cobb's pecan pie was famous throughout Alabama, having won 1st Place at the 1938 Mobile Fair. The recipe was such a closely guarded secret that only Alma, their Aunt Margaret, and now apparently Patricia knew how to make it.

"I cannot believe you just did said that," Sam said solemnly.

"Well, I did," Patricia returned firmly. "Now, if you excuse me, I have dinner guests to entertain."

With that last comment she went into the house, leading Charles by the arm towards the kitchen. Eric took one last look back at his brothers.

"Sorry fellas," he said, shrugging. "I don't think she wants to listen to reason."

"I heard that Eric! It's not too late for you to go home!" Patricia's voice came from the kitchen. Looking at Sam and David's forlorn faces, Eric shut the door.

It was very, very quiet as the three Cobbs and Alf stood looking at Patricia's front door.

"You know, they say that a woman starts to turn into her mother at about age twenty-one," David observed drily.

As if we're not in enough trouble, David, Sam thought.

"Was your mother like that when you were growing up?" Alf asked. All three boys looked at him deadpan.

"Mom was worse, actually," Sam observed. Both Nick and David looked at him, causing him to throw up his arms.

"Someone had to say it," he said resignedly.

"Your father has my utmost respect," Alf said. "If you gentlemen would like, you may join my wife and I for dinner. It is the least I can do after my son has gotten you in so much trouble."

"That's all right, Alf," David said. "We wouldn't want to impose and put you in the doghouse also."

Alf smiled appreciatively.

"There is that, although I am certain that she has cooked enough for twenty extra guests," the man replied. "But I suspect, from your dialect and fluency that you know how Russians cook."

"We have a guess, yes," Sam replied. He proceeded to quickly explain how they knew Russian.

"My Niole's parents are also White Russians," Alf stated. "They emigrated to California back in 1928."

"Thank you," he said, then looked at his watch. "Well, I had better hurry up and get inside so that I may eat before I go on shift."

"If you don't mind our asking, Alf, what do you do?" Sam queried. "It is a little surprising to find someone from Scandinavia in Hawai

The man smiled.

"*I* was born in Minnesota," Alf said with a smile. "But yes, my parents are from Scandinavia. You have a good ear."

No, just lots of interesting classmates, Sam thought.

"I work for the Pacific Bridge Company," Alf continued. "Which is a running joke, as there are clearly no bridges that need building here on Oahu."

"It was a might bit curious," Nick observed.

"There are many other things we do," Alf stated.

"Well, we don't want to keep you," Sam said.

"No worries," Alf said. "You have a good evening." The three brothers watched as the man moved back into his house, then stepped through the door with a wave.

"Isn't Alf sort of a weird name?" Nick asked once the front door had closed.

"It's Nordic," David replied. "He's probably from

Finland, which would explain how he ended up with a Russian wife."

"Well, I don't care of the man's a space alien, I'm hungry," Sam stated forcefully. "It looks like we better head back to your place and get some sandwiches, David."

"My place?!" David asked. "Why are you eating all my groceries?"

There was a whistle from the side of Patricia's house. All three men turned to look, seeing Jo standing just outside the kitchen door holding a box. Sam moved quickly, walking over to his friend.

"Your brother told me what happened," Jo whispered. "I didn't think you were stupid enough to punch a man your sister's sweet on right in our front yard. Doesn't mean I wouldn't put it past you to rough him up, just means I think you have enough brains not to do it in public."

Taking a whiff, Sam realized immediately what was in the box.

"You know, if you weren't my sister's housemate and a woman I respect and admire, I'd lay a big one right on you this instant," he whispered fiercely.

"Even though that's really sweet and the feeling's mutual, you kiss me right now in front of your brothers and you'll need more ice than Ensign Read," Jo replied, a sweet smile on her face. "You sort of let that ship sail."

"You know, your father should have named you Katherine," Sam observed, his tone droll.

"Why is that?" Jo queried, her eyes narrowing. "That seems familiar."

"Someone needs to brush up on her Shakespeare," Sam gloated.

"Yeah, yeah, get out of here before your sister comes out here and goes all berserk again," Jo replied with a grin. "Come on by in a couple of days, we'll do lunch."

"Will do. Take care of Eric, make sure Patricia doesn't poison him with her cooking," Sam said.

Jo raised an eyebrow.

"I cooked dinner tonight," she said quietly. Sam jerked back in surprise and was about to retort when he saw Eric's anguished face passing by the window.

That's his 'Mom's right behind me, flee you fools!' look, Sam thought. Giving Jo a quick hug, Sam darted around the corner of the house while signaling for his brothers to scram.

"You okay?" Jo asked, looking at Eric's pale face and sweating brow as she came back into the kitchen. The man didn't get a chance to answer, Patricia coming into the room behind him.

"I can't believe those three," she said, clucking her tongue. "I mean, I know they didn't actually hit Charles, but I'm sure that they had something to do with it." She rinsed out the washrag she was holding, looking pointedly at Eric.

"Did you see what happened?" she asked archly.

"Actually, it was an accident," he said, to which he received a look of disbelief.

"Fine Eric, if you don't want to tell me the truth, this is the last time I will ask," Patricia said, her voice clearly indicating that it wouldn't be the last time she thought of it. Charles chose that moment to come into the kitchen wearing just his t-shirt. Eric's eyes nearly bugged out of his head, causing Jo to start giggling. Patricia turned to look at her, raising an eyebrow.

"You've got blood on your shirt, Patricia," Jo said, pointing.

She looked down at her cream colored blouse in horror.

"Oh no," she said. "We've got to get that before it

COLLISIONS OF THE DAMNED

sets." She started to dab at the spot, but was stopped by Jo grabbing her.

"If you do that, you're going to ruin that shirt," Jo said. "And I know exactly how much it cost because I was about to buy one just like it."

The two women left, leaving Eric and Charles alone. Waiting until the door to his sister's room closed, Eric turned and gave Charles a hard look.

"And just how did my sister get blood on her shirt?" Eric asked quietly. Charles gave an exasperated sigh, throwing his hands in the air.

"You know, sir, I really don't know how," he said. "It might have been when she was putting the ice on my nose, it might've been when she was scrubbing the blood off my face, who knows? More importantly, who *cares*?"

With that last Charles drew himself up to his full height, looking Eric levelly in the eye as if expecting an argument.

It's about damn time you passed the test, Eric thought.

"*Finally*," he sighed aloud, causing Charles to be utterly bewildered.

"What are you talking about?" the younger officer asked, not understanding.

"*Finally* you display some damn backbone," Eric retorted, walking over and clapping his wingman on the back. "I was starting to wonder if my sister was going to be courted by a sissy."

"*What?*" Charles asked.

"Look, between you, me, and this kitchen, even if you have no intention of courting my sister, she's taken a shine to you," Eric replied. "I wasn't just arguing with my brothers for my health."

"So you mean to tell me your brothers were actually

177

trying to talk me out of seeing your sister?" Charles asked, incredulous.

"Oh yeah," Eric said, smiling. "I mean, she was rather upset about their friend going missing, and we all take protecting her rather seriously."

"How did your sister ever manage to get a date in high school?" Charles asked.

"It's not coincidence she ended up with my best friend," Eric said simply.

The sound of Patricia's door loudly squeaking open made Charles stop his reply.

"You know, one of these days we'll have to get that fixed," Jo said, her voice just a little louder than necessary. "Or maybe some nice gentlemen who nearly ruined a nice shirt could do it for us while I warm dinner back up."

Eric and Charles shared a look.

"That gentleman should probably put his arm back in its sling before he goes to doing any housework," Eric observed, gesturing at Charles' current state. "I think I can bend down to oil some hinges."

"Well he can use the oil can before he puts the sling back on," Jo said forcefully, fixing Eric with a level stare.

Apparently this is going to be a clash of wills day, Eric thought.

"Apparently you're being requested by description rather than name," Eric observed drily.

"Guess so," Charles replied, standing up. He looked around really quickly, then spotted what he was looking for. Grabbing the kitchen lard, he headed back into the house.

Jo gave Charles a rather obvious wink as she passed him coming into the kitchen.

Well I guess we know that Jo likes him, Eric thought with a smile.

"So, Patricia told me earlier you're the sanest of the

Cobb clan," Jo stated without preamble.

"Knowing my sister and brothers, you realize that's like saying I've got the slickest shell in a snail race, right?" Eric said with a slight smile. Jo laughed, her mind playing the mental image of the Cobbs as a bunch of snails.

"You know, I was trying to think of a metaphor that would aptly describe that statement earlier," Jo said. "I think you hit the nail right on the head."

"Well, they say realizing you're crazy is the first step to getting better," Eric said lightly. Seeing Jo trying to do several things at once, he stood up to help her. With a sharp pain, he felt his wounds remind him not to move so quickly.

I know I'm getting better, but sometimes I wonder if there's still something broke loose back there, he thought.

"Sit down, Eric," Jo said, seeing the look on his face. "The day I need help in a kitchen is the day that I need to think about being put down like a lame horse."

Eric raised an eyebrow.

"Well, never heard a woman that vehement about not needing help," he said. "My Mom used to always like it when us boys helped her in the kitchen."

"Having seen Sam, David, and Nick eat, I can definitely understand that," Jo replied, a comment that elicited a sharp bark of laughter from Eric. "Speaking of which, I prepared enough spaghetti for all of them, so you might as well take a dish for those three lunkheads."

"As good as that smells, it might not make it," Eric replied, taking a sniff. Jo gave a mock sniff of disbelief.

"You sure you weren't abandoned on your parents' doorstep?" Jo inquired playfully.

"No, I'd dare say I look the most like my father out of all of us," Eric replied.

"You know, Sam says the same thing," Jo pointed out.

"Yeah, if you crossed Dad with a gorilla," Eric snorted. "That big lug may have the same name, but he does *not* look anything like him."

"I wouldn't know," Jo said with a shrug, "given that Patricia has no pictures of your family."

"Funny thing about that when you leave in the middle of your wedding planning," Eric observed.

"You know, he never formally asked *me*," Patricia said petulantly as Charles and her came back into the room. Her arrival made Jo jump, nearly causing her to spill the pot of spaghetti sauce she was stirring.

Eric realized with a start his sister had completely changed her outfit, probably at Jo's insistence. While the cream blouse and black skirt she had been wearing before had looked very attractive, the black formal dress she had changed into made her absolutely stunning. Looking at Charles's face, Eric could see his wingman thought the same.

I'm not even sure Read heard me mention her prior engagement, he's so busy looking at her rear, Eric thought.

"Yeah, that's what you said in your letter too," Eric replied. "Or at least that's what I gathered once Mom was able to form coherent sentences again."

"I notice that you are not wearing a wedding band, Eric," Patricia shot back. "Why is it that you get to call of your engagement without repercussion yet I cannot break off a courtship that was basically forced upon me by Mom and Dad?"

Jo's neck nearly snapped she looked at Eric, clearly waiting on an answer.

"Well I guess we might as well have *this* discussion," Eric snapped at his sister. "You know da...*darn* good and well that I dumped Joyce because she tried to make me into a man I am not."

"She was scared, Eric," Patricia sighed.

"At the time of our engagement," Eric bit out, "Joyce made it seem like she understood the rigors involved in being a Navy wife. Specifically the part about I may have to give my life in the service of the Republic."

"Yes, and you don't think her brother being in the service hasn't helped her to rethink things?" Patricia asked plaintively. "Beau nearly got killed by a submarine a couple days after the war started."

Eric's eyes narrowed.

"She's written you, hasn't she?" Eric asked.

Patricia started to speak, then stopped.

"Out with it, Toots!" Eric demanded.

"Yes, Eric, she has," Patricia said heavily. "The poor thing's had her life made a living hell by Mom and the Duchess. She asked me for help with at least one of them."

Eric snorted.

"Yes, having you intercede on her behalf with Mom would be the very definition of…" Eric started, only to be interrupted by Josephine.

"I don't want to speak for Charles, but I for one don't want to sit through another broadcast of 'Cobb Family Follies,'" the smaller woman said.

Whoa, she does not look happy, Eric thought.

"There wouldn't be any 'Follies' if my brother had been just a tad bit more compassionate," Patricia observed archly.

"Not my fault that Joyce wasn't paying attention to the job description until I ended up swimming in the Atlantic," Eric snapped back. "Maybe that's something any woman intending to marry a military man should think about."

Patricia met her brother's icy gaze with a look that was as heated as his was cool.

"Do you think I have not learned what the worst thing

181

that can happen to a Navy wife is, Eric?" Patricia began. "Or did you forget Mrs. Hertling living with us for a week before moving out?"

"Patricia..." Jo started, realizing the argument was about to spiral out of control. Fortunately Eric, being used to his sister's strong will, was willing to concede the round.

"No, Patricia, I didn't. If any of us thought you were that stupid, we wouldn't have brought Charles with us tonight," Eric said, causing Charles to turn beet red and Jo to laugh. Standing up, he went over towards the stove to help serve up.

"But Joyce had a dream she wanted, and was willing to do just about anything to achieve it," Eric said simply. "At least you can tell yourself that Beau was an idiot even if it's not true."

"If she dated you for three years and wasn't ready to get married to the Navy, this Joyce person obviously wasn't that bright either," Jo said firmly, touching his arm. Eric looked up in surprise.

"Sorry, you're just not the first Navy man I've seen that happen to," Jo said quietly as their eyes met. Embarrassed, they both looked away, Jo flushing slightly.

*Okay, I am **not** going to try to hit on the daughter of Jacob Morton*, Eric thought. He watched as his sister came to stand by Charles, her hand brushing his. Eric saw his former wingman take her hand, squeezing it when he thought Eric wasn't looking.

Well, glad to see they finally broke the mutual ice, Eric thought.

"So, garlic bread?" Patricia asked, the sudden silence awkward.

"Good plan," Jo exhaled in a rush.

I hope her Dad keeps himself in one piece, Eric thought. *I think I want to ask his permission to court his daughter.*

CHAPTER 5: TO RULE THE HEAVENS

In the development of airpower one has to look ahead and not backwards and figure out what is going to happen, not too much what has happened—**Brigadier General Billy Mitchell**

No. 7 Group Headquarters
Darwin, Australia
0900 Local (1800 Eastern)
1 May (30 April) 1943

Russell Wolford adjusted his uniform cap as he approached the squat, single story building that currently housed No. 7 Group, Royal Australian Air Force. Located on Darwin's northern outskirts, the wooden structure looked utterly non-descript—which was probably why it had survived the Japanese carrier raid a little over thirty days before.

I'm guessing that's why they don't have any defensive emplacements surrounding it either, Russell thought. A tall, lanky soldier with a bayoneted rifle separated himself from the post he'd been leaning upon.

"G'day Flight Officer," he stated. "Can I help you find something?"

I'm sure I look quite suspicious in this borrowed uniform and bandages, Russell thought. *Unfortunately there wasn't any time to stop in Surabaya and grab my gear That is, if what's left of the squadron hadn't already boxed it up or stolen it.*

"It's actually Flight Lieutenant," Russell replied evenly. "I'm here to see Wing Commander Stokely. My

183

password is Birmingham."

The man gave Russell a long, hard look.

"Well, Sir, if you're some German commando or a very well disguised Japanese officer then I'm making a dog's breakfast of it," the soldier said. "We changed pass codes three days ago, but given what you're wearing I doubt you got the word."

"I've been trapped in a submarine, then in transport, sergeant," Russell observed. "So, no."

"I hope you gave them hell, sir," the digger replied.

"I think we gave as good as we got," Russell stated, surprised that he actually believed what he was saying.

Too bad it wasn't nearly enough, he thought. No. 625 Squadron had been officially withdrawn for refitting after the madness of the *Ryujo*.

*Good thing they're giving that **Boston** bloke a Victoria Cross*, Russell thought. *Too bad he had to earn it crashing into the carrier's deck. We'll never know if he did it on purpose, but either way that carrier's not going to be back for awhile.*

Walking through the staff sections arranged in a single common room, Russell hoped he didn't look as foolish as he felt in the uniform. His time in the DEI had shaved twelve pounds off his frame, and the flight officer whose shirt he was wearing had been heavyset before getting shot down defending the *Canberra*.

Poor Meadows, he thought. *Bloke was always a little unlucky.*

"Russell!" Wing Commander Stokely said, standing up from behind his desk before Russell could knock. "Glad to see the Royal Navy didn't press you into service." Tall, with a boxer's build, Stokely had the onsetting paunch and balding hair that was the lot of most men who saw middle age. Still, his blue eyes shone with alertness, and the decorations on his uniform jacket spoke to his service in the previous war.

I'm sure he was looking forward to a long retirement when he agreed to join the RAAF, Russell mused. *Oh well, so far I have no complaints.*

"I think it was due to my frightful appearance," Russell replied drily, gesturing to his bandages.

"My good man, I believe your appearance was frightful before some bastard shot you to pieces," Stokely replied. "I had a chance to talk to some of your blokes after the mission while you were catching your water taxi. Still, I'd like to get your view of it, and *Leftenant* Collins should be arriving shortly to take notes."

*I'm pretty sure the captain of the **Thrasher** would have sharp words without you for talking about his ship that way*, Russell thought with an inner smile.

There was a soft knock at the door, and Russell turned to see a bright, cheerful looking brunette in a WAAF uniform standing by the door. Her brown eyes looked over Russell, briefly lingering on his rank before she nodded to Wing Commander Stokely.

"Sir, you sent for me?" she asked, her accent telling Russell that she was not from around Darwin.

"Yes Deborah," Stokely replied. "We need to take down Flight Lieutenant Woolford's account of the Makassar Action. Russell, I want you to tell us everything. *Leftenant* Collins is cleared for anything you would know…as well as things she'd probably have to kill you for finding out."

Well that's interesting, Russell thought, seeing the woman blush at that comment. As soon as she gave her indication that she was ready for his notes, he began. Forty-five minutes later, including questions from Stokely, Russell realized he was sweating profusely and had a tic in his left hand.

Get a grip on yourself, he admonished himself mentally. Seeing Russell's state, Stokely stopped mid-question, reached down into his desk, and withdrew a bottle with three shot glasses.

"*Leftenant* Collins, I assume I will not offend your Auckland sensibilities if I offer you some schnapps?" Stokely asked.

"Most certainly not, sir," Deborah replied, working a cramp out of her right hand.

"Russell I'm not giving you a choice," Stokely continued, pouring the first glass.

"Sorry sir," Russell said, managing to stop his left hand's palsey finally.

"Nonsense!" Stokely guffawed, his laughter gallows. "I'd be more worried if you weren't affected telling me that account! Trust me lad, I lived through Bloody April. If you were totally calm, it'd mean you were either about to get the chop or blow your brains out."

"I assure you, sir, I have no intentions of catching a beer with Death after cheating the bastard," Russell replied. "The rest depends on when we get replacement aircraft."

Stokely shook his head at that.

"No, it doesn't," the Wing Commander said. "I have it on good authority that Vice Admiral Phillips is about to inform our Dutch friends the gig is up. We're losing too many ships."

"How bad is it?" Russell asked. "I understand there were a couple of scuffles last week."

"'Scuffles' is one way of putting it," Stokely snorted. "Massacre is another. Apparently the Dutch lost over half their fleet in ten minutes on one end of the Java Sea, and one of our task forces lost some ships on the other. The Japs will probably have Sumatra in under two weeks, and the Army refuses to commit any more soldiers to try and stop it."

"Well that's awfully sporting of them," Russell spat, then stopped himself. Stokely shrugged.

"Prime Minister Curtin has publicly stated it is time for Australia to see to our own defense," the senior officer replied. "The raid on Perth and that midget submarine business in Sydney a couple nights ago has everyone on edge."

"Midget submarine business, sir?" Russell asked.

"Couple of Japanese midget submarines snuck into Sydney Harbor and put two fish in the *Eagle*," Stokely replied. "Nearly hit some Yank cruiser while they were at it. Neither of them made it back out of the harbor, and there was another one that a couple of corvettes put paid to."

"What happened to the *Eagle*?" Russell asked, his face shocked.

"Apparently her captain was a lunatic and had had most of her hatches shut," Stokely responded. "Plus the Japanese midget skipper was a poor shot and hit her forward. Either way, she won't be going north to help provide air cover."

Probably lucky for her from what I saw, Russell said.

"Speaking of which, you'll be pleased to know that we're reequipping your squadron with *Mosquitoes*," Stokely continued. "The boffins figured out why the tails were coming off: the glue doesn't like the tropics."

Well that's problematic for a bloody wooden plane, Russell thought.

"Either way, I think that things will be over with before you have to worry about that," Stokely said. "The three squadrons of *Whirlwinds* and two of *Typhoons* we sent north will be the last help our friends the Dutch get from us."

Surabaya
1015 Local (2315 Eastern)
1 May (30 April)

The sound of air raid sirens was audible even deep within *Houston's* hull. A few moments later, the ship's own intercom crackled than began blaring the bugle call for air attack.

"Don't even think about it, sir," Lieutenant Ethan Sharpe, ship's assistant surgeon, muttered as he continued to work. "I'd really hate to leave a scar."

Jacob let out an exasperated snort, truly angry that he was being forced to remain laying on his left side in only his undershorts while Sharpe continued sewing shut the gash in his calf.

"Leave it to the Japanese to attack when I'm stuck with my pants on the damn deck," Jacob muttered.

"Oh, we've probably got a good thirty to forty minutes before they get here," Sharpe replied. "So far the Dutch have been pretty good about getting the word out early."

"Probably some poor bastard sitting with a pair of binoculars looking over the Jap airbase," Jacob muttered. "I'd hate to have that job."

"Well, it's not like ours is exactly risk free as of late, Sir," Sharpe said. He rubbed his eyes with his forearm.

"When was the last time you got some sleep, Sharpe?" Jacob asked worriedly. While the wound was far, far away from the Morton family jewels, he wasn't a big fan of getting jabbed anywhere with a needle.

"Sir, I'll sleep right after you, since you were quite adamant about being our last case," Sharpe replied. "I'm glad Captain Wallace wasn't given a chance to protest."

Well our good master did have a helmet that'd been almost cut in half, Jacob thought fearfully. *I don't think Chief Roberts will have to ever tell me to put mine on again.*

"You and me both agree on Captain Wallace not getting asked," Jacob replied. "Hopefully our Japanese friends won't get close enough to give you any new ones."

"I'm not too worried if they do," Sharpe replied.
"With the *Revenge* and *Hermes* on the other side of the
harbor, we're positively little fish."

"Don't envy those bastards," Jacob gasped out. "At
least *Australia* and *Phoenix* aren't sitting here also."

"Is it wrong of me to hope the bombers see them at
sea and decided to take their chances?" Sharpe asked tiredly,
finishing the last stitch.

"Probably, but I won't deny that wasn't the first thing
that ran through my mind," Jacob said, watching as the
medical officer grabbed a tin of sulfa and began applying it
liberally to the wound area.

*Strange, I'm almost glad the shoulder is distracting
me from the damn leg*, Jacob thought. While *Houston*'s XO
had insisted on waiting until the ship's surgeon had taken
care of the other wounded before stitching his leg, Sharpe
had thought it wise to readjust the shoulder immediately. It
had not been one of Jacob's finest moments, the event
bringing home to him the difference between a man in his
early twenties and one who was old enough to have a
daughter that age.

*Said daughter that is probably trapped in Hawaii
now*, Jacob thought. *I don't think they'll be lifting the non-
essential shipping restriction anytime soon after losing those
two baby carriers and the **California***. As horrible as Japan's
ability to strike across the breadth of the Pacific was, in a
way it was a relief to know that he probably didn't have to
worry about Jo getting a vessel blown out from under her.

Of course, I can't say the same for her old man, Jacob
thought. *Especially since we don't have time for another
Sydney trip.*

"Well Sir, that's all I can do for you," Sharpe said. "I
still strongly recommend you take some painkillers, but
Lieutenant Commander Frankes told me your response to
that suggestion earlier today."

"Yes, I need to be able to think clearly," Jacob replied.

"Well, if you change your mind, we've got plenty from our Dutch friends," Sharpe said, pointing to the boxes arranged against the far wall.

"Hopefully we won't need anymore of those," Jacob said. "But if we do, save them for people who are hurt worse than I am."

The distant sound of anti-aircraft guns made Jacob stop before he could reply.

"XO to Battle Two! I say again, XO to Battle Two," the loudspeaker squealed.

"Well, looks like our Japanese friends are moving a bit quicker than expected!" Jacob observed.

Splitting our force to come from two directions was a masterstroke,, Isoro thought to himself as he led his *chutai* down from their altitude advantage on the Dutch, Australian, and American fighters struggling to gain altitude. *Now we will see how well these men fight on the defense.*

Quickly scanning his targets, Isoro selected a twin-engined aircraft that he had not seen before. The machine's long, narrow fuselage and thin wings seemed dwarfed by its two massive engines, one under each wing. A bubble canopy was set just behind the two engines, while four fairly prominent cannon muzzles projected from the fighter's nose.

Whatever that is, I think it will burn, Isoro thought. Aiming just in front of the climbing Allied fighter, Isoro depressed both of his triggers. His fire stitched down the center of his prey's fuselage and out onto its starboard wing as the pilot reacted. It was far too late, as the fighter's engine burst into flames. Isoro pulled up to avoid a collision, passing over the damaged fighter in a half roll in order to watch it crash.

I must confirm the k...damn you! Isoro thought in

shock, the enemy pilot finding enough power to skid his nose. A moment later, the four cannon muzzles fired even as Isoro was finishing his roll. Thankfully Newtonian physics dragged the damaged fighter's aim off as it stalled, the tracers passing wildly behind Isoro's *Shiden*. Even as the plane began falling away, Sawato put another cannon burst into it. The twin-engined Allied fighter staggered in midair, then began falling like a leaf out of the sky, a dead man at the controls and the fire starting to spread across its wings.

Their aircraft are so rugged, Isoro thought, shaken as he looked around the chaotic sky. Seeing a pair of *Hurricanes* attempting to turn back towards the Japanese fighters, Isoro shoved his throttle to the firewall and snatched a few dozen feet of altitude. Kicking his rudder, he came around into a smooth turn that put the sun at his back, lining up on the trailing fighter. Waiting until he clearly saw the bright orange triangle of the DEI Air Force, Isoro fired his cannon. The stream of tracers walked up from the enemy's tail, through its cockpit, then to the fuel tank situated just in front of the unfortunate Dutchman. With a bright flash, the *Hurricane* exploded, killing its pilot instantly.

Continuing blindly on through his turn, the lead *Hurricane* sighted a *Zero* heading the other way. As it rolled, Isoro found himself staring at the aircraft's underside before he fired. The *Hurricane* pilot never knew what hit him, the storm of cannon and machine gun fire exploding up from the cockpit floor and ripping his port wing off. Amazingly, the fighter did not burn, corkscrewing crazily as it began its arc downward.

Isoro leveled off, once again climbing. Just as suddenly as the combat had begun, it was over, trails of smoke marking the funeral pyres of the vanquished.

The sky always clears so suddenly, Isoro thought. *It becomes empty in the same way as the sea.*

Looking over his starboard wing, he saw a formation

of aircraft turn towards a smoking Surabaya harbor.

The bombers are beginning their runs, he thought. *Strike hard, Eiji.*

"Okay, here the bastards come," Jacob muttered, standing on the deck outside of Battle Two as *Houston* began making her way towards sea.

"It would appear that you were right about them not wanting us," Lieutenant Foncier observed. "I count twenty-seven bombers, and they're all heading past us."

The *Houston's* anti-aircraft guns began tracking the approaching aircraft, waiting as the bombers began descending from just above the guns' maximum altitude on their attack runs. The *Houston's* crew watched the aircraft that the intelligence types were calling "Bettys" moving into their attack runs.

Their formations are so damn precise, Jacob thought, feeling a twinge of fear. *This must be what the rabbit feels like watching a redtail take its friend.* Only as they passed their initial point, incidentally entering the *Houston*'s range, did the bombers divide into three groups of nine. As if on cue, every Allied gun in Surabaya harbor opened up, the sound a cacophony of noise that pounded into Jacob's ears. Amazingly, the fire appeared to be reasonably accurate, the barrage good on height and only slightly off in speed.

"Looks like all the practice they've been giving us is starting to pay off!" Foncier shouted.

"Yeah, but not good...nevermind!" Jacob shouted back, his voice turning gleeful as two of the enemy bombers suddenly began to smoke. With a bright flash, one suddenly became an expanding fireball, one of its wings turning crazily out of the blast. The second began losing altitude and airspeed, clearly not making it towards the *Hermes* and *Revenge.* Putting its nose down, a streamer of flame and smoke flowing behind it, the aircraft continued in a gentle diving turn, the intent of which suddenly became clear.

"Goddammit!" Jacob shouted, feeling his sphincter clinch as the Japanese bomber began to gain in size. The *Houston* could not increase her speed or maneuver, Surabaya's channel being notoriously poorly marked.

Every AA gun on the *Houston* began firing towards the diving, flaming twin-engined *Betty*. As he watched, Jacob saw pieces of debris beginning to stream behind the aircraft, the heavy cruiser's guns doing damage that would have made any sane pilot break off his attack so that his crew could try and escape the aircraft. Looking at the bomber's direct path, it was quite obvious this particular pilot was not sane, or wanted some company when crossing the Styx.

C'mon dammit, hit the bastard! Jacob willed the cruiser's gunners.

In the end, it was the much-maligned 1.1-inch pom-poms that saved the *Houston*. One of the automatic weapons' shells punctured the diving bomber's all glass nose, passed through the bombardier's chest, and exploded on the co-pilot's control column. The resultant blast killed the co-pilot and blinded the pilot, causing the man to flinch backwards. Another 1.1-inch round them ensured the pilot would not make a correction or any other actions in this life.

With a roar, the G4M roared over Battle Two, so close that Jacob felt the rush of heat from the burning wing as he dropped to the deck. The bomber continued into the ocean barely thirty yards off the heavy cruiser's port side, its bombload exploding as it hit the ocean. Once again, *Houston*'s decks were swept with fragments, killing several and wounding a couple dozen more exposed crewmen.

I wish I hadn't made my comment about any more casualties, Jacob thought, pain shooting up his leg.

"Sweet Jesus, would people stop trying to kill us?" Foncier asked, his voice hoarse with emotion. Jacob was about to reply, but was struck silent as he stood up just in

193

JAMES YOUNG

time to see the bombers releasing their deadly loads against the *Hermes* and *Revenge*.Having been aware of their respective targets due to reconnaissance missions flown the day before, the Japanese had equipped those bombers going after the *Hermes* with lighter but more numerous 250-kilogram bombs while the *Revenge* was the target of heavier, 500-kg. armor-piercing weapons.

The two vessels' immobile states greatly aided the Japanese bombardiers' aim. To everyone's horror in the harbor, both ships were struck multiple times. In the case of the *Revenge*, one of the four bombs that hit the elderly battleship broke upon hitting her thick belt at an angle. The next exploded atop her previously battered X turret. Once again, the turret's crew was treated to the sound of an explosion right on top of their heads, the fragments clearing many of the tars manning her aft AA guns and holing both 15-inch guns. The next two bombs both expended their fury on the battleship's heavily armored main deck, causing many personnel casualties but not significantly affecting the vessel's fighting ability.

Similarly deluged by falling bombs, the *Hermes* fared equally in number of hits, taking four bombs and three near misses. Unlike the *Revenge,* however, the *Hermes* did not have multiple levels of thick deck armor designed to keep out heavy shells. Having jettisoned those *Sea Hurricanes* not already aloft at the time of her torpedoing, the old carrier was spared a hangar fire. In the end, this was to be of little consequence, as the first two bombs plunged down into her forward fire room and undid the extensive repair work that had almost been completed in the aftermath of her torpedo hit. Following closely behind, the third weapon wiped out the central damage control station and much of the communication throughout the ship. Last, but far from least, the fourth weapon hit the carrier's aftmost elevator and exploded in its shaft, blasting the lift device into uselessness

194

and starting a blaze in a paint locker. Hard hit, with her hull once again opened to the sea, the *Hermes* began to settle, listing to starboard with a good, strong plume of smoke beginning to rise from her aft elevator.

Their mission complete, the remaining bombers rejoined into their formation, seemingly unaffected by the strenuous barrage being thrown up by the vessels in Surabaya Harbor.

Isoro brought his *Shiden* alongside the lead bomber's port side, looking across at the battered aircraft. The aircraft's rear half resembled a sieve, the gunner's blister on his side blown completely out with the unfortunate man's torso hanging out in the slipstream. As Isoro watched, he could see a torrent of blood running down the bomber's side in the slip stream.

It's a miracle that he did not catch fire, Isoro thought. *It was be similarly miraculous if he makes it back to Borneo.*

Seeing that the lead aircraft was going to continue on, Isoro manipulated his throttle to drift back, looking for Eiji. Drawing even with the last vic, he saw his friend's aircraft and heaved a sigh of relief. The G4M looked unscathed, its crew manning their stations and the two pilots easily keeping formation. Rocking his wings to gain Eiji's attention, Isoro gave his friend a wave.

We have managed to survive another day. Looking across at his friends face, Isoro could see he felt the same way. Looking away from the bomber, he watched as *Zeroes* and *Shidens* began to form back up with their charges, the combined group turning back towards Balikpapan.

Far above the gathered group, a solitary twin-engined aircraft identical to Isoro's first kill that day moved into attack position up sun. One of No. 7 Wing's *Whirlwinds*, the aircraft had been constructed in Great Britain shortly before the Treaty of Kent, crated, and then shipped to Australia. Almost as well traveled as his mount, Flight Lieutenant George Buerling quickly surveyed the Japanese formation.

As the escort *Zeroes* began to slide into position, the Canadian made his final selection. A veteran of both Battles of Britain, the pilot knew there was little to be gained from dispatching one of the small and nimble single-engined fighters in lieu of a far more important bomber. Figuring the laboring, starting to smoke leader was done for, Buerling chose a bomber further back in the formation.

Here goes nothing, he thought, pushing over.

If there was one thing a fighter pilot learned, it was that there was no such thing as uncontested airspace. Whilst his peers obviously believed their jobs to be done, with some of them even going so far as to break into their pre-packed lunches, Isoro continued his scan. As a result, he sighted the Allied fighter diving out of the sun, arms and legs reacting instinctively to turn towards the hurtling aircraft.

In the end, even Isoro's vigilance did no good, the *Shiden*'s maneuverability insufficient to allow him to deter the diving enemy fighter. Realizing that he was too late, Isoro screamed at the top of his lungs in frustration as the enemy fighter's nose began to seemingly strobe in slow motion. To his amazement, the heavy fighter ignored him, literally firing past his climbing fighter. Stomping on his rudder pedals and throwing the stick over to invert the *Shiden*, Isoro had a momentary impression of Eijii's bomber converted into a flying crematorium. As he began his dive to chase the Allied fighter, a quick glance told him his initial thoughts were correct, flames shooting from the G4M's cabin and side windows, the starboard wing peeling back and away in the slipstream. The death of his friend had not even registered as Isoro finished his maneuver, determined to catch and kill the Allied aircraft.

In an instant, Isoro saw that his efforts were useless, his *Shiden* not able to gain on the fighter quickly enough. Still he pursued, his engine roaring in his ears. It was only the realization that his wingmen were behind him that made Isoro pull up, the taste of bile in his mouth.

I will not sacrifice three fighters for vengeance, he thought angrily. Adding insult to injury, he saw the enemy fighter waggle its wings as Isoro turned away. He felt tears of frustration welling up in his eyes.

I am samurai, not some weeping child, Isoro thought. *I will gain my solace in continuing to kill the Emperor's enemies.*

Strangely, that thought did not ease his pain, and he flashed back to his earlier conversation with Eiji. Suddenly, he realized his friend was right...their opponents did not fear something that would kill them one by one, and that was why the enemy had not attacked his *Shiden* or any of the other *Zeroes*. With this bitter thought, Isoro continued back towards his formation, ignoring the trail of smoke that led down to the Java Sea below.

Pensacola, Florida
1000 Local
2 May

Adam cursed in frustration as the squadron's formation disintegrated once more. Pulling up above the chaos, he uttered a quick oath as he narrowly dodged his predecessor's fate, Yellow Two nearly taking his tailplane off as Red and Yellow flights crossed paths.

"Goddammit! It's...one...freakin'...plane! Everyone can't screw the chicken at once!" he roared over the radio. "Yellow One, you lead your flight through mine once again I'll choke you myself! "

Bowles had returned to the squadron the evening

before, arrogant smugness radiating off of him. Adam had knocked that out of the junior officer very quickly, telling the captain he had to pull duty officer for the air wing. This had prevented him from going out to frequent any familiar haunts, as well as keeping him from having conjugal relations with Mrs. Burke or some other hapless wife.

I guess he must have been more upset than I realized, considering he just tried to kill me, Adam thought angrily.

"All right gentlemen, form back up by flight," Adam barked. "While you're pulling your heads out of your asses, let me remind you again that anything less than two aircraft, only one flight bounces…"

"Because there's always someone else up in the sun!" a familiar Irish voice interrupted. "Tallyho Colonials!"

Down from above them came eight *Spitfires*, diving out of the sun where not a single Marine was looking. Disgusted, Adam realized that even he had been caught by surprise thanks to Bowles' near miss.

If that had been a bounce, there'd be at least four or five of us dead, he thought angrily. He recognized the emerald green Seafire of Squadron Leader Connor O'Rourke, one of his former squadronmates from his time with the Royal Air Force. The eight Brits continued their charge after passing through VMF-21's, drawing away from the *Wildcats* as if the tubby fighters were dipped in molasses.

"Bastard," Adam muttered. There was dead silence over the net as he looked at his fuel gauge.

"All right Buccaneers, let's pack it up," he barked. "Time and fuel's awasting."

A thoroughly cowed VMF-21 formed up behind him, sliding into its usual perfect formation. As they circled over Pensacola Field in preparation for touchdown, Adam keyed his microphone.

"All pilots meet in front of my aircraft immediately after touchdown," he intoned. "Flight leaders acknowledge."

"Green, roger."

"Blue, roger."

There was silence immediately after Blue. After a few moments, Adam pressed his throat microphone again.

"Yellow One, acknowledge," Adam said sharply.

"Oh, sorry Red, didn't monitor your last transmission," Yellow One said.

You lying bastard, Adam thought. It would appear that Bowles was determined to test him.

I can't have you have an accident, but we'll get this settled up most quickly, Adam thought.

"Yellow One, I say again, meet me at my aircraft once we land," Adam replied. "Did you monitor that time, or are your brain and posterior still inverted from your leave?"

There was at least one audible intake of breath.

"*Roger* Red One, I understood your last transmission," Bowles replied in a faux British accent. "Won't bloody well happen again, I think."

There were a couple of chuckles over the net. Adam gripped the control stick so hard his knuckles popped from the force, then breathed out in a ragged exhalation. He so desperately wanted to turn his aircraft to starboard, charge his guns, and unleash a long burst of fire into Bowles cockpit.

It would be so damn easy, he thought to himself. Taking another deep breath, he forced himself to calm down.

A time and place for everything, Adam thought. *With this many witnesses is neither of those*. Bowles' time would come soon enough, judging from the reports from the Pacific. Comforting himself with that though, Adam keyed his mike.

"All Flight Leaders, we're starting a new policy effective immediately: For every time we get bounced by our British friends, a different flight will buy the drinks for the squadron and the British when we get back to Mustin Hall," Adam said. "Yellow One, thank you for volunteering your flight."

There was stunned silence over the net for a moment.

"And the preferred drink of Wing Commander O'Connor is gin, neat," Adam said. "Feel free to see if he appreciates your English accent, I'm sure your dentist will appreciate the business."

The last comment was answered with several whistles and catcalls about Bowles' bravery and general common sense. Adam allowed himself a small smile.

That'll teach him to remember that old saying about old age and treachery versus youth and exuberance, he thought to himself.

Forty-five minutes later Adam stood in front of the gathered pilots, the engine on his fighter ticking over behind him. The fifteen men all had various degrees of attentiveness, ranging from Bowles's glowering indifference to the rapt attention of a couple of the more junior pilots, fresh from the Pensacola aviation cadet class.

"Okay, what did we learn?" Adam began.

"That the *Spitfire* is faster than a *Wildcat*," Burke said grimly. There was murmured assent from around the group.

"In level speed, you're right," Adam said. "That is one thing all of you must remember—our fighter is *not* that fast."

"So what you're telling us is that we're all going to die when we go to war," Captain Bowles said, his tone just short of belligerence. "Guess my mother is going to be a widow and out her only child."

"Only if you're too dumb to listen," Adam replied. *I'm tired of this man.* "My father tells me that's a paternal trait, which makes it pretty obvious why you're a half orphan."

Bowles reacted exactly as Adam predicted he would, dropping his helmet and starting to stalk forward with an inarticulate cry. Adam waited for him to throw the first punch, a clumsy haymaker that he shifted most of the way out of, allowing the man to connect with his shoulder.

Having satisfied his right to self defense, Adam tripped the off balance captain while shoving him in the back.

Looks like all those years of tussling with the security folks taught me more than I thought, Adam observed as Bowles hit his face on the tarmac. Before the man had time to realize to gather his thoughts, Adam was swinging around to kick Bowles hard in his posterior. The blow sent the captain forward into a heap under the *Wildcat*'s wing.

"Thank you again, Captain Bowles, for volunteering so I can prove a point," Adam said simply, his voice sounding as steady as during classroom instruction. "As you can see, Captain Bowles is arguably faster, younger, and quicker than me. Yet he is the one who is currently up against the side of my *Wildcat*."

The entire squadron's attention was focused on him now, many of their mouths open in shock. Watching Bowles start to struggle to his feet out of the corner of his eye, Adam continued with his instruction.

"The reason this happened is that I took advantage of my inherent advantages," Adam continued. "In the case of the *Wildcat*, this aircraft's advantages are its rate of dive, especially against most European fighters. In a dive, the *Spitfire* is nowhere near as fast as the *Wildcat*."

Adam saw a flicker of movement out of the corner of his eye and turned into the blow that Bowles was throwing. To the bystanders it appeared that Bowles had caught him full on in the head, where in reality Adam's stepping into it had shortened the force by a considerable margin. If Bowles hadn't committed fully committed himself to the punch, Adam might have been in serious danger. As it was, it took him a second to get his balance back, but when he did it was behind a left-right-*left* combination that left Bowles unconscious on his back.

"Much like the *Spitfire*, Captain Bowles apparently cannot handle much punishment," Adam said, flexing his hands. "On the other hand, as you all saw a few weeks ago, the *Wildcat* is built to take a licking."

Scanning the squadron, Adam was shocked to see the Air Wing Commander, Lieutenant Colonel King. The man had a scowl on his face, but had yet to say anything.

Well I've got a whole squadron of witnesses that will say that bastard threw the first punch even if you didn't see it, sir, Adam thought angrily.

"This also means if you have to get into a head-on run with an enemy fighter, especially a Jap, you'll likely survive," Adam said. He looked down at Bowles's prostrate form and shook his head.

"Remember," he continued, looking back over the squadron, "air combat is *not* only about who has the fastest or prettiest plane."

I'm starting to make them understand, Adam thought with a glow of pride, seeing several of the men starting to nod their heads.

"It's who has the better tactics and keeps his head out of the cockpit," Adam finished. He took a moment to let that lesson sink in, then turned to Lieutenant Colonel King.

"Sir, do you have anything else to add?" Adam asked, his tone nonchalant.

"Captain Burke, Lieutenant Ratford, pick up young Captain Bowles and take him to the stockade," King snapped. "Turn him over to Commander Sherman with my compliments, he should know you are coming by the time you get there. Major Haynes, I need to see you in my office in thirty minutes after you get some ice on your knuckles."

With that, King turned to leave.

"Squadron attention!" Adam barked. After Lieutenant Colonel King walked off, he turned back to the assembled group.

"You guys are dismissed until 1700, at which point we will all meet at Mustin Hall so that Yellow Flight can ante up on the beers. Any questions?"

The pilots all looked back and forth at one another, at Burke and Ratford as the two officers picked the unconscious Bowles up, then back at Adam.

"All right, get out of here," Adam said. "See you in a few hours."

Precisely nineteen minutes later, Adam was standing in front of Major Anthony's desk. The slightly heavyset adjutant was looking at Adam with a bemused smile on his face.

"You know, you really have a knack for sticking a very short stick into hornets' nests," Anthony observed.

"It's a gift," Adam responded dryly.

"Major Anthony, if that's the good Major Haynes, please send him in," Lieutenant Colonel King boomed from his office. "I'll save him the trouble of knocking his knuckles on yet another hard object today."

Anthony gestured towards the office door, mouthing a 'good luck' for Adam's benefit. Adam strode into the wing commander's office and came to attention.

"Major Haynes repor…" he began.

"Dammit Haynes, you're not in trouble—much anyway," King snapped, cutting him off. The man stood in front of a small coffee pot, adding cream to a large porcelain mug. "Shut the damn door."

Adam complied with the order, then turned back around.

"Coffee, Major?" Lt. Col. King asked genially, his

203

tone nonchalant. The hairs rose on the back of Adam's neck, alarm bells going off in his head.

"No thank you, Sir," Adam replied.

"Oh, please, I insist," King replied. "I mean, given that you are apparently just a guest here in my wing, and not actually a subordinate officer, I must do my best to make you comfortable."

Adam practically felt the air around him drop in temperature as King's eyes met his.

*Oh sweet Jesus, he is **pissed**,* Adam thought.

"I mean, after all, conducting a mock dogfight with your former RAF buddies without my knowledge, teaching your pilots non-standard tactics, and, most importantly, goading one of your less-liked officers into striking you so that you may be rid of him are all indicators that you must have been frocked to lieutenant colonel by your friends in high places," King continued. "I guess the paperwork just hasn't crossed Major Anthony's desk yet or he would have informed me."

"Sir, we are at war," Adam said. "Like football, the only way I can get them ready for a game is to practice at game speeds. I was merely utilizing the resources at hand."

"Oh, so pray tell what would have happened if something had gone wrong?" King asked, his tone making it clear he was not buying what Adam was selling. "Like, oh, a collision? Say you killed one of our RCAF friends? Think your little analogy would keep anyone from sending you on a long vacation to Leavenworth?"

"Sir, while my training tactics are a bit unorthodox, they will save this wing several pilots once the bullets start to fly," Adam responded, his voice contrite. "With your permission, I would like to continue practicing with the British pilots."

"Permission denied," King said sharply, holding up his hand before Adam could continue. "I received the order last night to prepare this wing for transport, with a report date in San Diego within two weeks. The ground personnel are to be on trains within one week, we'll fly the aircraft out after that."

Adam's face registered his shock.

"Sir, who is going to provide fighter defense for Florida?" Adam asked.

"I'll get to that in a moment," King snapped. "When we get to San Diego, we will be traveling by ship to Hawaii." He handed Adam a copy of the orders so that the junior officer could quickly scan them.

"In Hawaii there are sufficient pilots and aircraft to form two composite squadrons from the Marines there," King said. "I have to leave one squadron here at Pensacola. Given that you are my most experienced squadron commander, I want to have you form the Hawaii composite squadron."

Adam felt as if someone had just taken a running start and kicked him in the stomach.

I'm being relieved, he thought. His face must have reflected his disbelief because King quickly raised his hand.

"Trust me Major, this is not be a relief or discipline action," King stated, tone slightly more amiable. "I have already contacted General Geiger with this proposal and he stated it was up to you, but he agrees that you're the best man for this job. You've only had the squadron for two weeks, so I think that it will cause little turmoil amongst your men."

King's statement made Adam think of something.

"Will West and Burke keep their flights if I go out to Hawaii?" Adam asked.

"That would be up to the incoming squadron commander," King replied. "At this time I do not know whom that would be."

Adam thought for a moment, then made his decision.

205

"Sir, I must respectfully refuse," Adam said simply.

King sighed, shaking his head.

"You realize this might be your last and best chance to get into the fight, don't you?" King said. "I mean, there are already murmurs about your relatively advanced age compared to the rest of the pilots."

"Sir, I can't abandon my men, even to get into the fight," Adam said. "With the exception of Bowles and his little coterie, they've all followed me and given 100% so far. If it means I get stuck here in Pensacola for eternity, then so be it."

"I knew you were going to say that, and so did General Geiger," King said. "This means I've got to drop the other shoe...we're taking your aircraft also. Your squadron is going to transfer to Bremerton to help form another wing."

"Sir, what good are we going to be without our aircraft?" Adam asked. "While I'm sure it's possible to shoot down Japanese aircraft with sidearms, I'd imagine it's a bit difficult."

"They need your aircraft pretty badly in the Pacific," King replied, smiling slightly at Adam's comment. "VMF-14 got torpedoed on the way to Wake Island and lost almost all of their pilots and all but four of their aircraft."

"Sweet Jesus," Adam said. "Are those some of the pilots that will be forming the composite squadron?"

"Yes, they are," King replied. "The two senior survivors are coming back for a War Bonds tour—they killed some Japanese aircraft during the Battle of Hawaii I'm told."

"Are they both getting promoted?" Adam asked, raising an eyebrow.

"No, they're both junior captains," King replied. "But that's not important."

"When does my squadron leave?" Adam inquired, taking the hint.

"You have one week," King replied. "Good news is that you'll fall in on new *Wildcats* when you get out there. Apparently they've got General Motors putting together planes now."

"I can only imagine that's like putting different color lipstick on a pig," Adam muttered.

"Either way, Major Anthony already has your orders cut," King said.

Adam looked at Lieutenant Colonel King in surprise.

I guess he really did know what I was going to do, he thought.

"Remember, Major Haynes, loyalty is an admirable trait in a commanding officer up to a certain point," King noted. "Once past that point, however, it becomes a fault."

"Understood, sir," Adam replied. "What are we going to do about Captain Bowles?"

"Well, if Commander Sherman does what I asked him to do, you'll be gone before Bowles even gets a chance to make a phone call," Lieutenant Colonel King observed. "He's going to be in pre-trial confinement on bread and water for the next two weeks. After that, it will be the post commander's headache as he will no longer be assigned to my wing or your squadron. But no, he won't get a court-martial if that's what you're asking."

"Dammit," Adam said, shaking his head.

"I don't disagree with your actions on a personal level, Major," King intoned, "but on a professional level I'd advise you to not do something like that ever again. In this case you have sixteen witnesses, including myself, that saw him take the first swing. Even so, if this were the peacetime Marines, I would have had to relieve you."

Adam took a deep breath and nodded.

I have to not let my temper get the better of me, he thought. *Still, bastard had it coming.*

"Still, striking at a superior officer is something no one above us can argue with, no matter how distraught the man was," Lieutenant Colonel King stated. "I'm not wasting any more of our time on him and neither are you. Get your orders from Major Anthony and start getting your men ready to depart."

"Aye-aye, sir," Adam responded, coming to attention and saluting.

"Major Haynes, it's been a pleasure," Lieutenant Colonel King said, his features softening as he returned the salute. "Good luck to you."

"The feeling is mutual, sir," Adam replied. "Good hunting, and give Mr. Tojo and his friends my regards."

"Will do," King replied.

Adam closed the door to the wing commander's office then turned to find Major Anthony. The adjutant smiled as he handed Adam several sheets of paperwork.

"Good luck to you, Major Haynes," Anthony said.

"No, good luck to *you*, Major Anthony," Adam stated. "You guys are the one going to a war zone."

"Somehow, I think that you'll find a way to the fight yourself," Anthony said, a slight smile on his face. "I don't see you missing your chance to kill someone…again."

Adam didn't quite know how to take the adjutant's comment. He was about to respond when the phone on Anthony's desk jangled.

"I'll let you get that," Adam said, giving a wave.

Distracted by what needed to be done, he stepped out of the headquarters door and nearly ran a woman over.

"Excuse me, how clumsy of me," Adam said, reaching his hand out to keep the woman from falling. With a flash he recognized her. "Mrs. Burke, I'm sorry."

The woman considered him with her eyes. A slight smile reached her lips.

"Are you truly sorry, Major Haynes?" she sneered. "Or were you already apologizing before you realized who it was?"

I don't think either one of us want me to answer that, Adam thought, stiffening. He was about to open his mouth to take his leave of Mrs. Burke before she placed a hand on his arm.

"Major Haynes, please, a moment," the woman said. Adam thought, looking her in the eyes.

"There is talk among the wives of a move to Hawaii," Mrs. Burke said. "Can you let me know if this is true?"

Adam looked at the woman, dumbstruck.

Okay, someone here is definitely blabbing to the wrong people, he thought, stunned. *Wait, I bet I know how she got that information from...*

"No I may not," Adam snarled. "I would advise you to speak to Chaplain Grimes or your husband, Mrs. Burke."

Mrs. Burke pursed her lips.

"Chaplain Grimes is no longer speaking with me, Major Haynes," she said quietly.

Adam gave the woman a hard look, his facial expression revealing his thoughts quite clearly: *If he hadn't found you nude in another officer's home, this might not be a problem.*

"Then I do not know what you are speaking about Mrs. Burke," Adam replied simply. "I do not know what rumors are being passed among the wives, nor do I care. If you'll excuse me."

With that, Adam took his arm out from under her hand, turning to leave. To his surprise, he could hear Mrs. Burke starting to follow him.

"You know, Major Haynes, people make mistakes and things are not always as they seem," Mrs. Burke called after him. Adam could have sworn that there was an element of hurt in her voice, but he had finally had enough.

"Mrs. Burke, you are married to one of the finest pilots in my squadron, yet you chose to and continue to *fuck*," Adam said, emphasizing the word to Mrs. Burke's obvious shock at being cursed at, "another one of my pilots. That is not a mistake, but an indication of character."

"Major Haynes, please, lower your voice…" Mrs. Burke said, her face pale and voice panicked as she looked over his shoulder.

"I was told that you had gone to live with your relatives, but apparently you do not have an ounce of shame in your body," Adam continued, his voice hot. "This is not my problem, but what is my problem is that you continue to be a distraction to my squadron and my pilots. If you wish for me to 'lower my voice', then please do not accost me again until such time as you have decided to honor your marital vows."

Mrs. Burke's hand flew to her mouth as she continued looking past Adam. Wondering what she was so fixated on, Adam turned to look behind him and found himself almost face-to-face with Virginia King, the wing commander's wife, standing behind him. A tall, regal-looking woman with graying brunette hair, she was looking at Adam in shock.

"Mrs. King," he nodded. "I apologize if my language offended you."

"Oh my God, you've ruined me," Mrs. Burke said lowly, her face remaining pallid. Turning from Adam she began walking up the sidewalk, hurrying away from him as quickly as possible.

No my lady, your lack of morals and restraint ruined you, he thought venomously. *Mrs. King overhearing was simply a fortuitous occurrence.*

"Major Haynes, I see that your reputation for being a bit of a firebrand is well-deserved," Mrs. King observed quietly.

210

"Ma'am, with all due respect, she had it coming," Adam replied. Mrs. King gave a slight smile at that comment.

"I am quite sure she did," Mrs. King replied. "Have a good day, Major Haynes."

"You too, Ma'am," Adam said, tipping his hat. With that he continued on his way, whistling an old Irish drinking tune as he headed towards his squadron's barracks.

*I.J.N.S. **Musashi***
Truk Lagoon
1000 Local (2200 Eastern)
3 May (2 May)

"Our reconnaissance planes indicate that the Hermes is resting on the bottom," Vice Admiral Jisaburo Ozawa stated. "The Revenge has escaped the harbor, and no aircraft have reported her whereabouts."

You mean 'no aircraft that have survived,' Yamaguchi thought wearily. *There was a transmission that got summarily cut off from east of Java.* The *Kido Butai*'s commander could see in Ozawa's face that the man was tired, and Yamaguchi resisted the urge to look down at his own clean, pressed uniform in comparison to Ozawa's ruffled, stained one.

He has won as many carrier battles as I have, Yamaguchi thought, feeling slightly threatened. *His maneuvers off of Ceylon were brilliant, and he likely saved Fukodome from certain defeat.*

"What is the status of your air groups with the new reinforcements?" Admiral Yamamoto asked. Yamaguchi could sense the man sounded almost as tired as Ozawa.

"I recommend we send the *Hiyo* and *Junyo* back to the Home Islands," Ozawa answered quickly. "We no longer need them to stage our fighters, and if the Fifth Fleet's reports are true the enemy no longer has any carriers to employ against them."

Yamamoto closed his eyes, rubbing his temples. His missing fingers were quite obvious as he did so.

"Kondo-san is correct," he stated. "It is well past time to stop trying to kill an elephant with arrows when we have perfectly good spears at hand."

Yamaguchi stiffened at the comment.

"I mean no insult, Yamaguchi-san," Yamamoto continued wearily. "As you said earlier, it is imprudent to misuse a well balanced katana as well."

"Sir, are you going to lead the attack?" Ozawa asked, his voice awed.

"No," Yamamoto said. "His Majesty has expressedly forbidden me leading the attack or using the *Yamato* or *Musashi* in it. Kondo-san will have the *Kongo*s and the older vessels, plus cruisers carrying *Sandaburo* warheads."

Hopefully we will not lose any more of those cruisers than we already have, Yamaguchi thought.

"When will the *Ise* and *Hyuga* arrive?" Yamamoto asked Ozawa.

"I am told they will arrive in two hours," Ozawa said. "I will give them ten hours to refuel and rearm, then we will depart."

"Very good," Yamamoto said. "Make sure you get some sleep, Ozawa-san. You have done very well in this war."

Ozawa came to attention and bowed.

"Thank you, Sir," he said.

CHAPTER 6: DANCE OF THE DAMNED

Something must be left to chance; nothing is sure in a Sea Fight beyond all others—**Lord Nelson: Plan of Attack, before Trafalgar, 9 October 1805**

Pearl Harbor
0700 Local (1230 Eastern)
3 May

Yawning, Nick Cobb opened the door to his small office, his arms sore and tired from his morning calisthenics. While exercising always hurt, it also woke him up and helped him to think more clearly, an attribute that was always helpful when going over collected dispatches and news from the front. Setting down the box of dispatches, reports, and orders collected for him by the previous night's duty staff, Nick began to absently whistle.

"You know, Mr. Crosby might have something to say about you butchering his music in such a manner," Agnes said from the doorway, causing him to jump. He realized that he had not heard the woman approaching as he turned, then saw why—she was standing in her barefeet in the hallway, her shoes in her hand.

"Hello Agnes," Nick said, smiling. "I thought I was going to be the only one here for at least another half hour."

"Yes, apparently. I take it you're an early riser like the admiral?"

"Old habits die hard, and the day starts pretty early for a midshipman. Will the admiral be in today?"

"Probably not, his son's memorial service will be this

afternoon. His wife has been pretty broken up Justin's death, and I think he'll want to be with her."

Nick nodded and exhaled heavily.

"He was a very good man. I cannot believe those yellow bastards murdered his crew like that."

Agnes shrugged, her eyes sad.

"Men are very cruel," she said simply. "All of us are only a few generations removed from being barbarians, and war brings out the worst in you."

Nick raised an eyebrow.

"You seem rather philosophical on this."

"I guess I am. A woman sees and hears many things when men forget she exists."

Nick smiled.

"I find it a bit hard to believe men forget you exist."

Agnes blushed a little, smiling.

"Men often forget that secretaries have ears also," she said quickly. "And a brain that can think about what those ears have heard."

A corner of Nick's mind, what he liked to call the Cobb family's inherent paranoia, thought briefly about that statement. The look must have shown on his face, as Agnes giggled.

"Don't worry, Nick, I'm not a spy," she said.

There was the sound of a door closing at the other end of the hallway.

"But I am about to be late for getting the coffee started, so I will go."

Watching her turn to leave, Nick suddenly remembered something.

"Hey Agnes," he said, stopping her before she got too far.

"Yes?" the secretary asked.

"I'm sorry I didn't call the other night," Nick said.

Agnes grinned at him.

"That's all right, you can make it up to me by coming over tonight. Seven o'clock all right again?"

"Yes," Nick replied. "I'll even bring over some wine."

Agnes fixed him with suspicious look.

"Lieutenant Cobb, I hope you realize that I am not the type of woman to get drunk and fall into the arms of every handsome young officer who gets assigned her."

"Agnes, I don't think many 'young' officers are unlucky or stupid enough to get assigned here, and you can rest assured I have no designs on your virtue."

"Good, because my roommate would likely kill you."

Nick was about to retort when Agnes's phone rang. Sighing, the woman gave him a quick wave then started to move out at a fast walk towards her desk.

Turning back to his desk, Nick started to read the first war dispatches to come from Europe. Three paragraphs into the dispatch, he found himself reaching for the National Geographic maps he had appropriated from the intelligence staff. Pulling out a map that included Poland, he moved his finger around until he found the place he was looking for.

"Damn lieutenant, I've seen navigational officers study maps less intently," Captain Donze said from the doorway. "What has you looking at…Poland, is it?"

"Apparently the Russian attack that started two weeks ago was them putting their heads into a noose. The Germans are claiming to have over two hundred thousand men trapped between Warsaw and some city called Grodno. The Russians are strangely quiet, with no dispatches coming from Moscow save to say that the 'Fascists will be crushed upon the forge of the masses', which I'm taking to mean that that the Germans aren't stretching the truth too far."

"Decent analysis," Donze allowed, "but what does it mean to our boats?"

"That if things keep going this poorly, we might have to start sending boats to the Atlantic to try and take some of the pressure off."

Donze laughed.

"While the Germans benefited from beating the Brits, there is still quite a shortage of targets for our boats. Might want to refine that thought process before taking that in front of RAdm. Graham when he gets back."

Nick fought to keep his face neutral.

Never did cotton to being laughed at, and it's not like I asked for this job, Nick thought.

"Don't worry, Lieutenant Cobb, you'll get the hang of this yet," Donze said, putting his hand on Nick shoulder. "Besides, even I just have an opinion—the President tried so hard to help the British that we almost left our own cupboard bare, so nothing's to say he won't try and do the same for the Russians."

"But I thought you just said that there was no way to really hurt the Germans with our navy?" Nick said, confused.

"Oh, there's ways to hurt the Germans with our navy, I'm just not sure our submarines would be much use in doing it," Captain Donze replied. "Not to mention I don't fancy taking a chance on getting confused for some U-boat and blown apart by our own side."

Can't say I disagree with you on that one.

"What news from the Far East?" Donze asked, going into the box of dispatches.

"Nothing much, except apparently the ACDA command is having all sorts of fun fighting the Japanese," Nick said. The implied *"unlike us"* was almost visible as it hung in the air.

"Well hopefully they're having better luck than this

fleet has," Donze replied. "It seems like every time we leave harbor we lose a battleship, and I'm pretty sure Washington has told Vice Admiral Halsey he's to hold what we already have before we all end up in San Diego."

Or a Japanese prison camp, Nick thought grimly.

"Still can't see why we can't send them some help," the younger officer said aloud.

"Come over and check the admiral's plot today," Donze said quietly. "You'll see things aren't quite as quiet as you may think."

Nick shook his head, feeling the frustration starting to rise.

"Sir, if there's no good news I can pass on or everyone finds out things before I do, why am I here and not on a boat?" Nick asked.

"Besides the fact that you're the first officer Agnes has ever gone out of her way to talk to?" Donze replied gently, causing Nick to start to blush. "Maybe because you have the willpower to keep trying to make sense out of all this rather than bitch and moan about how you're not out on a boat. You're doing quite well for someone whose first calling isn't intelligence work, so I think we'll probably keep you here just a little bit longer."

"Sir, I've got to know more if I'm to do my job," Nick said.

"We're working on that," Donze replied. "Soon, Lieutenant Cobb, you may know more than you ever wanted to. Ignorance is sometimes truly blissful."

Nick didn't like the look on the older officer's face.

He suddenly looks like he hasn't slept in days based on what he knows, Nick thought.

"But, anyway," Donze continued, stepping in and closing the door behind him, "before we go any further, let us talk about yourself and Agnes."

Nick felt himself starting to sub-consciously come to the position of attention and stopped himself.

I can get my ass chewed about trying to date the secretary, Nick thought, *but I'll be damned if I'll act like I'm doing something wrong.*

"Agnes is a very special woman to all of us, sort of like the daughter most of us never had or haven't seen in months," Donze said flatly. "We'd just like to make sure you take due care for her reputation."

"Sir, I never had any intentions of behaving other than an officer and a gentleman," Nick replied stiffly.

"You know, Lieutenant Cobb, I honestly never doubted that," Nick said. "Others in this office, on the other hand, just wanted to make sure someone sat you down and made sure you were aware of the situation. So consider this our talk, and don't do anything that's going to have you conning a Sugar boat in Alaska."

"Aye-aye, sir," Nick replied neutrally.

Donze grimaced at Nick's reply, then nodded.

"All right, I guess I'll go ahead and leave you to your work."

Nick watched as Donze headed back into the office.

Probably could've handled that a bit better, Nick thought after a moment. *Of course, if I piss them off enough, maybe I'll get out of this damn office.*

With that he turned back to the dispatches.

We may not be able to use our boats in the North Atlantic, he thought. *But I'm reasonably certain we could convince those damn Argentineans and Brazilians they picked the wrong side. Or maybe raid some of that oiler traffic going across the Red Sea.*

Looking at the map with the German pocket, he had a sudden onrush of fear.

We just might be losing this damn war, he thought.

Maybe Captain Donze is right, and I'm probably happier not knowing the full picture.

As if on cue, his office door swung open to reveal his superior. Captain Donze strode up to his desk, his face looking like the man was in great pain as he sat a recently opened envelope on Nick's desk.

"I may have been wrong," Donze said, his voice quivering. "There might be a use for our boats."

"Sir?" Nick asked, his stomach falling as he noted the other man's agitation.

"Read it, and then bring it back to me," Donze said. "Show no one, and I mean, *no one* else."

Nick waited until the door clicked shut then pulled the dispatch out of the envelope. Trimmed in red, with TOP SECRET in bold letters at the top, the document was three pages long. Taking a deep breath, Nick started to read it. Five minutes later, he put his shaking hands down, his stomach flip flopping. Suddenly he felt the overwhelming urge to vomit, just barely grabbing the trashcan in time.

My God, the Atlantic Fleet just got its ass kicked by the Germans, Nick thought. In the aftermath of the Second Battle of Britain, with the Germans managing to acquire two complete British battleships and a third being nearly finished building, the USN had greatly reinforced its Atlantic Fleet in anticipation of fighting a great battle to reinforce Iceland.

Well it appears that battle has been fought, and we lost, Nick thought, swilling his mouth out with some of the water that was on his desk. *The **New York, Mississippi,** and **New Mexico** lost. The **South Dakota, North Carolina,** and **Washington** severely damaged. Ten thousand Army troops, at least, gone.*

Donze came back into the room, his nose wrinkling as he smelled the fresh vomit in Nick's trash can.

"Sorry Sir," Nick said, his voice raspy.

"At least they got both German carriers the next day,"

Donze said, his voice shaken.

"How…how did they get past the escort?" Nick asked.

"They showed the main fleet what they wanted to see," Donze replied. "Apparently Admiral Kimmel took off after one German heavy group and got into a gunfight with them. We're not sure if it was the French, Italians, or Germans that snuck up on the convoy in the dark that night."

Nick looked down at the dispatch, fighting the urge to crumple it.

"Does it matter, sir? Three battleships for one of theirs, plus the two carriers, is a loss," Nick observed bitterly. "Throw in the transports, cruisers, and destroyers and this was a brutal defeat. How long can they hold Iceland?"

"Don't know," Captain Donze replied. "With the reinforcements landed there shortly before the war started, plus supplies, maybe another month if the Germans don't try to take it by force."

"Sweet mother of God," Nick muttered. "We *are* losing this war."

Topeka, Kansas
1430 Local (1530 Eastern)

With the subconscious survival instincts of a combat veteran, Adam suddenly realized that the conversation in the train car had almost completely stopped. Acting as if he was still reading the *The Grapes of Wrath*, Adam used his peripheral vision to glance across the aisle at Captain West. Seeing the man looking towards the front of the compartment with wide eyes and an agape jaw, Adam exhaled.

Only one things makes most men start to look like half their brain has up and melted away, and that's a woman, Adam thought. Realizing there was no danger, he went back to reading his book.

The sound of walking high heels stopped slowly at his small booth. Putting down the book, Adam looked up into the blue eyes of a tall, The woman's shoulders were obviously muscular, indicating that she had done her fair share of hard work, but not so much so that she lost her femininity. She wore a button up emerald dress, the hem of which came just above her knee, revealing well-muscled calves underneath her stockings.

"Is this seat open?" the woman asked, her voice distinctly Midwestern and quite pleasant. Her blue eyes were friendly and intelligent, looking directly into Adam's.

"Yes, it is," Adam replied pleasantly, gesturing nonchalantly with his hand. The woman nodded, sliding into the opposite bench and placing her purse beside her. Looking at Adam, the woman extended her hand.

"My name is Norah, Norah Hedglin."

"Adam Haynes."

Good firm grip she has, Adam thought. *Wonder what she does for a living?*

The thought was interrupted by the conductor coming up to collect Norah's ticket. Nodding at Adam as he handed the ticket back, the gray, balding man went back to his seat at the front of the now moving car. Looking outside, Adam could see a group of children attempting to catch some fish in the Kansas River, the body of water apparently uncharacteristically high.

"Boys will be lucky if they get any bites," Norah observed. "I've probably fished in that river two dozen times as a kid with no luck."

"There seems to be a story behind why you were fishing as a little girl," Adam said, drawing narrowed eyes from the young woman.

"When you're the oldest of five daughters, your Dad often teaches you things he would normally have taught his sons," Norah said. "Especially when it cuts down on the grocery bill."

"Wow, that must've been a crowded house," Adam said in awe.

Norah looked at him, a faint smile on her face.

"You sound like an only child, Mr. Haynes," Norah observed.

"My parents wisely decided I was bad enough on my own, I didn't need brothers or sisters to corrupt," Adam said.

Norah laughed politely at Adam's joke.

Well, fine, I guess it wasn't all that funny, he thought.

"Well, maybe I should choose another booth to sit at after all," she said in mock seriousness. "I thought you'd be safer since you were the only man who wasn't looking at me like they were in the desert and I was the last oasis they'd see for days."

Adam shrugged self-consciously.

"I guess I was just lucky to have a Mom who made me respect women," Adam said wistfully. He took a deep breath, the wound still a bit raw. Norah picked up on his discomfort.

"I'm sorry, I didn't mean to dredge up any bad memories," she said softly, putting her hand on his. Adam heard a muted comment from the booth two behind his on the other side. He turned and favored the three sailors gawking at Norah and him with a hard look whose intent was very clear. The three men quickly turned back to their acey-deucy game, not liking what they had seen in Adam's eyes.

"So, where are you heading, Mr. Haynes?" Norah asked, pulling a small, square container out of her purse. "That is, if you can tell me."

"Please, call me Adam, and we're headed for the West Coast."

"We?"

Adam nodded his head to where his flight leaders and their wingmen were busy playing poker in the booth beside them, studiously avoiding looking at their commander and his companion.

"My companions and I," Adam said, purposefully vague. "And you?"

"Well, since I'm not in the military, I can tell you specifically I'm heading to Seattle to take a job at Bremerton Naval Yard."

"Really? What do you do?"

"Well, up until a week ago, I was a nurse, but since I double-majored as an artist, I'm going to be doing drawing for the Navy."

Adam sat back, impressed.

"Surprised that a woman is that adventurous, or that I have a double major in college?" Norah asked, her voice neutral.

Okay, someone has a bit of a chip on her shoulder...probably for good reason, Adam thought.

"Impressed, actually," Adam responded amicably. "My mother was good friends with one of the few female doctors in New York, so I know a bit about nursing."

It was Norah's turn to be surprised, leaning back and crossing her legs. Adam noticed her hand was still on the table, not quite on his anymore but not back in her lap. Looking at her face, he guessed her to be only a couple years younger than him, and he noted that she did not have a wedding band or jewelry of any kind on.

"Well, she must be a truly impressive woman," Norah

"Yes, she was...she passed away a few months ago," Adam said quietly. "I never really got a chance to say goodbye."

Norah brought her hand up to her mouth in shock.

"I'm so sorry," she said. "I should have realized

when you were uncomfortable earlier, but I didn't realize it was that recent."

"That's okay, it's not like I'm wearing a black band or anything that would give people a clue," Adam replied, gesturing towards his arm. "She lived a full, wonderful life and was surrounded by people who loved her when she passed away."

I'll just leave out the part about her drowning in her own fluid, Adam thought quietly. *No cancer is a pleasant way to go, and I'll take a one way ticket down in a blazing fighter over that any day.*

"If I might ask, what were you doing in the Orient? I've always wanted to go there, but since the Japanese have started being such barbarians I've decided that can be something I do when I'm old and gray."

"What he was doing was killing said Japanese, or at least, that's what most people seem to believe," a voice with a soft Texas drawl said from over Adam's shoulder. Adam turned around in his seat, recognizing the voice but thinking that he had to be imagining things. One glance told him that he was not, as the person standing by his booth seemingly had everyone's attention.

"Well, well, that's a look that's not on your face that often," Trevor Fesselier, former Eagle Squadron member, said maliciously. "Why, one would almost think you expected to never see me alive again...of course, as you can see, you weren't far off."

Adam felt his stomach churn as he looked at the man standing before him. The man was wearing the uniform of an Army Air Corps captain, and that was the only thing that was well put together about him.

I know Connor caught a raw deal, but Fesslier's living proof that things could have been worse, Adam thought. Fesslier's face was horribly disfigured, the overwhelming majority of it disfigured burn tissue to include the misshapen lump of cartilage that passed for his nose. The only clear skin was that around his pale blue eyes, the outline clearly indicating that the man had been wearing goggles when the rest of him was literally put to the torch. His once full head of hair was nothing but several large tufts and patches of pale, thin white material that looked like thin pieces of pasta.

"My God," someone muttered, then began retching.

"Trevor," Adam said, nodding slowly, his face emotionless.

"My, my, how civil of you, considering that I wasn't good enough to fly with the last time you saw me," Trevor said. "How nice of you to deign to fly with us 'bloody colonials' again."

Adam could feel several of his men's eyes upon him. Opening his mouth, he was saved by another Army officer coming up behind Trevor. Looking, he recognized the other officer as one Paul Fussner, another former Eagle Squadron member. The man was also wearing an Army Air Corps uniform, but his was decorated with several ribbons, to include the French *Cross De Guerre* and British Distinguished Flying Cross.

"Captain Fesselier, I thought I made it quite clear that you were *not* to seek out Mist...Major Haynes," Fussner snapped, his voice harsh.

"Sir, I was just passing through to the dining car when I saw him..."

"Captain, I am giving you a direct damn order...return to our car *immediately*, is that clear?!" Fussner barked. Trevor snapped to attention, his scars stretching visibly as his jaw muscles clenched.

"Yes, sir!"

With that, the ruined man moved past Fussner towards the train's engine, disappearing quickly into the next car. Fussner watched him go, then turned back towards

225

Adam.

"Glad to see you made it out of England okay," Fussner said quietly, extending his hand. "Heard you were in the Dutch East Indies with your Poles...surprised to see you here."

Adam took Fussner's hand, clasping it firmly.

"I had to come back to take care of some family business."

"Oh. Well, I was heading back towards the dining hall if you care to join me for a soda or something, catch up on what's happened since London."

"Be delighted," Adam said, standing up. He turned towards Norah.

"Save my seat?" he asked, surprised to see the woman completely unshaken.

"Actually, I think a soda would seem quite nice right now," she replied, gathering her things. "It's not often I get to meet a man who apparently inspires great emotion in others."

Adam didn't quite know how to take that, but stepped aside to let Norah pass in front of him. Feeling a presence at his back, he turned to see Captains West and Burke filling the aisle behind him.

"I take it you guys are suddenly thirsty also?" Adam asked quietly. The two men looked at him, not knowing what to say.

"Fine, your sodas are on me. Let's go."

Five minutes later, after introductions were made all around, Adam turned to Fussner.

"Okay, so tell me just how Trevor makes it out of a blazing *Hurricane* in less than four thousand feet," Adam said. "Because that's the last I saw of him."

"Uh, sir, not to interrupt, but could we start a little

further back?" Captain West asked. "Because I know myself and the rest of the squadron have been curious since the first day we met Major Haynes."

Fussner laughed as Adam gave West a baleful gaze.

"He's got you there, Major Haynes," Norah chimed in. "Especially since the only hurricanes I know of happen off Florida, occasionally New York."

Adam shook his head, exhaling slowly.

"I arrived in England just after the Brits beat the Krauts the first time," Adam started. "Let me tell you, that was a great time to be a fighter pilot."

"I'll bet," Norah observed, narrowing her eyes at his tone.

Okay, not the best foot to start off on, Adam thought. *She's apparently more worldly than I thought.*

"Not that Adam would know, seeing as how he never left Biggin Hill," Fussner chimed in. Norah gave both Adam and him a skeptical look.

"No, seriously, I am telling the truth," Fussner said, holding up his hands. "He got so bad into asking questions that the station chief started to think he was a spy."

"I was just a little focused," Adam admitted sheepishly. "After Spain, I had a bit of a grudge…"

"Spain?!" West and Burke asked simultaneously. "As in, the Spanish Civil War?"

Fussner looked at Adam a bit amused.

"Yes, your squadron leader's gotten around quite a bit. Bet he didn't tell you that he had a price on his head either."

"What?!" Norah, West, and Burke asked simultaneously.

"You're getting ahead of the story," Adam snapped, glaring at Fussner.

"Okay, this is already getting a bit hard for this

Kansas girl to understand," Norah said. She reached in her purse and pulled out a case. Opening it, she pulled out a stick of chewing gum then offered pieces all around. Getting no takers, she put the gum back into her purse.

"Most women keep cigarettes in a case like that," Adam observed.

"They stink, and they make your teeth look funny," Norah replied. "I can't think of a *good* reason to smoke, and that's enough bad ones right there for me not to. But we're not talking about me, are we Mr. 'Price on His Head'?"

Adam gave Fussner another glare, then continued.

"The reason I was with the Poles was I had the good fortune to run into the former British military attache to Spain," Adam said simply.

"Damn sir, just how old are you?" West asked, then realized he may have overstepped himself. "I mean, Spain started a while back."

"I started flying early, Captain West," Adam said. "It helps to be young and idealistic when going off to war, especially one as chaotic as Spain. I'll be twenty-nine in June."

"How many kills did you have in Spain, anyway?" Fussner asked. "Just wondering, as all the sudden it becomes crystal clear why you did so well over Britain."

"Six confirmed, two probable," Adam said quietly. "I got out of there just as the Condor Legion was starting to make it really dangerous to be a Republican pilot."

"So, you weren't just spouting from the hip when you came in that first day," Burke said in quiet amazement.

"I am not a pretentious man, as Major Fussner can attest to," Adam said.

"Ain't that the truth," Fussner said. "Most men would have mentioned that he has a total of twenty-one kills if you add the ones in Spain. More if those rumors about you in the Dutch East Indies are true."

"Twenty-five at last count," Adam continued, starting to blush.

"Holy sh...crap," West said, mindful of their female companion. "You're only one behind Rickenbacker."

"Problem is, our government probably won't recognize most of those kills since he was technically a mercenary for several of them," Fussner said.

"What's more incredible is that he had fifteen kills during the Second Battle," Burke observed. "Everything I've read said that the Germans gained control of the air in the first two months."

"Not quite," Adam said. "Since the Eagles weren't expected to get into action until after 1 January, and I was obviously a man of prior experience, the RAF decided for some odd reason to billet me with the Poles."

"The Poles?" Burke asked.

"No. 303 squadron, moved up to Biggin Hill just after I arrived. Actually, I guess it was because I was fluent in French, which some of the Poles spoke."

"They didn't speak English?!" Norah asked. "How odd."

"Well, let me tell you, there was nothing wrong with their fighting spirit," Adam said. "I don't know how the Germans rolled that country as quick as they did if all of them were that crazy."

"Russians stabbed them in the back," Fussner observed.

"Anyway, I had barely been there two months when Bomber Command up and killed Hitler," Adam stated. "Bad move, that."

"Ah, but no one knew that at the time," Fussner said. "Of course, the British were quick to jump on the idea of a truce when Himmler offered one."

"Churchill tried to warn people the Germans weren't happy about Adolph getting killed," Adam said. "Should have known better when we found out Goering committed suicide. Supposedly."

"You had to admit, the only thing the Brits could do was fly some cross-Channel missions in order to get pilots," Fussner said. "Not one of Sholto Douglas's brighter ideas, God rest his soul."

"As far as I'm concerned, I hope the man's rotting in Hell along with Leigh-Mallory," Adam responded, getting a shocked look from Fussner. "That 'experience' was not worth it, especially come Spring '42."

"We'll just have to agree to disagree on that one," Fussner replied, waving his hand dismissively. "Regardless, it was during this time that Major Haynes and I first met. A contingent of us Eagles had heard about some crazy American flying with the Poles and figured we'd ask him to come join us."

"Of course, you guys were flying *Hurricanes*, so the answer was most certainly not," Adam replied, snorting in derision.

"The *Hurricane* is a type of British fighter," Fussner said, suddenly remembering that Norah didn't know what they were talking about.

"What were you flying?" Norah asked, turning to Adam.

"*Spitfires*," Adam replied.

"A *Hurricane* is a bit…" Fussner began.

Adam snorted at that.

"…slower than a *Spitfire*, but it could take more punishment," Fussner concluded. "It was also a steadier gun platform."

"You generally tried to avoid German fighters in a *Hurricane*," Adam said. "Of course, that's sorta hard to do when they're all faster than you."

"So is that the only reason you didn't join the Americans, sir?" Burke asked, sensing something else in Adam's tone. Fussner and Adam gave each other a short look, Adam glancing away uncomfortably.

"No, that's not the only reason," Fussner said finally. "But I'm not going to do Major Haynes's talking for him."

"Anyway, back to the original topic," Adam said. "Trevor."

"Yes, Trevor...well, gents, the Germans kicked off their big offensive in March," Fussner said. "I wasn't around for the First Battle, but what veterans there were told us the Second Battle of Britain started off worse than its predecessor was at its peak...and then it got really bad."

"We were all introduced to the Focke-Wulf 190, a.k.a. the 'Butcher Bird'," Adam said. "That and Me-109s with extended fuel tanks."

"Yeah, that was an unfortunate shock," Fussner said. "The intelligence boffins didn't want to believe us on either one, not until they started dumping their tanks over shore on their way inland and someone shot one of the damn 190s down almost right on top of Fighter Command HQ."

"But by that time things were already heading into the crapper," Adam followed up, holding his soda as he saw the events in his mind's eye. "Next thing you know, we can't even fly off of any Fighter Command airfields in southern England without a good chance of meeting Luftwaffe before our wheels are up."

"So we were forced to disperse, which is when we saw Adam again," Fussner said.

"We were scrambled out of Eastchurch, one flight of *Spitfires* and two of *Hurricanes*," Adam started, his jaw clenched. "For once we got the altitude advantage on the Germans, catching them as they were descending to strafe the field."

"Quite a dustup," Fussner said. "That's where Trevor got clobbered, and I nearly got killed myself if not for Adam."

"I never saw those Messerschmitts before they were all over you guys," Adam said sadly. "If it gives Trevor any solace, the bastard who got him is no longer with us."

"I don't think it will. It's his own damn fault for not flying with a damn flame hood under his helmet," Fussner said quietly. "His *Hurricane* landed in a sheep pond, which is why he's still alive."

"Jesus," Adam said. "Why was he flying one of the ones without self-sealing tanks anyway?"

"What are self-sealing tanks?" Norah asked Adam. "That seems a bit abnormal for putting fuel into."

"Self-sealing tanks are lined with vulcanized rubber," Adam said. "When they get penetrated, the rubber seals the hole, keeping the fuel from streaming out and turning the plane into a torch. It has nothing to do with how the fuel goes in."

"The *Hurricane* has a fuel tank in front of the pilot," Fussner said, seeing Norah starting to understand. "During the Battles of France and Britain, after many, many pilots were getting burned to death in their cockpits, the RAF supposedly modified all the existing *Hurricanes* to keep that tank from going up like a torch."

"Oh my word," Norah gasped, the mental image playing in her mind. "That's horrible."

"Yeah, Trevor's lucky to be alive, both because of the crash and the fact that the mud and water smothered the flames without drowning him."

Lucky to be alive is in the eye of the beholder, Adam thought.

"So what happened to you after the Treaty of Kent?" Fussner asked.

"I caught a ship out of Portsmouth to South Africa," Adam said. "From there, caught a South African tramp steamer to the Dutch East Indies—where I got hunted down by a man my father had sent to tell me Mom was dying."

"Jesus," Fussner said. "I'm sorry."

"Everyone's sorry," Adam said sadly, "which makes no sense, since they didn't give her the cancer."

Fussner looked at him uncomfortably.

"Sorry, that was awfully poor of me," Adam apologized. "I guess I just took it for granted that she'd always be there. So what's the Army Air Corps setup?"

"They're bringing a bunch of us Eagles together, yes," Fussner said, giving Norah a sidelong glance.

Ah, don't want to take a chance that our lovely Miss Norah might be a German spy, Adam thought.

"Let me guess—you're joining Don Blakeslee?" Adam asked with a smile.

"How did you know that?" Fussner asked, raising an eyebrow. Adam quickly told Fussner of his time waiting for the United States to allow him back into the country.

"Lot of sleeping, lot of poker playing," Adam said. "All the time wondering if my mother was going to die before I got home."

Fussner looked at his watch.

"Not to cut this short," Fussner said, "but that statement about sleep reminded me I should catch some shuteye before we get to Denver." With that, Fussner stood up, Adam sliding out of his chair right behind the Army officer. He extended his hand.

"Good luck to you," Adam said solemnly.

"You too, Major Haynes. Gentlemen," Fussner said, nodding to Burke and West.

"Sir," the two men replied nearly in unison. Looking at Norah still sitting down, then at Adam, they both nodded in Norah's direction.

"Nice meeting you ma'am," Burke said. "We've got to get back to our game."

"The pleasure is mutual," Norah said, smiling.

The three other pilots left, leaving Adam and Norah sitting alone. The dining car was starting to pick up in business, but Adam decided to go ahead and buy Norah another soda. He returned with it a moment later, the two of them staring at the plains of Kansas passing by. Adam looked off to the south and noticed the sky darkening, a massive thunderhead starting to form.

"You know, I've read the *Wizard of Oz...*" he started.

"I'm sure it'll miss us," Norah said, stopping him. There was another moment of silence as they watched the storm continuing to build. Finally, Norah turned to him, looking him square in the eyes.

"Forgive me for prying, and since there's a chance we'll never ever speak again I understand if you don't want to tell me," Norah started with a rush. "I just want to know what you said when the Americans asked you to join them in Britain."

Adam looked away, staring out into the Plains. As he looked out the window, his eyes started to glisten.

"That I didn't have the time or the inclination to teach and fly with a whole bunch of men who were going to be dead in six months anyway," Adam said quietly. "It's a statement that's haunted me ever since because I was right—out of the six men who came to see me, only Fussner and Trevor are still alive. Out of the three squadrons of Eagles that started the Second Battle, only seven of the original pilots remain."

Norah placed her hands on Adam's, startling him into looking at her.

"I'm no expert at fighting," Norah said. "I can't even beat up my sisters, much less shoot at some men I don't know. But I do know that those sound like pretty long odds, and I don't think you would've made much of a difference in them."

"I might've been able to do more, maybe taught them something," Adam said. "I was too focused on killing Germans to care…that's why I wanted to stay with the Poles so badly."

"Why do you hate Germans so much?" Norah asked, squeezing his hands as she looked into his face. Adam found himself wanting to tell her to mind her own business, then stopped.

"Do they teach you interrogation in nursing school?" he asked quietly.

"Usually they give us a scalpel," Norah joked quietly, causing Adam to laugh. "Seriously, they teach us to recognize pain, and you seem to have a lot of it."

"You're going to think me a bit strange," Adam replied.

"You have a price on your head, and you appear to be addicted to danger. Besides, you're talking to a woman who is traveling across the country to draw little lines on paper…I don't think I can comment much on strange."

"I loved a woman…" Adam started, then swallowed hard. "Her name was Zepherine, and she was a nurse. She and I were engaged, and we always joked we'd get married in Paris once all the insanity in Spain was over."

Once more, he looked out onto the Plains, this time with the tears actually starting to roll down his face. He angrily wiped them away.

"You know, it's all right for a man to cry," Norah said gently, glad to see they were still somewhat away from everyone.

"Oh, I know," Adam said. "My mother used to always yell at my Dad when he told me men don't cry. She'd remind him that it was a toss up who cried more when

235

I was born, me or Dad."

Norah laughed along with Adam, waiting for him to finish.

"Well, on April 26, 1937, Zepherine was in Guernica, Spain, at the hospital," Adam seethed. "It was clearly marked with Red Crosses, the town all but defenseless, but the Germans didn't care."

Adam could hear the bitterness in his own voice, the anger that always began to creep in when he thought about that day. He had been on his way to the town to tell Zepherine she needed to leave, to escape, to flee with him out of Spain.

Probably some folks who would have thought me a coward, Adam thought. *But the damn Fascists were starting to force us back towards Balboa.* To his utter regret, he had gotten to the outskirts of town just in time to see the air raid in all its awesome glory.

"The Germans razed the town," Adam continued. "Once their fighters had cleared the air, they came down to strafe, killing everyone, even women and children, in the streets. Only darkness stopped them from continuing to murder people from the skies."

"Adam, you're hurting my hands," Norah said calmly. Adam looked down, shocked, and realized that he had begun to grip with all his strength.

You would think that I would learn to stop holding a woman's hand when I'm talking about Germans, he thought, letting go and starting to pull his hands back in shame. Norah reached out with surprising speed and gripped them.

"It's all right," she said soothingly.

Adam could see the chaotic scene in his mind's eye, the flames leaping and throwing chaotic shadows in the gloom, the smoke choking his lungs as he desperately searched for his beloved. It was well after midnight when he had finally found her, her body amongst a score of others mowed down by machine gun fire, splayed in the crazy manner common to violent, sudden death.

I should have known better than to turn her over. Zepherdine's face had been down to the street, having fallen naturally into the hollow of her arm. Foolishly, Adam had rolled her over, meaning his last memory of her would be the ruin that the German bullets had made of the left side of her face. Adam had personally carried her to the graveyard that night, paying a local priest to perform the Catholic service over her grave.

"How much longer did you stay?" Norah asked.

"I didn't have any kills then," Adam said quietly. "I had damaged a few, gotten a couple off of Frank Tinker's tail, but not killed any of my own."

Looking away from the window, he looked directly at Norah, his face a terrible thing.

"That changed," Adam explained grimly. "I flew as much as possible over the next three weeks, until I wouldn't be able to get out of my aircraft at night because my arms were spaghetti. I flew mainly ground attack missions because I figured I'd kill more of the bastards that way."

"What made you stop?" Norah asked, her voice trembling slightly at Adam's transformation.

"Tinker made me stop, actually," Adam said. "Part of it was because I finally passed him in total number of kills, most of it was because there was only one other way my little campaign was going to end."

"I'm surprised you stopped when he told you to," Norah observed.

"Funny thing about being told if you'd be shot if you ever stepped into a cockpit again, it tends to persuade a person to stop doing so really quick," Adam said. "In retrospect, Tinker saved my life. Or at least, I ended up better than he did."

"What do you mean?" Norah asked.

"Poor man shot himself after Spain fell to Franco's men," Adam said. "Guess he couldn't handle it. I just came home and nearly got myself disinherited by my father."

"What?"

"My father had lots of German contacts," Adam said. "He was enthralled by what Hitler did in bringing Germany out of the ashes, so he started helping those idiots in early '38, just after I got home."

From the look on her face, I think she can figure out why that might not have gone over well, Adam thought. In a way, it was fortunate that Adam had relatives out in California, because going to visit them was likely the only thing that had kept him and his father from coming to blows. Seth Haynes had not approved of his son's romantic adventurism in the first place, much less when it started to interfere with the *his* business dealings.

"Do you and your father still talk to one another?" Norah asked.

"We buried the hatchet when I was finally let back into the country," Adam said. "The *Lufwaffe* firebombing and gassing London...well, that really put things in perspective for him."

"Did you see London after the Germans bombed it?" Norah asked.

"Not much," Adam stated, feeling uncomfortable as he remembered whom he'd been with at the time. "Tried to find a friend's mother and wife, but there was too much fire and gas."

"I still can't believe the Royal Family fled," Norah observed.

"I can't believe the King is dead," Adam replied wearily. "At least, minus South Africa, almost everyone decided to fight on."

"Judging from Mr. Churchill's speeches," Norah said, "the Commonwealth won't rest until they see Germany destroyed."

Well Churchill says a lot of things, Adam thought. *They should have listened to him during those nine months of 'peace' after Hitler died.*

"Lots of war to fight yet," Adam allowed. "opefully the Russians are able to hold on, or good ol' Winston can give all the speeches he wants."

"You seem skeptical," Norah snorted.

"With the Vichies throwing in with the Krauts, that's a lot of ground to fight over to Germany," Adam replied.

"But you just mentioned the Russians…" Norah began.

"I had a chance to talk with a very interesting gentleman, a White Russian, on the way to South Africa from Great Britain," Adam said, his tone forlorn. "Some of the things he told me were going on in Russia, with Stalin…let's just say allying with that man's like cutting a deal with the Devil himself."

"Now *you* sound like Mr. Churchill," Norah laughed.

"Mr. Churchill's no dummy," Adam retorted. "I think he knows Mr. Stalin probably has more blood on his hands than Hitler, the former'ss just a little more keen on keeping things in house."

Norah sighed, shaking her head.

"I think that you have led a very interesting life, Adam, and we better get back to our booth before people start to think we've snuck back to the sleeper cars," Norah said.

Adam gave her a wry look.

"That would be mighty forward of me, I think," Adam stated.

"And very foolish to attempt," Norah glowered.

Hey, you brought it up, Adam thought.

"Do you play gin rummy?" Adam said, changing the

subject. "I've got a deck of cards in my travel bag."

"No, but I'm willing to learn," Norah said. "I think we've got a couple more days on this train ride until Seattle."

"Yeah, at least," Adam said, standing up to pull out Norah's chair. "But I guess it beats being chased over southern England by a bunch of murderous Germans."

"I would certainly hope my company wasn't that trying," Norah snickered, giving Adam a hard look.

"No, not *that* trying," Adam said, then quickly dodged her playful swat at him. The two of them headed back towards the car, Adam walking behind Norah.

Nope, not that trying at all…and the view is certainly better, Adam thought.

Houston
1500 Local (0300 Eastern)
5 May (4 May)

"Well, that tears it," Captain Wallace said, reading the signal being relayed from the *Hobart*, the next ship forward in the Allied formation. "XO, looks like we'll be seeing action in about two hours."

The signal was quite brief, it ending before 'action' had been out of Captain Wallace's mouth.

ENEMY SIGHTED, 60 MILES N, NW. ALL SHIPS FOLLOW LEADERS, PHILLIPS SENDS.

"About damn time, I'm tired of dodging air strikes," Jacob observed. "Let's give these yellow bastards a kick in the teeth so they'll go home."

Dumb bastards should've came after they bombed Surabaya, Jacob thought. *Although they definitely do seem to be giving it the college try today.*

The day so far had been a festival of dodging almost hourly air attacks, most of which had been relatively inaccurate thanks to the intermittent cloud cover. Judging from the radio traffic, there was a significant aerial battle occurring both to the west and east, with fighters from both sides feasting on the bombers attempting attack the respective fleets. All Jacob knew was that the Japanese were not their normally accurate self, which was quite all right with him, especially since there had been none of the dreaded torpedo bombers.

I hope they're out of torpedoes, because they've more than made their money with those attacks, Jacob thought. *Not that the **Revenge** handled being bombed very well.* While the elderly British battleship hadn't succumbed, her hasty underwater patch job had started to give way before she'd made it to the south side of Java. The last Jacob had heard, it was questionable whether the ship would make it to Ceylon or Sydney. As for the *Hermes*, her own crew and a Royal Navy repair vessel were desperately trying to patch her damage, but it was not looking good for the venerable carrier if Phillips' force failed to turn back the Japanese invasion thrust.

"Sir, the vessel is ready in all respects," Jacob said. "We've got enough fuel and ammo to get through this fight, probably another if it comes to that."

Although I really don't think this is going to be a two step brawl, Jacob thought. *This has the air of a grand finale.* The reconnaissance reports, while confused, were pretty clear about one thing: Japanese battleships were coming down the Makassar Strait in numbers. To meet them, Admiral Phillips had consolidated all of his heavy units south of Java, then brought them north into the Java Sea under the aegis of land-based air cover.

Then again, as slow as those old battleships are, we might have to two step just so they can get close to the enemy, Jacob thought, annoyed. In a concession to the battlecruisers *Repulse* and *Renown*'s thin armor and acknowledgment of the IJN battleline's superior speed, Phillips had split his force into two groups. The faster vessels he placed under the control of Vice Admiral Crutchley aboard the *Prince of Wales*. Crutchley's reputation, stemming from the Victoria Cross he had won in the First World War and the Battle of Narvik, had many of the Allied captains believing the fight would be over by afternoon.

Crutchley is probably glad to be finally engaging in a daylight fight, Jacob thought. *Nightfall has not been friendly to the Royal Australian Navy.*

"I cannot believe that Admiral King specifically ordered Admiral Hart ashore," Captain Wallace observed, startling Jacob.

Then again, we are both looking at the same fast ships and wondering if we're going to be fast enough, Jacob thought.

"I think he's still upset about Rear Admiral Glassford's death," Jacob stated.

Or put less diplomatically, Admiral King thinks there are too many star-wearing corpses in this war already, Jacob thought uncharitably. *With that idiot Admiral Jensen and most of his staff getting killed, that Army bastard riding the Shark to the bottom, plus Rear Admiral Glassford, the Navy's not going to run out of ship names for the next decade.*

"This is what a naval officer lives for, and he's earned this right," Wallace stated. "I don't think Admiral Phillips was very happy to be overruled."

Guess Jacob thought. *Those chimps alone are going to be two or three perfectly good destroyers with bad names.*

"At least it's not that damn Dutchman again," Jacob muttered lowly. Captain Wallace gave him a glance, staring back into the bridge to make sure that the Dutch liaison officer, a commander from Admiral Helfrich's staff, hadn't overheard him.

"XO, it's probably time for you to head back to Battle Two," Wallace said tightly. "Try to keep your opinions of our hosts to yourself."

"Aye-aye, sir," Jacob said, saluting. "Good luck to you."

"And to you, XO," Wallace replied, his face softening somewhat. "Try not to get any more stitches."

"Sir, you try not to get a splinter haircut," Jacob said, heading down to the main deck. He turned and looked as the *Houston* began to turn to starboard, following the *Hobart.* As the cruiser went through her maneuvers, Jacob had an opportunity to take in the group of slower vessels.

Even if they're more than old enough to vote, they look impressive enough, Jacob allowed. Leading the line was the H.M.C.S. *Ramilles,* sister ship to the *Revenge*, and likewise armed with a main battery of eight 15-inch guns. Next in line were the identically armed *Valiant,* Phillips' flag, and *Malaya,* both of the slightly faster *Queen Elizabeth*-class. Trailing the three battleships were the heavy cruisers *Cornwall* and *Devonshire*, while nine destroyers circled protectively. As Jacob watched, the Commonwealth vessels all began running up their massive battle pennants, the famous "red duster, white ensign."

Well, can't have them showing us up, can we, Jacob thought. Turning, he was about to grab a runner when he heard the sound of rustling cloth. Looking up, he saw the largest Stars and Stripes he had ever seen making its own way up the *Houston's* flagstaff. For a moment he felt a lump in his throat, then forced it out with a loud cheer. Startled at the uncharacteristic display of emotion from their XO, the men around him were silent, until several of the older, saltier chiefs began shouting in turn. In moments, the *Houston's* top decks were pandemonium.

Somewhere up there, Jones, Farragut, and Decatur are watching with a smile on their face, Jacob thought. *This is the navy that they built, and we will do them proud today.*

Continuing aft, Jacob suddenly realized the men were breaking into 'Anchors Aweigh'. As he entered Battle Two, he could see several of the older hands eyes glistening with pride, and fought down his own tears by picking up his binoculars to look aft over the ships behind the *Houston.*

The fast group was arranged with the *Hobart* in the van, followed by the *Houston*, the ever pugnacious *Exeter*, the twin battlecruisers *Renown* and *Repulse*, the *Prince of Wales*, the damaged *De Ruyter*, *Achilles*, *Ajax*, and finally the H.M.C.S. *Dorsetshire*. The destroyer screen, arrayed so as to protect against any interfering submarines, consisted of the Dutch destroyers *Piet Hein*, *Van Ghent*, the Commonwealth and Australian destroyers *Express, Eclipse, Encounter, Intrepid, Arunta, Jupiter*, and the new American arrivals *Tucker* and *Smith.*

*We **are** going to kick those bastards' asses today*, Jacob thought. *Then it'll be the Krauts' turn.*

If Jacob could have been sixty-five miles away, he might have had a little less confidence. The IJN battleline had been placed under the command of Vice Admiral Nobutake Kondo, commander of the Third Japanese Fleet. Unlike the unfortunate Admrial Hart, Kondo had not been prevented from placing his flag on the battleship *Mutsu.* Like Phillips, Kondo had disposed the battleline into two groups based on speed. Steaming south, his westernmost column consisted of the fast battleships *Kongo, Hiei, Haruna*, and *Kirishima* in that order, each with eight 14-inch guns. They were supported by the *Suzuya, Atago, Aoba, Kinugasa, Furutaka*, and *Kako*, all 8-inch heavy cruisers.

In the slower column were IJN's older battleships.

Leading the column were the sisters *Ise* and *Hyuga,* with their archaic arrangement of twelve 14-inch guns. Behind them were the similarly armed *Fuso* and *Yamashiro*, followed by the more heavily armed and armored 16-inch *Mutsu* and *Nagato*. Screening this massive force were sixteen destroyers and four light cruisers, the excess light forces being gained by leaving the transports of the invasion force in Balikpapan with only six destroyers as their escort.

The Japanese plan was quite simple, a miniature of the plan they had intended to utilize against the American Pacific Fleet in their planned 'Decisive Battle'. First, the *Kongo*s, cruisers, and destroyers would press forward to gain contact with Phillips' fleet. Upon making contact, the fast forces would conduct a long-range torpedo attack utilizing their Long Lances, the intent to cause confusion and attrit the enemy's heavy forces. Once the enemy fleet was in disarray, the slower Japanese battleships would close and complete the destruction of the Allied forces utilizing their superior firepower. Seemingly simple on paper, in reality it would require a delicate combination of timing, accuracy, and luck to succeed.

With hoisted flags and hastily blinkered signals, the plan was set into motion. Smoke pouring from their stacks, the four *Kongos* and all Japanese light forces except for six destroyers surged forward, accelerating to twenty-six knots. With only limited intelligence on each others' forces due to the great violence being wrought in the skies above, Phillips and Kondo moved towards each other to being the Second Battle of the Java Sea.

In the end, Captain Wallace was off in his estimate of time. The two columns had been steaming along at a relatively stately twenty knots for just over an hour when the first contact was made.

"Lookouts report smoke bearing three four oh,"

Seaman First Class Donald Dewey, Wedgewood's replacement, intoned from the back of Battle Two.

"Well, either that was the quickest two hours I've ever experienced, or our opposite numbers are as eager to get this over with as we are," Jacob muttered, looking at his watch. He grabbed his steel helmet, putting the pan-shaped headgear on and making sure everyone else did the same.

"Damage control parties ready in all respects, sir," Chief Roberts said. Jacob started to reply, suddenly finding his mouth dry. Swallowing quickly, he nodded.

"Range thirty-five thousand yards to enemy contacts," Dewey sang out. "*Prince of Wales* is ordering an increase in speed and preparation to come to port to unmask all guns."

Jacob nodded, getting a mental image of the geometry in his head. If the faster column came to port, that would give the slower vessels room to turn in column behind them. When complete, the turn would establish a single long line of Allied heavy guns, with the destroyers and Commonwealth cruisers going forward to conduct torpedo attacks.

Best to keep the plan simple, I guess, Jacob thought. *We're nowhere close to a well-honed squadron.* He felt the *Houston* starting to heel over, not her sharpest turn but definitely not as stately as a peacetime column maneuver.

"Range is thirty-two thousand yards, contacts are tentatively identified as four battleships and six heavy cruisers."

Jacob, turning, saw the *Houston's* aft turret trained as far forward as it could go, the guns elevated near maximum. Looking back, he saw the *Exeter's* forward turrets in the same condition, then more distantly the *Renown, Repulse,* and *Prince of Wales.* As the *Houston* came around he could see the aft turret starting to traverse, tracking the approaching Japanese.

For their part, the Japanese had no interest in

reenacting the German High Seas Fleet at the Battle of Jutland. As Jacob brought up his binoculars he could see the lead vessels starting to change their orientation to present their broadsides, the *Kongos* discernibly larger than their accompanying vessels. Behind the four fast battleships, the Japanese heavy cruisers began to make smoke as they increased speed, their own turn more gradual so that they did not foul their larger brethrens firing solution. Listening to the talker chanting down the range, Jacob suddenly felt his sphincter tightening and his mouth turning to cotton.

"Range is twenty-eight thousand yards, all ships are cleared to fire," Dewey said with finality.

Jacob nodded, imagining Commander Sloan going through the computations up in the *Houston's* director. Long range daylight gunnery was the U.S. Navy's standard doctrine, the one event towards which all of its equipment, training, and tactics were geared towards. Whereas the night fights had been confusing, bizarre affairs, this was what Jacob and every other officer and sailor aboard the *Houston* had trained for.

If this is supposed to be normal, then why do I feel like a nervous groom on his wedding night? Jacob thought.

Houston's firing gong began to ring. Looking at the aft turret's orientation, Jacob winced and ducked back inside Battle Two. He was just in time, as with a massive roar all nine of *Houston's* rifles spoke, the vessel shaking with the force.

That fucking idiot Sloan fired a full broadside! Jacob was beside himself in fury as he brought his binoculars up. Standard practice was to stagger the fire of a vessel's guns when the range was unknown, the intent being to shorten the amount of time between ranging shots. By firing a full broadside, the *Houston's* turrets would still be in the midst of their firing cycle when the first shells landed. This meant if Sloan had to make a radical range correction the process would take far more time.

I'm going to wring his neck, Jacob thought, stepping up to the spotting glasses on the bridge rail. Dimly, he heard several more blasts, and paused to look astern at the extended Allied line. The *Renown* and *Prince of Wales* had been the only other ships to fire, the other vessels either unable to induce the necessary elevation or unwilling to spend the rounds. Jacob turned back to the glasses just as he heard the sound of cheering from inside the aft turret.

"Hit! We got a hit!" Dewey shouted excitedly a moment later, nearly jumping out of his chair in his excitement.

"Good, now sit down!" Chief Roberts barked, pushing firmly on the young sailor's shoulder.

Jacob could not believe his eyes. *Houston's* initial salvo had been on in range, speed, and course through either dumb luck or Sloan's skill. Smoke poured from just abaft the *Suzuya's* bridge. .

"I can't believe it! We've got to be the luckiest bastards in this fleet," Jacob shouted.

The next thirty seconds swiftly disproved Jacob's nascent hypothesis, as the *Renown* demonstrated why she'd been a former Home Fleet gunnery champion. Like Sloan, her gunnery officer had fired a full broadside, having learned to rely on the range and bearing provided by the modern fire-control radar located on her mainmast. Even with the technological addition, hitting on the first salvo at twenty-seven thousand yards was a feat previously unheard of in naval warfare.

While the hitting was not as much a matter of luck as a testament to *Renown's* greater experience, the placement was enough to convince a vocal atheist of divine intervention. Almost twenty-six years before, at the Battle of Jutland, the Royal Navy's ammunition had been a critical reason large portions of the German fleet had escaped. Well aware of this fact, the Royal Navy had spent much of the intervening time period refining and developing new shells for its battleship weapons for just such an occasion as Second Java Sea. Falling from its apogee, *Renown's* 15-inch, 1938-lb. shell developed a massive amount of kinetic energy, more than enough to defeat even *Kongo's* modified deck before terminating its flight in the forward port secondaries' magazine.

With a bright flash and puff of black smoke, the magazine exploded. In and of itself, this would have been a grievous but possibly not fatal wound. What finished the former battlecruiser, ironically constructed in her assailant's homeland, was the same thing that had finished her cousins at Jutland—unstable cordite. In the split second after the explosion of the secondary magazine registered, the vessel's forward powder magazine followed, snapping the vessel in half forward of the bridge. The fast battleship rolled to starboard onto her beam ends, the steel of her massive pagoda bridge structure screeching as it dug into the unyielding sea and bent backwards with the vessel's momentum.

Aboard the *Hiei*, the stunned captain and officers in the vessel's conning tower saw the pristine stern come out of the water, props still turning as it slid underneath the waves. Barking commands that quickly began to bring his ship closer towards the enemy while still maintaining her broadside, the captain looked and saw only a spreading oil slick where the *Kongo's* bow had been. Feeling the vessel starting to turn, the captain's next inquiry, icily delivered, was to ask why the *Hiei's* own guns were not speaking. His answer was the booming of the eight 14-inch rifles, a move that sparked the rest of the stunned Japanese line into action.

JAMES YOUNG

"Damn, if the Limeys keep shooting like that this is going to be a short fucking war!" Jacob said in exultation, just as the Japanese riposte roared from their guns. All three remaining *Kongos* and the heavy cruisers opened fire, their gunnery officers choosing to utilize the more traditional range gathering methods in absence of radar.

To his utter dismay, Jacob realized that the Japanese shells were discernible as they began their plunge. His mind dimly realized that there were five dots coming towards him with the characteristic rushing sound, then the shells were passing overhead to thunder in a tight group six hundred yards behind *Houston*. Turning around, he was just in time to see the *Kinugasa* fire the second half of its salvo.

There was a dull *whump!* forward, and he turned to see *Hobart*'s Y turret lurching in train, smoke issuing from a small hole near the structure's forward edge. Jacob was so busy concentrating on the light cruiser that he did not hear *Houston's* firing gong. The heavy cruiser's gun blast startled him, and he was suddenly glad that the heavy cruiser was at near broadside presentation to the enemy. The blast had no sooner dissipated, his hearing dimly returning, then *Kinugasa*'s second salvo arrived, the shells barely two hundred yards beyond *Houston* and almost one hundred behind her.

Bastards don't realize just how fast this vessel is, Jacob thought. Once more he checked the line, hearing the tail end of a vessel reporting damage. Astern, he saw that there were *two* vessels with damage, both the *Exeter* and *Dorsetshire* trailing thin streams of smoke from holes in their side. The *Prince of Wales* did not look like she was doing so well either, her forward quad turret silent and having returned to minimum elevation. Looking, Jacob could see no clear damage, but it appeared the battleship was working through some sort of issue.

"Sir, we're reducing speed...the *Repulse* and *Renown*

250

are both reporting leaks forward," Chief Roberts said.

"So much for this being a 'fast' group," Jacob muttered, the *Houston*'s engines starting to audibly slow. Turning his binoculars further aft, he could see the Japanese destroyers and light cruisers turning towards the 'slow' group of vessels as the distance between the two Allied forces steadily increased. The sound of snapping flags was suddenly audible, and he turned towards *Houston*'s signal bridge. This time he heard the firing gong and braced himself as Sloan sent the cruiser's third salvo towards her opponents. Jacob turned to see the spot of shell and was just in time to see a bright flash high on the *Hiei*'s massive pagoda.

*Even if they cannot keep up their speed, the **Repulse** and **Renown** are both shooting lights out*, Jacob thought exuberantly.

"The Dutch are turning out of line to attack the Jap destroyers," Dewey called out.

Jacob turned around, raising an eyebrow and cocking an ear to listen to the speaker mounted on Battle Two's aft bulkhead. Due to his inattention, he did not hear *Kinugasa*'s third offering coming in. It was an almost fatal lapse, as the Japanese heavy cruiser nearly found the range. With a high whine and several *thunks!*, Battle Two was scoured by several splinters and some spray. Belatedly ducking as his front was soaked, Jacob turned towards the structure's side.

Holy shit! he thought, startled at the three gouges barely a couple of feet ahead of him. Shaken, Jacob looked down to realize that the spotting glasses he had just been looking through a moment before were shattered, the storm of splinters having jaggedly removed the left side.

Well that was a little bit closer than I would have liked, Jacob thought, stomach churning. Forcing the bile down, he turned towards Foncier.

"Damage report," he said crisply, startling the

younger officer out of his own shock. With a rush, the lieutenant turned towards the talker, just as *Houston* began a gradual course change towards the Japanese line.

Captain Wallace has started chasing salvos...this ought to be interesting, Jacob mused.

The at first tidy sea fight was starting to degenerate into a disjointed brawl. Realizing that the Japanese forces were closing for purposes of a torpedo attack, Phillips was forced to begin turning his slower vessels to present a narrower angle. This had the effect of allowing the range to begin opening, the end result being only *Valiant* was able to fire a pair of salvoes at the faster *Kongos* before they were out of range. This was fortunate for the fast battleships, as *Repulse* and *Renown's* fire alone continued to be dangerously accurate, but quite terrible for the Japanese light forces. In moments, the charging destroyers and light cruisers found themselves running a gauntlet of heavy shells as they attempted to close the range for their Long Lances.

For their part, the Japanese heavy elements continued to gradually close the range. With their initial accuracy having left much to be desired, the Japanese seemed to suddenly land a flurry of hits. *Exeter,* having just fired her fifth salvo, was suddenly struck with two *Atago* shells. One shell, a dud, lanced into her aid station, killing the ship's surgeon, while the second shell detonated in her captain's cabin, causing minor casualties.

Dorsetshire and *Hobart* were in some ways luckier than their Commonwealth fellow, in other ways worse off. Like *Exeter*, both of the first shells to come aboard were duds, each killing a couple of unfortunate sailors but doing little other damage. It was the second shell that caused significant dismay in each case, hitting the *Dorsetshire's* torpedo flat and devastating *Hobart's* A turret. In both cases, rapid damage control measures prevented things from being worse, the *Dorsetshire* jettisoning her torpedoes while *Hobart's* crew quickly brought her fire under control.

Jacob had just watched *Hobart* receive her hit forward when he heard the familiar ripping canvas sound of an incoming salvo. Ducking, he felt the *Houston* shudder, the sound of rending metal coming from forward. When there was no subsequent explosion, he quickly stood up.

"Dud forward, into the secondaries," Chief Roberts said, forestalling his question. "And there are minor leaks from the near-miss, but otherwise the old girl is fine."

Houston's own batteries roared back at the Japanese line, Sloan firing another full broadside. The *Suzuya* had begun evasive maneuvers, also chasing salvoes. Like *Houston*, staying in line necessitated only gentle turns, and the Japanese heavy cruiser's luck was similar. While the maneuver prevented her from being dead center in *Houston's* salvo, it intersected her primary 8-inch director with a shell from No. 3 turret. With a bright flash, *Houston* turned the position to junk, killing *Suzuya's* gunnery officer and blasting large segments of steel into exposed personnel forward. The heavy cruiser lost precious moments as her gunnery department began switching control of her main battery over to secondary directors, a respite the *Hobart's* crew was extremely grateful for.

Once more, Jacob turned and checked the Allied line. *Hobart* and *Dorsetshire* were not alone in their damage, it appeared. *Prince of Wales*'s A turret looked like it had been hit, but the four guns were finally elevated and trained out towards their target. Further aft, the battleship looked like she had taken a couple more hits in her belt, but without anything significant being struck. Beyond her, only the unfortunate *Dorsetshire* was clearly showing damage within the fast battle line.

Beyond the last Commonwealth cruiser, however, was the nautical equivalent of Dante's Inferno as the two light forces were engaging one another. From those forces that had originally been with Admiral Phillips, Jacob could see the *De Ruyter* down by the bow, her forward turrets silent, while the destroyer *Vendetta* was smoking heavily amidships and coming to a stop. As Jacob watched, the destroyer took another two hits forward, one on her superstructure the other at the extreme limit of her bow. Just beyond her, the *U.S.S. Parker* was curving out of line, siren shrieking and a breakdown flag running up from her signal bridge.

Swinging his glasses to look at the steadily advancing Japanese line, Jacob saw that there was at least one vessel, a light cruiser by the looks of it, burning heavily and in obvious distress. Another destroyer was circling aimlessly, the sea alive with shells from the Allied vessels closing. As he watched, one of the other light cruisers was lost in a forest of 15" shells, and his mind quickly counted that there were only seven splashes.

Lucky bastard, he thought, realizing that the eighth shell had been a dud. *There seems to be something wrong with everyone's ordnance today.*

"Holy shit, look at that big Jap bastard burn!" someone screamed. Jacob turned his glasses back, seeing that the 'big Jap bastard' in question was the third *Kongo* in line. The vessel was indeed hard hit, fire, smoke, and steam pouring from her amidships. For an instant, Jacob found himself hoping for a repeat explosion, but as the cloud turned noticeably lighter in color he could see that it was not a magazine that was afire.

Must be an engine room, he thought.

Jacob's guess was correct in many ways. The hit vessels was the *Haruna*, and she had been trading fire with

254

the *Prince of Wales*. In the end, as Jacob had noted, the Japanese vessel did not have heavy enough guns to penetrate her target's belt or turrets at long range, In contrast, the *Prince of Wales*'s 14-inch guns were doing an excellent job piercing IJN armor at the extended range.

Fortunately for *Haruna*'s crew, the lesson was not delivered with as much dispatch as it had been for *Kongo*. Whereas *Renown*'s shell had been the equivalent of a bullet to the brain, *Prince of Wales*' hit in *Haruna*'s forward starboard engine room was buckshot across the legs. Bursting against one of the vessel's turbines, the shell instantly laid most of the black gang out, carving many of them into unrecognizable detritus of war. The disintegrating turbine and blast opened the space to the sea while simultaneously opening leaks in the adjacent fire room's bulkhead.

Aboard the *Mutsu,* Vice Admiral Kondo had seen enough. With the *Haruna*'s crippling, his force was now heavily outgunned as well as outnumbered. Looking towards the west, he could see that the sun was rapidly setting and would be down within two hours, putting the Japanese Navy back in its preferred environment. Realizing that the geometry of the situation was against his forces, he realized that he needed a diversion. Turning to his signals officer, he gave his commands.

"Sir, the battleships are turning away," Foncier reported. Enemy cruisers turning in towards us!"

"What in the Hell are they doing?" Jacob asked no one in particular. He had thought his eyes were telling him something crazy, but now he saw that insanity wasn't residing in his head.

"That's awfully nice of the Japanese admiral to ask his boys to cover his retreat against three battleships and a bunch of heavy cruisers," Chief Roberts drily remarked.

"If he wants to sacrifice his vessels, so much the better."

A bright flash astern caught Jacob's eye, and he turned to see the horrible sight of an unidentified Allied vessel exploding, the ship's forward magazines detonating as fire reached them.

"What vessel was that?" Jacob asked.

"The *Express,* Sir."

From the looks of it, the British destroyer wasn't about to be alone. There were at least four or five vessels on each side that were in dire straits. One Japanese vessel was stopped and burning heavily yet still surrounded by shell splashes. The range between the two light forces, with their combined closing speeds, had swiftly drifted to under twenty thousand yards with expected results for increased lethality.

I wonder when those boys are going to admit they've had enough? Jacob thought. Some small part of him had to admire the Japanese destroyermen's aggressiveness even as he hoped and prayed for every rapidly maneuvering vessel to get blown out of the water. Jacob was not about to question the bravery of any man who was willing to charge into the face of guns large enough to sink his vessel with a single shot.

That's a lot of ground to cover to get into torpedo range, he mused. As if reading his mind, the Japanese forces began to turn away from attempting to catch Admiral Phillips' vessels. Jacob was about to continue watching their battle when *Houston's* guns began speaking again.

Sloan must've finished computing the new closure rate, Jacob thought. Spinning his glasses around, he was suddenly shocked.

"Those bastards are turning straight in!" he remarked. The Japanese heavy cruisers were turning directly into the Allied broadsides, permitting their T to get capped by the extended Allied line. The move was tantamount to suicide, even with the reduced profile presented by being practically head on. Beginning to make smoke, the Japanese cruisers charged in a staggered line, *Suzuya* still leading. The *Houston's* shells landed to starboard of the heavy cruiser, on in range but off in direction.

She's not chasing salvoes anymore, Jacob observed. *Sloan will hit her next time we fire*. Ahead, the *Hobart* fired another salvo, her six-inch guns finally able to contribute. Tracking the vessel's shots, Jacob could see that she was also firing at the lead Japanese cruiser, a flash indicating that she had hit even as her guns fired again.

*Glad we've got dye in our shells, or I'd be a tad bit pissed off that she's firing at **our** target.* *Houston* shuddered with another broadside, the nine guns at a noticeably lower elevation. Glancing at the advancing Japanese, Jacob guessed the range at roughly 18,000 yards.

That's a long, hot way to go to torpedo range. As if to reinforce that thought, one of *Houston's* shells slammed into the heavy cruiser's massive superstructure, again finding the cruiser's director just as the space was being remanned. This time *Houston's* shell burst in the midst of the sensitive equipment instead of clearing the director's crew, starting a major fire among the electrical wiring. Whereas the last hit had been relatively temporary, the second shell effectively destroyed *Suzuya's* main director until the vessel returned to harbor.

"Another hit on that bastard!" someone observed. "The *Prince* is shooting her butt off!"

The comment was quite apparent, the *Haruna's* pagoda structure clearly trailing a thick stream of smoke. Still slowing, with her two healthy sisters starting to open the distance, the *Haruna* was beginning to get into dire straits with her continued flooding and the *Prince of Wales* sharpshooting. Even as her own guns raggedly answered, it was clear that unless something drastic occurred the Japanese battleship would not be long for this earth.

"Torpedoes astern!" a lookout shouted.

Submarines! Just what we need! Jacob thought.

Jacob could be understood for being wrong about the origin of the Japanese torpedoes, as no Western weapon could have made the sixteen thousand yard trip from the light forces melee even on slow setting. While the geometry was all wrong for the long-range shots fired by the *Oi, Naka,* and four of their DDs, the Allies had helped the situation by turning to pursue the three *Kongos.* Admiral Ozawa had not specifically ordered his screen commander, the newly returned Rear Admiral Tanaka, to fire torpedoes as he was withdrawing, but the still healing admiral had determined to take the chance. Launching from a shallowly converging course, the barrage of sixty-five torpedoes were a wild throw of the dice, caused by a sense of desperation.

Jacob saw one of the deadly weapons broach two hundred yards from *Houston's* starboard quarter, the cigar-shaped cylinder seemingly incredibly long. Even as he saw it go back underneath the water, he realized that the weapons were almost wakeless. From their approach angle of forty-five degrees off the stern and at the range that they had been sighted, there was nothing that could be done. Having been firmly in the Allied camp for the majority of the battle, Lady Luck abruptly changed sides and struck against those who had seemed to have her favor, the *Renown* and *Prince of Wales.* Three of the large 24-inch torpedoes hit the former, while one hit the latter astern.

Renown's builders had never intended for the vessel to be subject to one, much less three, of the Long Lance's warheads. The first torpedo hit one of the old lady's port engine rooms, sending the crew into oblivion before most of them had a chance to know what happened. The vessel was still whipsawing from that hit when the second hit her stern just forward of the rudder. The blast destroyed *Renown*'s steering and knocking one of her props askew with tremendous vibration. Finally, just as the vessel's commander was giving orders for the vessel to be brought to a halt, the third torpedo did it for him, opening her second engine room to the sea. With the loss of power went any chance for *Renown's* survival, and the battlecruiser quickly started an alarming list to starboard. Before the startled eyes of the entire battlegroup, the old battlecruiser shuddered to a stop and continued to settle.

The *Prince of Wales* had been slightly luckier than her cohort. While her underwater protection had not been designed with Long Lances in mind, the system was still fairly sound unless hit in a few vulnerable spots. Directly abaft the #1 port engine room was not such a location, the torpedo's warhead hitting the thickest part of the battleship's sub-waterline armor . While necessitating the abandonment of the engine room with subsequent loss of speed, the vessel was not in any danger of sinking.

Seeing the Allied fleet turning away in an attempt to clear the torpedo water, the Japanese light forces chose their opportunity to lay smoke and reverse course back towards their own battle line. Believing that he was turning away from a submarine ambush, Vice Admiral Crutchley was in no mood to give chase, radioing this fact to Admiral Phillips who heartily concurred. With his own light forces in disarray, and a few Type 93s having been sighted by his own lookouts, Admiral Phillips was determined to wait until nightfall when he felt that he would have an advantage.

As the heavier vessels continued their retreat, the Allied light forces began to clear the battlefield, their Japanese counterparts firing a few desultory torpedoes at crippled vessels as they left. One such weapon found the *Vendetta*, the drifting destroyer's back broken by the weapon. Her demise somehow missed in the milling confusion, the vessel's crew would be subject to shark attacks and exposure over the next four days until they drifted ashore on Java.

The losses were far heavier for the Japanese. The light cruiser *Sendai*, having suffered a direct hit from the *Malaya*, was burning so fiercely for several minutes it seemed no more Allied attention would be necessary. However, as she was approached by the *John Paul Jones, Pillsbury,* and *Edsall*, the forward turret fired two rapid shots at the latter. This was enough for the Americans, and three 21-inch torpedoes made the light cruiser's demise much more rapid. Their good humor already weakened by the stresses of the last few days and various damages suffered in the present fight, the American destroyers decided it was far more important to search for *Renown's* survivors than help men who clearly did not know when to surrender.

While not as damaged as the *Sendai*, the destroyer *Shigure* found herself barely able to make fifteen knots. This was completely insufficient for escape purposes, as the Dutch squadron fell upon the destroyer with great fury. Angry at the loss of their comrades, the threat to their homes, and their allies open contempt for them, the Dutchmen quickly smothered the Japanese destroyer. True to their national heritage, the Japanese did not surrender, the destroyer firing her final shots even as she sank stern first beneath the waves. Their bloodlust up, the *Piet Hein* and *Van Ghent* steamed through the wreckage, their hulls and screws depleting the number of *Shigure* survivors even further and simultaneously adding more blood to attract the Indies underwater denizens. Even worse, on their second pass through, the two Dutch destroyers dropped several depth charges apiece. In the end, no member of *Shigure's* complement would see their homeland again.

As *Shigure* was suffering her fate, the *Renown's* battered hull finally gave out. With very little warning, the battlecruiser lurched then began to capsize. Her complement, the majority of which had already been ordered topside, quickly found themselves in the water. As the vessel continued over, her massive wounds were exposed for a brief moment to the sky. Pouring oil, the *Renown* briefly resembled a bleeding, injured whale before plunging her bow under and disappearing with a deep rumble.

Standing aboard *Houston*, Jacob saw the several attending destroyers moving in to begin picking up the *Renown's* survivors.

We were lucky. If that Jap cruiser could shoot, we just might be swimming right now also, Jacob thought. *Jesus, it's like you can die any moment out here.* With that thought, he went inside and began to start directing damage control actions.

The next sixty minutes, like all times when a person was extremely busy, passed quickly. Jacob made a quick tour through the vessel's compartments, stopping to talk and surreptitiously inspect several of the damage control parties as he went. Finding everything in order, he returned to Battle Two just as the tropical sunset was commencing in all of its beauty. From his position Jacob could just see the sun beneath the cloud cover as the red orb headed for the sea. As per usual, sunset proceeded quickly, Sol seeming to plunge itself into the sea. Feeling the *Houston* starting to come around, he caught a glimpse of the *Exeter* lit up by the red sun, the white field of her battle ensign almost blood red. Jacob suddenly felt a chill, as if the colors were a portent. Laughing at himself, he stepped back into Battle Two.

"Sir, the captain requests you forward," Lieutenant Foncier said, nearly running into him in the hatchway.

Jacob nodded his assent and turned slowly around, his stitched wound having apparently reopened itself during his trip around the ship.

Strange, I didn't feel that a few minutes ago, he thought. *Adrenaline is a wonderful thing until it wears out.*

Gingerly coming down to the main deck, Jacob made his way painfully forward. As he passed through the anti-aircraft positions he could see the ship's chaplain, Lieutenant Commander Cody Mulcahy, providing last rites over a sheet shrouded body. Taking off his helmet as he passed, Jacob gave a slight nod to the chaplain. The man, his face drawn and pale, nodded back then continued his work.

Upon reaching the bridge, Jacob moved slowly out to the starboard wing. Lieutenant Commander Sloan and Lieutenant Connor were also present, the engineering officer soaking wet from the waist down. Jacob didn't have time to ask Connor how he got wet, the captain starting as soon as he came out onto the deck.

"XO, you look like you've seen better days," Captain Wallace said, all three officers noting Jacob's ginger movements.

"Sorry sir, leg wound opened back up," Jacob said. "I'll get doc to look at it if I've got the time."

"XO, you need to make the time," Wallace replied, his voice clearly conveying it wasn't a suggestion.

"Aye-aye, Sir," Jacob replied, grimacing.

"Gentlemen, we'll go around the horn quickly," Wallace began, turning to Sloan. "Guns, damn good shooting. How many shells do we have left?"

"About a hundred per gun, sir," Sloan said. "Turret No. 1 is shooting the new rounds we got from BuOrd off the *President Jackson.* We didn't have a problem at long-range, but the rate of fire will be a little slower at shorter range given their heavier weight."

"Noted," Captain Wallace said wearily. "Is that all, guns?"

"Yes, Sir," Sloan said slowly. Wallace gestured for Lieutenant Connor to go next.

"Sir, we've plugged the leaks from the near misses," Connor reported. "The firing shook some fittings loose, but we'll be able to give you full speed without any problems."

"Good enough, Lieutenant Connor," Wallace said. "Gentlemen, you are dismissed."

Both men came to attention and saluted. Wallace returned the gesture, then waited for them to go inside the bridge.

"Commander Morton, I have recommended to Admiral Hart that you be returned Stateside," Captain Wallace said.

Jacob could not have been more shocked if Wallace had started speaking Japanese.

"Sir?" he asked tremulously.

"Relax XO," Wallace said, looking as if he was having trouble focusing his thoughts. "I suggested Admiral Hart promote you and place you in command of new construction. Your work out here has been exemplary."

"Thank you, sir," Jacob said, going from shock to pride.

"Your actions over the last six months have been exemplary for someone in your position," Wallace continued. "I hope that you have another chance to excel in a couple of hours."

I hope I survive it! Jacob thought.

"Now let's get back to work," Wallace said. Jacob came to attention and saluted, the gesture returned by his captain.

"It has been an honor serving with you, sir," Jacob said.

"Likewise, XO," Captain Wallace replied, extending his hand. The two men shook, then Jacob turned to make his way gingerly to sick bay. Beneath his feet he felt *Houston's* engines starting to accelerate once more, followed by the bugle call for General Quarters, then Air Action. Deciding his leg could wait, he headed aft to Battle Two, barking for a report as soon as he was through the door.

"Sir, *Prince of Wales* is reporting two air contacts relative bearing one eight zero, course one seven nine," Foncier reported as he stepped in.

"Understood," Jacob said coolly.

Well, if this is to be the last time I'm aboard this vessel, the Japanese are at least making it memorable, Jacob thought.

The two aircraft, flying in trail, were the harbingers of Admiral Kondo's forces returning to the fray. Unfortunately for them, it was not quite yet dark enough for all the Allied aircraft to depart the area. Guided by the *Prince of Wales'* FDO, four Australian *Whirlwinds* reversed course from returning to Surabaya. While not as polished as his compatriot on *Australia*, the *Prince of Wales'* FDO was pretty darn good. Bringing the four fighters in from the east so their opponents would be silhouetted against the lighter western sky, the FDO set the stage for a brilliant interception.

Neither *Jake* had a chance, the two crews being immolated within seconds of one another by the two Australian section leaders. Having succeeded in poking out Kondo's eyes, Admiral Phillips came north in what he intended to be a complete evisceration of the Japanese main body.

Watching the flaming comets fall from altitude, Jacob was once again struck by the wonders of the new device, this "radar".

Like a damn magic lantern, Jacob thought. *An all seeing eye that gives us one hell of an advantage over the Japs.*

Darkness at sea level had arrived with its customary suddenness, and Jacob was startled to see Battle Two was steeped in the usual gloom of blacked out operations. The

Allied Fleet was still short of its night time dispositions, the ragged column being held up by the Dutch squadron and the last two destroyers that had been searching for *Renown* survivors. The *Houston* was still being trailed by the *Exeter, Repulse,* then *Prince of Wales*, the battleship having slowed to twenty-three knots to ease the pressure on her torpedo wound. Behind her the slower *Valiant, Ramilles,* and *Malaya* were slowly gaining ground, roughly five thousand yards behind their faster and younger relative. The remaining Commonwealth and Dutch cruisers were just starting to reform into a loose column eight thousand yards off the *Houston's* port quarter, *Hobart* in the lead. Once that column was formed, the *Houston* was to break off from her position, steam down the starboard side of the battleships, then form up behind the tail of the cruisers, but that was still twenty to thirty minutes off.

"Sir, *Prince of Wales* reports multiple contacts bearing two six nine relative, range twenty-eight thousand yards," Dewey reported.

Yeah, definitely an all seeing eye, Jacob thought, looking out to the *Houston's* port side. The skies were still partially cloudy, obscuring a portion of the moon's light. If he had to venture a guess, and knowing the general range to the barely visible *Prince of Wales*, Jacob would guess naked eye visibility at just over twelve thousand yards. He could see several other shapes as other vessels moved to join the column, but he could not have identified them if his life depended on it.

"*Prince of Wales* requesting permission to open fire," Dewey stated breathlessly.

There was silence over the Talk Between Ships (TBS) circuit. Jacob, looking at the ship clock, watched as two, then three minutes passed.

"Permission denied," the speaker crackled. "Friendly vessels fouling range. Destroyers free to conduct torpedo attack, all other vessels clear for action."

What vessels is he talking about? Jacob asked, moving to the plot board. *There shouldn't be anything out there...oh, wait.*

Twenty thousand yards to *Prince of Wales's* port, the destroyers *Express* and *Encounter* were steaming pell mell back towards the Allied squadron. Having heard the *Prince of Wales* sighting report and realizing that meant there were enemy vessels less than nine thousand yards astern, the destroyers were literally running for their lives. Their decks full of *Renown* survivors, both vessels were clearing for action as well as they could. To a man, their complements could still hear the sounds of the men they had been forced to leave behind in the water. Straining their eyes abaft, the two vessels' lookouts peered into the darkness desperately looking for signs of enemy vessels.

The men could have saved their eyes, as death stalked them from the shadows. Realizing that tying his own light vessels to his relatively slow battleline would be suicide, Admiral Kondo had conducted reorganization of his battered light forces as he came up. In the end, his force had been disposed into two columns of light vessels with the battleships in line abreast in the center.

The port, or easternmost, column was led by the light cruiser *Oi*. Behind her were thirteen of the large Japanese destroyers with their heavy gun armament and torpedo tubes. To starboard, or west of the battleline the *Kitakami*, *Oi's* sister ship and similarly modified with an extensive torpedo battery of forty 24-inch tubes, led the damaged *Naka* then also thirteen destroyers. In the center, the *Hiei* was the furthermost battleship to port, then came her two sister ships, then the *Fuso, Yamashiro, Ise, Hyuga, Mutsu, Nagato,* then the eight heavy cruisers that made up the remainder of the force.

VAdm. Kondo's plan was simple in concept. The light forces would make contact with a night torpedo attack, eschewing their guns until they had fired at least one torpedo salvo. Once this attack was made, these same vessels would illuminate the enemy fleet as they reloaded their torpedoes, allowing the battle line to bombard from a distance with impunity. While battle losses and other needs had meant his force was a hodgepodge of different squadrons, this operation had been practiced so many times in tough, realistic pre-war maneuvers Kondo had no doubt it would succeed. Ships had collided and sailors had died to ensure the IJN's proficiency, an investment that he fully intended to reap in the next few hours.

There were two things the pre-war maneuvers had not counted on. The first of these was free-floating, hastily laid Dutch minefields. So recent that they had not been known to Admiral Phillips, these would have surely led to disastrous results if not for Allied turn away from Japanese torpedo water. Drifting with the currents, the weapons were now squarely in the path of Kondo's westernmost squadron. With no minesweepers, Kondo's forces had no idea of what lay before them.

The second oversight had of been the Royal Navy's aggressive nature. There was no excuse for this lapse, as the Imperial Japanese Navy's own traditions were based on those of her former allies'. Admiral Phillips, not considered to be in the Nelsonian mold by many of his contemporaries, rose far above his diminutive stature in his bold order to dispatch the destroyers. Whilst if he had known the relative disparity in light forces his decisions may have been different, Phillips' aggressive maneuver had meant that both sides' light forces would meet far in advance of the battleships.

Thus, as the *Oi* ran pell mell into three of the Dutch mines and burst into a mass of flames, the Allied destroyers were already charging forward to conduct their torpedo runs. Initially stunned by the sudden explosion of their flagship, the thirteen Japanese destroyers behind quickly reacted by throwing their helms to starboard and simultaneously hurling a monkey wrench in Admiral Kondo's plans.

"Holy shit!" Jacob heard a lookout shout, the bright explosions and mass of flames far closer than he would have expected. Bringing up his night glasses, he focused on the furiously burning pyre and could see shapes elongating and turning broadside in the darkness. In the next instant, he was nearly thrown off his feet as *Houston* suddenly turned to starboard, her engines changing in pitch as they went full astern.

"Shoal water dead ahead!" Seaman Dewey reported, his feet braced as the heavy cruiser listed away from her turn.

"What?!" Foncier, Jacob, and Chief Roberts asked in unison.

"Message from the *De Ruyter*," Dewey said sheepishly.

"Nice of her navigator to suddenly look up and do his job!" Jacob muttered, even as he turned back out to port.

The message had completely discombobulated the Allied formation, the *Hobart* having also initially turned to starboard, a course that would have taken her right in front of the swiftly turning *Repulse* if both vessels captains hadn't reacted quickly. Like a rippling whipcrack, the subsequent avoidances caused vessels to heel out of line or, even more dangerously, stop. Only the nimbleness of the smaller cruisers and the relatively slow speed of the battlewagons prevented any collisions, and only at the cost of preventing all but the *Dorsetshire* and the *Exeter* from getting off any salvos for three critical minutes.

The Japanese had no such issues, the discovered port column opening fire with starshell at their approaching counterparts and the milling battleships and cruisers beyond.

Aboard the *Houston*, Jacob suddenly found himself bathed in a glare so bright he could have read by it without straining his eyes. Shielding his eyes from the glare, he saw that the majority of the Allied battleline was similarly outlined.

Not good, not good at all, he thought, even as he saw similar sunbursts exploding over the Japanese port wing destroyers. Then the night became a cacophony of exchanging tracer rounds as the destroyers began engaging one another.

The *Express* and *Encounter,* already being tracked by both sides of Japanese vessels, were the first to suffer. Having heard Phillips order, the two vessels had been reversing course back towards the radar contacts even as *Oi* was impaling herself in the Dutch minefield. While an example in British bravery, with both decks full of survivors both ships might have been better served in continuing south to join their rapidly advancing comrades.

The starboard wing of Japanese light forces, still stealthily approaching, held their gunfire and most of their torpedoes, only the *Harusame* and *Kawakaze* firing their forward quad tubes at the two turning destroyers as they presented their broadsides. The eight torpedoes missed behind the speeding two vessels, hurtling into the darkness back towards the unaware Japanese battleline, already starting to execute their simultaneous turn to form line ahead. While it would have been extremely perverse if the Long Lances had found the sides of friendly battleships instead of their intended prey, Fortune gave the IJN her first favor of the night.

The port wing, with starshells already bursting over their heads, had no reason to maintain their stealth. Indeed, several of the destroyers went so far as to illuminate the *Express* and *Encounter* with searchlights, the hapless destroyers finding themselves the focus of at least six enemy vessels at under ten thousand yards. Even as the former engaged the *Fubuki* and the latter the *Yugumo*, the Japanese were already straddling the wildly maneuvering destroyers and threatening to cross their 'T' as they finished reversing course. Porting their helms further to port, the two vessels adopted a near parallel course with the retreating port wing, the range a brutal seven thousand yards.

As neither vessel's master nor any other officer for that matter survived the subsequent fight, the next five minutes would remain the subject of historian conjecture for years. The citation for Lieutenant Commander Morgan and Cartwright's Victoria Crosses would simply read 'intrepidly maneuvered their vessels in such a manner as to cause maximum damage to the enemy'. These were staid and subdued wording for the act of throwing ones vessel against incredibly superior odds and likely saving many of their comrades at the cost of their own, for the two destroyers' launched such a valiant counterattack, guns and torpedoes blazing, that they further threw the port wing into chaos.

While it was not known what went through most of the crew's minds in those moments, what was known was the damage they caused. Equipped with four quick-firing 4.7" guns, both vessels were capable of firing a salvo every eight to ten seconds with their well-trained crews. While their own wild maneuvers initially threw the guncrews off, as the two light forces sped westward the *Encounter* landed a hit on the *Yugumo* with her fourth salvo, the round severing the destroyer's steering cables as it detonated. *Express* did even better, hitting the *Fubuki* with a shell that started an intense fire in that vessel's fire room. Hard hit, that vessel began rapidly slowing and started to turn away, a maneuver that would normally have had little effect except the *Yugumo* was the next vessel behind her. The collision was terrible, the *Yugumo* slicing into the *Fubuki* abaft of her 'Y' turret as that vessel turned and nearly severing her stern.

Spying the opportunity, *Encounter* fired eight

torpedoes at the stopped ships. It would be her last act, as a 'Long Lance' from the *Nowaki* arrived at that moment. Hitting the destroyer in her boilers, the torpedo's warhead snapped her keel. The subsequent force from the vessel's forward movement finished the destruction, ripping her in half at her forward funnel. For a few moments the stern half surged forward, almost passing the bow before stopping then tilting up and plunging into the sea. Due to the suddenness of the sinking, the destroyer's depth charges had not been set to 'safe'. The fifty or so men who had been on the vessel's deck and survived the torpedoing, to include a large proportion of *Renown* survivors bitterly complaining about their second dunking, had just enough time to begin looking for debris to cling to when the explosive canisters began detonating with terrible results. Fortunately for those on the bow section, itself following two minutes later, all the explosions had ceased by the time it was their turn to enter the water.

Having seen the demise of her sister ship aft and realizing that thirteen to one odds were insane, the *Express* had just started to turn away when it seemed as if all of her assailants got the range at once. Having just fired her own torpedoes as she started to turn away, the *Express* was hit by twelve shells within the space of thirty seconds. One of these found her aft magazine, with the results to be expected, the other hits merely hastening her sinking.

Sighting the white wakes of the incoming torpedoes, those Japanese vessels that could avoid quickly turned to comb the tracks, the maneuver simultaneously putting them bows on with the other rapidly closing Allied light forces. The unfortunate *Fubuki* and *Yugumo,* in effect one large target even as they separated, each collected a single torpedo. Unlike their American cousins, the British torpedoes had been extensively tested for function during their development. While not as impressively fatal as the Long Lance, the 21" torpedoes made more than a large enough hole to see off a destroyer. The maelstrom of battle continued even as the two vessels foundered, their depth charges' detonation increasing the night's body count.

"Enemy cruisers, bearing oh three oh!"

"The *Express* and *Encounter* have sunk!"

"*John Paul Jones* reports enemy battleships sighted!"

Jacob suddenly felt himself overwhelmed by the shouted orders and general cacophony of battle. The *Houston*, her path of fire now cleared, was steadily seeking targets in a sea that seemed full of them. The vessel's aft turret had changed orientation at least three times that Jacob could notice, the Lieutenant Commander Sloan obviously unable to clearly discern prey. Judging from the numerous shell splashes, none fortunately closer than two hundred yards at the moment, that sea full of targets seemed to also be seeking her.

I hope Sloan stops acting like a damn teenage boy at the town social and picks someone out, Jacob thought, because I sure don't hear the...

As if the gunnery officer was reading his mind, *Houston's* forward turrets erupted. Jacob could not see the target the shells were aimed at, but he could see that they weren't the same ones being illuminated by the 5-inch guns. Not wanting to question Sloan's judgment, he attempted to pierce the gloom, something hard to do with yet another starshell bursting overhead.

In the next instant he suddenly had help as the area *Houston* had been shooting at became alive with dim flashes. Fixing on the location, Jacob could make out dim shapes, shapes that were beginning to turn away. *Houston's* guns roared again, the nine waterspouts just visible in Jacob's field of view as Sloan was slightly short, failing to account for the enemy's change of orientation. As the enemy ships' shapes began to change, the series of flashes began once more, the maneuver starting to trigger some sort of memory in Jacob's mind.

His thoughts were interrupted by the freight train sound of incoming ordnance, the ripping canvas incredibly loud and extremely close. As in the earlier fight, his veteran's instincts saved him and most of the crew of Battle Two, the space once more swept with splinters and, alarmingly, spray. Out of the corner of his eye, Jacob could see that the towering waterspouts were far higher than any he had ever seen, a development that could mean only one thing: battleships.

"Oh fuck!" Chief Roberts cried. Turning, Jacob could see that the man's abdomen was a mess of goo, the blood black in the harsh light of the starshells. In light of Battle Two's seemingly magnetic attraction for shell splinters, Lieutenant Sharpe had determined placing a corpsman in the space would be prudent. Jacob cast around looking for the medical professional and saw the man already tending to a sailor that had collapsed in a heap at the port entrance to Battle Two. Jacob started to take a step towards Chief Roberts and was cut off by Lieutenant Foncier.

"I got it Sir, keep in the fight!" Foncier shouted. Jacob realized the wisdom of the younger officer's words as the *Houston* started to heel over.

I have no idea why we're turning and that's not good, he thought, the ship vibrating as her guns fired again.

"Status report!" he shouted at one of the talkers. The man did not hear him, continuing to look at Foncier tending Chief Roberts. Jacob took two quick strides and hit the man atop his helmet, the sailor looking at him in shock.

"Status report, dammit!" Jacob roared. He could hear the radio squawk box behind the man, the device a babble of ships talking as chaos reigned in the Allied fleet. The talker, shaking himself out of his shock, began listening to his headset. Jacob was almost ready to throttle him when there were two distinct explosions, one of them forward the other quite close to Battle Two in the vicinity of the secondaries. Turning away from the sailor, Jacob sprinted to the port side of Battle Two to try and look down the *Houston's* length towards her bow. His view was obscured by the horrifically bright blaze burning on starboard #1 secondary.

Why are we still turning? Jacob suddenly thought as he realized the ship was starting to orient back towards the Allied line. He leaned back into Battle Two to ask that question and got his answer before he had a chance.

"Fire in #1 5-inch!" the talker said rapidly, then stopped, his face pale. Taking a deep breath, he continued. "The bridge is hit!"

"Assume control!" Jacob shouted to the auxiliary helmsman. The man threw several switches then seized the vessel's auxiliary wheel.

"I have the helm, aye!"

"Rudder amidships!" Jacob barked, seeing the *Repulse* and *Prince of Wales* following the heavy cruiser around. "Have damage control let me know if the bridge is destroyed!"

"Aye-aye, Sir!" the talker replied.

Judging from the lack of inquiry from the bridge as to why Battle Two had assumed control, Jacob had assumed that the captain was wounded or dead. If the bridge was gone, that meant he would have to continue to fight the vessel from his location, not the optimal place for a fight. However, if the bridge's control apparatus were still intact, he would make his way forward.

"Gunnery is inquiring as to our next actions, Sir!"

Calmly, Jacob took stock of what he knew of the battle's geometry in his head. The *Houston* was starting to steam back past the surging Allied battle line, the *Prince of Wales* and *Repulse* in tow. Apparently the *Ramilles* had realized the American heavy cruiser was out of control and had continued on her original path, firing at the now visible Japanese battle line. Dimly, he could hear Admiral Phillips voice on the TBS inquiring into their condition and why the *Houston* had turned out of line. That was followed by the *De Ruyter* reporting that she was taking friendly fire.

"Tell Commander Sloan fire at the next target he sees, we're coming back into the fight! Hard a port, make your course two seven zero."

"Two seven zero, aye-aye!"

If Jacob's guess was correct, *Houston's* turn would carry her several hundred yards aft of the Allied battleline, at which point he would be able to make another turn and gradually arc to a location on the battleships starboard quarter. Thinking, he suddenly remembered what had made the initial turn so chaotic in the first place. He looked at the plot, the young ensign in charge furiously making notations. Casting a glance at the map, Jacob nodded to himself, sure that the *Houston* would clear. As he glanced at the map, seeing the geometry, the reason for the white flashes along the Japanese line suddenly hit him.

"Shit! Torpedoes...tell the *Valiant* she is entering torpedo water!" Jacob shouted.

Even if Jacob had been aboard the three British battleships his warning would have been far too late. Fired at roughly twelve to fourteen thousand yards, the Type 93s had been set to their faster, forty-eight knot setting, while their smaller 21-inch cousins had been set for forty-two. This meant the torpedoes had an approximately five to seven minute run before impact, virtually an eternity in naval warfare. For many of the crew of one vessel, the light cruiser *Naka,* the passage took on a literal meaning. Having had the misfortune to be set afire by the *Dorsetshire,* the *Naka* attracted the attention of most of the Allied fleet, especially those vessels which had not been in night combat previously.

Smothered by a storm of smaller caliber shells, her armor barely above that of a destroyer, the *Naka* strangely enough did not explode and sink despite being set afire from bow to stern. Instead, her hull finally pierced numerous times, the light cruiser rolled over and sank just as the first Japanese torpedoes were starting to arrive.

Whilst the only vessel of the port wing to be sunk, *Naka* was not the only vessel to be damaged. Indeed, if not for the disorienting effects of darkness, poor lighting, and the confusion caused by the Allies' emergency turn, the Imperial Japanese Navy would have found itself missing many stalwart destroyermen when the sun next rose over the Java Sea. As it was, only one of the light vessels would come through unscathed, with the remainder seeing from two months to a year in various yards.

In less than three minutes all of this damage was more than made up for. First to suffer, despite not being the primary targets, were the Allied cruisers. Far faster and nimbler than the battleships, the cruisers had managed to surge ahead so as not to foul the battleships range. The surge had brought them directly into the easternmost edge of 'torpedo water', meaning that only the lead vessels were in danger. Relatively, the odds of any one ship being hit were small due to the long range and changing geometry, the chance so small that even if they had been aware of the torpedoes the cruisers' captains probably would have continued on their course.

If not for the presence of the *Kitakami* and her extensive torpedo tubes, such a gamble would have likely been successful. However, when the *Kitakami's* forty torpedoes were added to the fray this meant that the seven leading vessels in the Allied formation were steaming through a tremendous amount of torpedo water. When put into this perspective the *Hobart, Cornwall, Exeter, Devonshire, De Ruyter, Danae*, and *Dragon* were fortunate to only have ten hits spread between them.

The first vessel to be struck was the *De Ruyter*. One moment the vessel's guns were steadily engaging a Japanese destroyer with some success, the next the vessel was staggering and afire as one torpedo eviscerated her powerplant spaces and the other blew off her stern. In an instant the Dutch cruiser was a wreck, afire and rapidly flooding with no means to stop either problem. Despite the valiant efforts of her crew, the vessel was doomed and would sink sixteen minutes after first being struck.

The *Danae*, throwing her helm hard over to starboard to avoid the derelict *De Ruyter,* saved herself from being hit. As the light cruiser passed by her stricken companion the *De Ruyter's* crew could be heard cheering encouragement even as they struggled to save their vessel. Unfortunately for the *Danae* passing between a burning vessel and the enemy was not the most prudent course of action, resulting in her receiving three shells aboard. One of these destroyed the light cruiser's 'Y' turret, setting off the ready ammunition and powder in the hoists. Making smoke, the light cruiser turned away from the enemy.

Forward of the *De Ruyter* and *Danae*, the *Devonshire* and *Cornwall's* masters had just enough time to wonder what had happened to the lead Dutch cruiser just before they found out first hand. *Devonshire* was fortunate, taking one of the smaller 21-inch torpedoes than a larger 'Long Lance'. The 21-inch torpedo hit far aft, damaging one of the heavy cruiser's props and opening a portion of her stern, while the 'Long Lance' snuffed out the vessel's boilers. Coasting to a stop, the heavy cruiser was passed by her compatriots, her crew turning to the grim business of fighting the inrush of seawater and attempting to regain power before any Japanese units returned.

Cornwall, her turrets still punching rounds into the burning *Naka*, never realized the danger she was in before two 24-inch torpedoes found her. Like the *Devonshire*, the first 'Long Lance' found her boilers, this one killing the entire crew and snapping the vessel's keel just before the second did the same for the engine rooms. Adding insult to injury a third 'Long Lance' hit as the cruiser was coming to a stop. Striking the vessel in her aircraft fuel bunkerage, this 'Long Lance' caused the area between the third stack and 'X' turret to erupt into a blazing cauldron. Without power, and suddenly the most attractive target amongst many for Japanese gunners, the heavy cruiser's crew began to abandon ship.

Hobart, lead Allied cruiser, and Dragon, the last ship to pass through the torpedo water, were the final victims. The Australian vessel, her captain having just commented on her improved luck from the afternoon's engagement, received two torpedoes. The elderly British cruiser, her antiquated equipment and relatively poor training having prevented her from effectively contributing to either of the battles, received only one. The end result was the same, as the vessels' thin armor belts failed to prevent high explosive from detonating in fuel spaces. For the Hobart, the last HMAS vessel to have avoided damage in the Australian fleet, the second hit only hastened what was already a fatal wound. Coasting to a stop, the light cruiser capsized to starboard in a little under ten minutes, the Java Sea putting out her flames as it claimed over three quarters of her crew. The Dragon received no such succor, the brilliant fire continuing to spread despite all efforts to fight it. Clearly finished, she was left to burn by both sides, her crew abandoning ship. It would take a little over thirty minutes for the fire to reach a magazine, the light cruiser breaking in half and sinking when this occurred.

Having been unmasked by the cruisers' surge, the Ramilles, Malaya, and Valiant had begun engaging their opposite numbers as soon as the vessels had been illuminated by starshells from the Prince of Wales then their light forces. This fire had been kept up even through the Houston's

278

impromptu turn from formation, and it began to tell even as Japanese battleships were still attempting to find the range and their torpedoes were decimating the Allied cruiser line.

The *Ramilles* had begun firing on the *Yamashiro*, and began hitting on her tenth salvo. The first 15-inch shell, identical to those fired by *Renown* in her earlier engagement, had a much flatter arc at the shorter ranges of the current fight, resulting in it hitting the Japanese battleship in her much thicker belt. However, at seventeen thousand yards this merely meant that the penetration was not obscene, merely effective. Piercing the barbette for No. 2 turret, the shell vented its fury into the ammo hoists for that mount. If not for the sealed scuttles and protective apparatus installed as a result of the British experience at Jutland, *Yamashiro*'s carcass would have immediately joined that of *Kongo*'s on the bottom of the Java Sea.

As it was, the hit started a fairly large blaze that greatly aided *Ramilles* aim, resulting in her hitting with her next salvo. This shell also easily overmatched the Japanese vessel's belt and detonated in her engine room. With a cascade of sparks and a muffled *boom*! the armor-piercing shell destroyed one of the vessel's massive turbines, the resultant spall greatly increasing the IJN's casualty notification branch's workload. Not the swiftest vessel in the best of conditions, the *Yamashiro* was slowed to twelve knots and forced to turn out of line.

Malaya and *Valiant* both engaged the *Fuso*, *Yamashiro*'s sister ship, with devastating results despite a loss of accuracy due to their over concentration. The first to hit, *Malaya*'s put three shells into the Japanese battleship in quick succession, starting a tremendous blaze amidships, smashing her No. 1 turret, and holing her engine room. Believing the Japanese battleship to be finished, and with a plethora of targets shooting back at his vessel, *Malaya*'s gunnery officer shifted off the battleship while *Valiant*'s continued to engage. With flames shooting to the height of her massive pagoda mast and the problem of over concentration suddenly solved, *Valiant* even outshot her sister with four hits.

With the *Valiant's* first two hits simultaneously clearing the vessel's signal bridge and turning her conning tower's inhabitants into something resembling that which came out of a sausage factory, the vessel's command fell upon her executive officer. While not a lightweight vessel by any means, the *Fuso* had never been intended to stand up to such a pummeling. The junior captain had just enough time to be informed of his impromptu promotion when *Valiant's* third shell ended his tenure. The fourth shell, hitting almost immediately thereafter and cutting the battleship's fire mains, ensured the hapless man had plenty of company for the journey to meet his ancestors. With the loss of water pressure, the raging amidships fire swept like a hurricane into the magazine servicing No. 3 turret, causing that compartment to erupt in a massive explosion that had debris landing around the *Mutsu*.

Admiral Kondo, seeing the burning *Yamashiro* turning out of line and the *Fuso's* explosion, realized that he would lose all of Japan's battleline in one fell swoop if he was not careful. Screaming at his staff, he began ordering the battleships to turn away. It would be up to the destroyers and cruisers to damage the Allied battleline so that their Japanese opposite numbers could return to finish off cripples.

"I'm going forward!" Jacob shouted above the din of *Houston's* main battery firing again. "Lieutenant Foncier, you have the con!"

"Aye-aye, Sir!"

Jacob slid down the ladder to the main deck and began rushing forward. His leg attempted to buckle under him and he stopped, looking down to see that his previous wound had darkened his pants with blood. Biting down hard, he forced himself to move quickly past the firing port 5-inch guns in order to avoid hindering the firefighters still battling the blaze on the starboard guns. Looking around once more he realized that the *Houston* was still in the dark even though her 8-inch guns were like giant strobe lights whenever they fired. Looking out towards the enemy, he saw what could only be several Allied vessels afire. As he watched one of the three-funneled Commonwealth cruisers, her silhouette lined in flame, had her aft magazines detonate with a thunderous *whoooooommmmmpppp!* that was audible almost four miles away.

Jesus Christ on rollerskates! Jacob thought. *We're getting creamed!*

With a roar the *Prince of Wales* fired at some distant target, the six shells proscribing a lazy arc towards the horizon. Aft of her, *Repulse* also fired her forward guns at a distant target. There was a flash then a bright burning on the far horizon.

Maybe not, as long as those Limey battleships keep hitting.

The "Limey battleships" in question were indeed hitting well. Unfortunately, despite their brilliant shooting, the Japanese retort was about to arrive. Even with the ten torpedoes absorbed by their cruiser escorts still over one hundred remained. Slow, cumbersome, and utterly fixated on their opposite numbers which they were so brilliantly pummeling, it was only in the last few moments that anyone aboard the three battleships realized the danger they were in. Whilst errors in Japanese aiming and a misjudgment of the vessel's true speed made the number of torpedoes with a realistic chance of hitting maybe a third of those launched, that was more than enough.

Ramilles was the first vessel hit. The 'R'-class battleship had been designed to slug it out with her German counterparts in the North Sea which meant that almost a third of her weight was devoted to armor. Unfortunately, little of this was below the waterline to resist the two 'Long Lances', one amidships and one aft, that hit the elderly battleship. The first hit was like a stroke from a massive warhammer, ripping a gigantic hole in the vessel's side at the point where the engine and boiler rooms adjoined one another. The second was like a whirling backhand blow with the same blunt object, opening another appalling gash just a couple dozen feet aft of where the first wound ended. Powerless, with a severe fire making her a beacon, the *Ramilles* came to a stop and began to list, her guns still trained to starboard. Realizing from the reports coming in that her fate was sealed, the battlewagon's captain swallowed hard and made the hardest decision any captain could face. Twenty minutes later, with the majority of the survivors off, the old battleship proved the wisdom of his decision as she capsized to starboard and sank.

Malaya, in one of the strangest flukes in naval history, was somehow missed. From the locations of the damaged cruisers, her captain would later determine the torpedoes that would have had the best opportunity to hit her had already eviscerated the *Cornwall* and *Devonshire*. Putting her helm over to port in order to pass the mortally wounded *Ramilles*, the *Malaya* checked fire as she did so. As a result her crew had a ringside seat to the worst sight of the night for the Allied side: the death of *Valiant*.

The *Valiant* had just fired her first salvo at her next target, the *Mutsu*, when she was struck by two 'Long Lances'. The first one, running shallow, hit the battleship in her armored belt, the thick armor minimizing the damage of the blast. Shuddering slightly, the battleship had enough time to fire another salvo when she was struck by the second 'Long Lance'. Seeming almost guided by a malevolent force, the 'Long Lance' more than made up for its earlier companion by running almost as deep as it had shallow.

Hitting the battleship between A and B turrets at the point where her belt was starting to thin as the hull curved, the 'Long Lance' sent hot fragments and debris into the vessel's main forward magazine. While the *Valiant*'s propellant had been modified to provide added stability after the keen lessons of Jutland, its nature was to explode. Like the scorpion in the children's fable it was unable to deny its nature in the face of opportunity.

Hauling himself up the bridge ladder, Jacob was suddenly stopped dead by an explosion that made that of the British heavy cruiser seem like a child's firecracker. The bright flash lit up his face, followed a few moments later by a gust of warm wind. Turning to look at its source, he felt he suddenly felt faint, nearly falling off the ladder. As he wildly flailed and managed to hang on, his mind screamed in terror at what his eyes were telling him. The *Valiant*'s aft end was starkly outlined by the inferno blazing in her fore half, the flagship clearly down by the bow.

*Oh sweet Lord...*Jacob thought.

He never had time to finish his prayer as suddenly it was raining all around the *Houston*. First there was a massive splash roughly five hundred yards off the port bow, some large portion of the Commonwealth battleship smacking into the water. Then there were shouts of surprise followed by screams of horror as several mortal remains of the *Valiant*'s crew began falling on the heavy cruiser, several falling wetly on the deck below where Jason was climbing the ladder.

The revulsion snapped Jacob out of it.

I don't want to end up damn chum for some fuckin' shark! he thought angrily. Fighting down the urge to vomit, he fought himself up the ladder and onto the bridge.

Stepping into the structure, he was confronted with bedlam. Whereas pieces of the *Valiant*'s crew had been landing on the

283

Houston's deck, those of most of the bridge's inhabitants were strung all about the structure. As he took another step forward he nearly slipped, going down to one hand and one knee in a blinding bit of pain. Feeling his hand wet, he looked down to see his hand covered in the normal aftermath of a violent death.

"Corpsman!" Jacob barked. A senior chief looked towards him, surprised to see the XO. Just as the man started to come towards Jacob the *Houston's* guns roared again, the blast rustling through the bridge.

"Aye-aye, Sir?!" the man asked.

"Get some freaking sand up here before someone kills themselves!" Jacob barked. "On the double!"

"Sir, we've got wounded..." the man protested.

"Unless you want me to toss you off *my* fucking ship, sailor, you will damn well comply with my order!" Jacob bellowed. "Now move!"

The sailor moved away, shocked into action. Jacob cast his eyes around the compartment. Looking, he saw a man sitting in the corner, holding his knees to his chest and softly sobbing. The man was covered in blood, but judging from the lack of corpsman attention was otherwise not hurt. Looking, Jacob realized that the man was an officer, likely the Junior Officer of the Deck. Not recognizing him, he realized the man must be a *Boise* survivor. Moving over to the man, Jacob grabbed him. The officer recoiled away, giving a frightened cry.

"Ensign," Jacob said quietly, forcing the man to look at him. "Ensign!" he barked. The officer stopped shaking and looked at him.

"W-w-we're all going to *die!*" the man sobbed. "Oh God..."

"Listen ensign," Jacob said quietly and firmly, resisting the urge to slap the man silly. "We're not going to die. I need you to get up and take the wheel."

For a moment it did not appear as if the officer was going to come out of it. Then, catching himself, the man nodded.

"Aye-aye, Sir," he said, unclenching himself. *Houston's* guns fired again, the vessel starting to come around to port. The heavy cruiser was bathed in the bright light of starshells again, causing Jacob to curse under his breath.

"Son, what's your name?" he asked.

"E-ensign Carlyle, sir," the stunned officer said.

"All right Carlyle, let's get back into this fight—the Limeys look like they could use a hand," Jacob said calmly.

The speaker at the back of the compartment crackled, a faint and tremulous voice coming over it.

"All...vessels. All vessels, this is Admiral Phillips.," a strained voice said. "Admiral Crutchley is in command. God...save...the King!"

Jacob looked out towards where *Valiant* was still burning furiously. As he watched, several salvoes of shells arrived near simultaneously, at least two battleship shells hitting the sinking flagship.

"Goddammit, those little yellow bastards are pounding her!" someone cried.

Jacob felt his own stomach do flip flops. The *Valiant* was obviously finished, the fact that the Japanese were still firing on her demonstrating their foes implacable nature. Then he had no more time to reflect as an enemy salvo bracketed the *Houston* once more with massive waterspouts.

"It'd be nice if someone would pick on a vessel their own size!" Jacob muttered. The *Houston's* guns barked back in defiance, Jacob sincerely hoping that Sloan was not playing tag with a battleship, new shells or no. There was silence on the bridge, and suddenly he realized all eyes were staring at him because no one was manning the wheel.

Shit, we've go to move or we're dead! Jacob thought.

"Carlyle, take the helm! You," Jacob barked, pointing at a corpsman who was busy pulling a shroud over one of the bridge's many dead, "are now my talker. First thing, tell Lieutenant Foncier to send me a talker on the double. Second, figure out what Commander Sloan is shooting at."

The corpsman quickly dropped the shroud over the corpse he was tending and jumped for the voice-powered telephone. Slipping in his predecessor's blood, the man's feet flew out from under him, causing him to slam backwards to the deck despite furiously windmilling his arms to try and regain his balance. The wind obviously knocked out of him, the sailor still managed to struggle into the talker's chair. Jacob turned away as soon as the man was able to start talking, bringing his binoculars up so he could try and get a feel for what was going on.

Off the port bow about five thousand yards he could see the *Malaya* continuing to fire towards the distant enemy battleline. Waterspouts all around the maneuvering battleship indicated that her opposite numbers were firing back, and the rapidly firing 6-inch secondaries meant that there were enemy light forces still about. Beyond *Malaya*, the *Dorsetshire* and *Exeter* were firing at their full rate at a furiously burning target far to their starboard, approximately the same range as the enemy battle line but aft of those vessels. Other than those two vessels, Jacob could not see any other clearly friendly vessels. The radio was eerily silent, and Jacob suddenly realized that the Allied fleet was for all purposes decimated.

"Sir, we are engaging a heavy cruiser or small battleship," the man replied. "Commander Sloan reports that the enemy vessels are turning away."

Thank God, Jacob thought. *I hope it's the former, as the words 'small battleship' are a rather big misnomer.* The talk between ships suddenly crackled into life.

"All vessels, all vessels, *scrum*, I say again, *scrum*," Admiral Crutchley's voice came from the speaker. Crutchley, an avid rugby fan, had jokingly recommended "scrum" as the code word for all ships retreating. Jacob doubted that the man was laughing now.

Someone has wisely decided to wait and fight another day rather than immolate themselves on the pyre of sacrifice. Turning to Carlyle, Jacob quickly thought of what course needed to be steered.

"Bring your helm to course two six five relative, full speed ahead. Order all hands to release rafts and boats for the survivors."

"I can't believe we're running," someone muttered. Jacob started to whirl on whomever had spoke then realized he was now the vessel's master and thus not to be trifled with minor matters like the lower deck's opinion. After a moment's pause he realized that someone else was had the same opinion he did.

"It's going to be a long war, friend," the other man's voice said out of the darkness. "These fuckers have won the first mile, we'll see how they do over the next twenty-five."

"Sir, signal from *Prince of Wales*—she's ordering us to retire and put out our fires," Lieutenant Foncier said, stepping into the bridge. "Lieutenant Morgan has Battle Two," he spoke before Jacob could ask.

"Good enough, have a seat over as the talker," Jacob said. "Corpsman, you may continue getting these bodies out of here."

"Sir, you're bleeding," Lieutenant Foncier observed.

"I'll be all right, damn stitches just opened up," Jacob said.

"Aye-aye, sir," Foncier replied, his voice skeptical.

"I need a damage report from all division chiefs on the double, and someone tell me when we've got that fire out," Jacob ordered.

"Aye-aye, Sir," Foncier said. *Houston's* No. 3 turret roared again, the only guns able to bear as the heavy cruiser moved away. Foncier gave a whoop.

"Commander Sloan reports hit!"

Unbeknownst to Sloan, he had already struck his target, the *Chikuma*, three times prior to his current hit. It was the fourth shell, however, that had the greatest effect while simultaneously highlighting the problem with putting a seaplane carrier, albeit a heavily armed and armored one, in the line of battle. The heavy 8" shell performed as advertised, going through *Chikuma's* belt like a brick through a plate glass window, passing through the forward bulkhead of the vessel's generator room, and detonating against her avgas storage. With a *whoomp!* that was audible aboard the Japanese cruisers forward and aft the seaplanes' fuel ignited, the brilliant fireball making it seem as if the vessel had suffered a magazine explosion.

Fortunately for those crewmembers whose action stations were not in adjacent compartments, the explosion was not as severe as it could have been due to the fullness of the tank. While the immolation of the generator room rendered the vessel without electric power and the loss of battery power only exacerbated this issue, the heavy cruiser was still controllable and able to turn out of line, heavily ablaze.

"Sir, Commander Sloan reports target suffered explosion! Looks like a magazine!" Foncier said excitedly.

The riposte from whatever Japanese ships were firing on the *Houston* was well astern, the heavy cruiser having finally moved out of the starshell patterns. Simultaneously, Sloan decided to check fire, the *Prince of Wales* potentially fouling his aim. The British battleship had no such issues,

288

firing her aft guns again at a distant target.

"Course two six five relative! Speed thirty-one knots!"

"Fire secured in secondaries, Sir," Foncier said. "Division chiefs are sending runners with the damage reports."

"Corpsman!" Jacob barked, looking for the petty officer whom had begun to spread the just arrived sand on the bridge deck.

"Aye-aye, Sir?" the man asked from behind him.

"When you get done with that, tell the surgeon I need a casualty count."

"Aye-aye, Sir," the petty officer replied.

Jacob turned back to conning his ship, the stiff breeze from the shattered bridge windows hitting him full in the face. Now that the immediate danger was past, he could smell the aroma of burnt gunpowder and blood, the mixture making his stomach turn. He was suddenly thankful for the vessel's darkened light conditions, as the bridge likely resembled a butcher shop.

"*Prince of Wales* is turning back to cover the retreat of our destroyers. She's signaling for us to hove to and remain in this area as a rally ship."

"Signal our assent and bring her around. Where in the hell are those damage reports?"

The Second Java Sea, like many naval fights, seemed to gradually grind to a stop rather than end. While Jacob's ultimate prognosis might have been correct, in the short term *Malaya*'s continued accuracy as well as that of *Prince of Wales* and the two Commonwealth heavy cruisers gave Admiral Kondo enough of a pause to order his own forces to withdraw in order for the destroyers to reload torpedoes. Disengaging from their spirited fight with their Allied opposite numbers, most of whom would never realize how fortunate they were that the Japanese destroyermen had expended their torpedoes before engaging.

In turn, the relative inexperience of the newer Commonwealth crews, long range and poor angles presented by rapidly turning destroyers, and the wretched capabilities of the American contingent's torpedoes meant that Japanese losses were similarly light. Indeed, the only vessel to be hit by a functional torpedo was the *Kitakami,* and that one of the elderly Mk. 8s. Set ablaze in her engineering spaces, the light cruiser was further flayed by the *Malaya's* secondaries but managed to escape into smoke lain by the Japanese destroyer *Suzukaze.*

It was this smoke, as well as that from many other ships, that allowed the two sides to extricate themselves with relatively little difficulty. On the Japanese side, this allowed Admiral Kondo to take quick stock. With *Fuso* and *Kongo* destroyed, *Yamashiro* a near wreck, *Haruna* damaged from the afternoon battle, and the *Hiei* and *Ise* having received moderate damage from the *Prince of Wales* and *Malaya* respectively, Kondo swiftly determined he would try to further attrit the enemy force with his heavy cruisers and destroyers before bringing his battleline forward again. Barking orders for reorganization, he sent eight of his destroyers forward to determine the situation while the shuffling of the fleet was accomplished.

These eight vessels returned to the battlefield a little more than an hour after Kondo had given the order to turn away. As they continued pressing south, they found a sea dotted with two cripples, the *Devonshire* and *De Ruyter* still struggling for life. Circling around the two cruisers were three destroyers, mostly concentrating on picking up survivors. With sixty-four torpedoes between them, and believing themselves to be undetected, the eight destroyers began maneuvering to deliver a devastating close range torpedo attack.

Things did not progress much further than preparation as the sky was suddenly lit up over the eight vessels as *Prince of Wales* fired starshells. Having been detached by Jacob as a hedge against the Japanese battleline returning, *Prince of Wales* quickly opened fire with her main battery at the eight contacts, causing the destroyers to scatter in evasive maneuvers. The battleship was joined a few moments later by the other undamaged vessels, the fire prompting the eight destroyer captains to determine that discretion was the better part of valor as they fired their torpedoes and turned away. Outside of some splinter damage, the eight vessels managed to escape without being hit.

Roughly seven minutes later four of these torpedoes ended the hopes of saving *Devonshire* and *De Ruyter*, three hitting the former and causing her to quickly sink, one hitting the other and causing her to catch fire. Having watched the *Sumatra* explode just minutes before, the *De Ruyter's* crew did not hesitate in abandoning ship. Twenty minutes later, as the Japanese fleet reappeared at the outer edges of *Prince of Wales'* radar screen, the *Exeter* sank the blazing hulk with a pair of torpedoes. That unenviable task complete, the Allied vessels headed away from the advancing Japanese cruisers and destroyers. Amongst the lost was Admiral Doorman, last sighted on the *De Ruyter's* bridge with her captain.

Finding nothing but open sea and not really having any desire to duel battleships he could not see, the Japanese cruiser commander made a half-hearted attempt to regain contact then rejoined Admiral Kondo's main force. It was an act of timidity that would earn Rear Admiral Upper Half Gunichi Mikawa a shore billet at Singapore for the remainder of the war, the position coming with the express order that he was *not* to commit *seppuku* to atone for his sins.

Beaten, dejected, and far weaker than when the fight had begun, the Allied forces straggled back towards the circling *Houston*. It would be well after dawn before all the vessels arrived, but nowhere near that long for all present to realize that the East Indies were now irrevocably doomed. For their part, the Japanese fell back towards Borneo to regroup and prepare to launch the final and decisive assault, that against Java.

Honolulu
1000 Local (1530 Eastern)
5 May

"Are you sure you don't want to come to the movie, Jo?" Patricia called from the bathroom. "C'mon, *Casablanca* won't be around forever!"

In the living room, Jo looked up from her pulp detective novel. The paperback was one of her father's, the twenty boxes of books in the attic running the gamut from the classical to the disposable. Looking at her watch, she shook her head at Patricia.

"Gee, let me think…why would I want to go down to the middle of Honolulu, in a city that's getting more and more packed with sailors who will likely ogle, jostle, and perhaps grope me?"

*Not to mention that would mean that **three** of us were going to a movie, and we all know that's the definition of a crowd*, Jo thought.

Jo could almost hear the wheels of disapproval turning in her friend's head. Not hearing anything for a few minutes, she turned back to her book. As she read, a small part of her mind began wandering in idle daydream to the last time her father had walked through the door. Everything had seemed so different five months prior, and she found herself wishing with all her heart that she could return to that time.

Patricia came into the living room and stood looking down at Jo she put in her earrings. The youngest Cobb was wearing a green blouse and yellow skirt, the latter falling straight and coming to her knee. Her hair was pinned up tight to her head in a hairstyle that appeared to use all of America's annual production of bobby pins but did well in emphasizing her pretty face, neck, and shoulders. As per usual, Patricia was wearing only lipstick, opting for a soft rouge shade. All in all she was the epitome of understated beauty.

"You know, we could call Eric if you didn't want to be an odd person," Patricia said. Jo gave her a look, causing her to begin stammering. "N-n-ot that I'm saying…"

"The look was in regard to the 'odd person' comment, Patricia, not to your absolutely absurd attempts to set me up with your brother," Jo said.

Patricia colored slightly in embarrassment.

"I think you're doing quite well setting yourself up with Eric," Patricia observed.

"Like you have a problem with that," Jo teased.

"Maybe I do," Patricia retorted.

"And I'm the Virgin Mary," Jo said snarkily.

"Your name is not Mary, that is most definitely true," Patricia said teasingly, her voice clearly indicating that Jo's name wasn't the only hangup. Jo threw a cushion at her, groaning in disgust. Patricia dodged with a squeak, Jo surprised at the woman's agility in high heels since she had never seen her roommate wear them.

"Look, just because some of us had the misfortune to be surrounded by highly sexed and persuasive men our entire life does not mean we should be looked down upon."

Patricia smiled sweetly at her roommate.

"Well, I was surrounded by highly sexed and persuasive men and *I* didn't lose my virtue."

"That's because all of them *were related to you*," Jo pointed out. "Now, if I'm wrong and Alabama shares more than a first letter with Arkansas, let me know."

Patricia let her jaw drop, her mouth forming a perfect

'O' of shock.

"I cannot believe you would even *suggest* such a thing," she replied. To Jo's amazement the woman looked like she was actually about to be ill.

"I was joking," Jo said, her own eyes widening. Patricia suddenly closed her mouth and smiled broadly.

"Gotcha."

Jo reached for another pillow just as there was a knock at the door. Patricia wagged a finger at her then turned and went to answer it. Looking through the eyehole, her features broke into a smile. Jo waited until she opened the door, then wound up.

"Hi Charl…" Patricia started, right before she was hit hard in the side of the head by the thrown pillow.. The impact staggered her, nearly causing her to fall before. Charles moved swiftly, stepping across the threshold and steadying Patricia by putting his arm on her shoulder. Jo watched as Patricia regained her balance, her eyes meeting Charles.

I think I'm going to be ill, Jo thought quietly. *Really, really ill.*

"Thank you," Patricia said softly, her eyes still looking into Charles's. The man closed the door behind him, his arm still on Patricia's shoulder.

"You're welcome," Charles replied with a nervous grin. "Sorry if I was a bit forward."

"Oh no, you weren't forward at all," Patricia replied breathlessly.

Okay, time to break this up because I'll be damned if I'm going to watch these two smooch, Jo said. She cleared her throat quite loudly, abruptly killing the mood without looking up from her book. The couple broke awkwardly apart, Charles fumbling to get the bouquet of flowers out of his left hand to his right.

"I got these for you," he said quietly.

"They're beautiful, thank you! I'll go put them in some water."

Jo didn't look up as her roommate walked past, concentrating intently on the last few pages of her book. As soon as she heard the water start running she looked up at Charles, the officer standing quietly inside the living room looking at pictures. Jo was about to offer him a seat when there was suddenly frenzied knocking at the door. Startled, Charles and she looked at each other, then at Jo when she came in.

I wonder who in the hell that is, Jo thought, waving her roommate away from the door. Looking through the peephole she was surprised to see Eric and Nick Cobb, both resplendent in dress whites, standing on her doorstep.

"This is a bit weird," she said, opening the door. Both Cobbs looked at her in her shirts and floral print shirt like she had grown an extra head.

"Okay boys, I know there aren't that many white women on this island, but surely you've seen one that's not related to you in the last few hours, so please stop staring at me like that," Jo said drily. All three men suddenly got matching looks of horror on their face.

"Let me guess…no one called you guys?" Nick asked grimly, looking at his watch.

"Called us guys *what?!*" Patricia asked, stepping around the corner. Both of her brothers looked at her, then at Charles, then back at her.

"Yes, it's called a date," Patricia snapped. "Now would you two stooges care to tell me what's going on? Where's David and Sam?"

"Probably sweating out the most anxious forty-five minutes of any man's life," Eric quipped. "Well, next to…"

"Look, we don't have time for riddles…*sir*," Nick said, seeing the look his brother was giving him when he didn't add the last word. "Sam and David are down at the church getting David's preacher to sign a marriage license."

"What?!" Patricia asked.

"Yes, you heard correctly…Sadie wanted to get married in the church since they only had a civil ceremony last year. Let's just say there are reasons this ceremony needs to be rushed," Eric said.

Jo and Patricia looked at each other, then back at Eric.

"You guys were supposed to get called this morning by Sadie's friend Cindy, her bridesmaid," Nick continued. "Since you guys were never called, and now no one can seem to find Cindy, we're going to assume that she took to the hills, which means that Sadie is going to need a stand in."

"Doesn't she have to get dressed and everything?" Patricia asked.

"Things change, little sis…you may have noticed there's this whole war thing on," Nick chided. "Since you're dressed, and Lord knows ain't no way a woman can get ready in fifteen minutes," he said, looking at Jo, "you'll do."

Jo raised an eyebrow at that comment.

"If one of you louts will stay here to lead me to where the wedding is, I'll make a liar out of you, Nick Cobb."

"Right, and next you'll tell me there really is a Santa Claus," Nick replied, laughing. "No matter, Eric can stay, I've got to pick up my date."

Eric and Patricia both did a double take at that comment.

"You have a *date*?"

"Yes, dear sister, you are not the only one who can have those. Now, let us go before all heck breaks loose down at the church."

Jo was moving even before the others finished going out the door. Starting to unbutton her shirt as she headed towards her bedroom, she looked back over her shoulder at

Eric.

"There's lemonade in the fridge if you're thirsty! This shouldn't take but a few minutes."

"Thanks. Do you want a glass?"

"Yes, please, I'll get it when I get out of my room."

With that, Jo entered her bedroom and shrugged out of her shirt. Opening her closet she quickly decided to go with a solid, lightweight black dress. While arguably it would be inappropriate to wear black to a wedding as a woman, she just didn't have the time nor inclination to try and impress anyone. Quickly putting the dress on, she stood and looked at herself in the full-length mirror.

"Okay, obviously someone here has been losing weight without determining to inform the brain," she muttered. The dress wasn't as formless as a gunny sack, but it definitely didn't do her any favors on where it curved.

"Screw it, I'm only getting invited because some brainless nitwit forgot to call the remainder of the Cobbs," Jo muttered. Reaching around to zip the dress up, Jo opened her dresser drawer to pull out a pair of nylons. Pulling them on, Jo silently thanked her lucky stars that she had taken a bath and shaved her legs despite being off that day.

I swear, it wasn't just because I wanted to feel better about Patricia having a date and me being without one, Jo thought. *Or at least, that's what I'll keep telling myself.*

Looking at the clock, Jo gave a slight smile.

"Shows what that knucklehead Nick knows," she muttered. "I've still got eight minutes to spare." Throwing on a pair of flats, she moved out into the living room. Like Charles before him, Eric was staring at the pictures on the bedroom wall. When Jo saw the specific one he was looking at she felt the blood rush to her cheeks.

"What is it with men and staring at pictures?" she snapped. Striding over to the one Eric was looking at, she quickly took it off of its hook.

"So who's the lucky young lieutenant with you and your father?" Eric asked, the needling quite apparent in his voice.

"Lieutenant Gary Foster," Jo replied. "And that's the last question you get to ask about him." Looking around, Jo spotted her lemonade and beat a quick retreat towards it across the room.

Eric raised an eyebrow at that. From all reports as well as his own observations, Jo did not seem rather unflappable about most topics. Sam and David both thought that she seemed to be a good, stabilizing influence on Patricia, and was the primary reason that their younger sister had made a smooth transition into *womanhood*, to allude to her earlier statements in the hospital. Nick, after initially giving Eric a hard time for asking, had echoed those sentiments as well as pointing out that Commander Morton had quietly paid Patricia's first two months of rent, a fact that only Jo and he knew. The money Patricia had given Jo for her half of the rent was currently accruing interest as a 'rainy day' fund back on the mainland and would be released to Patricia once she moved out. All in all, it appeared that the Mortons, both Jo and her father, were really good people.

So why did she just react like a scalded cat when I asked her about this lieutenant? Eric wondered.

"Okay, I've obviously struck a nerve," Eric observed. "Why do I only get one question about him?"

"Because I don't ask you questions about Joyce Cotner," Jo replied icily. "Even though she's still alive, unlike Lieutenant Foster."

Eric let that one wash over him like a ship passing through a particularly high wave—it hurt a bit, but he was after an objective.

"So you're saying Lieutenant Foster and you were engaged?" he asked. "That would explain why you guys look so chummy."

"Dammit, Eric, I said that we were *not* going to discuss him. Now, if you can't handle that, you need to get the *hell* out of my house!" Jo said, her voice breaking into a sob at the last part. Taking a deep breath, she grabbed a napkin off the nearby table and dabbed at her eyes.

"Now look what you've made me go and do, damn you," she sniffled. "*We* don't know each other well enough for you to be making me cry, Eric. Maybe you need to be going to your brother's wedding by yourself."

It wasn't intentional, if that helps, Eric thought helplessly. He placed his lemonade on the nearby coffee table and went walking across the room.

"I'm sorry," he said, stopping just outside of arms reach. "I didn't mean to pick a scab."

"Oh no, you completely meant to pick a scab, you just didn't mean to make me cry about it," Jo said, laughing mirthlessly. "I don't know why, but all of you Cobbs seem to have this innate urge to pry at people."

Eric cautiously went to embrace Jo. His arms were almost all the way around her when she put a hand to his chest.

"No," she said, pushing him back.

What the hell?

"You're wearing whites, genius. Trust me, you do *not* want to try and get makeup out of whites."

"Oh," Eric said. *Practical even when she's upset, and did I mention pretty?* While all three of his brothers had all sung the praises of Jo as a person, not one of them had ever mentioned her looks. While Eric would readily admit she didn't have the porcelain doll beauty of the women he and his brothers had usually dated, he saw nothing that made him think Josephine was anything but beautiful.

I'm not saying I'm in love with her or anything, I just

think she's really, really pretty, Eric told himself.

"Not to mention that you'd have to explain that to your brothers, and if there's one thing the Cobb family utterly lacks it's the ability to avoid teasing someone when the opportunity presents itself."

"You say an awful lot about our family for only having known us for a couple of years," Eric chided.

"I think having met you all now I'm able to make an informed judgment," Jo replied. "Now go on, you'll be late."

"Hey, what do you mean *I'll* be late. You're coming too," Eric said.

"No, I'm not," Jo said, stepping out of his arms. Eric touched her arm, just above her burn scar. Jo looked down in surprise, then up at him.

"What?" Eric asked.

"Most men avoid touching my scar," she said quietly. "You're the first I've ever met who hasn't."

Eric shrugged as he watched the play of emotions over her face.

"Everyone has scars," he said, simply, then stopped as he realized how idiotic that sounded. "I mean…"

Jo stopped him with a finger to his lips, looking up at him.

"That is probably one of the most profound things a person has ever said, Eric, because we all do have scars." Looking at where she had placed the picture of her dad, Lieutenant Foster, and herself, she swallowed. "Just not all of them visible. Now let's hurry up before people start talking bad about us."

In the end, they weren't as late as the bride. Of course, once Sadie walked into the small room, everyone stopped looking at clocks. In her white wedding dress, veil, and heels Sadie was an image of beauty, outshining every other woman in the room. The ceremony was quick, the pastor speeding things along even as he maintained the decorum and seriousness of the situation.

Twenty minutes later, after the bride and groom had stolen away to parts unknown, the four Cobbs not joined in a state of matrimony, Charles, and Jo found themselves standing outside David and Sadie's church.

"You know, you're still welcome to come with us, Jo," Patricia said, looking at her watch. "Now that you're dressed and everything, you might as well catch a movie."

Jo pondered for a moment, then seeing a gang of sailors walking by and quite obviously gawking at Patricia's backside, she shook her head.

"No, if you want to go play zoo exhibit, that's fine with me," Jo replied. "I've got a good detective novel to finish." Looking at Sam, she suddenly felt very sad for the big lug. The man was staring despondently into space, and he looked all the world like a small child whose playmate had left for good. "Sam, why don't you go with your sister?"

Startled, Sam turned to look at Jo.

"Huh?"

"I said, why don't you go with your sister to *Casablanca*," Jo said, smiling. "It'll be a great time."

"No, unfortunately I've got to get back and get David and I's stuff ready for…uh, nevermind," Sam said, having said far more than he meant to. Patricia cocked an eyebrow at her brother.

"Ready for what?" she asked.

"Nothing you should be asking your brother about on a crowded street," Jo said. Patricia turned to look at her friend then closed her mouth, seeing Jo was in deadly earnest.

"We'll go with you," Nick said, Agnes nodding her assent. Looking at the woman Jo had to admit Nick had done

301

damn well for himself.

Pretty girl, although I'm not sure if Nick realizes how tough she is, Jo thought. *If he's not careful she'll eat him for lunch*, Jo thought.

"Eric?" Patricia asked, turning to her other brother.

"Nah, I think I'll walk back to BOQs and catch some rack time," Eric said. "It'll be pretty dead with most everyone on duty. Walk you back, Jo?"

Jo saw a slight, knowing smile cross Agnes's face, the expression so quick most people would have missed it.

Okay sweetie, it's not like you didn't fall for some Cobb magic yourself, Jo thought.

"Sure, let's go," Jo replied. "We'll see you guys later."

"Okay," Patricia said, waving. With that the two couples moved off, leaving Sam, Eric, and Jo.

"Thanks Jo," Eric said. "I'd hate to get my nuts ripped off because someone overheard the conversation."

"Eric!" Sam thundered

"What?" Eric asked, nonplussed at his brother's anger.

"That's no language to use in front of a lady!" Sam snapped. "You were raised better than that."

"Sam, I passed biology and I've been around the Navy forever—I am aware that men have nuts, balls, di…" Jo started.

"You know, do you kiss your mother…" Eric started to ask, then stammered to a stop as he realized that was a very dumb and improper question. "Sorry."

Jo just looked at him, utterly amazed that a grown man could be so befuddled.

I truly hope that you're a better flier than you are a smart-aleck or I think I'm starting to understand how you keep ending up in the hospital, Jo thought uncharitably.

"Notice that I am only saying these things around two men, one of whom that I only recently got to stop treating me like I was a nun, and not loudly where everyone can hear me. I realize that you're not used to it, but we women have brains and stuff, we're not just pretty pictures."

"I guess now I know where Patricia got her 'I am a woman' speech from," Eric said quietly.

"I think if we're going to get along," Jo continued levelly, prompting a bit of a snicker from Sam, "you'll have to get used to my bluntness. Your brothers have managed to accept that not every woman is a delicate Southern belle who desperately needs a man to protect her from the world's wickedness or who may occasionally say something a bit stronger than 'shoot', so there's no excuse for you not doing the same."

Eric inhaled sharply, suddenly seeing Jo in a whole new light.

I'll be damned if I'm going to hide around just one man. If, and it was an 'if' the size of most continents, Jo was going to truly get serious with Eric he would have to learn to take her warts and all. Studying his face, she suddenly found herself caring about his opinion.

Not so much that I'm going to change, however, Jo thought.

"Well, if my brothers can do it, guess I can't very well complain, can I? Especially since it's kinda hard to get a home cooked meal around here, and I get the sinking suspicion that I would be banned from your house by 'Toots'."

"Heck, David, Nick, and I still haven't been allowed back," Sam observed. "And we didn't even hit Charles."

"She's forgiven you guys for that, she's just too enamored with her new beau to get around to having you guys over."

The pained look on Sam's face was something to

behold. Jo gave him a slight smile.

"Yes, it is something that she's going to regret not having done in, unless I miss my guess, about seventy-two hours. Just how did Sadie get back from her school's trip to the outer islands, anyway?"

"Someone in the Patrol Wing owed David a favor, and some of our bosses are hopeless romantics," Sam replied.

"Those Distinguished Flying Crosses that you guys are up for probably helped," Eric said wistfully. He clasped his hands together and looked up at Sam, batting his eyelashes. "You're my hero, Sam," he said falsetto.

"Don't be jealous," Sam laughed. He looked at his watch and gave a slight smile. "And as much as I'd like to sit here and shoot the bull, I've got to go."

"Make sure you stop by the house, you big lug," Jo said, stepping up and giving Sam a hug. There were a few whistles from behind Sam, one brave soul starting a cat call until the big man turned around and scanned the crowd. Suddenly, the dozen sailors that had conducted the whistling found something else to do and in another direction.

"I'll see you around, Sam," Eric said, the *before you leave* remaining unspoken.

With a nod, Sam turned and headed back towards where he had left the bicycle he had pedaled up from Pearl.

"That man is not going to know what to do with himself tonight," Jo observed. "At least Sadie didn't actually chain him to a lamp post like she threatened to."

Eric looked over at Jo in surprise.

"I like Sam, but it's got to be a pain having him constantly underfoot," Jo said.

"Yes, but I didn't think he was over at their house all that often," Eric replied.

"Don't give me that line of crap," Jo said. "I started to wonder how they kept their fighters from getting tangled in their Siamese bonds."

"Well, you know with twins you get either completely sick of each other or you're incredibly close," Eric replied. "I'm just glad it wasn't the former, we had enough strife at home between Nick and I."

"You guys used to fight?" Jo asked.

"Oh yeah...Dad would wear his belt out on us, and that was after either Sam or David usually gave us a pretty good tarring," Eric said, then mocked his brothers. "'You don't fight with family.'"

"Bet that went over real well," Jo observed with a throaty laugh.

"Yeah, but as you can guess, if you fought David or Sam you fought them both," Eric said. "That was always painful, especially when they went through their growth spurt. I guess around the time I was twelve Nick and I stopped being like cats and dogs."

Jo sighed wistfully, causing Eric to give her a funny look.

"Sorry, I just never got to go through that," Jo said quietly. "After Mom died it was just Dad and I. That wasn't fun, let me tell you...I always felt like I was way older than everyone else in school, and I do mean almost everyone, because I was always around Dad and his friends. Nothing like just becoming a woman and the most important woman in your life drops dead right in front of you."

Hope I don't sound too bitter, Jo thought. *I hate pity.*

"I'm sorry about what I started to say back there," Eric said after a short pause.

Guess not, Jo noted.

"Why? Because I can't kiss my mother with this mouth or because you honestly don't think less of a woman if she says 'fuck' every once in awhile?" Jo asked, then took a deep breath. Eric was looking at her like she had turned into a wild animal and tried to bite him.

"Okay, now *I'm* sorry," Jo said. "You didn't deserve that, and I'm way too sensitive about people feeling pity for me."

"I'm not feeling pity for you," Eric said. "And I guess it's a little bit of both, although I can't believe you just said f...*fuck* in public."

"Wow, glad to see that you're not rushing for the nearest sink to wash your own mouth out. I was starting to be afraid you were some sort of mama's boy," Jo teased.

Eric gave her a hard look, making her wonder if she'd struck a nerve, then smiled at her apprehension.

"Please, Nick was the Momma's boy," Eric observed. "Between Mom and Patricia I'm surprised he didn't arrive at the Academy a sissy."

"My, aren't we nice," Jo said. "Given that other than David he was the only Cobb there with a date, and a dish at that, I wouldn't be so hard on him."

"I didn't notice you with a companion, Miss Morton," Eric replied.

"Ah, but I was a woman flanked by two unattached men, three if you count Charles. Do you really think anyone in that building thought I was alone?" Jo stated mischievously. "I could have looked like Medusa and they would've thought one of you was my date."

"Gee, glad to see you don't have a confidence problem," Eric replied.

Thanks for not taking that opportunity to tell me I don't look hideous, jerk, Jo thought uncharitably.

"Just stating the facts, and I'm glad to see you didn't touch the Medusa comment," Jo said, tossing the proverbial softball over the plate again.

Eric stopped, causing Jo to also pause and look at him quizzically.

"You don't honestly think you look like Medusa, do you?" Eric asked, incredulous.

Jo laughed, the chortle having a bit of a rough edge to it.

Well he didn't exactly take that one over the fence, did he? she thought, shaking her head.

"I'm well aware of where I stand on the beauty scale, Eric," Jo said. "I don't need you to confirm or deny my self-perception."

"Really? So where do you think you stand?" Eric asked, his face neutral.

"Remember Lieutenant Foster?" Jo inquired.

"Yes," Eric replied, not understanding where Jo was going.

"Well, you'll get me to answer another question about him before I answer that one," Jo said, turning towards her front door. Eric stopped just at the edge of the yard, causing Jo to turn around and look at him.

"What, you still trying to figure out whether you should press your luck?" Jo asked. "Or have you decided there are some things you can live without knowing?"

"No, I'm just wondering if I'm still kicked out of your house or not?" Eric said.

Jo stopped and seemed to adopt a reflective pose, her chin on her hand as she looked up at the sky. After a few moments she looked back at Eric and was taken aback by the look on his face.

Okay, I've seen lust, and that's not it, she thought.

"For the record, Josephine, you *are* beautiful," Eric said softly. "And I guess I'll leave you with that."

Jo felt her face grow warm as Eric turned smartly on one heel and started walking off.

"Hey!" she called. "What are you doing for dinner tonight?"

"I've got duty officer," Eric replied. "But I'm free tomorrow."

"Good enough, it's a date then," Jo said. Eric gave her a wave and continued walking off towards Pearl. Jo watched him head out of sight, then turned to go back inside. She saw a movement out of the corner of her eye and found herself looking at Niole, who was standing just at the edge of her property. The woman looked at Jo, then towards where Eric had just turned the corner and gave a knowing smile.

"I would've chose the bigger one, but he is a good choice nonetheless," Niole said in heavily accented English.

"I'm not..." Jo started.

"I may be Russian but some things do not need translation," Niole laughed. "It is obvious in the way you look at him that you care for him. It is not love yet, but it may well grow if he is a good man."

Jo was about to answer when there was a crash inside Niole's house.

"Excuse me, but my ears tell me that it is probably time for some punishment," Niole stated, exasperated.

Jo watched the Russian go back into her home, confused yet happy at the same time. If Niole was right, and she was falling in love, then there were far worse things. Watching a military sedan go slowly past, two men in full dress whites in front and a rabbi in the backseat, she shuddered.

Far, far worse things, she thought to herself.

Bremerton, Washington
0900 Local (1200 Eastern)
6 May

"Does it *ever* stop raining here?" Adam asked disgustedly as he doffed his cap and hung it on a nearby hat rack. VMF-21's train had arrived the previous day, a Sunday, in Seattle. Adam had disembarked to find a messenger waiting for him. The young Navy lieutenant had handed him a message directing him to report to Rear Admiral (Upper Half) Piedmont, commander of the Northwest Military District, by 0930 Monday morning.

"In July," an older, gray-haired woman said from the corner of the room behind her desk. She was typing something up, not even bothering to look up at Adam as he came in. Other than the coat rack, the only other furniture were two straight-backed seats with navy blue cushions. Looking around, Adam noted the utter lack of usual flag-officer sycophants.

Someone's running a fairly efficient ship around here, Adam thought. *Only one secretary, and I only saw a barebones staff downstairs. Usually flag officers need at least ten people to hold their hand.*

"You must be Major Haynes," she said. "You're half an hour early."

"A good officer never keeps an admiral waiting," Adam replied, noting that the nameplate on the woman's desk read 'Mrs. Corinth'. The older woman gave him a wry look.

"Well, you're a lot smarter than most people who come in here," Mrs. Corinth replied, standing up. "I'll see if the admiral's ready to see you."

"Thank you," Adam said, taking a seat. Mrs. Corinth headed back up the hallway to the admiral's office. A few moments later, she came back.

"Admiral Piedmont will see you now," she said, sitting back down. Adam nodded politely and headed back to the admiral's office. Not seeing the man as he looked into the partially-opened door, he knocked three times.

"Come in, come in, Major Haynes," a deep male voice said. Adam pushed the door open to find the admiral staring out the window, his hands clasped behind his back. Piedmont was a tall man, standing well over six feet, with black hair graying at the temples. He turned to Adam, revealing the face of a man who obviously took care of himself, looking almost two decades younger than his sixty-three years.

"Major Haynes reporting as ordered," Adam said, saluting.

"Have a seat, Major Haynes," the admiral said, returning Adam's salute. "I was just looking outside to see if it was still pissing all over us. Damn terrible weather up here."

"Yes, sir, it truly is," Adam said with a slight smile. "Your receptionist was telling me it doesn't stop raining until July."

"Amanda's an optimist…it just rains less. Of course, she's lived her all of her life, so she's probably the better person to ask," Piedmont continued. "Anyway, you're not here to ask about my secretary, so let's get down to brass tacks. I am told by Commander Tolby, my air officer, that your squadron is at full strength. Is that correct?"

"Sir, I've got twelve pilots—we were raided pretty well in Pensacola."

"Well, I'm afraid you're in for more of the same here—I've been ordered to stand up two more squadrons."

"Sir?" Adam asked, surprised.

"The Navy Department has directed for two more Marine squadrons to be raised here at Bremerton, with their squadron numbers to be assigned officers immediately. I am assured that more pilots will be en route to fill out the squadrons, to include commanders."

"Roger Sir," Adam said, stunned.

"I'm sorry, Haynes, but if it makes you feel any better I don't have any planes for you anyway—I just put all of our *Wildcats* on the next boat to Hawaii," Piedmont said. "I'm assured that we've got first priority for the next ones off the Grumman line, but somehow I doubt that given recent events in both theatres."

Adam nodded. The "Battle of Iceland" had been in the papers the last few days. Scuttlebutt had it that the *Ranger* and *Wasp* themselves had not been damaged.

I sincerely dout their air groups came through unscathed, however, Adam thought.

"I'm told that you were pushing your squadron pretty hard in Pensacola," Piedmont said. "I'm sure they will not lose their edge in a few weeks."

"Sir, I certainly hope not," Adam replied. "Do we have any trainers or any other aircraft in the area?"

"The only folks with surplus aircraft are the Commonwealth, and those are the aircraft that came off the *Illustrious*."

Adam winced at that.

"Sir, that's quite all right—*Fulmars* and *Sea Hurricanes* won't be much help for us."

Piedmont nodded his approval at Adam's knowledge and opinion.

"Yes, I'm told that you have a little bit of experience with the Commonwealth," Piedmont said simply. "There are those who believe that to be a negative factor."

Adam tried to read Piedmont's face while keeping his own blank. The admiral laughed, waving away Adam's concerns.

"Major, you are probably a killer poker player, but you really have nothing to worry about," the senior officer replied. "I will tell you that you have made some enemies in high places with your treatment of one Captain Bowles, but it's hard to defend a cuckold, much less one who assaults his superior officer."

"Sir, with all due respect, Captain Bowles was a little

311

too wrapped up in politics for being in the middle of a war," Adam said grimly.

"Oh, I concur," Piedmont said. "Which is why I politely told some of the enemies you made that as long as I was in command of this District, and that will be a long time since Secretary Knox placed me here himself, that you will be treated with the utmost professionalism."

Hopefully you're not blowing a smokescreen, Adam thought. *Because I'm really tired of dealing with assholes from Annapolis.*

"Since we've got some time, why don't you tell me a bit about yourself," Piedmont said. "I'm friendly with Air Marshal Barrow, and he says you still have quite a reputation in the Royal Air Force."

"Sir, I don't know all about that, I just had good pilots around me," Adam said. "Anyone surviving the Second Battle was basically lucky, and I was just luckier than most."

There was a soft knock on the door, followed by Mrs. Corinth putting her head around the corner.

"Admiral Piedmont, Admiral King is on the phone for you."

Adam knew a good time to leave when he heard one, already standing up as Piedmont reached for the phone.

"Another time, Major Haynes," the older man said. "Turn those names into Captain McAdams, my air officer, by Friday—you'll find him downstairs."

"Yes Sir," Adam said, saluting. Piedmont returned it, picking up the phone. Exiting his office and closing the door behind him, Adam passed back by Mrs. Corinth.

"Well, that was quick," she observed, still banging away on her paperwork. "As much as the Admiral's been looking forward to actually meeting you in the flesh I figured he'd have you hang around until he was done."

Adam shrugged.

"I guess one doesn't get called by the CNO every day," Adam replied.

Mrs. Corinth gave a slight smile, as if Adam was some poor, misguided soul.

"Of course not," she replied. "I'll let you know when you can schedule another sit down, as I don't think you'll be getting off this easily."

"Well, let's hope it's after the weather changes," Adam said, "because I'd hate to drown the next time I have to come over."

"You don't resemble a turkey, Major, so I think you'll be okay," Mrs. Corinth said. "See you in a couple of weeks, at most."

"Yes ma'am," Adam replied, grabbing his hat and heading out the door. Cursing as he realized that, if anything, it was raining harder than when he had gone in, he closed his overcoat. Stepping out into the rain, he began to think.

Four days to figure out who's leaving, even though I've already got a pretty good idea who it should be, and since I hate breaking up flights, I guess that means I've got my eight pilots, Adam thought. *I just hope Burke and West are ready to stand up for themselves once they get new commanders.*

CHAPTER 7: ENTRIES AND EXITS

Fight on my, my men, Sir Andrew says,
A little I'm hurt, but not yet slain
I'll lie me down and bleed awhile,
And then I'll rise and fight again!—**Ballad, Sir Andrew**
Barton

Sydney, Australia
1450 Local (2350 Eastern)
15 May (14 May) 1943

"Commander Morton, this is one of the rare pleasures I have had in the last few weeks," Admiral Hart said, a genuine smile on his face. Turning to his chief of staff, the flag officer continued firmly, "Publish the orders."

As Captain McPherson read the citation for his Navy Cross, Jacob fought the urge to look to his right or left to ensure Admiral Hart had the right person. Those members of the *Houston*'s crew not involved in her extensive repairs stood gathered in tightly packed ranks under turret No. 1, the recently replaced 8-inch guns gleaming with fresh paint in the afternoon sun.

I feel like a fraud, Jason thought. *Captain Wallace was getting ready to send me home before he was killed. It's almost like I benefited from some Jap destroyer gunner's lucky shot.* Looking up towards the bridge, Jason could see the faint outline of the shot plug that would be in place until the cruiser could be taken into dry dock.

We got off lightly, Jacob thought, then immediately felt guilty as he thought of the heavy cruiser's fifty-three dead and seventy-nine wounded. For a brief moment there as a slight stinging in his eyes, and he blinked rapidly to clear it as he returned Admiral Hart's salute.

314

Chief Roberts would have a field day with me right now, Jacob thought. *I'm sure he's looking down at me shaking his head. Houston* had had eight of her casualties succumb to wounds en route to Sydney. Chief Roberts had been the last, taking his last breath less than six hours out from the harbor.

I can't believe he's gone, Jacob thought. One of his first acts after the *Houston* had completed her initial offloading of casualties and hasty repairs had been to write the gruff non-commissioned officer's wife and three daughters.

"Well deserved, Commander Morton, well deserved," Hart said. "As is this."

Before Jacob could figure out what "this" was, Captain McPherson was starting to read a second set of orders.

"By order of the Chief of Naval Operations, Admiral Ernest J. King, and as a direct result of his demonstrable skill in preparing and commanding the U.S.S. *Houston* for her participation in the Battle of the South China Sea, First Battle of the Java Sea, and Second Battle of the Java Sea," McPherson said, his voice ringing out over the cruiser's suddenly silent deck, "Commander Jacob Thoreau Morton his hereby promoted to the rank of Captain. Signed, Admiral Ernest J. King, Washington, D.C., May 10, 1943."

Jacob was in shock, standing numbly as Lieutenant Commander Sloan smoothly executed a right face and, in concert with Admiral Hart, began changing his epaulettes to the cheers of the *Houston*'s crew.

"With all due respect, Sir, if you try and kiss me I will be forced to maim you," Sloan said quietly. Admiral Hart chuckled at the comment, finishing his job of changing Jacob's epaulettes far more quickly than the gunnery officer. Looking, Jacob realized that the epaulettes were slightly faded and of a different style than the more recent captain's epaulettes. With a start, he realized that they were more than likely Admiral Hart's.

"Don't laugh too long, *Commander* Sloan," Hart said, producing another pair of epaulettes. "Some poor bastard has to take *Captain* Morton's place as executive officer."

Jacob didn't even try to fight his laughter as Sloan's face fell.

Unfortunately, this likely means we'll both be leaving the Houston, Jacob thought. Lots of men in the queue for command back in the States, and I'm pretty sure that BuPers isn't going to change the seniority rules just because there's a war on.

Looking across the harbor at the *Phoenix* as he finished affixing Commander Sloan's epaulettes, Jacob allowed himself a slight smile.

Although I can handle waiting a few months to take command if it means getting a new cruiser rather than this rather distinguished lady, Jacob thought without a twinge of guilt. *I get the feeling that this war will not be over for a couple years at least, and I'd like better odds at surviving it.*

"Well Captain, I believe we have some more men to decorate," Admiral Hart said with a smile. "Adjutant, publish the orders!"

Three hours later, Jacob found himself making his first captain's call to Admiral Hart's headquarters. After that afternoon's ceremony, with the crew dispersing back to their work tasks, the reality of the Allied situation had come pressing back in like a ton of bricks. The Dutch East Indies were officially lost, the last Australian troops evacuating Java a mere three days before.

Strange the Japanese didn't press the invasion fleet harder, Jacob thought. *Of course, having **Prince of Wales**, **Repulse**, and **Malaya** as backup plus the **Ark Royal** and **Biter** providing air cover might have had something to do* *with that*. The ACDA's command intelligence apparatus had been beside themselves trying to explain why the IJN had not forced the issue. There was a whole slew of theories on the enemy's lack of aggressive spirit, ranging from it being a sign that Japanese losses had been heavier than believed at Second Java to signs that the IJN was preparing for an offensive elsewhere, perhaps against New Guinea.

If the Japs take New Guinea, we've got huge problems, Jacob mused. Fortunately he wasn't the only one who could read a map, the Australians continuing to fortify a moderate-sized town named Port Moresby. With three airfields already having been constructed during the defense of the East Indies and some of the combat hardened troops from those same islands taking up residence, Port Moresby was going to be a tough nut for the Japanese to crack when they got around to it.

Not that stiff defenses stopped them in the Dutch East Indies, Jacob thought. The Dutch resistance had proved almost fanatical, it taking a direct order from Admiral Hart as theater commander to get them to board the evacuating ships rather than fight to defend their families and homes. That order was becoming more and more controversial as reports filtered out of Borneo of the Japanese treatment of prisoners and Dutch families there, with things being done in the name of the Emperor that would nauseate a hardened criminal.

Upon entering the small hotel Admiral Hart was using for his headquarters, Jacob made a beeline for the men's room. He was just finishing washing his hands when the door to the restroom opened. Turning, Jacob suddenly found himself staring at what he was sure was a ghost, that of one Commander Damien Thomason.

I thought he was dead, Jacob thought, *and it looks like I was almost right*. Thomason's empty right sleeve was pinned up to his uniform tunic, and an eye patch covered his right eye. The man's head was shaven, with a long series of vicious looking gashes running in a half circle through the black eye patch, down past his nose, and out of view around his neck.

"If you are quite done staring, Comm…*Captain* Morton, I would like to use the head," Thomason said stiffly. Jacob muttered an apology and stepped out of the man's way, letting the Australian head for the urinals. Jacob opened the restroom door and moved out quickly, feeling suddenly short of breath and sick to his stomach.

I wonder what in the hell happened to him? The *Perth* had sunk rather quickly, and while *Houston* herself hadn't been involved in rescue efforts, the scuttlebutt had been that less than fifty men had made it from the Australian cruiser.

Although it doesn't look like Thomason should be too happy about his close shave, Jacob thought as he entered the briefing room. Looking around, he saw that almost every seat was taken, the sole the sole remaining berth being in the front row next to *Phoenix's* master, Captain Nathan Beckham.

*You know, with the **Phoenix** heading back stateside for a new bow I wonder if they'll give **Houston** to Beckham?* Jacob mused. *It would probably save them having to ship someone out here. Beckham's not an Annapolis man, but I imagine BuPers wouldn't care about that.*

"Well, let me be one of the first to congratulate the newest captain in the fleet," Beckham said, extending his hand. Jacob took it, shaking firmly.

"Thank you," Jacob replied, still somewhat distracted.

"You look like you just met the Grim Reaper," Beckham said, his face curious.

"No, just ran into a man I thought was dead and looked like he wished he was," Jacob replied. Beckham nodded, his face registering cognition.

"Let me guess, Commander Thomason, Royal

Australian Navy?"

"Yes, how'd you know?" Jacob asked, surprised.

"Well, that poor bastard is the only man I know of in this headquarters that fits that description," Beckham said lowly. "Got mauled by a shark right before getting picked up."

"Yeah, he was the liaison officer to *Houston* right after war was declared," Jacob stated in return. "Gave me some good advice on damage control that I'm really glad I took."

"Oh really?" Beckham asked, surprised. "I'm always looking for ways to keep from going swimming—with your permission, I'd like to send my XO over to talk with yours."

Jacob was surprised at that one, even more so when he realized other officers were listening to what he was saying.

"Good enough," Jacob replied. "I'll let Commander Sloan know that he should expect company."

"Gentlemen, Admiral Hart!" someone barked from the back of the room. Jacob and everyone else started to come to attention in a cacophony of sliding chairs.

"Have a seat, have a seat," Admiral Hart said, passing through the group. "I don't need any more officers in the hospital because someone put a chair into someone's knees."

There was a ripple of polite laughter as Hart mounted the stage. He was followed by Admiral Crutchley, and with a start Jacob realized the Commonwealth admiral was wearing the new epaulettes of a Vice Admiral. Whilst there were some who probably thought that the promotion was simply because Admiral Phillips had gotten himself killed, Jacob was glad to see it.

The man got us out of Second Java alive, then went back and evacuated most of the Allied soldiers. He's a good man, Jacob thought.

"As you gentlemen can probably see, we have *Sir* Crutchley, the Commonwealth's newest Vice Admiral, with us," Admiral Hart said. The room broke into a bedlam of applause and lusty cheers from the Australian and New Zealand contingent. Admiral Hart waited for it to simmer down, then continued.

"Gentlemen, we also have a new captain amongst us. Jacob, why don't you stand up?" Admiral Hart said.

Jacob was caught by surprise, but not so much that he couldn't stand and turn to face the room.

"I think I'm going to embarrass Jacob a little bit, but as you know he currently is in command of the *Houston*," Admiral Hart said. "What most of you may not realize is that the *Houston* has fought in every straight up gunnery fight in this conflict."

Once again, there were cheers and applause. Jacob successfully fought the urge to blush like a young schoolboy, acknowledging the accolades with a simple nod of thanks.

"There has been some speculation amongst members of my staff and various wardrooms around the fleet that I'm going to send ol' Captain Morton here back to the States to take new construction and let some other lucky bastard get the fightingest heavy cruiser in the Navy. Well, let me just put that to bed right now—Captain Sean Wallace was a fighter, and he trained his wardroom to all be fighters," Hart said fiercely, his face grim.

"Despite the belief of BuPers and some other gentlemen here, *I* choose the commanders of my vessels, and recent experience has taught me that I need a few more fighters. So, as long as the U.S.S. *Houston* remains in the Southwest Pacific, Captain Morton will be her master," Hart finished.

Jacob was stunned in amazement and full of pride at the same time as Beckham and the other U.S. captains sprung to their feet, backslapping him and shaking his hand.

COLLISIONS OF THE DAMNED

I feel like I just had another baby, he thought, then suddenly felt his bright mood lessen. *Shit! This means I'm not going to Hawaii anytime soon.*

Pearl Harbor, Hawaii
0950 Local (1420 Eastern)
15 May

"Gentlemen, I'd like to remind everyone that this briefing is classified SECRET," Nick Cobb said quietly as he looked around the small auditorium at the gathered officers. Most of them were Pacific Fleet submarine officers, but in a move that had utterly surprised Rear Admiral Graham and all of his subordinates, Vice Admiral Halsey had decided to attend the situational briefing Nick had put together. The craggy old aviator had come in with little fanfare or staff, bringing only a solitary captain. Indeed, if the *Tautog* had tied up on time, it was likely Admiral Halsey would have snuck in without being noticed. It appeared to be the man's style as acting fleet commander.

Of course, that's how one finds out the true information, by just appearing and listening.

"Gentlemen, this briefing will last forty-five minutes. At the end of this time, you will have an understanding to the strategic situation facing the United States. Most of this, to be frank, is far above our pay grades. However, as you will soon see, the current situation my require some of your reassignment's to the Atlantic or Indian Oceans—hopefully this will allow you to be in the know when you get there. Lights please."

The lights went dim, leaving Nick alone on the stage with a projected map of Europe. Most of the continent was covered in black, signifying the advance of the Nazi's ground forces. Nick felt a strange sense of calm as he regarded the map—he had practiced the briefing five times in the last two

321

days, the final dry run being at 0500 that morning. The first two times, he had felt physically ill at the end—it was not easy confronting the fact that the war was going terribly. However, by the third time he had started to realize there were some hopeful signs of an ultimate Allied victory, or as Agnes had put it, 'a German overreach'.

Once again, I am glad my girlfriend has a clearance...and doesn't mind cooking breakfast, Nick thought.

"In the last two weeks, the German Army has finished subduing the Grodno pocket, with the death or imprisonment of over half a million Russians," Nick began. That number elicited a murmur that was rapidly silenced by each vessel's commanding officer.

"After eliminating the last of the Russian forces, the Germans advanced across the old borders of the U.S.S.R.. In doing this, it is believed they have suffered heavy casualties despite their advances. The Soviets have decided to trade ground for time, and appear to be doing it fairly well. Next slide, please."

The next projection was a map of the southwest U.S.S.R., from the Black Sea to Smolensk. Marked prominently was the Ukraine, the region in black and red hash marks.

"They were doing a much better job of it before the Nazis broadcast that, should the Ukraine rebel, they would recognize the nationalist movement of one General Yuris Melnikova. General Melnikova is a traitor, but apparently a popular one since the Ukrainians took the bait."

Nick brought his pointer to rest over the city of Kiev, which was the lone area in the region to be a solid red.

"The Germans proceeded to drop five airborne divisions in the vicinity of Kiev, and now the region doesn't really belong to either side. As a result, the Russians have had to retreat to line running from Novgorod, which is north of this map, to Smolensk, through the Ukraine, then down to Odessa on the Black Sea. As you can see, that leaves a dangerous bulge in the southern Russian line."

Nick could tell he was starting to lose his audience...and he couldn't blame them.

Heck, I barely care about some ground fight half a world away myself, but it is pertinent.

"This applies to us here in the Pacific for the following reason—it might force Russia to *leave the war*," Nick stated forcefully, his tone grabbing several of the more aloof officers' attention. " While the Japanese have strangely not attacked the Russians yet, they probably will if and when the Russians move forces from Siberia. If the Russians *do not* move forces from Siberia, the Germans will likely carve them up and take Moscow—which means we face the damn Krauts by ourselves."

*And this is why Agnes and I got drunk two nights ago, because it looks like the Fascists are winning **everywhere**,* Nick thought. *The stories she can tell me from right next door are scary enough as is. I can't imagine what Europe will be like if the Germans take the Russians—but I know I won't be visiting there for the next fifty years.*

"We kicked their ass once before!" someone shouted in the darkened room, followed by several murmurs of assent.

"Ah yes, I was hoping someone would point that out," Nick said quietly. "Next slide!"

This time there was a map of the eastern Atlantic, with England colored a neutral blue, but ominously all the rest of Western Europe except Switzerland and Portugal shaded black.

"I think, as you gentlemen probably recall from history, that we had the French on our side," Nick said. "Once Vichy France threw in with Germany and the Usurper took England's throne it wasn't very hard to persuade Spain,

323

Ireland, and Sweden that it was a good idea to join the Nazis," Nick continued. "Switzerland agreed to stop dispensing occupied nations' gold reserves, so even though she's technically neutral her stance means a lot of our allies are technically flat broke."

Nick paused for a second to look out into the auditorium.

"In short, gentleman, that means we're not just fighting Germany, but most of Europe," Nick continued.

The proverbial pin would've sounded like a hand grenade in the now silent room. Nick had certainly gotten the gathered groups' attention with his statement, which had been his intent.

There's always at least one smartass in the room, and now that asshole's going to keep his mouth shut, Nick thought. *There are lots of things one learns from being the youngest sibling.*

"Before you all decide to leave here and go drown your sorrows in whiskey while learning how to speak German, there is good news," Nick said, gesturing for the overhead to be changed.

A map of the Mediterranean was projected onto the screen. Nick paused a moment to let everyone get their bearings.

"The Spanish 'encouraged' the English to give up Gibraltar, and in pristine condition," Nick said. "From all accounts, the Commonwealth commander was prepared to fight it out—until he was informed that the entire garrison would be put to the sword once the post was captured."

Given that the good admiral's family, as well as those of many of his officers, was present, he made a wise decision, Nick thought bitterly.

"As a result, the Axis now have a first rate harbor and fleet facility at the west end of the Med," Nick continued.

"When do you get to the good news?!" some

catcalled from the back of the room. Nick smiled.

"The *good* news is in their hurry to base the fleet there, the Italians forgot to change the minefields," Nick said easily. "As a result, the British submarine *Upholder* slipped into harbor and sank the battleship *Andrea Doria* at her moorings."

There were several appreciative murmurs about the the British captain's skill and some speculation whether his testicles could be used for church clappers. Nick gestured for the next map.

"Moving east, the Commonwealth has conducted several small commando raids throughout the Levant and North Africa," Nick said. "However, it is unlikely that there will be any major activity in light of recent events in the Dutch East Indies and Indian Ocean."

He did not need to gesture for the next slide, the map of the Indian Ocean looking as if red ink had been spilled across it.

"The Vichy French have reinforced Madagascar, and South Africa remains neutral at this time," Nick stated. "The South African ambassador has expressed his regret to President Roosevelt, but with neither claimant to the English Throne recognized by their parliament, they feel compelled to sit this one out."

Once again there were angry murmurs, but no outbursts.

I think that some folks in Pretoria better hope that the Germans win, Nick thought angrily. *I don't think the Queen is a very forgiving woman.*

"India continues to be the scene of unrest given the new government's decision to back the Allies," Nick said. "Without getting into details I don't have, I will merely state that it appears someone named Ghandi is advocating that India remain removed from either Commonwealth or British affairs."

From what I understand, the only reason the Indian government is allowing the Brits to still use Ceylon is they need grain, Nick thought.

"As you may have heard, there were a couple of fights between the Commonwealth and some Japanese carriers off of Ceylon and again near Australia," Nick continued. "All that needs to be said about that is the Japanese carriers are no longer operating in the Indian Ocean, and the Commonwealth will not likely tangle with our friends across the Pacific anytime soon."

*Biplanes versus **Zeroes** ends poorly every time*, Nick thought bitterly. *Not that we did much better last month.*

Agnes, once again anticipating Nick, brought up a map of the Pacific.

We really do make a good team, he thought, fighting the urge to smile at her.

"Finally, we are here in the Pacific," Nick said. "While many of you know the status of our own fleet, you may not know what has been going on in the Dutch East Indies…."

Five minutes later, as the lights flicked back on, Nick realized that the overwhelming majority of those gathered in front of him had not known how bad things were. There were many pale, somber faces as he scanned the rows.

"What is not known is what the next Japanese move will be," Nick said. "ONI believes that they still retain enough power to strike at Australia or, on the outside, even here at Hawaii. I will be followed by Rear Admiral Graham."

Nick quickly turned to his right as Graham approached, handing the senior officer the pointer. Once fully out of the screen's way, he did turn and give Agnes a slight smirk, causing her to smile in return. Scanning the room, he saw Admiral Halsey and the captain who had accompanied him talking earnestly in low tones.

"Okay men, I have 1025," Rear Admiral Graham said. "Take ten and come back in here no later than 1035 hours. Dismissed."

The auditorium cleared out quickly, men heading for the exits to catch some fresh air. Agnes stood from the projector and started to head over him, her smile broadening.

I am really, really lucky to have her, Nick thought. There was a diplomatic clearing of throat behind him, and he looked to see VAdm. Halsey and his staff officer standing with Rear Admiral Graham. Nick snapped to attention, his heartbeat accelerating.

"Vice Admiral Halsey, I would like you to meet Lieutenant Nick Cobb," Rear Admiral Graham said. Halsey extended his hand, Nick taking it.

"Sir, it's a pleasure to meet you," Nick said, hoping his voice didn't sound as breathless as he sounded.

"Son, that was a great briefing," Halsey said. "And you didn't even reveal anything that you weren't supposed to."

Uh, actually that's because I don't know all that much, Nick thought, seeing Rear Admiral Graham looking a bit uncomfortable.

"Thank you, Sir," Nick said. "I had plenty of help putting it together, I just got to stand up there and give it."

"Well, it was good enough Captain Browning here tried to snatch you up for our staff," Halsey said, gesturing towards the disgruntled looking captain, "but Rear Admiral Graham assures me you're about to go out to sea here soon."

The look of shock must've crossed Nick's face because Graham quickly broke in.

"Yes sir, Lieutenant Cobb will be shipping out as XO on the *Plunger* as soon as she returns from her war patrol."

Nick could tell Captain Browning was not buying Rear Admiral Graham's statement, nor was Vice Admiral

Halsey. However, whereas the former was visibly restraining himself, Halsey just gave a small smile.

"It seems like your family's name keeps coming up in my reports," Halsey continued, a twinkle in his eye. "I look forward to hearing more about you in the future. For now, we've got to get down to the Navy yard and see how things are progressing with the *Maryland*."

In other words, VAdm. Halsey's going to check and make sure I get on board a boat and gone, Nick thought. *Great, I go from being the 'forgotten lieutenant' to admiral chew toy.*

After the two other officers had left, Graham turned to Nick, a wry smile on his face.

"Well, I knew I couldn't keep you in the office forever," the admiral said. Captain Donze chose that moment to join them after having come down from headquarters.

"I just saw the old man leave...did he have anything critical to say?"

Rear Admiral Graham and Nick both looked at Donze.

"Just that Lieutenant Cobb has about two weeks before he'll be on his next war patrol," Rear Admiral Graham replied sadly. Donze turned towards Nick with a look of dismay, then slight anger. The officer was about to say something when Rear Admiral Graham stopped him.

"It's not Nick's fault, it's mine," Graham said, then outlined the whole situation.

"Dammit," Donze said when his boss was done. "Lieutenant Cobb, you were getting damn good at your job...in retrospect, I guess too good." Looking at his watch as well as the rapidly returning officers, Graham realized that it was about time for him to resume speaking to the gathered men.

"Well, guess you better go tell Agnes before she finds

out through the orders crossing her desk. I'd hate to see her kill you," Captain Donze said. Nick turned to see Agnes looking at the gathered officers with a worried look on her face.

She knows something is up, which means I'd better take Captain Donze's advice and go talk to her, Nick thought.

Moving like a man who had been condemned to the firing squad, Nick pushed against the tide of incoming officers to head for the stairs to the projection room, acknowledging congratulations for his briefing along the way. At the top of the stairs he stopped and straightened his uniform, then turned the knob to go in. To his shock, Agnes was turned away from where Rear Admiral Graham was starting to speak to look at him.

"You stopped to straighten out your uniform and gather your thoughts...something you only do when you are about to get chewed out or are nervous," Agnes observed quietly. "Since I look nothing like Captain Donze, I must assume it is the latter."

"Aye...yes, it is," Nick said, breaking into a smile at his discomfiture.

"So, let me see...you are either going to work for Captain Browning" Agnes began, "or you are going to sea. Given that your brothers would encourage you to stab Captain Browning in the neck at the earliest opportunity and working for him is an assignment which I have heard likened to being flayed alive, it is probably the latter."

*Once again I realize why I lo...I mean, **like** this woman,* Nick thought to himself. It was rare to have such beauty and brains in the same package, and with the addition of her matter of fact take on life Agnes was, to quote his brother Sam, "a keeper".

"I just found out that I am going to be going out on the *Plunger*," Nick replied. Agnes gave no reaction except to place both her hands in her lap, regarding him carefully as if expecting more. When nothing more came, she raised an eyebrow and started to turn back around, then stopped herself. Sighing, she shook her head.

"I have to remind myself that you mainlanders are a bit...*different*," Agnes said. "Well, that and the difference in our upbringings. Nick, do you love me?"

Nick was caught flatfooted at Agnes's directness, his jaw dropping open. Reading it wrongly, Agnes pressed her lips into a thin line and completed turning away, looking down where Rear Admiral Graham was continuing his speech.

"Y-yes," Nick said, placing a hand on her back and starting to turn her chair around as he pulled up the other chair in the small room. Initially resisting, Agnes let him complete the maneuver. To his surprise, he saw that her eyes were glistening.

"Then why is it that you haven't said something?" Agnes said quietly, her voice catching. "Because I love you, and I think if I was possibly leaving you forever I'd want to make sure you knew that."

"But the *Plunger*'s not due back for..."

"The *Plunger* will be back in harbor within four days. The reason she needs a new XO is that her current one 'cracked up' because her captain has been so damn aggressive since she went out on patrol right after the war started."

"Jesus..." Nick said.

"Yes, there are advantages to having the admiral's secretary as your girlfriend," Agnes said drily, wiping her eyes. "One of them is you get to find out that your dream assignment may actually be a nightmare."

"So you're worried that I'm going to be XO for an insane man?" Nick asked.

"I'm worried that you're going to get killed, you

idiot," Agnes snapped fiercely. "Your captain's sanity or lack thereof does not concern me as long as *you're* safe."

Nick put his arms around Agnes, embracing her.

"I'll come ba...oof!" he started, stopping as Agnes slammed her hand into his chest.

"I am not some idiotic schoolgirl, Nick," she said. "Do not make promises you cannot keep, it only makes it worse. Haven't you ever wondered why I refused the advances of every man before you?"

"Well, sort of..."

"But you just thought you were so suave and handsome that I couldn't help myself?" Agnes asked sarcastically, then stopped him before he could answer. "I know that's not the case, Nick. Part of why I love you is that you understand humility and your place in the world. Few people have that gift."

Nick found himself blushing slightly at the compliment.

"It comes from being the youngest," he said.

"Partially, I am sure it does come from your parents," Agnes said. "But I think even more of it comes from you and who you are."

"So you're saying I'm not humble *and* handsome?" Nick asked lightly. Agnes laughed, then kissed him, hard. Breaking off after several moments, she pulled a handkerchief out of her purse and dabbed at the lipstick she had left behind.

"No, Nick, you are handsome, caring, and a wonderful man," Agnes said. "Which is what finally made me overcome my fear of you ending up like William."

"You know I can't promise you..." Nick started, only to have Agnes silence him with another kiss.

"I know, Nick," she said. They were interrupted by the scraping of several chairs beneath them. They both

331

turned to see that Rear Admiral Graham had finished speaking with the gathered group of officers.

"I'd better get back down there," Nick said.

"Nick, wait," Agnes said, placing a hand on his arm. "I want you to know that I will love you, no matter what happens. We can continue this discussion tonight, when you come over for dinner."

Nick caught himself looking at her face as he detected her tone.

I may not be all that experienced with women, but I could swear that she just basically told me that I had best plan for breakfast the tomorrow morning also, Nick said.

"Agnes, I...I don't know what to say," he started, then was stopped by Agnes pressing her finger to his lips, followed by kissing him again.

"Say yes," she said simply. "All I am *asking* for is dinner...both now and forever. Anything else is up to you."

"I don't think you mean a game of checkers when you say anything else, do you?" Nick said, still a bit flustered. Agnes gave him a soft smile.

"I do not want you to think less of me, Nick, so I will not answer that," she said. "Just understand that my heart belongs to you, and I hope that yours belongs to me also. I understand that you weren't, as you Americans say, 'brought up that way', so if all that happens is we enjoy some good food, I will still love you as much as I do now."

You know, my Dad used to say war speeds everything up, Nick thought, reflecting on the last time he and his father had spoken before he came out to the Pacific. *I guess I know what he means now...and I completely understand why. I need to make a stop by a jewelers before I go over tonight.*

"I think I'll be seeing you at seven, then," he said, gently. Leaning in, he kissed Angela again, then got up to head downstairs.

Roughly twelve miles away and twelve thousand feet above his younger brother, Eric found himself thinking similar sentiments regarding the speed of conflict.

Eight weeks ago, I got put into a hospital bed, he thought. *Now here I am, about three weeks earlier than the doctors expected, trying to regain my flying touch.*

"C'mon Eric, just settle down and trust your instincts," Lieutenant Chad O'Shannon, formerly of Pensacola and now check pilot for VB-11 (Provisional), stated from the Curtiss SNC's backseat. Pressing his lips together, Eric nodded took a deep breath, and concentrated on trying not to overfly the light monoplane. After another ten minutes, he was finally able to move around the sky without feeling like every turn was going to lead to a possible stall.

"See, just like riding a bike…now why don't you go ahead and take us back to Ford Island?" O'Shannon asked. Eric was sure the man was writing something down, but decided to worry about flying more than how his check ride was going. Putting the aircraft in a gentle bank, he continued to scan the skies around him. Seeing two dots in the distance, he felt his pulse starting to pick up.

"Bogeys, two of them, eleven o'clock," he said, his voice slightly more intense than he intended. He could hear O'Shannon look up, then bring his binoculars to his eyes.

"Army boys," he said, as the two aircraft turned towards their SNC. "Probably out on patrol."

Eric realized with a start that he had some sweat running down his face. Shaking his head, he forced himself to remain calm.

You'd think it was me who got shot down, not Charles, Eric thought grimly. His former wingman had been reassigned to VB-5 off of *Yorktown*, in no small part because the man was involved with Eric's sister.

Hopefully 'involved' is not a euphemism in this case,
Eric thought. *Although it's no more my business than Jo and
I are Tootsie's.*

"Bastards are going to use us for target practice,"
O'Shannon muttered, seeing the two Army pursuits curving
around for a simulated pass. The next instant the backseat
pilot was crying out in shock, Eric whipping the SNC into a
tight turn into the two Army pursuits.

"No body uses a Cobb for a damn firing dummy,"
Eric said, the two P-40s rolling out of their turns as he put his
nose into them. Waggling their wings, the two fighters
pulled up and moved off.

"You know, a little warning before you decided to
hassle around with someone would be nice!" O'Shannon said
harshly. "Especially since your checksheet just went out the
canopy!"

Eric started to turn around.

"Oh shit, I'm..." Eric stammered.

"Gotcha," O'Shannon said, holding up the clipboard
where Eric could see. "I think we can skip the solo. If
you're ready to mix it up with two planes in this crate, I think
you're fine to start flying again."

"Good enough," Eric replied, suddenly euphoric. He
turned the SNC towards Ford Island, putting it into a shallow
dive to get back faster. Clearing his approach with the tower
and air defense commands, he circled into the island's busy
pattern. As he went, he looked down at the harbor, noting
the empty holes in Battleship Row.

Bastards got a pretty good lick in on us, he thought
grimly. *Fleet's been back on its heels for the past two
months, but I think we're about to start swinging back.*

It was easy for any one with eyes to see that
Yorktown, Enterprise, and *Illustrious,* after multiple weeks
patrolling around the islands, were taking on a large number
of provisions. Carriers didn't take on a large number of

provisions just to circle around their homebases. Given that Charles had nearly slipped up and made a comment when Patricia had made a reference to doing something in a couple of weeks, Eric figured the Pacific Fleet was about to get in the business of dishing out punishment rather than taking it.

About damn time, too, Eric thought as he dropped down for his final approach. Thinking about how his sister was clearly falling deeper in love with the young Lieutenant Read, he hoped that she was really aware of what she was doing.

Jo's tried to tell her time and time again that maybe she should have learned her lesson from last time, but Patricia doesn't want to listen, Eric thought. Eric could tell that Jo was getting frustrated with his sister's naïve, idealistic view of wartime life. Both Nick and he had jointly decided to stay out of the fight between the two housemates, Eric because he didn't want to have to choose between his girlfriend and his sister, Nick because when he wasn't eating at Agnes's there was always room for him at Patricia and Jo's table.

Little idiot must take after Mom more than we thought, Eric thought, *because Lord knows I've had to start pushing the rehab a little bit harder to keep fitting in my uniform.* The hospital doctors had been less than pleased with his pushing the envelope, but they couldn't argue with the results. While he wasn't even close to approaching his pre-injury level of fitness, he was a lot close than most men should have been.

Touching down with chirp of tires, Eric brought the throttle back and taxied the SNC over to the hangar. Twenty minutes after touching down he was off the inter-harbor ferry and headed for the small building the orphaned *ad hoc* Air Group Eleven had taken over as its headquarters. The ramshackle building wasn't much to look at, and quite frankly Eric hoped that the dockyard workers were wrong and the *Hornet* was repaired well before June was done.

With Vice Admiral Halsey driving the dockyard workers like it's 1843, not 1943, I'm sure that just might happen. There were rumors going around that Halsey, tired of all the complaining being done by the long hours, had gotten a quick block of instruction and taken a hand in repairing some of the damage to the *Maryland* himself when that vessel had been pulled into drydock. While Eric was certain the story was apocryphal, and the lack of bitching had more to do with the fact that fleet intelligence expected the Japanese back any time after they had finished digesting the Dutch East Indies, it was certainly plausible given Halsey's personality.

You can tell he wants to be out there hitting at the enemy, not back here playing fleet commander, Eric thought. *Can't say that I blame him, not after missing out on the fleet's one big battle.*

"Well, the prodigal son returns," a familiar voice observed drily as he passed the VB-11's airman's room. Turning, he was pleasantly surprised to see Radioman 1st Class Brown.

"Sir, I was starting to wonder if the Japs had got you after all," Brown said, extending his hand. Eric took it, shaking it firmly. While he was sure many officers would have been surprised at the familiarity, as far as he was concerned maintaining mutual respect wasn't encouraged by treating enlisted flight crew like pariahs.

"No, just banged me up enough to scare me," Eric replied, letting O'Shannon past him in the narrow hallway. "I heard that they tried to transfer you to the gunner's pool."

"Yeah, until I told the…"

"Lieutenant Cobb, get your ass in here, *now*," Lieutenant Commander Ernest Hitchcock bellowed from the officer ready room. Eric saw Brown roll his eyes and step away.

"Sorry Sir, I guess you shouldn't be seen touching the unwashed masses," he murmured. Eric turned around to see the new squadron commander standing and looking at him from within the squadron ready room.

"Aye-aye, sir," Eric said, moving smartly past the door.

"Close the fucking door, Cobb," Hitchcock snarled. Eric, seeing O'Shannon braced at the position of attention, did what he was told and came over, looking somewhat bemused.

"You know, when I was a midshipman, I learned that if one of my classmates was at attention getting chewed out, that probably meant I should do the same," Hitchcock said quietly. "Now, while I expect such behavior from a ninety-day wonder like this genius, I would think that Annapolis hasn't changed that much in the last 14 years."

Eric came slowly and snidely to a loose position of attention.

I'll be damned...no, I'll be goddamned if I'm going to let some piece of shit who has yet to hear a shot fired in anger give me grief about military courtesy, Eric thought.

"O'Shannon here tells me this freaking mark on your evaluation sheet," Hitchcock continued, pointing to a long line through the middle of the form, "is due to unauthorized maneuvering with Army aircraft. Is this true?"

Eric looked straight past Hitchcock, staring at the wall.

"Yes sir, I reacted to a…" Eric began.

"Don't bullshit me, Cobb," Hitchcock snapped. "I asked a simple question, yes or no…or have they eliminated the four basic responses also."

"No sir," Eric bit out.

"Do you *want* to be a fighter pilot, Cobb?" Hitchcock asked. "Maybe on one of those damn tubs that brought us our replacement aircraft?"

"No sir," Eric replied.

"Then don't ever let me hear about you trying to be one again, or I'll see that you get cross-trained on *Wildcats* shortly thereafter," Hitchcock continued. "Now, let's discuss proper senior/subordinate relationships since I'm told you have an issue on this topic."

Eric snapped his eyes down and looked at Hitchcock, his face puzzled.

"Oh, don't give me that puzzled look...I was appraised of why I had to transfer an experienced pilot because one of my officers set his wingmen up with his sister," Hitchcock sneered.

"Sir, with all due respect, I do not believe my personal life is any of your business," Eric said, lowly.

"But it is my business when I see you talking with an enlisted man like your best buddies," Hitchcock snapped. "And unless you plan on adding a charge of belligerency to your packet, I suggest you keep a civil tongue in your head."

Eric suddenly realized why he had never heard of Hitchcock in carrier aviation circles—the man was an "accident" waiting to happen.

You're not going to make it more than thirty days in combat, Eric realized. *I can only hope you're not going to take someone with you.* The knowledge gave him a strange sense of peace.

"Aye-aye, Sir," Eric replied, his tone suddenly neutral. Hitchcock gave him a hard gaze for a few moments, then looked back down at the sheet he held.

"O'Shannon says your ready to fly, but I'm not convinced you have what it takes," Hitchcock said. "You'll fly as my wingman until further notice."

Eric bit back the urge to tell Hitchcock to go fuck himself. Flying as anyone's wingman, much less the squadron leader's, was an insult to someone as senior as Eric. Looking into Hitchcock's eyes, he saw that this was what the man was waiting on.

"Sir, when do I need to report for our first flight?" he asked simply. *Because getting a front row seat to your demise will be completely worth it.*

Six hours after Eric found himself in his unenviable position, another Cobb was in one potentially as dire, if far from as uncomfortable. Charles' left arm was cinched firmly but lovingly around her, the two of them passionately clinging to one another on the couch. She could feel evidence of Charles' arousal pressing into insistently into her side, his hand passing lightly up her leg as if it was leaving fire in its wake.

*I...can't...oh...that feels...*she thought.

"Charles, stop," Patricia gasped, grabbing her boyfriend's hand as it continued moving well past the hemline of her sundress. Moving it back down to her knee, and feeling quite breathless, she took a couple moments to gather her thoughts.

"Does the word incorrigible mean anything to you?" she asked, seeing the disappointed look on Charles's face. "How about persistent, or relentless?"

"Unless they're all synonyms for utterly and passionately in love, they don't apply to this situation," Charles replied, breathless himself. Patricia was suddenly glad she had established very early on that both of them had to remain sitting if they were going to do anything more than hold hands. While not overly familiar with the male form, Patricia had four brothers, was well aware of the differences between men and women, and was very sure that her elbow hadn't been brushing up against loose change when the two of them had just been kissing.

Not unless he has a strategically placed roll of

quarters, her mind thought unbidden, causing her face to suddenly color. Charles leaned back and looked at her, and she began to think that he was mistaking the look on her face, when she realized his face was wearing a very strange expression.

"You know, I don't think I've ever realized how beautiful you are when you're really embarrassed," Charles said, reaching up to brush her cheek. "I'd ask what you were thinking, if for no other reason than you'd stay that way forever."

Patricia chuckled nervously.

"What, you mean red as a beet?" she asked. "Or mortified?"

"Okay, I'll bite—why were you mortified?" Charles said.

Patricia felt herself blushing again and stood up.

"You did that on purpose, Charles," she drawled in mock severity. "For that, you get to have a timeout while I go make some lemonade. Maybe a drink will keep your hands where they belong."

"I didn't think you minded," Charles said lecherously. Patricia turned to look at him, and he recoiled from the cool look she was giving him.

"I may not have, but thank you very much I know where babies come from—and strongly suspect that was where your hand was headed," she said. "I think when I return I'll be sitting in the chair, *alone*."

As she walked to the kitchen, she was glad her boyfriend had yet to figure out how to read her guilty looks.

*Because yes, you bastard, I **did** like the way you were touching me, and I'm not sure I trust myself to keep you from just "touching,"* she thought, well aware of the need that was more than just slightly urgent between her legs.

I wish Jo was here, Patricia thought, exhaling as her

hands shook while she began pulling items out of the refrigerator. Jo was currently at the library and likely wouldn't be home for at least another hour or more. The two of them had started taking opposite shifts, as much to keep from getting on each other's nerves as to give the other one some sort of privacy at least some of the time.

Little Ms. Holier-Than-Thou acts like she's pure as a mountain stream, Patricia thought haughtily as she sliced a couple of lemons. Not paying attention, she cut herself…and immediately realized that there were worse things than salt in a wound.

"Dammit!" she cried, striding over to the sink and turning the water on.

Damn man's got me so flustered I'm lucky I didn't slice my finger off! If the two of them hadn't been using the knives so much, she probably would have—one of the few things Jo was fanatical about was having her knives as keen as they could be. As she washed her hands, she heard Charles get up and start to come into the kitchen.

"Don't touch me, Charles Bedford Read," Patricia said firmly as he started to approach her. "I think you've done quite enough of that this afternoon." Reaching for the first aid kit Jo had thoughtfully affixed to the bottom of the cabinets, she took out some gauze and tape.

I cannot, for the life of me, understand why that woman insisted on keeping her knives sharper than King Arthur kept Excalibur, Patricia thought as she worked on her finger. Eventually her skill with wielding knives had improved to the point that this was the first time she had cut herself in months. Turning to look at Charles, she leaned back on the counter, clutching her hand to her abdomen.

"Do you have any idea how hard," she thought, then colored as her earlier thoughts about Charles' arousal returned to her mind, "how *difficult* it is to stop you sometimes?"

"You know, you're the one who started kissing me this time," Charles observed coolly. "After the last ten times of getting pushed, shoved, and slapped away, I sorta figured you were one of those women who believed in aggressively saving herself for marriage. Then you go and kiss me like you're dying of thirst and I'm the only water fountain in Honolulu."

Patricia crossed her arms, then realized how bad her finger still hurt. Having a horrible thought, she looked down to make sure she hadn't got her dress bloody.

"So, I suppose this is all my fault?" she asked.

Charles threw up his hands in exasperation and started to stand up.

"You know, I'm not interested in assigning blame or playing games, Patricia," he snapped, his voice raw. "In case you haven't noticed, there's a war on, and I go out..." Stopping, he visibly shut his mouth.

Patricia suddenly felt like a great weight had settled on her chest.

"You go out where?" she asked quietly, the words barely loud enough to carry. Charles looked past her at the open window, then crossed the room to stand closer to her.

"I go out to sea on Tuesday," he said quietly, standing a couple of feet away from her.

Patricia felt her knees going weak, and fought it. She turned and looked Charles in the face, compressing her lips in a thin line.

"So, wanting to get a final piece of tail before you go off to face the Japanese fleet, is that it? A man has needs, after all."

Charles visibly recoiled at her iciness.

"I would certainly hope, after the last month, that you did not honestly believe that was my intention," he said, hurt in his voice.

Patricia realized she may have overstepped her bounds as he started to turn away. She grabbed him and pulled him back into her, simultaneously pulling his head down so she could kiss him. Pushing her body up against him, she felt him stiffen, then start to push her away.

"No, stop," he started to say, then she kissed him again. He responded this time, his right hand sliding up her side, then over to her front. She broke off, causing him to groan deep in his throat.

"Shush, Charles," she said, placing her hand on his chest. "Tell me, do you love me?"

"Yes," Charles answered, without hesitation. "With all my heart."

"Promise me that you'll come back," she said.

"I promise," Charles replied. Searching his eyes, she could see that he meant it. Taking a deep breath, she began speaking slowly and deliberately.

"Jo won't be home for at least an hour, and we have to be done by then," Patricia said, looking him in the eyes. "I think we'll be safe. In every sense of the word."

Charles looked at her, stunned.

"Patricia, I don't want to…" Charles began.

"Charles, you could be *dead* in a week," Patricia said. "I'll be damned if I'm going to spend the next week, month, or year wondering if I should have done this."

I cannot believe I am doing this, she thought as he reached down and took his hand.

"Patricia, I don't *want to* sleep with you because you think I'm going to die," Charles said, firmly pushing her away.

"*What?!*" Shocked, Patricia took a step back.

"I love you and respect you too much to do that," Charles said, holding her hands.

"That's not what you were saying a few min…"

Patricia started to say.

"Yes, and that was before I promised I'll be back," Charles replied. "I don't want to leave you single and in the family way, and while I love you, I don't want to be one of those people who get married just because I'm going to war."

You mean like half the couples frequenting the courthouse these days? Patricia almost asked, then stopped.

"I said I'll be back," Charles said, taking a deep, shuddering breath. "I meant it. Then we can get married if you still feel that way."

Patricia felt as if her heart had started to drain into her stomach. Suddenly she understood what her mother had been talking about when she used to say 'your father made my heart melt'. Reaching up, she kissed Charles again, this time far more softly.

"I think, Charles Read, that I love you a lot more than I did ten minutes ago," she said, meaning every word. Charles have her a slight smile.

"Ten minutes ago you sliced your finger open, probably because I didn't have you thinking straight," Charles said.

"No one likes a cocky person," Patricia replied severely, then kissed him again. As they embraced she found herself having to fight down the cold fear that even then was starting to gnaw in her belly.

He's going to sea, she thought. *Oh my God, he's going to sea.*

"Let's go to the bedroom, and you can just hold me, okay?" Patricia said. She felt her eyes starting to tear up again and blinked the water away.

He'll be fine, and I'll be fine, and we'll both laugh about this in ten years, Patricia told herself desperately. Stepping away from Charles, she grabbed his hand and started to tug him back towards her bedroom.

I'm also going to do a lot more than hold you, Charles Read, she thought fiercely. *Sometimes having a widely read girlfriend has its advantages, as you're about to find out.*

"So then the bastard tells me I get to be his wingman," Eric said bitterly. "I was this close to telling him to go fuck himself." Suddenly realizing what he had just said, he colored, much to Jo's pleasure.

"Wow, I am rubbing off on you," Jo said, then looked at him mischievously. "Soon I'll have you losing the last of your moral hang-ups and living like a complete heathen!"

Or hey, at least I'll get you to make a pass at me, she thought. *Quite frankly I think Charles has probably gotten further with your sister than you've even thought about with me.*

Eric gave her a bemused look, and she could tell she had struck a nerve.

"Why are you so pushy? I thought women wanted a man to act like a gentleman," he drawled as they came to the end of their walk. Jo turned and looked up at him, then joined her eyes together and looked at him while batting her eyelashes. With her current white blouse and conservative skirt, she looked every inch the prim, proper, and naïve young woman.

"Why, Eric, whatever do you mean, pushy? I'm just a sweet, innocent…" Jo started coquettishly.

Eric raised and eyebrow.

"Jo, you swear more than most *men* our age, and you've made it abundantly clear that you want to do more than shake hands with me," Eric said.

"Then what is the holdup, Eric?" she asked, turning to get her and Patricia's mail. "I mean, I don't want you to rip my clothes off and ravish me like some savage, but it'd be nice if I could tell a difference between how you kiss me and the way you kiss Patricia," Jo said, trying to keep her voice light to take a bit of the edge off her words. Turning to look at Eric, she saw that her attempt had failed.

You know, Eric would be cute when he was angry...except for being a dead ringer for a crazed killer who just found a way out of the handcuffs. While Jo knew Eric would never raise a hand to her, she knew that she was definitely picking at a wounded man given how bad a day he'd had. Eric worked his mouth as he obviously through through several replies.

Here it comes, Jo thought, bracing for a truly acidic comment. Eric did not disappoint her.

"Well, I'm sorry if your little fling gave the impression all men are rutting animals who can't control themselves," Eric said. "Or was it more a case of your time with *him* gave you an appetite for fornication?"

Jo closed her eyes, Eric's words cutting her far sharper than he realized. Taking a shuddering breath, she bit down hard on her lip. Opening them to look at Eric, she could see he was horrified by what he had just said.

"Josephine, I'm…" Eric stammered.

"What, sorry for telling the truth as you see it?" Jo asked conversationally, proud that the hurt didn't make it into her voice. "You know, I was just starting to think that you were a special man, Eric. Now I see that you're just like the rest, ready to twist something against a woman if given half a chance."

I mean, you of all people should not be throwing the past at someone, Jo thought angrily. She realized pausing had been a mistake as she felt the first hot tears start to go down her cheeks.

"Look, Eric, how about we don't see each other for awhile, okay?" Jo asked, not looking at him.

"How long is awhile?" Eric asked. The tremor in his voice told Jo that he realized he was lucky to be getting that

346

much.

"I don't know, *a while*," Jo said bitterly. "When I figure out if I want to keep going out with a man who can't seem to determine whether I am an utter harlot or a woman who has 'lived a little', to quote him last week."

Eric recoiled from her comment, getting a small smile that didn't even approach Jo's eyes.

"See, having one's words or past twisted against them isn't very comfortable," she said sweetly, then pushed past him for her door. Hearing him starting to follow, she quickly opened the door then leaned back against it, slamming it in his face.

"Jo," Eric said, trying the door only to find it locked. "Jo, c'mon, please let me in."

Feeling her eyes really starting to swim, she turned and faced out the small window.

"*A while most certainly isn't five minutes!*" she sobbed at him. "*Go away!*" With that, she turned away to see a very bedraggled looking Patricia and Charles gazing at her from the couch.

Well that's just peachy, she thought. Before either one of them could speak, she gave them both a patronizing smile.

"Oh look, it's the *chaste* lovebirds," she snarled. "Am I disturbing you? I'm sorry, but for some reason I thought you two would be sitting on the couch looking deep into each other's eyes as you maintained exactly the proper distance of good little boys and girls."

"Jo, I don't know what's going on…" Patricia started to say, self-consciously starting to arrange her hair.

"Oh, well, let me fill you in, oh dear *Tootsie*," Jo snapped. "Whereas your flyboy seems quite happy to try his hand at landing on your deck, your brother is treating me like the whore of Babylon. I was thinking it was a family trait until I came in to find you guys apparently just having finished a friendly game of doctor."

Patricia went pale as a sheet.

"Why you bit…" she started to say, before Charles grabbed her shoulder.

"Jo, I am ashamed of you," he said, even as he brought the shaking Patricia in.

"Oh where do you get off?!" Jo snapped at him. "You're busy trying your damndest to deflower the world's most naïve virgin here, and you have the nerve to tell me that you're ashamed of me?"

"Yes, I do," Charles replied, his Missouri accent thick. "Because I thought you were a far better woman than the type that throws stones. Patricia's never tossed them at you."

Holy shit, he actually means it, Jo thought. *Well, guess my day is suitably complete.*

"I'm sorry," she sobbed. "I'm so sorry." With that, she ran past the couple to her bedroom, closing the door behind her. Changing out of her clothes, she flopped down onto the bed, quietly sobbing as she looked up at the ceiling.

Well, I've gone and made a fine mess of things, she thought once she was cried out. *Guess I'll be putting a want ad for another roommate in the paper before too long.*

With that pleasant thought, she started to roll over when the door slowly opened. Realizing it was probably Patricia, justifiably with a butcher knife, she turned to face the entryway. Seeing that it was indeed her housemate, albeit unarmed, she rolled away to face the wall.

"You know, most people wouldn't be standing here right now," Patricia said coolly. "That was a very hurtful thing for you to say to me."

Jo gave a short laugh that sounded crazy even to her.

"Oh, I'm sorry oh Saint Patricia," she said sarcastically. "I'll try to be less hateful next time my heart gets ripped out *by your brother* in the future. That is if you're even still wanting to live with me."

Jo could hear Patricia coming over to the bed and steeled herself for a fight, rolling back to face her roommate.

I'm giving her one free lick...I've insulted her that much, Jo thought. *But after that I'm going to show her having four older brothers is nothing compared to fighting another woman.*

To her shock, Patricia pulled up a chair, sitting with her arms folded on the top of it.

"I'm no saint, Jo," Patricia said, quietly. "I'm just a woman who realizes that she owes a lot to you and your father. One who also realizes that her idiot brother said some very, very hateful things, which is why he gets to eat Navy mess food for *awhile*, as long as that is."

Jo was shocked, so much so that she didn't start when Patricia reached over and teasingly closed her mouth.

"I asked him what happened," Patricia continued. "My mother would skin him alive if she knew what he'd said, and I will not have a brother who treats my best friend like that."

"Patricia, I…" Jo started.

"Even if that best friend is acting like a hypocrite," Patricia stated coolly.

Well, guess I'm still not off the hook, Jo said.

"I'm not…" Jo started to defend herself.

"Oh? Isn't that what they call someone who cries about being judged yet rushes to judge someone else who may or may not have done the same thing?" Patricia asked, raising an eyebrow.

Jo sighed, realizing Patricia had her boxed on that one.

"For the record, not that it's any of your business, *that* did not happen," Patricia said. "Charles is, despite what you apparently think, a perfect gentleman. He's also going to sea next week."

"Oh Jesus," Jo said, sitting up and reaching to hug her friend. Patricia stopped her.

"If there's one thing you've taught me, it's bawling my eyes out every time someone leaves is going to make my eyes very sore before this war is over," Patricia said. "I might need you whenever he leaves, but I want to try and stand on my own…it's something a very good woman taught me."

Jo sat back down, looking at her friend.

Somewhere in the last couple of months, Patricia's grown up, Jo thought.

"While you were in here, Nick came by also," Patricia said. "He's becoming executive officer of the *Plunger*."

"When?" Jo asked, feeling her face pale.

"'Soon,' he said in that voice Navy men seem to take when they're trying to keep secrets," Patricia said, pulling an imitation of the tone in question. "I don't know how soon, but he's about to ask Agnes to marry him."

"Get out of here," Jo said, smiling in excitement. "Little ol' Nick? Ladies man of ladies men?"

"Yeah, Mr. "I don't want to be set up" himself," Patricia said, laughing. She grew sober. "Speaking of engagement, I think it's time we cover why Eric's being a bit, hesitant, shall we say."

Jo held up her hand.

"Patricia, we don't have to…"

"In case you haven't noticed, I'm most of my brother's confidantes," Patricia said. "Everyone except for Eric, that is. He was always happy to play dolls, chess, or games with me, but when it came to telling me anything, forget it. That is, until a half hour ago while you were still in here hating yourself."

Jo sighed.

I'd apologize again, but we both know I'm sorry and it's just wasting breath saying it again at this point, Jo thought resignedly.

"So, with that being said, you can imagine my surprise when he started to spill his guts about his last relationship and how it was affecting this one," Patricia continued. "Let me just say, if I ever should happen to cross paths with one Joyce Cotner, I'm clawing that bitch's eyes out."

Whoa, I've never seen Patricia this upset, Jo thought. *I hope I never break Eric's heart, I don't look good with a cane and dog.*

Patricia regained her composure, visibly forcing herself to brighten.

"Anyway, it appears that Ms. Cotner and my brother became lovers," Patricia said. "It seems to be a funny way of thinking with my brothers—that 'ring on the finger' doesn't seem to have to be a wedding band for them to sew their wild oats."

"I think that's far more common than you think, Patricia," Jo said. "Especially in time of war."

"I once thought that if my mother *ever* found out, they wouldn't have to worry about that problem, or that act, ever again," Patricia stated. "However, I'm not a math whiz, and I know nine months before February is barely the month Mom and Dad got married."

"I thought Sam and David were premature?" Jo said slyly.

"Right," Patricia replied deadpan. "Because they both look like babies that were early and sickly."

"But your mother's not here," Jo said, "and I guess that means we know why Nick bought an engagement ring today."

Patricia stopped, her mouth making an 'O' of shock and terror.

"Oh no, I've got to…" she started to say, standing up. Jo grabbed her arm.

"Agnes and Nick are big kids," Jo said quietly. "And in case you haven't noticed, probably more in love than any other couple you can think of."

Patricia sat back down, obviously still wanting to run off and save her brother's virtue. Looking at her, Jo finally started to snicker.

"What's so funny?!" Patricia asked.

"Nothing, except you are *so* obviously the only daughter in a house full of boys," Jo replied. "It's humorous to watch."

"You're not amusing, Jo," Patricia said, then composed herself. "But anyway, Eric's reticence is because he's afraid that you'll leave him just like Joyce did, and believe it or not we Cobbs aren't exactly fond of collecting bedpost notches."

"Gee, so wholesome I could be ill," Jo said, getting a look from Patricia.

"Anyway, that's why he's afraid to really do anything with you, despite your apparent willingness," Patricia said. "Which I'm understanding a whole lot more of, by the way."

"Oh?" Jo asked, giving Patricia a suitably skeptical look.

Nothing happened my ass, Jo thought.

"I know what you're thinking, and I'm serious, I will still be wearing white on my wedding day," Patricia said with a great deal of pique.

"Will that be white, or an off cream?" Jo asked, widening her eyes innocently.

"Do you really want to know?" Patricia asked, her voice calm. Jo looked at her, in shock, a feeling that quickly evaporated.

"Because if you really want to know, you can ask God when you get to Heaven since neither one of us is ever going to tell you," the youngest Cobb snapped.

Jo shook her head.

"Look, let's go make dinner, you ninny," she said. "It'll be nice to have just the two of us for once."

"Yeah, actually," Patricia said. "I can tell you about my growing love affair with Edgar Rice Burroughs."

Tacoma, Washington
1730 Local (2030 Eastern)
20 May

The Green Clover was a modest restaurant, by any stretch of the imagination. Consisting of a single-story, roughly L-shaped building with booths all along the short end, tables the length of the long end, and a kitchen in the slightly thicker link, the diner specialized more in traditional American than Irish cuisine.

Well this place isn't exactly inspiring confidence, Adam thought as he crossed the threshold.

"Come on, Adam," Norah said gently. "Tabitha warned us that the décor might look old, but the food is to die for."

Looking over at his date, Adam gave a wan grin.

"You know, I have a problem saying no to the most attractive woman in the room," he stated solemnly, causing Norah to color.

"Well I'll let her know that when I see her," Norah replied with a smile, self-consciously running a hand through her curled locks. Let down to the shoulders of her homemade but well-tailored blue dress, the hair do only accentuated the attention the nurse was receiving from the establishment's mainly male clientele.

The only reason I'm not putting that Army sergeant's eyes back into his head is his wife looks like she's about to rip his balls off, Adam thought, giving the man a hard look. *Sweet Jesus, how did I not notice she's a damn knockout while we were riding up from Kansas.*

The sergeant looked like he wanted to say something until he fully read Adam's expression. It took a moment, but the older gentleman realized the relatively plain gray suit, blue shirt, and gray and red tie was more than offset by military bearing. Narrowing his eyes, he turned away from Adam's gaze and fixed his companion with a glare that matched hers. To Adam's disgust, the woman looked down at her plate.

"You're not doing her any favors even if you broke his jaw," Norah said lowly. "I recognize the type."

Before Adam could respond, a harried looking hostess finally came up to greet them.

"Y'all need a seat for two?" the long-haired, slender brunette asked in a deep, rich Texas accent that surprised both Adam and Norah.Her nametag said Leslie. Adam did a doubletake, giving her a strange look.

"No, your ears aren't playing tricks on you, I'm from Amarillo," the woman said. "I guess you get nice, wet and dreary for nine months out of the year when you marry an Irishman."

Adam and Norah both chuckled at that comment, Adam because he knew quite a few Irishman and Norah because it didn't take that much of a journey back up her family tree to find people from the Emerald Isle.

"Actually, we'll take a booth for two," Adam said. Looking around, he suddenly realized what was missing— cigarette smoke. As they walked towards their booth, he remarked on the especially clean air to Leslie.

"Kinda hard to open a window when you're basically

underwater," Leslie replied in response to Adam's query, gesturing towards the rain coming down in sheets outside. "Since the kitchen smoke is bad enough, we sure don't want to have people having to decide whether to cough or chew."

"Can't argue with that," Adam said.

Although I can't imagine it's good for business, Adam thought. *But what clientele you get are probably very loyal.*

"Why are there so many military men in here?" Norah asked as Adam let her sit down in the booth first, then took the bench with his back to the door.

"Honey, this is the best food around Fort Lewis and McChord Field," Leslie replied. "Trust me, if a man ain't married and doesn't want to go out and get drunk, they come here."

"Well, we brought our appetites," Adam replied. Leslie smiled at that.

"I'll send Debbie right over," she replied. "Do you guys want anything to drink?" Adam looked at Norah, indicating for her to go first.

"I'll have a Coke and a glass of ice," Norah said.

"I'll have coffee," Adam replied.

"Good enough," Leslie said, obviously committing their drinks to memory before she pulled out two menus, put them on the table, then moved swiftly back towards the door. Adam saw Norah regarding him as they both sat down at their table, the woman placing her head on her linked hands.

"So, Mr. Haynes, what have you been up to for the past three weeks?" she asked impishly. "Because I could have sworn that someone fitting your description said that he would take me out to dinner almost a month ago."

Adam diplomatically cleared this throat, somewhat embarrassed as he thought of something to say.

"Uh, I was flying?" he joked weakly.

"So, the Marine Corps is testing a flying submarine?" Norah replied in a chiding voice. "Because I'm quite interested to hear how they plan on using *that.*"

"Dear lady, I am starting to wonder if you are a spy," Adam said in a mock British accent. "Well, I guess that would be in league with my previous luck in love."

Norah winced even as she laughed.

"That's a rather bitter way of looking at things, but I guess if you can laugh you're obviously feeling better."

"I have present company to thank for that," Adam said earnestly, his sudden seriousness throwing Norah off. "Who would have known that reading the *Grapes of Wrath* would prove so fortuitous."

"Somehow I don't think you would have been staring at me like a walking T-bone steak even if you hadn't been reading, Adam," Norah said.

"No, probably not," Adam replied. Debbie, a slim brunette who looked like a younger version of Leslie, chose that moment to arrive with their drinks.

"Y'all ready to order?" she asked, her accent confirming that the two women were somehow related. Adam and Norah looked at each other sheepishly, realizing their menus were still unopened. Debbie smiled broadly, then reached down for her notebook.

"You guys want to just have the special? It's corned beef with glazed apples and mixed vegetables," Debbie said.

"Sure," Adam and Norah said simultaneously, causing Debbie to laugh.

"So how long have you two been going out?" Debbie asked as she wrote. Norah blushed as Adam looked sorta sheepish.

"This is our first date, actually," Norah said. Debbie flashed a knowing smile at that one.

"Well, hopefully we'll see you guys back here next

week," she said, putting her notebook in her apron pocket. "I'll be right back with your plates."

"So, do you like Washington better than Florida?" Norah asked, sipping her soda.

Adam gave her a slightly bemused look.

"Yes, because I'm always happy to be living like a fish," Adam said.

"Silly man, I meant the change of commanders," Norah replied. "Besides, the humidity just actually falls as rain here. I'm told Florida is like taking a bath with your clothes on."

"Touche. I guess I can't complain about the change ," Adam stated. He searched for something he could tell Norah without revealing war information. "Found out that I'm really getting too old to play football against the mechanics."

"You play against the enlisted men?"

"Yes," Adam replied, somewhat surprised at her question.

"I thought officers and enlisted weren't allowed to fraternize," Norah said. Adam raised an eyebrow, surprised at her knowledge.

I truly hope I'm the only man you're seeing right now. While he had no one to blame but himself if he wasn't, but that wouldn't make it any less painful. Norah looked at him, smiling even broader.

"You know, every time something starts to bother you, you put on your poker face," she chuckled. "I mean, I'm sure it works with people who don't know you very well, but if someone's been around you for more than a couple of days it's pretty easy to tell."

Adam wiped the blank expression off his face and spitefully replacing it with a full, broad grin that caused Norah to burst out into genuine laughter.

"Is this better?" Adam asked through his teeth. "Can you tell what I'm thinking now?"

"Oh my," Norah said, fighting to keep her laughter quiet as other patrons started to look at her. She began blushing again, her face matching her hair.

"Well, I guess I don't need to be all that observant to see what you're thinking," Adam said quietly, and started to take a sip of his coffee when Norah kicked him under the table.

Ouch, she's got strong legs, he thought to himself.

"So what was bothering you, anyway?" Norah asked, once again setting her chin on her clasped hands.

Adam paused for a moment, then decided that honesty was the best policy.

"I was wondering why you seemed to know so much about the military," Adam replied.

"And you were wondering if there was another fella in the picture since you'd been standing me up for a month?"

"Yes," Adam replied, waiting to see what her reaction would be.

"Well, I am seeing another man," Norah said simply, taking a sip of her soda after speaking and looking at Adam over the glass. Looking at her eyes, Adam could see a devilish gleam in them.

"Okay, what's the part you're leaving out?" Adam asked.

"That the other man happens to be my sister's intended, one Major Mark Price, United States Army Air Corps," Norah said.

"Ah," Adam said. "Let me guess—he's one of those, 'don't associate with the help' kind of fellows?"

"Well, no, not actually—but his commander, a lieutenant colonel Perry, seems to take a dim view to the officers and enlisted mixing."

"Then the man's a fool," Adam said simply. "A unit's enlisted men work long hours to make sure we all get into the air, and most of them are just trying to serve their country like everyone else."

"Well, that's quite a different approach than most people seem to have," Norah said. "I'm kind of curious as to why you have it, actually."

Adam gave her a strained smile.

I really don't think this topic is something fit for date conversation, and I've already bared a lot of my soul to you during the train ride, Adam thought, then examined his feelings.

"That's either you 'I just swallowed a hot pepper and I'm trying not to scream' look or you have a particularly bad memory," Norah said, her eyes narrowing as she studied him.

Debbie arrived at that moment with their food. Looking at the plates, Adam suddenly realized he was very, very hungry—which was good, because there was plenty to eat. Norah looked at the food in horror as soon as Debbie moved off.

"I can't eat all of this," Norah said. "I'll burst out of this dress."

Adam looked up, his eyes slightly wider than normal and a hopeful look on his face.

Let's hope I haven't misjudged her sense of humor, he thought.

"Oh, the horror, the horror," the Marine officer said mockingly, bringing his hand up to his mouth as if he were aghast. Norah looked at him for a long moment, her face severe.

Whoops, fucked that up, Adam thought.

"I don't know whether to slap you or make a retort," Norah said finally, breaking into a broad grin.

"Well, hurry up and make a decision, people gotta eat

359

here," Adam said jokingly.

Norah shook her head in frustration.

"You know, someday I'll understand men," she said, starting to cut into her beef.

"Yes, well, I'm sure that will be long before men start to understand you women," Adam observed. Norah's response was immediate, her foot hitting Adam in the shin again.

"You know, I'm going to be black and blue if you keep kicking me so hard," Adam said grimly.

"Maybe you should modify your behavior then," she replied.

"Well, you must admit, women are far more complex than men," Adam said as Norah chewed. Giving him a harsh look and swallowing quickly, Norah took a drink of her soda to clear her throat then started speaking.

"Only because men care about two things, one of them being fighting and the other one not really mentionable in polite company," she snapped.

Adam leaned back against the booth, studying Norah for a few moments. She continued to eat, looking back at him as she chewed until she finally got exasperated.

"Why are you looking at me like that?" she asked, setting down her knife and fork.

"Just wondering what man was foolish enough to hurt you so badly," Adam said quietly.

Norah looked at him, then turned away to look out the window.

"Oh, so you can pick my brain apart all the way across country yet I don't even get to find out why you are so bitter against men? That sounds like a really square deal," Adam chided.

Norah turned back and was about to answer when a pair of men came into the restaurant, causing a slight murmur to go through some of the gathered individuals. Adam turned to look at the pair and saw why there had been a stir. Either one of the men looked like he could have ripped the place apart with their bare hands. Together they made Adam glad to see their Marine khakis and captain's insignia.

Hmm, there's something about them that's tickling my memory, Adam thought.

"Who are those men, and why are they famous?" Adam asked. Norah looked at him like he had been hiding under a rock.

"They're the Cobb brothers," she said simply. "They were both awarded the Distinguished Flying Cross for the Battle of Oahu and have been giving war bonds speeches all over the area."

"Oh," Adam said. "I didn't know that...and how did you know that?"

"Well, before you decided to try and pry open my brain, I was intending to tell you I got a job at Boeing—I start next week," Norah said.

"Oh," Adam said, surprised. "I thought you were going to be a draftsperson?"

"I am, but not for ships—they've already got all the spots filled at Bremerton," Norah said.

Leslie was bringing the two pilots over towards the booths, all of the tables being full. Adam turned back around to face Norah, who was busy looking at the two pilots in obvious admiration.

Well now I know how every other woman in this place felt when Norah came in the door, Adam thought. Clearing his throat diplomatically, he got Norah's attention and was pleased to see her color slightly.

"It's just I've never been around real live heroes before," she gushed, then reconsidered. "Present company excluded."

"Uh-huh," Adam said, taking a bite. Norah studied him for a moment.

"You're not really upset, are you?"

"Of course not, for I am but a simple creature," Adam said sarcastically. "Since I would clearly lose if I started a fight with either of those man mountains, and am quite disinterested in committing an act of sodomy, they are of little importance to me."

"Excuse me, but are you Major Haynes?" a Southern drawl asked from behind him.

Adam turned around slowly, sincerely hoping whomever was speaking to him hadn't heard his attempt at being a smart aleck. He found himself facing the larger of the two brothers.

"Yes I am, and you are…?" Adam asked.

"Captain Samuel Cobb, Sir, and I truly hope you can save our lives," the man replied, his face conveying that he meant every word.

Fifteen minutes later, as they watched the major leave with his very attractive date, David was still half stunned.

"I cannot believe you basically *begged* that man to bring us into his squadron," the smaller Cobb was saying. "If I were out with some great-looking dame like that, I sure as hell wouldn't want someone disturbing us!"

Sam regarded his brother.

"This bond drive shit is *killing me*, David," Sam said. He puffed his chest out and put both his fists on his legs, looking all the world like some poofed up superhero. "Remember, only you can give us the tools to do the job. Buy war bonds—our lives may depend on it."

David looked around, aghast.

"Sam! Are you trying to get us painting rocks?" David asked. "Perhaps being pet captains to some admiral or general? Have you taken a look around? There are far, far worse things than giving bond tours!"

"Yeah, and I wish I was doing most of them," Sam replied. "I mean, damn David, our brothers *are being shot at*, and we're sitting here doing nothing."

"Look, you know neither one of them are getting shot at right now, so calm down," David replied, looking up as Debbie brought them their food. The waitress gave Sam a lingering look as she walked off, putting a little extra sway in her hips. David turned from watching to see that Sam was not paying attention, his head bent in prayer. Fighting down a sigh, David said his blessing also, then tore into his brother.

"Sam, we will get our opportunity soon enough," David said archly. "For right now, why don't you enjoy yourself and do something like watch a movie, or go out dancing, or hey, pick up on that well-formed waitress who's sending you so many smoke signals Sitting Bull is wondering where is firewood went."

Sam stopped with his food halfway to his mouth.

You know, I think my 'little' brother's gone yellow, Sam thought. *Let's nip that shit in the bud.*

"I'll ignore for the moment that you're looking at another woman's posterior when Sadie arrives in town in how many days?" Sam stated evenly. "Instead, I will point out that there's something wrong with a man not wanting to get back into the fight."

"Look, you of all people should know I ain't ran from a fight a day in my life," David said darkly. "Just pardon me if I'd like an opportunity to start a family or enjoy married life before my brother goes volunteering us to get our fool heads shot off."

"You know, there are thousands of men who will never get the chance to see their wives again," Sam replied.

"Yeah, well, I'm not in a hurry to join them," David replied.

363

"Oh, really? You think I am?" Sam asked.

"Well, you're certainly going out of your way to get us back to flying," David snapped. "It doesn't take a rocket scientist to realize where every Marine squadron that has planes is headed, and I think been nearly killed enough to last three wars."

"So, you are feeling yellow then?" Sam asked simply.

"Call me a coward again and there's going to be an ugly scene," David growled, his eyes narrowing. Sam looked at him as if considering whether or not to push his brother's buttons some more.

I haven't lost a fight to you since we were ten, and that includes knocking you clean out during plebe boxing, Sam thought. *Yeah, Commander Cook was a cruel man to have us fighting each other, but you sure as hell didn't hold back either.*

"Fine, you're not a coward, but you must really love Sadie if you'd rather spend time with her than fly," Sam observed.

David got a wistful look on his face, nearly causing Sam to lose his dinner.

Oh, here we go, he thought. *Love testimonial number three hundred and...*

"Someday you'll understand," David began. "I mean, when I see..."

"Hey, isn't that...oh, nevermind," Sam said, cutting his brother off in the interest of saving his food.

"Fine, be a smart-aleck," David replied. "You just wait—someday you'll get smitten."

"Right, and then we'll have the Second Coming. Let's just say I'll believe I'll get smitten if we show up at work Monday and there are new orders waiting for us, the sun is shining, and there are actually planes."

"Well, if you're begging was successful, perhaps

we'll have a reason to go to church next Sunday," David said. "Not that you have been to church lately."

"I'm not holding my breath that there will be planes," Sam stated, pointedly ignoring his brother's chiding.

"Probably a good thing—you don't look good blue, and I really hate lugging your big butt around after you pass out from oxygen deprivation," David replied.

Sam looked up as the doors opened to admit another four servicemen, all of them in Army uniforms. The oldest of the bunch didn't look a day over nineteen, and he had serious doubts about the youngest one being old enough to shave, much less go and die for his country. Suddenly somber, he turned to look at David and saw that his brother also had a grim look on his face.

"Babes to the slaughter," David remarked.

"That's the way it always is," Sam said. Looking down at his plate, he realized he had suddenly lost his appetite. "Let's get out of here...we've got to go to some place called Yakima in the morning."

"Yeah, that we do," David said, looking at the time. "Remember your coat, it's supposed to be still cold as hell there."

"Well, as long as the sun is shining, I don't care," Sam said, leaving enough to cover the bill plus a healthy tip as he got up. Following his brother out the door, he could feel the young soldiers' eyes upon them.

I wonder what they think of us? Sam thought to himself. *No matter, they'll know why we look so grim soon enough.*

Tokyo, Japan
1700 Local (0300 Eastern)
22 May (21 May)

These baths always leave me feeling like a wrinkled prune, Vice Admiral Yamaguchi thought to himself. Feeling the hot steam beating upon him, he forced himself to ignore his discomfort as he regarded his host, Admiral Yamamoto. The man was enjoying a vigorous back rub, provided to him by his favorite geisha and mistress, Chioko Kawai. Looking at Yamamoto, Yamaguchi could not help feeling a bit envious. His thoughts were interrupted by the door to the room sliding open, a Navy captain in full dress entering and bowing respectfully to the three men in the bath. Upon rising, the man rendered his report.

"Respectful Sirs, the building is clear of any listening devices or Army spies," the slight man said. "My men have secured the perimeter against any future intruders."

"Thank you, Captain Mused," Yamamoto said somberly. Stopping Chioko, he indicated that she should leave. Looking at the two of them, Yamaguchi could see that there was true affection there. The geisha turned and curtsied to Yamaguchi and Yamamoto's other guest, Vice Admiral Inoue, then left quietly.

It is so sad that so great a man is unable to marry the woman he truly loves, Yamaguchi thought. *However, we must all make sacrifices for the good of Japan, and such scandal would be ruinous at this time.*

"Now then, let us discuss business," Yamamoto said. "Inoue-san, you first."

"Our air arm is crippled for the next two to three months, and that is only if we do not undertake any other major operations," Inouye said quietly. "Due to the heavier-than-expected resistance from the Australians and Dutch, we will have difficulty fielding six full carrier groups *and* maintaining contingents in the Dutch East Indies."

"Admiral Yamaguchi?"

"You are aware of the damage to the *Shokaku* putting her out of action until August," Yamaguchi stated simply.

"The *Kaga* is in desperate need of a refit, which means I have an effective strength of three carriers at this time. If I add *Zuiho*, I will have the equivalent of four."

Yamamoto nodded sagely, processing the information. His brow furrowed in thought, he shifted back in the hot tub. Yamaguchi could see the man was obviously uncomfortable with what he was coming up with.

"Even with the destruction of the *Saratoga, Lexington,* and *Hornet*, the Germans believe the Americans will have six more carriers available by the end of the year," Yamamoto said heavily. "That will give them a total of nine with the *Enterprise, Yorktown*, and *Victorious*."

Yamaguchi winced at that news as Yamamoto continued.

"I promised the Emperor six months to a year of running wild," the senior officer said. "If we are still fighting this war by 1944, then things will be far worse than I imagined."

"Would it be possible to trap the three carriers in the South Pacific while we massed all of our carriers against them?" Inoue asked, brow furrowed in thought.

"Our German allies, in between their anxious bleating for us to attack the Russians, have indicated that the Allies may be preparing to invade Madagascar," Yamamoto said. "If they do, they will surely need carriers to cover their attack with South Africa remaining neutral. If this occurs, yes, we may be able to trap whatever forces they use."

I am not sure that I would rely on trapping the Allies twice in the Indian Ocean, Yamaguchi thought. *Ozawa-san was lucky to sink the **Furious** while losing only **Shoho**.*

"The Germans may get their wish soon enough," Inouye observed, the contempt clear in his voice. "Already those fools in the Army are stating that since we allowed the bulk of the Australians to get away, we must help knock Russia out of the war to obtain a possible peace."

"I have already discussed the war situation with His Majesty," Yamamoto replied. "He agrees that the damage done to our battleline endangers the nation, and thus the last thing we need to do is fight an opponent who has bested us once before."

Normally, I would argue this point, but with the current carrier weakness, Yamamoto is correct. Vice Admiral Kondo's woes had not ceased with the Second Battle of the Java Sea's cessation. In addition to the loss of *Kongo* and *Fuso* and severe damage to other vessels, an Allied submarine had put a pair of torpedoes into the *Nagato* two days after the battle. While not enough damage to sink the battleship, it had been enough to necessitate her diversion to Singapore and reduced the active Japanese battleline to *Yamato, Musashi, Mutsu,* and *Kirishima.*

It is as if the navy is deteriorating before our eyes, Yamaguchi thought. *Even if **Shinano** is completed by the end of next month and worked up by August as the staff states she will, we run the risk of being overwhelmed.*

"Perhaps then it is best for us all if we allow the Army to carry out their foolish ambition," Inoue observed. "If they succeed, then we will have greatly increased the odds the Germans will finish off Russia, thus requiring the Americans to send more vessels to the Atlantic. If not, then it is likely they will support our desire to conduct a limited expansion of our defensive sphere."

Yamamoto grunted in agreement with Inoue's reasoning, still looking troubled. He turned to Yamaguchi.

"Do you see a flaw in this, Yamaguchi?"

"The fact that time does not aid us," Yamaguchi replied. "If we are to strike, we must do so in the next six months, preferably in such a manner that Australia decides to leave the war. Once that is done, we must turn and strike the Americans with all of our strength in hopes of gaining a great victory before they gather enough strength to shatter our fleet."

"How are we to gather enough strength for both of these blows?" Inouye snapped.

"By careful planning and conservation," Yamamoto said before Yamaguchi could answer. "Our faith must, as always, lie in the Decisive Battle. Hopefully it will be at the time and place of our choosing."

"But with what vessels?" Inouye asked. "Our battleline is greatly diminished…"

"I have spoken with Admiral Nagano, who in turn has spoken with the Emperor," Yamamoto said. "His Majesty has decreed that the *Shinano* and *Taiho* are now 'national priorities', which will hopefully garner us more resources to complete them."

Okay, maybe they are not being optimistic about the **Shinano**, Yamaguchi thought, nodding at his superior's words. *Now the question remains if the Yamato-class are truly the equal of two or three of our opponents' vessels.*

"At any rate, we have no choice in our actions," Yamamoto continued after a moment's reflection. "Now that we have started this war, we must finish it or else Nippon's enemies will completely devastate us. I do not intend to allow this to happen while I still live."

Neither of the man's subordinates doubted his words as they returned to planning the Imperial Navy's future moves.

Several miles away, at the Yokosuka Naval Yard, Isoro Honda found himself staring off into space at his small desk. Before him was a blank sheet of paper, the ninth to occupy that space since he had sat down to begin his task.

Who would have thought writing a dear friend's family would be so difficult? Isoro thought to himself. In his mind's eye, he could see Ikuko, Eiji's little sister, with her broad smile and infectious laughter. It had been an open secret that Eiji's parents had desired that Isoro and Ikuko would someday become wed, cementing the ties between the two families. Isoro had intended it to be this year once Japan was victorious.

I was a little too optimistic in that guess, he thought, tears threatening to well up in his eyes. *I always imagined our children would be screaming "Uncle Eiji, Uncle Eiji." Now I am not even sure I will survive. How do I tell someone that I will not be coming to visit them again because I failed my friend?*

Looking down at the paper, Isoro was surprised to see wet splotches. With a start, he realized that he was crying. Cursing, he fiercely wadded up the paper and tossed it to join its others.

Samurai do not cry! He thought angrily. *Samurai accomplish their task.*

With his newfound determination, Isoro bent back to the paper and began to write.

I will avenge you, Eiji, he thought. *There will not be enough water in the Pacific to wash away the blood I will spill in your name.* As he finished his short letter, he reflected back to their conversation regarding their relative importance.

The Emperor's enemies are many, but not so many that they cannot all be smote one by one, Isoro thought. *May the gods grant me strength to carry out that task now that you cannot.*

With that thought, Isoro folded the letter and placed it in its envelope. Seeing the time, he turned off his desk lamp, then climbed into his cot.

Tomorrow will bring me one day closer to killing my enemies. With that thought foremost in his mind, Lieutenant Isoro Honda, currently Japan's leading ace with thirty-five kills, laid back and stared at the ceiling while waiting for blissful unconsciousness.

Dramatis Personae

U.S.S. Houston
Commander Jacob Thoreau Morton

Chief Petty Officer Roberts

Seaman Third Class Teague

Captain Sean Wallace

Lieutenant Adam Connor

Lieutenant Commander David Sloan

VMF-21
Major Adam Jefferson Haynes

Captain Scott Walters

Captain Keith Seidel

Captain William Kennedy

Captain Jacob Bowles

Captain David West

Captain Todd Burke

Wing Commander Connor O'Rourke

VMF-14
Captains Samuel and David Cobb

Major Max Bowden

Pearl Harbor and Oahu
Rear Admiral Daniel Graham

Captain Daniel Davis

Lieutenant Nicholas "Nick" Elrod Cobb

Miss Agnes Nunes

Commander Jason Freeman

Patricia Ann Cobb

Josephine Marie Morton

Joanna "Sadie" Cobb

Nurse Beverly Bowden

Nurse Nancy Hertling

Lieutenant Eric Melville Cobb

Ensign Charles Read

Radioman First Class Willie Brown

Alabama
Alma Cobb nee Lee

Samuel Cobb

COLLISIONS OF THE DAMNED

Elma Cotner

Theodore Cotner

Joyce Cotner

Beauregard Forrest Cotner

Afterword

Whomever said the second novel in a series can be harder was telling the truth. *Acts of War* was a labor of the many, and this novel was no different. First, I'd like to thank Anita for her support and for helping with the drawings. In the former, considering that the final months of this novel overlapped with a busy Con schedule, she was much more tolerant of long writing absences than I imagine most folks would be. In the second, often she received some horrible chicken scratch notes and a picture that was then turned into the outlines you see at the front of the book. There's a reason that, in addition to continuing her own writing (*The Architects of Lore*-series), she's now going back to school for graphic design. As noted in my previous books, when you get your "franchise spouse" on the first go obviously someone's looking out for you.

Second, I'd like to thank my editor, Mallie Rust. Any errors in editing throughout the document are the fault of the writer who told her, "Oh, I'll have the chapter to you next week..." while forgetting he had a Con. I look forward to future editing endeavors going forward, and if anyone is looking for editing help I'll be hanging her shingle on my website once she goes "fully live." In addition to Mallie, the usual suspects (Kat Mitchell, Alma Boykin, and Heather Kitzman) were joined by several other people in in marketing this thing before it was done. I'd particularly like to thank authors Sarah Hoyt (for mentorship and taking time out of her schedule to prod her fans) and David Weber (for carrying me in his online web store) at this time. Finally, I'd be remiss in not thanking the many independent bookstores and Cons that have allowed me to do book signings or grab a table.

Other than advancing the construction or fielding time of various units based on Axis nations' resource reallocation, I've tried to maintain historical accuracy throughout this book. In addition to Martin Caidin, John Toland, and the inestimable Samuel Eliot Morrison's works on the Dutch East Indies campaigns, I'd like to specifically recognize Jeffrey Cox's *Rising Sun, Falling Skies* as being a particular useful reference. I'd also like to thank Jonathan Parshall and Anthony Tully both for answering e-mails as well as running the website Combinedfleet.com. While there are numerous sites that are helpful with World War II research, Parshall and Tully's is *the* "go to" site for most things IJN.

Thank you, again, for purchasing this book. Please tell your family and friends about it, and if you liked it give it a rating on Amazon. If this is the first *Usurper's War* book you have purchased, please check out *Acts of War* and *Pandora's Memories* for more alternative history. Merchandise associated with the series is available on Redbubble and CafePress.

67985272R00217

Made in the USA
San Bernardino, CA
29 January 2018